A NOTE BEFORE THE TITLE PAGE

NOVELS with prefaces are like pictures with inscriptions below them; there is a confession that something was left over and had to be expressed by an addendum. But the note which is offered here is not a preface so much as a protest, and in token therefore it is put before the title-page and does not figure in the list of contents. It is a protest against certain stock tricks of the book reviewer and certain prevalent vulgarities about books. They concern the treatment of opinion in works of fiction and what is called " putting people into novels."

This book, then, *The World of William Clissold*, is a novel. It is claimed to be a complete full-dress novel, that and nothing more. William Clissold is a fictitious character, and his thoughts and ideas throughout are the thoughts and ideas natural to his mental and social type. He is (to the best of his author's ability) his own self and not his author's self, in his emotional reactions, in his hard wilfulness, in his faith, in his political ideas, in his judgments. He is a specimen of modern liberalism, using liberalism in its broadest sense. He is a study of a modern type seeking modes of self-realisation. His circumstances and his views are fitted together with the utmost care to make one consistent personality. His views run very close at times—but not always—to the views his author has in his own person expressed; nevertheless, is it too much to ask that they should be treated here as his own? Naturally his point of view is like Mr. Wells'. That was to be expected. How can one imagine and invent the whole interior world of an uncongenial type? Every author must write of the reactions he knows; he must be near enough to them to *feel* them sympathetically. It is unreasonable to expect the author of this book to write of the inner life of such people as the devout Mr. Belloc, for example, or the aristocratic Duke of Northumberland, or the political Mr. Ramsay MacDonald. He can only comment on such types from an inaccessible remoteness, attack them, admire them, state his differences from them. Their ultimate processes are inconceivable to him. There never was a character created by an imaginative author from the inside which did not contain this quite unavoidable element of self-projection. Even Hamlet is believed to be a self-projection of Shakespeare. But while this is forgiven and taken for granted in the criticism of most authors it is made a stock grievance against the present writer. It would be a great kindness to a no doubt undeserving author if in this instance William Clissold could be treated as William Clissold, and if Mr. Wells could be spared the standard charge of having changed his views afresh, and so forth and so on, because William Clissold sees many things from a different angle than did Mr. Polly, George Ponderevo, Susan Ponderevo, Mr. Preemby, Dr. Devizes, Dr. Martineau, Remington, Kipps, the artilleryman in *The War of the Worlds*, Uncle Nobby, Benham, Billy Prothero, and the many other characters who have been identified as mouthpieces and exponents of Mr. Wells' scandalously varied views and attitudes. And it is a point worth considering in this period of successful personal memoirs that if the author had wanted to write a mental autobiography instead of a novel, there is no conceivable reason why he should not have done so.

Clearly he did not want to do so.

Which brings us to the second point in this intimate but necessary plea. This is not a *roman à clé*. It is a work of fiction, purely and completely. One thing which is something of an innovation has to be noted. A great number of real people are actually named in this story. It is, the author submits, impossible to get the full effect of contemporary life in which living ideas and movements play a dominant part without doing that. You cannot have a man like William Clissold going about the world of to-day and never meeting anybody one has ever heard of. Some of these living personages are not only mentioned but more or less described. But always under their proper names. Dr. Jung is made to talk in a London flat. It is very much as he talked in a London flat. He appears because certain original ideas of his have been taken and woven into the Clissold point of view, and it was at once ungracious not to acknowledge the far-reaching suggestions that came from him and clumsy and self-important to make a footnote or a prefatory note. Shaw, again, the Shaw of the 'eighties, blows into a Kensington evening, and Keynes lunches with Clissold. These are affectionate hospitalities; they do not wound nor injure and can awaken no resentment.

With one transparent exception, the vignette of a great scientific man at home in Book I., which is partially a portrait, every character that appears in the book under a fictitious name is an entirely fictitious character. The more nearly they may approach to living instances, the more fictitious they are. They say and do things that living people are saying and doing. That is inevitable in a picture of contemporary life. If one were to write a story in which a Prime Minister had to figure during the Balfour régime, it would be necessary to have a Prime Minister rather like Lord Balfour—or everything would have to be different. If an August Personage has to descend into the narrative, it would have to be drawn to the figure of the August Personage of the period. A beggar or a policeman must be something like some beggar or policeman one actually knows. People must be more or less similar to real people up and down the scale, so long as one is writing a novel and not a fantasy. But though you made your Prime Minister as Balfouresque as possible or your Prince as princely, it would be for atmosphere and not for statement, and the last imputation that is permissible against a novelist is that he is trying to say or insinuate this or that about an individual without daring to say it plainly and directly to the proper address. Cannot this sort of imputation be checked? Cannot those who criticise books and write about books cease to pander to that favourite amusement of vulgar, half-educated, curious but ill-informed people, the hunt for the imaginary "originals" of every fictitious character—for those who will, for example, discover in the present case that X or

Y or Z, who is an advertising specialist, " sat for " the brother Dickon of this story, or that Lady Steinhart is some particular resident in Cannes or Nice—because she has a large garden ? And that it is all great fun and very malicious and not for a moment to be treated as serious literature. This identification of " originals " is an old trick of the Victorian novelist and publisher ; it was, I suppose, an attempt to enhance interest by that faint intimation of libel. It is really not just to the spirit and intention of a book of this type.

An inanimate instance from this book will make the matter clearer without touching upon any personal note. There is written here the most exact and detailed description of the *mas*, which is the scene of nearly the whole novel. Rooms in that house are described, bits of its garden, the view from the windows. It is possible to locate that *mas* within a few miles of Grasse ; it is possible to find not one but a score of views closely similar to the view pictured so explicitly, a similar *mas* is to be found. But the actual *mas* no one will ever find, nor the precise rooms, nor the exact view. That *mas* does not exist. That view does not exist. It is the case of Mr. Britling's home over again, which everyone who did not know Mr. Wells' home in Essex very well, knew so surely was an exact account of Easton Glebe. The less these identifiers knew about it, the more they appreciated the photographic quality of the picture. The less they knew Mr. Wells, the more certainly they recognised him in Mr. Britling. Enthusiastic strangers still invade Mr. Wells at times with the demand to see the place where he wept when he heard that his eldest son was killed. It is embarrassing to encounter such intrusive sympathy for an entirely imaginary loss. And matters become complicated when " originals " volunteer and surrender to the detectives. A charming contemporary has just confided to the world that she was the " original " of Beatrice in *Tono Bungay*. It is the first intimation that has reached the author of this interesting fact. No one would have suspected it.

But this time may we have a truce to such artless tributes to the novelist's art ? It was William Clissold, an entirely fictitious character, who thought out most of the problems

4

of his life and made belated love to his fictitious Clementina in a fictitious *mas* in Provence, and in spite of the entirely imaginary wreckage of an automobile in the road to Thorenc the author survives. It is no good to look for that stone, with its simple inscription, in the Magagnosc cemetery. To the best of his knowledge and belief the author has never been buried anywhere. Even brother Dickon's allusion to William's good looks is not to be regarded as modest self-revelation. All novelists use actual experiences in their work. They must know things before they tell about them. But all novelists rearrange, sublimate, intensify. One turns over the sketch-book of one's memories and uses what one needs. One takes a lifted eyebrow here and a mimosa in flower there. The imagination discovers a certain congruity between some actual situation and some constructive necessity, and works in as much of the situation as it needs. But it alters and rearranges without scruple. The eyebrow is not a portrait; the parallelism of a situation is not a report. Surely there is enough to read in this book without reading between the lines.

And one other question may be glanced at here before this note concludes. There is much discussion of opinion in this book. Does that make it anything but a novel? Is it not quite as much "life" to meet and deal with a new idea as to meet and deal with a new lover? Must the characters in our English and American novels be for evermore as cleaned of thought as a rabbit is of its bowels, before they can be served up for consumption? This book, which contains religious, historical, economic, and sociological discussions, which expresses fits of temper and moods of doubt, is at any rate submitted as a novel, as a whole novel, and nothing but a novel, as the story of one man's adventure, body, soul, and intelligence, in life. If you are the sort of person who will not accept it as a novel, then please leave it alone. You are not getting sly peeps at something more real than the reality of art, and your attempts to squint through will only make you squint very unbecomingly.

THE WORLD OF WILLIAM CLISSOLD

Παντα ῥει

THE WORLD OF WILLIAM CLISSOLD

A Novel at a New Angle

by

H. G. WELLS

VOL. I

LONDON 48 PALL MALL
W. COLLINS SONS & CO LTD
GLASGOW SYDNEY AUCKLAND

Copyright

Printed in Great Britain

CONTENTS

THE DIVISIONS OF THE NOVEL

THE WORLD OF
WILLIAM CLISSOLD

BOOK THE FIRST
The Frame of the Picture

BOOK THE SECOND
*The Story of the Clissolds—My Father
and the Flow of Things*

BOOK THE THIRD
The Story of the Clissolds—Essence of Dickon

BOOK THE FIRST
THE FRAME OF THE PICTURE

THE FRAME OF THE PICTURE

THE SECTIONS

YESTERDAY I was fifty-nine, and in a year I shall be sixty—"getting on for seventy," as the unpleasant old phrase goes. I was born in November, 1865, and this is November, 1924. The average duration of life in England is fifty-one and a half, so I am already eight years and a half beyond the common lot. The percentage of people who live beyond sixty is forty-seven. Beyond seventy it is thirty. Only one in five thousand lives beyond one hundred, and of this small body of centenarians two-thirds are women. My expectation of life, says the table in the Almanac, is fourteen years and four months. That table in the Almanac is not a mathematical marvel, but it is close enough to the truth to serve my purpose here.

In the face of these figures I cannot hide from myself that the greater part of my life has been lived. So far I have had but few physical reminders of the ebb of the years. I do not feel that I am even beginning to be old. Perhaps I grow tired more readily than I did at thirty, and my tennis is neither so hard nor so quick-witted as it used to be, but my arteries, the doctors tell me, are still young arteries. I cannot read Bradshaw nowadays, I must put on spectacles for that, and I do not like to swim in cold water any more. Yet in good daylight I can still read ordinary print with unaided eyes, and, come to think of it, I have always gasped in cold water. Maybe I have not so much lost endurance as learnt wisdom. And generally my vigour is unimpaired. It is the dates and figures that will not be denied. They show quite plainly that at most only two decades remain for me, and when they are spent my strongest will be a white-faced, rather shrunken, assisted old man—"wonderful," they will say. I know because I say it now of Sir Rupert York and old Hayes. The greater chance is that I shall be no more than a jarful of ashes and a fading memory.

Possibly they may make something in time for me from these monkey glands they talk about; but I distrust these rejuvenescent extracts. I do not want merely to prolong my years as an unpleasant experiment. I may go on for some time yet by my own unaided strength, unless a serious illness catches me. Then, I have observed, if one comes back at all one comes back "aged."

I do not complain that I have to grow old. It is not a thing that I think about habitually. But the birthdays come round to remind me, and this year some journalist got hold of my date but added up the years wrong, and in the *Evening Standard* I found myself subjected to congratulations on attaining sixty.   I was so startled that I did a little sum at once on the margin of the paper.   For a moment I felt just as though I had missed a bank-note from a not too distended purse.

His mistake.

But to-day I find myself retrospective.   I have been caught up for a couple of days in London before I go back to my sunshine in Provence and I am all alone.   Outside it is not so much day as a saturated piece of dingy time, a stretch of chewed and damp and dirty fourth dimension between two nights.   It rains fitfully, now in fine clouds, now in hysterical downpours, now in phases of drizzling undecided intermission ; and the shops are lit and there are lights in the windows.   There is a sort of grey discoloration filtering down from above that I suppose one must admit to be daylight.   Wet omnibuses, wet taxicabs and automobiles splash and blunder by, there are a few reluctant foot passengers under wet umbrellas.   Everything shines greasily with the rain like the backs of rolling porpoises.   What a climate !   This intolerable place, they say, is the healthiest city in the world.   Thank Heaven !   I leave it to-morrow

I do not venture outside this room to-day.   At any rate I will lunch here.   These excellent chambers of my brother's are kept by a French couple who combine English comfort with French cookery.   No wonder old Dickon grows fat.   He is in Brussels now—probably growing fatter Inadvertently.   He does not want to grow fat.   He is dining with a curious little society for the promotion of scientific finance, of which he is one of the founders.   That is all I know about his business in Brussels.   Then he is going on into Germany, still in pursuit of monetary ideas.   His energy and industry in the cause he has taken up are prodigious—and he is nearly three years older than I.   He thrives on it.   No wonder he needs a comfortable resting-place here.   From these rooms one might imagine him sedentary.   They make me feel sedentary.   But even his sedentariness has directness and vigour.   There is something about this room in particular, and this desk of his and this chair of his, remarkably conducive to not going out.   To-day especially.

Before me are good square sheets of paper and quillpens and every provocation to write.   The lamp is admirably shaded.   So why should not write, and forget altogether that visible chill, that inky catarrh of climate which is snivelling against the window-panes ?

§ 2

FOR some time now I have had the idea of writing a book dominating my mind and never quite settling down to a positive beginning. I have wanted to begin so much, the thing has become so important to me that the very strength of my desire has restrained me. I have written one or two books before, but they have been technical works of no significance to the unspecialised reader. I have written various reports, too, and between thirty and forty scientific papers. Such things seem to write themselves. The book I have in mind now is something altogether more human and difficult than that.

It is not exactly an autobiography I want to write, and not exactly a book of confessions. My life has been largely spent in work ; my only scandal was a public scandal and very fully reported. I do not see why I should repeat the newspapers again ; much of my business I can only discuss in general terms because of my obligations to my firm and our associates, and there remains little for me to confess, even if I had the Rousseau streak in me. It is with larger affairs than my own that my projected book would deal. It is nothing, indeed, so systematic as a general philosophy of life I contemplate, but it is something rather more in that way than an autobiography would be. I should say that a description of my world best expresses what I have in view ; my world and my will.

I want it to be a picture of everything as it is reflected in my brain. I want it to be a comprehensive picture. The book, as I see it, should begin with my—I suppose I shall have to say—" metaphysics " ; it should display my *orbis terrarum*, and then it should come down to the spectacle of mankind as I apprehend it and my place in that history, and so to the immediate affairs of everyday life, to moods, passions, experiences, lessons, and at last to the faith and purpose that sustain me and fill my mind at the present time and make living on worth while. The main objective is that faith and purpose. All the rest will lead up to that, to how and why I accept life and go on living.

My metaphysics I can set about at once. I shall have chiefly to explain why I have no metaphysics. The reader need fear no elaboration of a system, not even a negative system. It is not so much a statement of scepticism that I have to make, as a confession of accepted ignorance. Yet that does not mean that I am—what is the word ?—a Positivist.

I find most of the world that other people describe or take for granted much more hard and clear and definite than mine is. I am at once vaguer and more acutely critical. I don't believe so fully and unquestioningly in this " common-sense " world in which we meet and exchange ideas, this world of fact, as most people seem to do. I have a feeling that this common-sense world is not *final*. It is necessitated in many ways by the conditions under which we think and communicate, and I do not regard these conditions as being fundamental to existence. The common-sense world is a practical working world and so far true, but it is not necessarily ultimately true. There are times when I feel as though it was less the sphere that enclosed me and made my all, than a sort of magic crystal into which I peered and saw myself living. I have, as it were, a sense of externality and a feeling that perhaps it might be possible, though I cannot imagine how it could be possible, to turn away and look at something else quite different from this common-sense world—another world.

I never get to more than that in the way of detachment. I never get further from philosophical Positivism than that. Could anything be vaguer? It is the shadow of the ghost of a doubt. The individual in that crystal globe of time and space has a hundred thousand traits by which I know him for myself. How, then, can I be the onlooker also, of whom I know nothing at all except that he sees? This sense of externality is, perhaps, no more than a trick of my brain, like a moment of giddiness as one walks along the street. It certainly has no practical significance.

I am reminded as I write of this of a queer little thing that happened to me at times, most frequently in my adolescence and when I was a young man. I do not think that it has occurred at all during the last ten or fifteen years. It was this: The visible world, remaining just as bright and clear as ever it had been, would suddenly appear to be *minute*. People became midgets, the houses and the furniture, dolls'-houses and furniture, the trees, mere moss-fronds. I myself did not seem to shrink to scale; it was only the universe about me that shrank. This effect would last for a few seconds or for a few minutes, and then it would pass away. I have not found anyone else who has had this particular experience, but I am sure it has happened to many other people. I have never had the converse effect of enlargement.

I suppose a slight momentary change in my blood or breathing produced a change of phase in my nervous state, I perceived a difference in the *feel* of my vision, and my mind, a little perplexed, interpreted it in this fashion. If so there may be drugs that would have the same effect.

Or there may have been some little transitory fluctuation in my sensations of optical adjustment. Mental specialists connect doubts and confusions about one's identity in dreams and in cases of mental disorder with changes in bodily feeling. Yet one may argue that a conviction of reality which is so finely poised that it totters at a slight excess or defect of oxygen or suchlike factor in the blood cannot be a very soundly established one.

But it is not my intention to be mystical. It is the world in the crystal

I want to write about, this crystal into which I seem to have been looking now and living for nine-and-fifty years. I will not question the reality or quality of the crystal further. It does not matter for my present purpose whether that is the final reality, or only a transitory moving picture produced by some stir of chemicals in a membrane of grey-matter inside my skull. I want to write of the motives of action in it, of its pains and pleasures, of its beauty and provocation, before my mental strength begins, as it must so soon do now, to ebb. I want to write of love and curiosity and habit and inertia and all the other motives that have kept me going. I shall write as a fairly fortunate and happy man, glad to have lived and very glad still to be alive, but wonderingly, more than a little regretful that this perplexing, interesting fabric of display and experiences, so incomplete still, so challenging a tangle of riddles, is drawing towards its inexorable end.

I do not want to go yet. I am sorry to have so little time before me. I wish before the ebb carries me right out of things altogether that I could know more—and know better. I came into the world with a clutter of protest; my mind is still haunted by protesting questions too vague for me to put into any form that would admit of an answer. If I had more time, I would like, just for a little while, in a winter's fireside talk, as it were, to have things made clearer before I go.

§ 3

My life, I confess, seems to me to be short, distressingly short, preposterously short in comparison both with the vast range of my thoughts in space, and with the huge perspectives of the past and the future in which we think nowadays. I doubt if man had quite the same sense of abbreviation before this measuring by astronomical distances and geological ages began. And life is not only short, but things in it are out of proportion. The rules of perspective are reversed, and the remotest memories loom largest and are the most vivid. Things that happened five-and-twenty years ago are often distant and obscure enough, but the things that happened in my childhood are things of yesterday. I am no longer the young man I was. He and I have almost lost identity. Nevertheless, I am still intensely the child I used to be.

I suppose this is because most things are first seen and heard and felt in childhood, and our minds file these early impressions as key-pictures and refer the later ones to them. So they are continually refreshed. But later experiences are no longer used as new points of reference.

A hundred times, perhaps, in the course of my life and in a score of places, for example, I have seen autumnal horse-chestnut leaves reflected in brown water and the branches of a horse-chestnut tree coming down close to that still mirror, but it is definitely as a child that I think of seeing them, and all the other occasions are in comparison vague and unassigned. I was in the old punt on the great pond at Mowbray. The silvery sheet of water had that convex effect one always got there upon a day of absolute calm. It was like a very smooth broad buckler. I think that effect of curvature must have been due to the way the reeds and bushes shaded the edges, or perhaps to some trick in the angle of the reflection of the pines up the slope. Far away against a background of dark bushes, some of them still deep green and some a rusty red, floated a little squadron of motionless swans, the old bird marvellously tranquillised since his days of terrifying aggression in the early summer. Even the ducks and the friendly attendant dab-chick among the lily leaves were silent. Everything was so still that I remember being startled by the sudden " plop " of a falling husk into the crystalline water behind me.

I suppose it is the sodden horse-chestnut leaves scattered over the wet stone pavement in the yard behind this house that have released this group of memories. The arm-chair and Dickon's study fade to nothingness. I sit again in the punt with a row of glossy brown conkers all neatly bored beside me. I have bored them with a long nail rather tediously and have

had to be careful of the palm of my hand. One or two I have broken.
There are leaves in the bottom of the punt, and a thin and scattered remnant
clinging insecurely here and there among the branches about me. I have
been seeking a perfectly golden leaf without a patch of green or brown
upon it, I have tried the taste of a horse-chestnut and have disapproved
of it and spat out and watched the fragments of my mouthful sinking slowly
and eddying down through the clear water, and thought how queer it
was that some should spin and whirl about and some sink swift and
straight, and I have wondered if the hooflike end of the leaf-stem accounts
for the name of the tree. And now I am sitting motionless, suddenly
aware of the tremendous quiet of the day.

It is as if the whole world paused. It is as if God was present, God whom
they talk about so much in church. . . .

Yes, I am almost as much back there as I am present in this
room. Perhaps for the first time in my life I observed serenity on that day.

Half a century ago that was, right at the other end of life, and it is more
vivid than yesterday. That must have been our first year at Mowbray
in the beginnings of my strange father's last burst of success before his
tragic downfall. We went to Mowbray from Bexhill, and everything was
new and larger and finer about us.

I was nearly eight then, and at Mowbray I seem to have awakened quite
suddenly to beauty and wonder. I do not recall any perception of beauty
and loveliness at Bexhill. I think the summer must have been exceptionally
fine and kindly. At that age I was entering upon a fresh phase of development, and the novelty and spaciousness of the new life stimulated me.
As I sit here brooding at this writing-pad I live again a score of vivid,
small, and yet intensely significant moments, and most of them are in the
open air in the park and particularly round and about the great pond.
Hardly any are indoors. I do not recall very much of the Mowbray
interiors. Indoors at that time, I think, I was always reading, reading,
reading.

In that punt it was I first became aware of the science of optics. I
discovered something remarkable about the handle of a little fishing-net
that I had put into the water. I was holding it quite still in the hope of
presently whipping it up with some minnows, and I perceived that it was
bent sharply at the surface of the water. I forgot the minnows and began
to move the net to and fro and higher and deeper. It seemed bent, but it
was not really bent. The bending shifted as I shifted the net. I puzzled
over that distortion.

And in that old punt I puzzled over the riddle of reflection as well as
of refraction. I found that if I crouched down with my nose just above
the side of the punt I saw nothing of the bottom at all, only blue sky and

tree branches. Then, as I rose, suddenly the still bottom with its roots and dead leaves and slimy weeds and the shoals of minute fish hovering above it came into view. I experimented. I extended and retracted myself. I tried to catch the exact moment between squatting and standing, when the mirror became transparent and the bottom appeared.

There was an afternoon at Mowbray, it must have been earlier in the year, in the summer, when I first discovered forget-me-nots. At the upper end of the pond near where the stream came in there were shallows and floating masses of green weed with pink blossoms and thick, widespread clumps of sedges, and half hidden amidst these sedges were clouds of flowers of a divine, incredible blue. Either I had never seen forget-me-nots growing before or I had never observed them. I went to and fro peering from the bank, and then took off my shoes and stockings and waded into the water and mud until my knickerbockers, in spite of all the tucking up I gave them, were soaked. And I picked handfuls of these the loveliest of all English wild-flowers.

Then suddenly came horror, the unqualified horror of childhood. My legs were streaming with blood. The sharp blades of the sedge leaves had cut them in a score of places. Fresh gouts of blood gathered thickly along the cuts, and then darted a bright red ribbon down my wet and muddy skin. " Oh ! Oh ! " I cried in profound dismay, struggling and splashing back to the bank and still holding my forget-me-nots with both hands.

Still do I remember most vividly my astonishment at the treachery of that golden, flushed, and sapphire-eyed day.

That it should turn on me !

§ 4

THINKING of one's childhood is like opening a great neglected volume haphazard and reading in it. There must be many thousands of such pages that I might turn over, still bright, still fresh. The earliest pictures are the most fragmentary ; they are vignetted in the unknown. One very early moment of self-discovery comes to mind when I was lying naked on my back gazing in a sort of incredulous wonder at my belly and knees. That must have been at Bexhill, although I have forgotten the background, and I could not have been more than three years old.

" *Me ?* " I thought.

Use and wont have dulled that first astonishment at the conscious sight of my body, but I still retain something of the early incredulity. Mine is that baby body still, though my grandchildren would not believe it if I told them so ; it is changed, but not out of recognition, it is younger than my face, yet in quite a little while now I shall see it for the last time and cease to see or feel it any more, and it will be altogether finished with, material for the undertaker and the crematorium. And that, I suppose, will be the end of all the pictures, and the volume will never be added to nor opened again. I know of no attic or store-room to which that great tome will go—even to moulder. It will, it seems, vanish.

I stare at this prospect in very much the same mood of wonder in which I stared at my foreshortened body fifty-odd years ago. My approaching disintegration is even more amazing than my realised appearance.

I think that discovery of my body must be one of the earliest pictures in my volume. But these vignettes of one's infancy are not firmly bound in nor properly arranged. Perhaps I was put to meditate upon that bed quite frequently. I remember my pink belly and the fat knees and toes that I recognised as myself, and how that then or later—it is not distinct— I discovered a most remarkable and most unaccountable button in the middle of my belly. At that point, though I did not know it, I had been cut off from the tree of life and made a separate individual.

Mixed up with that exploration of my navel is the hard long line of the rail of the bedstead and a memory of my mother standing at the foot of the bed and—strange and startling thing for my infant intelligence to realise— weeping very bitterly. I do not think I said or did anything about that, probably my mother never imagined I had observed it, but I remember it very plainly.

All these impressions are bright and immense in my mind. The later things in my life, even when they are as vivid, are not as large. This I perceive is the common lot ; nearly all autobiographers are disposed to develop the childish or adolescent experiences out of all proportion to the central realities of the life. But I shall not do that here; it is the maturer relationships with which I am concerned. . . .

For a time I must discontinue making these notes altogether, for old Sir Rupert York has rung me up. He has discovered I am in London, and this dismal downpour has afflicted him so that he cannot endure to be alone. He must not stir abroad in the wet, so I shall break my resolution to keep in this room to-day and go out and lunch with him. I must make my apologies to Madame Deland.

§ 5

" WONDERFUL " is certainly the word for Sir Rupert; he is close upon eighty, but his mind is as bright as it has ever been. He talks and moves slowly, and he confesses that he feels no longer disposed to work hard and is easily tired by any effort, but he misses no point in one's talk and his thought is candid and serene. On his desk were drawings and a photograph and a plaster-cast of a gorilla's foot; some American has been writing unwisely of the use of the ape's big toe in walking, and Sir Rupert has been demolishing him, patiently, unhurryingly, and completely. He is also feeling his way towards the use of a peculiar sort of early stone implement with a beaked end, and the room is littered with specimens.

He looks better than when I saw him last two years ago. Then he seemed to me to be greatly fallen away, and his skin had that rather shrivelled white delicacy that comes with age; now either I was prepared for it or it has really recovered tone and texture. He ate a good lunch; he is still far from the days of digestive paps, and in spite of the wet he came out on his doorstep without thinking of a coat to stand and smile his farewell.

Big and smiling he is and in some subtle way noble, and it is a comfort to me to have been with him, for in his case at any rate old age has not meant a lean and slippered egotism and jealousy of youth.

I told him about my project of writing a book, and he confessed he had had similar thoughts. They have come to nothing with him because rostro-carinate implements and suchlike riddles are more interesting to him than himself. But it was curious to see how different was his conception of autobiography. He is the least metaphysical of men; he has no doubts of the reality of our world of time and space; he will not trouble his mind with any speculations about his identity or consider any system outside the universe of science; he is even disregardful and a little impatient with the later analyses of modern physics. And the story he would tell would be a matter-of-fact record beginning with a sturdy boy full of material curiosities, fascinated by the discovery of strange mammalian bones in the Crag, and going on from that to collecting, to the systematic study of geology and morphology, and so to a fair full life of material gathered, generalisations sifted, facts insisted upon, and false conclusions exposed. I have always had a great affection for Sir Rupert since years ago we did some work together on the fracture of flints and bones; he had asked me to help him with an optical examination of flint under strain ; and he still seems to me in several ways the greatest scientific man I have known, the greatest and the simplest. He is as simple as some fine animal that has grown to its full development under favourable conditions.

My own scientific work gives me the measure of his. He makes me feel no better than an excursionist in this world of science in which he is a prince. An excursionist or a prospector. I was not simple after his fashion. Wonder touched me as it did him in boyhood. It was not fossils that seized upon my imagination, but the riddle of double refraction and the perplexities of what we still thought of in those days as the " shapes " of atoms and molecules. Some of my work was quite respectable. Other men have gone along the road I opened ; it was a sound piece of road. But I did not keep on whole-heartedly. In the end I deserted science altogether, as I shall have to explain. I am what passes for a rich man, an industrialist. I am one of the active directors of Romer, Steinhart, Crest and Co., and I have a share and a voice in most of their affiliated activities. I hold a considerable number of patents, and I am an exploiter of secret processes, which I recognise are offensive to science. The essence of science is open statement. During the war I was what they called an expert, and after the war I was foolish enough to dabble in politics. I thought a new and greater age was beginning and that the war had taught us a lesson. It did. But the lesson is slow in digesting, and I have experimented and tried this way and that in my effort to express and realise my conception of it. And I have let women deflect my life very considerably. I have been greedy for property and freedom and influence and for many sorts of experience I had better have avoided. But Sir Rupert with a large modesty and devotion has gone on serving the truth in that field to which he was called.

I do not think there has ever been any great conflict of motives in his life. Quite early and quite without reservations he determined to give himself to natural history. Other things have had to accommodate themselves to that. His circumstances made the gift easy ; Professor Huxley was a frequent visitor to his home and Charles Darwin patted his head. And to be a naturalist then was a great adventure ; science had challenged tradition and dogma, and the warfare that followed in the minds of men was an epic warfare. We live in the liberties of thought that were won for us then. He has never married, and though I suspect him of no excesses of chastity, I perceive that the mixture of sexual need and the hunger for a dear companion that has so disturbed me has had no equivalent influence upon him. Nor has he ever displayed any religious impulse beyond an upright, unswerving devotion to his sense of truth. He has accepted the work that lay before him single-mindedly, living comfortably and happily and without any sense of sacrifice. He has done that work magnificently. Abundant it has been, and sound and wide, and strictly within the limitations of things as they plainly are. He questions so ably because he accepts so completely. Before I went to him to-day I had intended, forgetting a little his quality, to put my conception of the provisional reality of life before him and discuss it with him. Such an exchange would be as possible with a pensive lion in the Zoo.

Ever and again, as we talked together and ranged from this to that, he would return to gnaw the bones of his American professor. " You see," he would resume in a pause, " if anyone had been trying to make a case and deliberately faking the photograph, he could not have put the foot in a better light for his own ends than this fellow has done. If he made the photograph. But did he ? He doesn't say whether he did or not. It may be the other way round. He may just have seen it somewhere and picked it up and run away with a misconception. That's not so bad. Then he's merely careless—and obstinate. He wanted to take up an original point of view and this made it seem plausible. But while this cast here of mine is from a living gorilla, *his* sketch is made from a photograph of doubtful origin of a foot which I am fairly certain has been taken out of spirits. . . . Queer. . . . All through he shows a sort of eagerness. . . .

" Some of these Americans live too near the newspapers. They get the headline spirit. They want to make startling discoveries and startling reversals in a hurry. . . .

" One has to understand one can't do that sort of thing. . . .

" They must live under bad conditions over there. I don't understand what sort of surroundings a biologist can have—in a Western university, for example. They seem to be restless, excessively sensitive to cheap judgments. Over there—— "

Sir Rupert paused and his manner became very earnest. " *They will let newspaper interviewers come into their discussions !* " he said. " They will let interviewers make statements for them, and they will attend to the stuff interviewers and paragraphists put on to other people. They seem to have no feeling for precisions in such things. . . . This man seems to be afraid to admit details that tell against him. . . . As though he might lose something. . . .

" And yet, you see, they will make the rashest attacks. . . .

" He brought it on himself."

He reflected for a moment and patted the plaster cast beside him on the table, and regarded it with a benevolent expression. He had brought it in from the study to the dining-room. He has the charming habit of carrying about with him everywhere the implements and bones that are interesting him. I have heard of him sitting at a large dinner party with a

2

polished rhinoceros bone from which he would not be separated beside his plate, just as a child will insist on sitting at meals with some very dear new toy on the table.

He disentangled his mind from the cast and remembered his duty as a host.

" You like this Château Margaux ?   1917.   Good year, 1917."

§ 6

I WISH I knew more of the practical side of literature. I suppose that after a craftsman has written six or seven " works " he learns so well how to set about his business that he writes on strongly and confidently from the very first word, and has—I think Stevenson explains as much somewhere —the end of his book latent in his opening paragraph. But I have been beating about the bush for five sections and making notes for various matters that must come in later, and still I doubt if I have told anything at all about my world. Instead I have written about my childhood and made a sketch of my host at lunch. It is like the way one draws on the blotting-paper in a board-room. Unless—unpleasant thought !—it is the onset of the garrulous stage.

I shall keep the morning's writing and this note upon Sir Rupert at hand, but I shall try a fresh commencement here. Perhaps, after all, the proper way is to go directly to the core of the matter. Even though that may mean stiff going for a bit for both writer and reader. How in the most general terms do I apprehend life ?

Metaphysically I have never been able to get very far beyond Schopenhauer's phrase : *Die Welt als Wille und Vorstellung.* Life to me as to him, when he wrote that title at least, is a spectacle, a show, with a drive in it.

Is there a plot to the show ; is it a drama moving through a vast complexity to a definite end, or at any rate moving in a definite direction ? To that question the various religions have given their various answers, and I will say at once that I have found none of their answers satisfactory. There is some invincible fact or group of facts outside of, or positively inconsistent with all their explanations. Yet every one of them has some half-truth in it for me. Either the whole is too complex for me to perceive a plot or recognise the one the teachers would have me see, or there is no plot.

I admit a tremendous splendour, beauty, and delight in much of the scenery. The lighting effects are superb. For more than fifty years I have been turning the pages of the book of sunsets and never have I wearied. The texture and quality of the costumes, the subtlety, charm, and humour of the cast again, are often amazing. I rejoice perhaps excessively in the loveliness of the bodies in which we are clothed. But plot to hold together this vast display in one comprehensive system I cannot see. My mind seeks it and needs it ; the spectacle remains incoherent in spite of all my seeking.

2*

It is like one of those rummage-sale outbreaks of disconnected cleverness they give in the theatres nowadays and call revues. And some of the scenes and some of the actors are infernally dull, some of the cleverness is harsh and base, some of the turns bore to the limits of endurance, ugly and offensive things come on and spoil an act and will not go off for all my manifested disapproval. And like an Elizabethan gentleman I am upon the stage and not in the auditorium, and ever and again my stool is kicked from under me and I have to answer an unexpected cue, pull myself together, as people say, and improvise a part. Passive or active, I am always in the centre of this show of mine.

The shifting values of the scene at any particular moment, the distribution of importance and quality, come, I perceive, mainly from three groups of things. Firstly, there is what is fed to us—*dietary* shall I call it ?—in which I include not only meat and drink and the want of them, but the reception or lack of all we can inhale or inject into our systems, fresh air or unexpected ideas. Secondly, come *infections and injuries* bodily and mental, and their feverish distressful stimulations. Thirdly, there is *irradiation*, by which I mean all that we call the weather, and heat and cold and sounds and light, and those subtler magic rhythms of colour and harmony that flow through eyes and ears and the substance of my body, to exalt or debase me. These three groups of things charge my life with its current quality and determine whether the mood of my part shall be urgency or valiant resistance, gay confidence, anger, respose, or despair. They determine, too, whether the tone shall be strong or weak, concentrated or diffused. There seems to be little or nothing in me that can resist these determinations. But manifest through all the phases they create there is an intermittent urgency of self-assertion and aggression upon which my poor simplifying and integrating human mind imposes a unity and continuity. This is the Me.

This urgency is, in the broader sense of the word, sexual : in that broad sense of the new psychology which makes sexual almost co-extensive with racial. Its drive is the drive of what Shaw calls the " life force " and Schopenhauer the " will to live." But it is concentrated about my egoism and divided off from the general life force of the world. It is protean ; it involves an anxiety for present and future things outside myself it seeks expression and recognition and response. Occasionally it becomes barely and plainly a clamour for woman. But—I speak for myself— it is reluctant to embody its desire in any particular woman for any length of time. Even when desire has run—as it has done once or twice in my life—deep and narrow and direct and passionate for a particular woman my rationalising mind has still been disposed to invent generalisations that broadened and mitigated the intensity of that desire. There is a counterbalancing disposition of this force to admit the claim of a wider obligation, and to reconcile the narrower and intenser drive with that. This widening has increased with the years ; the sexual has become more racial, and the will to live for myself has changed more and more into a will to live for life

Such are the ingredients of my role in this tremendous, terrifying, delightful, exciting, unequal, indifferent, and irrelevant revue of existence. This is my personal analysis of life. This is the composition of my life as it presents itself to me. These are the threads of the stitches in the tapestry, the elements of my hours.

§ 7

WHEN the curtain of death comes down, is the *revue* over ?

So far as William Clissold goes, I think it is. I think that death is a thing I shall never experience, for when it comes to me I shall be dead. I may see it coming, I may hope for it or fear it, but I shall never know it come. I shall never know it has come just as I never know that sleep has come. I do not believe in personal immortality. In my youth I struggled against the idea of individual extinction, but now I accept it quite tranquilly. I think there may be something immortal in me, and what that is I will do my best to explain in subsequent sections, but I do not think that immortal part contains any of the distinctive factors that individualise me. The sound of my voice, the oddities of my mind, my likes and dislikes, and the great volume of my personal memories will, I think, end when my heart ceases to beat.

I have still enough greediness for personal experience to want, if not complete immortality, at least a little extension of my time. I am like a well-behaved child who is willing to go to bed but would prefer to sit up a while longer. But I can find no tittle of evidence that experience goes on after physical death. The phenomena of fainting, sleep, and unconsciousness all sustain my conviction that the immobility of the dead is also subjective. And I am quite unable to imagine any sort of living at all, any sort of conscious existence, without hands that feel, eyes that see, a sense of material substance, and a stir of bodily feeling. It is not strength but weakness of the imagination that enables people to think of themselves as bodiless " spirits." The idea that man is a threefold being of body, soul, and spirit, all separable and mysteriously endowed with his personality, seems to me a survival of remote barbaric speculations. I can no more think of myself living on as a spirit than as living on as a moving photograph.

The decay of the established religious beliefs which wrapped the life after death in a sacred reticence has let loose much popular necromancy. I was sufficiently involved with these curiosities at one time to be a member of the Society for Psychical Research and to follow up some of the alleged evidence for personal survival after death. I found evidence of much deception and still more self-deception. And even if I had admitted the reality of all the phenomena tendered, which I would be very loth to do, they would have proved nothing except the survival of fragments of persona will and memory. Suppose a medium to produce some trivial secret between myself and some departed intimate, known to no one else ; that no more proves that my friend is still mentally alive than a corrupting fragment of his face with a characteristic scar would prove his bodily survival. The mere fact of the medium being in possession of this confidence suggests helplessness and insensibility in the departed. Generally the supposed messages from the dead display great mental degeneration. The mediums produce no more than a shrivelled phantom of the sought-after dead. When Victor Hugo was summoned back from the shades, Anatole France told me, he had forgotten *Hernani* and *Ruy Blas* altogether, and acquired nothing to make up for this but the sort of moral platitudes one might get from an intoxicated concierge. If we are to believe the stuff at all, we must believe on the evidence that the next life will be no better than a tattered fragment of this. I had rather have the flame of my life extinguished at once than turned down and down to flicker at last in such a fashion.

The revelations of Sir Oliver Lodge's *Raymond* and of Sir Arthur Conan Doyle and the lucubrations of Mr. Vale Owen confirm this view. The effect is not so much as if they had drawn the veil from a vision of deep and mighty things, as that the curate has bought a cheap magic lantern and got an enthusiastic and humourless spinster to daub his slides. I am prepared to believe the universe can be deeply tragic and evil or wonderful and beautiful, but not that it can be fundamentally silly. On the whole my presumption that there is nothing immortal in our individualities is strengthened rather than weakened by the evidence of this cloud of all too explicit witnesses to the contrary that has arisen in the past few years.

§ 8

THOUGH this is all that I can make of life, my mind is not entirely content to rest at this. I do not think that life is as entirely chancey and miscellaneous as my statement may seem to leave it. I do not believe that it is a succession of moods and impulses in an aimless confusion. There is order in the universe ; there is law, essential and inexorable law. It is law outside of and independent of our wills, and perhaps irrelevant to our wills. But it is there.

It is not, I think, a habit of mind derived from early religious teaching that sustains this belief. It is much more closely related to the assumption of my scientific work. The world is in the nature of rational and explicable. At the same time it is not in any way subservient to human feelings and human ends.

I am reminded of a dear little grey kitten I had last year—I hope I have her still—at the Villa Jasmin. She was much intrigued by my cheval glass. She saw her reflection in it and she was greatly perplexed because she could not get at it. She struggled with the riddle. It was clear to me that she believed the damned thing could be understood. But it was more and more evident to me that her nice, quick, and in many ways very clever little brain had nothing at all in it to enable her to apprehend the nature of a reflection. She would pat the glass with her paw—after a time she patted the glass and did not attempt to put her paw through it—and then dodge round very quickly behind the mirror. Then still more quickly she would return to the front. She would stiffen her legs and bristle her hair and stalk off in a silly endearing way she had. It was just as though she raised her eyebrows and shrugged her shoulders. It was in the spirit of that grimace. She would give it up and affect boredom and go out of the room. And come back presently to give it up again. She gave it up on different days, a dozen times perhaps. But now she has probably given it up altogether.

But though she cannot understand it the thing can be understood. That is the tantalising aspect of my own insufficiency. If I were God enough I might so contrive it, not by adding anything absolutely fresh to her ganglia, but simply by strengthening and expanding one or another faculty, that she would theorise about light—to the Newtonian level. And with a little more knowledge and training to the level of Einstein and Weyl. And if there were a God above me, and it is just as possible as not there are intelligent beings above me capable of watching my mental proceedings just as I watch hers—how should I know about them if there were ?— I too might be expanded to—anyhow, a larger sphere of comprehension.

I have always had a persuasion that I have never got anything like its full possibilities out of my brain. Even for what it is, it may not be anything near its maximum of effectiveness. Ever and again I have been astonished to find myself in a phase of exceptional lucidity, I have seen my way through a game of chess or grasped a mathematical problem with a directness quite beyond my normal possibilities. Or I have had a rush of creative energy, and invented lovely things very rapidly and expressed them with unpremeditated skill. Something happened then to my brain, some exceptional aeration or other stimulation. It showed what it could do. But all the time it was no other than the rather foggy and uncertain brain of my everyday life. It is quite conceivable that our present atmosphere is not the best of all possible atmospheres for the working of the human brain, nor the normal current in our arteries its most stimulating food.

The inhabitants of Venus, if there are any inhabitants upon that steamy planet, see no sun in their sky. There is, the astronomers suppose, a complete cloud shell between its surface and outer space. Life beneath that canopy must be life in the hot twilight of a tropical forest ; daybreak must be a mere rosy or orange brightening of the grey, and night a darkling into blackness. But perhaps there are storms there, and then on some rare occasion that flocculent, dense welkin may be rent and swept aside, and the stars may shine or the naked sun blaze down upon the tossing, waving jungle. A thousand things, faintly suspected, dimly apprehended hitherto, must be revealed for a little while, stark and plain.

But my everyday mind is a cloudy and misty mind. I grope, I do not see. So far as I can judge, most of my fellow-creatures are groping too, and many of them do not even suspect this possibility of clairvoyance. They think that what they do with their minds is all that can be done with their minds. I do not agree, but I have never worked out any very effective rules for bettering my mental operations. I have never been able to trace to my own satisfaction the causes that brought about those rare occasions of exceptional brilliance. I have never secured any command over them. But they have filled me with the haunting sense of something quite graspable if only I could close my fingers upon it, something just a very little way beyond my reach, quite visible had my eyes but a tithe more sensitiveness.

Yet even if some hitherto unsuspected God were to pour illumination into my mind so that, with all that intense realisation of beauty which is inseparable from discovery, a hundred obdurate riddles dissolved into obvious necessity, still I should have made, I feel, only one more step up an endless staircase. My kitten, could I put Newton's brain in control of its furry paws, would even then be patting pebbles on the margin of an illimitable ocean.

It had been necessary for me to keep in touch with current speculations about the constitution of matter, the nature of time and space. I have watched physical science, sternly self-disciplined, probing further and further, not only from ordinary human understanding, but from ordinary human feeling. The analysis of matter, in the last quarter of a century, has reached a point when it has ceased to be in any human sense wonderful. It is incomprehensible. Every statement is a paradox ; every formula an outrage upon common sense. One is left baffled as by the hieroglyphics of some insane scribbler. In my curious childhood, when I browsed among what were then already old-fashioned books in the Mowbray library, I read of atoms and molecules almost as kindly and human as Dutch cheeses. I write Dutch cheeses because I remember how later—I was just twelve and my mother had taken Dickon and me for a sudden furtive holiday in Holland to escape, as I realised years afterwards, from the sight of news-paper placards proclaiming the Clissold Smash, Clissold in the Dock, Clissold's Cross-Examination—when I saw the golden cheeses piled all over the market place, and the quaintly costumed porters carrying them in exact geometrically arranged batches to and fro between the gaily painted barges and the market, it seemed to me that in quite that fashion it must be that molecules moved about, and the atoms of matter combined and were distributed and re-combined. Everybody in those days thought of atoms as tangible things, and of space as a framework of three dimensions as rectangular as a window sash. The ether, the now vanished ether, wrapped about us like a garment, and time was like a star and dwelt apart. I remember when I was a science student, greatly torn between my search for knowledge and the urgent need of escaping from the wreckage of our family disaster, that in the college debating society we were already dis-cussing the ideas of time being conceivable as a fourth dimension, and of a limit existing to material rectitude and exactness of repetition.

Since then all those easy old imaginings of quasi-tangible atoms and infinite incessant space have dissolved away insensibly. We have followed our deductions further and further into a stirring crystalline complex of multi-dimensional curvatures and throbbing reactions. Energy is and it is not, and then again it is, all Being flickers in and out of Not-being, there is an irrational bound set to motion, there is a limit to the range of temperature. Space is bent in some incomprehensible fashion so that straight lines re-enter into themselves, gravitation is a necessary consequence of dura-tion, and atoms are the orbits and harmonies of infinitesimal electrical charges. Einstein's own description for popular enlightenment of his space-time system with its bent and possibly unstable co-ordinates, reads to me like the description of a clear vibrating four dimensional haggis. Weyl goes wider and further, and Bohr has imposed a rippling intermission upon the whole universe. In the depths or heights of physics, for one word seems as good as the other when all direction is lost, I find my mind sitting down at last exhausted of effort in much the mood of Albrecht Dürer's *Melencolia*. I have gone far along that way, and I can go no farther into that wilderness of vanishing forms and puffs of energy in a quadri-dimensional field of force.

The science of the elements is becoming too difficult for ordinary men to grasp—which must gratify every intelligent priest. But the mystical God of force and substance—if one may use the word " God " for so remote a conception—to whom the endless winding staircase of molecular science mounts for ever and never attains is, I feel, no priest's God of sentiment and morality, no friend of man and pitiful judge of our peccadillos, but a God of austere complexity, a God of variable and evasive rhythms and unfathomable intricacy, the God of a philosophical mathematician.

I note as I write this that something has passed insensibly out of my mind since my youth, and that hitherto I have not observed its departure. And that is, *the awe of the inorganic*. During my student days I was drawn by an overwhelming fascination to the lovely facts of crystalline structure, and particularly of double refraction and the interference of light. I went into these mysteries exalted and intoxicated with wonder. Partly it was an intellectual exaltation ; but partly it was sensuous, like the joy women find in the deep beauty of precious stones. Did I, in those days, in some faintly anthropomorphic way regard the glittering planes and beams and passages and patterning in those translucent depths into which I pried, as being accessible, as being physically accessible ? Did I somehow conceive of myself as presently walking out of the ordinary paths of everyday into those magic palaces ?

At any rate I cannot bring back any remnant of that wonder now. Neither in that connection nor in connection with that other profundity, space. There was a time, a rather earlier time in my life, when my little soul shone and was uplifted at the starry enigma of the sky. That has gone ; gone absolutely. I could not have imagined that it would ever go. While I was still a little fellow at Mowbray I remember looking at the stars one winter night upon the terrace—it must have been a night in winter because Orion was there—and I was in an ecstasy. I was rapt in a passion of wonder. I was lost to all other feeling. I had slipped out without a coat and did not care that afterwards my governess scolded me. For a time I did not hear her calling close at hand. But now I can go out and look at the stars as I look at the pattern on the wall-paper of a railway station waiting-room. About them I have become prosaically reasonable. If they were not there, there would be something else as casual, as indifferently sublime.

The more I have learnt about them the more coldly aloof from me have they become. What has happened to me ? Is it the story of my little grey kitten over again ? Have I grown tired of patting behind the glass ?

§ 9

I RETURN from the *coulisses* of physics and the deep dark outlook of astronomy, from the underworld and outerworld of material mysteries, to the spectacle upon the stage.

I have compared it in its casual inconsecutiveness to a London or New York revue. I cannot ignore the valiant attempts men have made to impose a coherent and comprehensive story upon it, to explain it as a drama with a beginning, a middle, and an end. Judaism and Islam give good but inadequate histories of how it all happened, and Christian teaching carries over some inexplicable gaps very ably and bravely; Buddhism, too, tells a tale with a curious affinity to the modern scientific spirit in its conception of impersonal retributions and its recognition of vast æons. But Hindu thought is saturated with the cyclic delusion that things come back again. As my vision of the world has grown plainer and more assured, the last tinge of credibility has faded from these various dramatic diagrams of the universe. They have followed the fairies that I could still half hope to see and play with, when I lay down amidst the bracken of Mowbray Park.

I wish I could recall more of my early religious life. It developed in that late Victorian period when nothing had gone from the creeds but everything had weakened; people still believed in hell but did not like to have it talked about. Instruction was vague and allusive. I should call my upbringing " disintegrating Protestant." The idea of God was very much entangled with the disciplines of my nurse and governess, and the most vivid memory I have of the divinity teaching of my Bexhill days, was a highly illuminated card in an Oxford frame bearing the words—

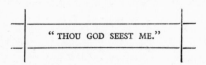

" THOU GOD SEEST ME."

I believed that firmly, and it abased my private dignity to a reluctant propitiatory restraint of my private thoughts. I would try to pretend that I was not thinking something that I was actually thinking. I was told repeatedly that I ought to love God, but I cannot remember feeling the slightest gleam of affection for that silent, invisible, dominating, and dangerous spectator. Dangerous !—he could strike me dead, and was quite capable of doing so. On some mere technical point. How could one love a Being of that sort?

But certainly I never ventured to think that I did not love him. I was too afraid of him.

So was Dickon, although he was more than two years older than I. But we said very little about it to each other.

There was scant mention of the Crucifixion in our early teaching. I was told of it as a harsh matter of fact, but it was not dwelt upon. I saw pictures of it, and they filled me with horror that God should permit it, and there was a lesson from the New Testament read in church on Easter Sunday that dismayed and depressed a small soul already suffering from a surfeit of very new hot-cross buns. I was told to love this victim on the cross also, and there was nothing in my heart to respond. I felt that as a member of the deity he need not have put this dreadful thing upon me.

It was some transitory governess who insisted upon my loving the crucified one. I have forgotten her name, but she had a very long body in a green dress, a thick pink neck that rolled up over a slight swell of chin into a pink face, and a voice that impressed me as being rich. She always seemed to be leaning forward. When she found no spark of gratitude in us for the cross and thorns, she tried another aspect of her faith, and showed us a brightly coloured picture of Christ with a crowd of children about him and one upon his knee.

" Wouldn't *you* like to come to him? " she said, watching our faces for intimations of a response.

That estranged us in a different way.

I remember Dickon with his little freckled hands half thrust into his first knickerbocker pockets, looking very obdurate and saying nothing.

We wouldn't commit ourselves. . . .

That is how I was taught about Jesus Christ. It is only in recent years that a personality has emerged through that curtain of mingled horror and mawkishness that was woven before him in my childhood. . . .

My mother went to church and had us go to church. Under cross-examination she would perhaps have admitted finally, and with qualifications and evident distaste, that she was a Christian, but she would have agreed at once and cordially that she was a Churchwoman, and even a " good Churchwoman." I do not recall any occasion when she spoke to us herself of Christ or Salvation or any such topic, nor did any of our nurses or governesses except that one I have just mentioned. Our home had a religion, but it was an extremely restrained religion; it was felt to have passed beyond the bounds of delicacy; it was referred to rather than actually produced. At church one did not listen much, and only the more anæmic hymns were sung. Even those abbreviated Anglican services seemed tediously unnecessary. "Now to God the Father, God the Son, and God the Holy Ghost." I recalled my wandering thoughts. I might move about again. Pouf! what a relief! Nevertheless, the idea of God gripped me as a terrible idea.

For the life of me I cannot reconstruct the phases by which my mind recovered from the suggestion of that all-seeing, all-pervading, disapproving, and restraining deity. But when I was a science student I was in full revolt against that obsession and, more than a little scared at my own daring, I would invent "funny" blasphemous stories about "my friend Mr. G." I would pretend to have special communications and revelations from this mythical person and to be exceptionally influential in my prayers. Sometimes I would call him "the other Mr. G.," because in those days British Liberalism was disastrously dominated by that astounding irrepressible person Mr. Gladstone, and it was the custom of the reluctant impotent party his energy hauled after him to refer to him with a breathless reverential familiarity as "Mr. G." There was a certain spice in confusing these two holy terrors, which lost none of its savour when presently, during my student days, the earthly Mr. G. embarked upon a ridiculously ignorant defence of the Book of Genesis as a trustworthy summary of palæontology. He had so much the manner of a distinguished author replying to his reviewers. . . .

Professor Huxley, his antagonist in the *Nineteenth Century* controversy, became a great hero to me, the valiant anatomist, the grave white-haired, yellow-faced dean of our college, who stood up alone and undismayed against both the Mr. G.'s and exorcised them together from innumerable minds that had formerly been oppressed by them.

I do not think enough attention has been given to the difference of our religious reactions at successive phases in our development. The great religions of the world come down to us from a time when the average age was shorter, when the world was relatively fuller of children and young people, when the emotional atmosphere was more in the key of adolescence than it is to-day. Life was short and thought was leisurely. Normally one believed what one was told. There were few things that were recognised as new and there was no appetite for novelty. The spirit of the times was against it. Ideas trickled then; in our times they jet. Notes of interrogation, those mosquitoes of the modern world, were scarcely known. Now they swarm on every path and infect us with a fever of doubt. Only a very few people grew out of the fears and beliefs they had acquired in childhood. Now very many of us do, and our unembarrassed actions and our freely expressed thoughts bring on the minds of many of the young towards our own stage far more rapidly than they would have come of their own accord.

It is difficult for me to judge how far the current generation is repeating the phases through which Dickon and I passed forty odd years ago, and whether there is the same necessity to minimise an early horror of God by familiar jesting. The edifying literature of our boyhood was pervaded by the idea of Providence, a fussy, uncertain, preposterous interference in human affairs, and we made my Mr. G. a symbol for all the petty malignities and kindnesses of the weather, and the chances of hill and road, and the turn of the cards, for all those caprices of accident indeed that were then called "Providential." And for every oddity of nature that jarred with our preconceptions of dignified benevolence. Our Mr. G., by our insistence on his human absurdity, became indeed a caricature and a defiance of all anthropomorphic gods. "Upon any supposition," we would say of the hyena, of the wart-hog at the Zoo, or of the slug in the salad, "why did Mr. G. make *that*? If he hadn't been ashamed of his slug he wouldn't have hidden it in the lettuce leaf. And what a sell if Eve had obeyed him! She had free-will. What would he have done with all these nasty creatures? Dis-created them? . . ."

Dickon had a wonderful imagination of the Six Nights of Creation. These, he fabled, came after the Fall. So Eve was restored to her theological freedom. Mr. G., he represented, after her vexatious indiscretions, in secret and much embittered, sabotaged a once perfect universe; for six nefarious nights he sabotaged it, put the taste of sin into his work, disharmonised sounds, invented stinks, created all the disease bacteria, supplied the wasps with stings, the flies with unsavoury instincts, and changed ten thousand once honest species into malignant parasites. Dickon would lie in bed shrieking with laughter, unable for a time to expound some new and still more awful dislocation that had just occurred to him.

"Didn't care what he did!" choked Dickon. "He *was* wild! Simply didn't care."

That old jest can still shock and please. Only this last June it was that I expounded the moods and character of our Mr. G. to my dear ridiculous Clem. We were walking up a winding, stony path, the old road from this place to that unaccountable village of Gourdon, which perches so high and splendidly above the Loup, and we sat down at a bend in the road which gives a particularly good view of the blue crests of the Esterel. In a flash she was up again with a short, sharp scream, and more than half disposed to scold me for the fact that she had put her hand upon a stunted little shrub smothered in a seething mass of nasty little crawling things, soft and distended purple larvæ that were just exuding from the cobwebby nest in which I suppose they had been hatched.

"That was Mr. G.'s bad hour," said I.

"What *do* you mean?" she asked.

The hour when the insects were made, an hour, I said, of feverish, fiddling, cruel industry, a morbid muddling of matter into life. " Well, wasn't it so ? " I demanded, at the protest of her raised eyebrows.

I dilated, in accents of reproach, upon the innumerable varieties of insect species, upon their stings, bites, poisonings, infections, burrowings into living flesh, cannibalisms and hideous parasitisms, I enlarged upon the tortures they inflict and the filthy preoccupations of their activities, their immense destructiveness and exasperating uselessness. They and the spiders and lice and all the noxious creeping things betrayed a morbid streak in creation. " What was Mr. G. thinking of then ? What was he about ? Before the Fall, you know ! Before the Fall ! "

It was better than the view to see Clem's face—at the onset of an idea she ceases to be beautiful and becomes elfin—manifestly scared but much more delighted by the flavour of release in this new version of the Bridge-water treatises.

" After all," she said, coming up bravely to my level, " your Mr. G. made this view."

" And almost prevented your seeing it—by an ungentlemanly trick." . . .

We grow out of belief.   All children are naturally and essentially believers. They begin with a sense of being completely protected ; they trust un-questioningly.   A cared-for child cannot conceive that there is a funda-mental insecurity of life ; that is an idea outside its circle of thought. It believes it is completely looked after and that all its proceedings are known ; if it is good it will be made happy, and if it is naughty it will be punished.   Only later does it begin to chafe and question under the restrictions of the law, and even then it doubts the justice of the control long before it doubts the existence of the control.   Much of this childish mind persists with many people into middle age and even into old age. You will find quite old people under some mishap cry out upon the in-justice of fate as though a promise had been broken.   The other day I was told that Margaret Payton, that valiant sceptic and most clear-headed woman, had had a painful minor operation.   Half submerged by the chloroform she betrayed her older, still persistent, preconceptions. " What have I *done*," she asked and asked again and murmured and muttered, " that God should make me suffer like this ? . . . What have I *done*? . . . What right has God ? . . . It is not just to me."

But we who really go right through into the completely adult stage come out at last beyond any sense of providence or responsibility. We realise the complete indifference of the universe to us and our behaviour. We know we are exposed and unprotected. " The Lord is my Shepherd," said the Psalmist, " therefore will I fear no evil."   And again, " God is our refuge and strength, a very present help in time of trouble."   But

I cherish no illusions about my shepherd. For good or evil no God is dogging me. There is no shield at my back and no friend to guard me from the ambush. But no-one reads my private thoughts before I can read them myself as they well up in me. No-one holds me accountable for my motives. No-one complicates my conscience and thwarts my will by arbitrary imperatives. If I tell the truth it is because lying seems to me a servility or a treachery and I do not like it, and if I go out of my way to be kind it is just as if I went out of my way to visit a pleasant corner in a garden.

§ 10

IN my earlier harsher phases of disbelief, while my conceptions of mental processes were still crude, I was very severe in my judgments upon the teachers and priests and professional servants of a revealed religion that was manifestly wrong in its revelations. I thought, for example, that it was only necessary to go to a clergyman and explain to him simply and clearly how this new Darwinism—how new it was in those days!—had swept away the historical Fall of Man, the very foundation of his scheme of salvation, to oblige him to cast aside his clerical collar and his specially cut garments, and, leaving them as a gift for any casual tramp, set out, in shirt and socks and braces so to speak, upon a search for some less super-seded costume and some more justifiable occupation than the cure of souls. And when I saw the churches still open everywhere, and the preachers still preaching in the old terms and the congregations standing up to sing the old hymns and kneeling down to pray in the old confidence, I did not know whether most to blame the stupidity or the dishonesty of mankind.

And I still recall quite vividly my fellow-student, Davidson, at the College of Science, and how he would shrink and retract from my efforts to talk about the theological applications of the new biology. We shared a bench during the opening course of physics. He would lose his wind like a punctured tyre at the mere intimation of this topic ; he would pant and his ears would grow red. He had a way of turning from me at the bench so that of all his features I saw just his red ear. It is only nowadays that I begin to understand the fear and disgust he felt for me. " I want to get on with my work," he would gasp at last, and there was hatred in his eye. " I don't want to talk to you. Not in the least. . . . Please, don't speak to me please."

Although he had been quite willing to talk about all sorts of things before he discovered my heretical bent.

I do not know if Davidson is still in the world or whether he may read this, but at any rate I will offer him my belated apologies for my intrusions upon the sacred places of his mind. They were sacred and they had no defences. I was already so much at large then, and still so young, that I could not understand how rooted and vitally entangled he remained. Religion is only formally a thing of the intelligence ; its substance is feeling and a way of life. Every religion pretends to rest upon facts and statements, but no religion really does so. The ordinary man has a private and personal world which is more or less completely ensphered in his religious beliefs, they give him a sense of being protected and of being accountable and of having a definite personal importance in the scheme of things. It is practically instinctive with him that this sphere of assurance and confidence must not be shattered. If it is, life will become as impossible for him as it is for the chick of a prematurely broken egg. And so he resists, and, indeed, becomes incapable of considering the most conclusive arguments against the formula on which his security depends.

He will not have them even as a recognised error in his world.

The other afternoon I was set thinking very vigorously by the face and behaviour of a priest, a man perhaps twenty years younger than myself, whom Clem and I found in the train at Vence. We two had been walking over the hills since the early morning, and we were very happy and a little tired and full of sweet air. We just caught the afternoon train with a run, and we got in breathless and a little clumsily and with a gasp of laughter ; we threw a jest at each other about my Mr. G.—he'd almost caught us that time and had he meant to catch us or was it just his playfulness ?—and disputed a little about the position of a cliff, the Baou des Blancs, marked on the map, and relapsed each into our own thoughts. And then I became aware of this fellow.

He was not looking at Clem. I have never seen anyone not look at anything with a more positive intensity. It was the exact converse of a hard stare. He was not looking more particularly at her flushed face and her pretty neck, his eyes were fixed on the panorama outside the window and his brow was knit and his lips moved—repeating some mental purge sovereign, I suppose, for such occasions.

It was as if his inner world was opened to me. I contemplated it as an explorer might do who has come over a crest to a tremendous declivity and contemplates a strange land. For the first time I think I realised fully the enormous distances between my peculiar world and the worlds in which the greater part of mankind are still living. I tried to put myself in his place and to imagine what sort of thoughts my ordinary thoughts would seem to him if suddenly they began to unfold themselves in his brain instead of mine, and what it would feel like to him to find himself living involuntarily for a day, let us say, as I live, neglecting all his offices, taking all my freedoms.

I used to think that bishops and clergymen and priests and teachers and all the Davidsons in the world doubted and went on from doubt to disbelief, and meanly concealed their disbelief in order to keep their incomes and positions. But indeed most of them are as capable of plunging into a sustained criticism of their beliefs as a passenger upon an ocean liner is capable of leaping the two hundred odd feet from the promenade deck to the Atlantic, in order to have a little swim in the sea. The liner has got him. And their worlds have got all these people, and no little cracks of inconsistent reality will be allowed to flood their mental holds with doubt

At once the pumps will get to work, the lips will be busy in exorcism.

What was my priest thinking, down there beneath the mists of his mind ? I doubt if his thoughts were very definite. Here was a life different from his own, not merely in contrast with it, but in antagonism to it, and yet it was happy and betrayed no sense of Sin. It was evidently on the easiest terms with the hills and the sun. It jested—had he some English and did he understand our jest ? And God permitted it ! Suppose after one's years of meagre fare and tedious observances and shameful clothing and meek bearing and bitter and dismal restraint, suppose it should be that God could tolerate such freedoms ? Suppose that God was different from what one had been taught ? Suppose oneself, too, might have possessed some such glowing slip of slender womankind ? To do with as one pleased ! Help ! Ave Maria ! Help ! Such thoughts were perhaps too clear for him, and yet I think a shadow after that fashion fell across his mind. And he muttered his time-honoured Latin specific : " Ave Maria, gratia plena, Dominus tecum," or some such stuff, and did not look, oh ! did not look.

My impression of this particular priest was that he was a fairly good priest ; he had a grey distressed complexion, he was untidy and disturbed. But he was not disturbed enough to be dislocated. There must be priests who have gone much further than he from the perfect obedience of childish faith. There must be priests who neglect offices systematically, who drink or smoke unseasonably or excessively, or who have pilfered and continue to pilfer, who have mistresses and sustain intrigues. Here in the South of France there is much sly jesting about the priests' house-keepers. One sturdy fellow over the hills associates almost openly with a past or present mistress, goes to dine with her every day, and is the father of her son. I am filled with curiosity about the inner life of such priests. I find it incredible that many of these sinful priests are unbelievers. There must be a strange jumble in their minds, and they must be accustomed to hiding themselves from the all-seeing God to their own satisfaction amidst the jumble. They must try not to think of him too closely. But they must feel that he is there still, the Hound of Heaven upon their track. Probably they find a consolation in exaggerating his mercy or in elaborating some fantastic childish belief in a propitiatory saint, a saint who is almost accessory to the offence. The good Saint Anthony will balance the cooked accounts. The Blessed Virgin loved greatly and is full of pity. God knows everything, it is true, but he ignores much.

Dickon told me a story the other day which shows how curious the jumble of a priest's world may become. Someone—Dickon or a friend of Dickon's, whichever it was—had taken a room for the night in an obscure and not too respectable hotel in a back street in Brussels. I think a railway connection had been missed or something of that sort, a cabman's advice

taken too hastily, but I forget that part of the story. I rather fancy that
Dickon, too, forgot that part of the story. In the dining-room was a
priest, a big fat grave paternal man, dining rather guiltily with a woman
He had a rich unsubjugated voice, and he was doing his best to restrain her
too public manifestations of personal devotion. Deponent's bedroom to
which he retired some hours later, like most hotel bedrooms, had doors,
locked of course, which communicated with the rooms on either side, and
through one of these doors there presently transpired—an excellent word
in this connection—the sounds of an acutely amorous encounter. Deponent
moved about noisily and coughed, but the passions at large next door were
too imperious for silence. They abated for a while, but a fresh and more
violent storm followed the lull. The unseen lover, it became evident
was the priest who had been dining downstairs. There could not be such
another voice in the world. In the morning he was visible in the corridor
departing, still grave, still paternal. But before he departed—and this
is really all that matters in this distressing but necessary anecdote—he was
plainly audible, very gently and sincerely, giving his fellow-sinner absolution
for all that had occurred.

And she no doubt received it with an equal piety.

She, poor sinner, must have believed that that absolution was perfectly
valid, and so believing she was absolved and troubled no other priest with
the affair, but his case was not quite so simple. There were highly technical
points about the matter, points above her understanding. She little knew
what he had done for her. To cover a carnal he had committed a mortal
sin, he had absolved an accomplice, and that the Church has very wisely
forbidden. For a week or ten days perhaps he must have remained in
danger of hell-fire, incapable of priestly functions, a man uncleansed. No
doubt he was in Brussels away from his parish—if he had a parish. He
confessed at once most probably, but absolution would have been reserved
—for some days. Automatically an application must have been made to
the bishop, naming no names, and automatically a faculty given to absolve
Then this curious transaction was completed and every shade of anxiety wiped
from the soul of the wanderer. He, too, was safe once more. He could
go his way in peace—until the next occasion.

He must have thought this out before and during his little encounter
He must have found it necessary to reassure his frail admirer. Perhaps he
had not anticipated that necessity. How subtle and wonderful is th
power of the human mind over contradictions ! Both these people imagined
they were living in the sight of God. Both of them believed that they
believed that God was seeing them and seeing through them body and soul
all the time ! And both believed that what they did was Sin and point
blank defiance of His will.

Here again in this spiritual book-keeping and quittance, in this simple deal between the carnal and the divine, is a glimpse of a mental world as remote from my present state as the life of some other planet from our earth's.

The human mind is at once complex and artless. Membership of a great organisation like the Catholic Church, which continues to fight for existence and power, must do much to develop the instincts and assumptions of partisanship. A priest, even a gravely erring priest, may still feel that he is on God's side and that God is on his side. Against a Protestant and still more against such a sceptic as myself, it must be easy for him to suppose himself a champion of God, and to feel in consequence a certain preferential claim upon Him. And even when the evasion of God's all-seeing eye has become habitual and loyalty has faded to nothing, that habitual evasion and that chilled devotion will still be far from positive denial.

I can imagine nothing more terrific than the outlook of a priest who really permits himself to disbelieve and allows his disbelief to be known. Before him are appalling difficulties and disciplines, difficult interrogations, struggles with his own still deeply rooted habits of submission, and at last expulsion into a vast, wild, windy, uncharted world of change and unknown dangers. Its usages are strange to him ; it eats, dresses, washes even, in an unaccustomed fashion. He has for his stock in trade his poor ineffectual Latin learning. He left his family when he became a priest, and he has no friends now, no circle at all. For a very important part of the world, for the community naturally nearest to him that he knows best, he will be now a man with a black mark set against his name. To all the rest of the world he will be *queer*. I do not know what the market price of an unfrocked priest can be, but surely, unless he has what is called a " gift," he is among the cheapest of homeless men. Who will find work for him ?

So I can understand that many a poor devil on the margin of the Church and with thoughts of rebellion in his soul, has stared out doubtfully at this greater world in which we live to-day, and felt the beauty of its breadth and freedom and heard the call of its ampler life, and then shivered and fled back headlong into the close and cramping but less perilous fastnesses of the faith, misapplying and crying, perhaps not altogether sincerely but with heartfelt passion, that ancient appeal ; " Lord, I believe. Help thou mine unbelief ! "

Were someone to discover some interesting well-paid employment for ex-priests, I do not know what would happen to the Roman Catholic Church. I believe it would collapse like a pricked sawdust doll. Its personnel would come pouring out.

With less vivid contrasts and a milder quality of tragedy, the inner history of a great multitude of people outside the Catholic Church must be

very similar to that of the doubting priest; Anglican clergymen and ministers of Protestant sects and schoolmasters and schoolmistresses and the like,
upon which the continuous active practice of religion is imposed. But
outside the very precise and inquisitory disciplines of the watchful mother
church, there is much greater latitude of accommodation, and the tragedy
of apostasy is qualified by the comedy of prevarication.

It is very easy for me to be uncharitable in these matters. And perhaps
I am. I have never had the least temptation to complicate my own thoughts
about faith and philosophy, and so it is difficult for me to understand
tortuousness in religion. What I believed and professed did not affect
my material everyday life in the least. I had not even a friend who could
be distressed by my opinions. It happened so. Dickon and I fell out of
a shattered nest at my father's suicide, and if we found ourselves without
any security we also found ourselves without any restraints. This is
unusual freedom. Even the ordinary layman is obstructed in his free-think-
ing by a tangle of associations, by fear of hurting people he loves, by fear
of offending people with whom he wishes to stand well, by an indisposition
to break habits and reconstruct his days, and above all by the fact that as
one goes out from formal religious associations one goes out from a complete
institutional system into the wilderness, into a void. Negation has no
schools, no ceremonies. Marriage and birth and death and the education
of one's children must still, to a large extent, occur upon lines originally
religious. There has been no revolution in religious opinion during the
last hundred years, no new system ousting an old system, but only a creeping
change, a crumbling down and a release. People drop one by one from
perfect faith to imperfect faith and so to explanatory doubt, but there is
never a day when they say en masse, " a new age has begun."

No new age has begun.

But while the Catholic Church, so elaborately organised, so stupendously
systematic, has to a large extent kept its footing and stayed where it was,
the Protestant world has passed through phase after phase of insufficient
adjustment and is still as unstably adjusted as ever.

Throughout all my life there has been a great display of Protestant teachers
who, if they were not precisely pouring new wine into old bottles, were at
least trying to add just as much new wine to the old wine and pour out just
as much of the old wine to make way for the new, as they thought the bottles
would stand. The bottles were rectories, vicarages, manses, schoolhouses,
college rooms, and cathedral closes; the bottles were habits and associations; the bottles were the phrases of creeds and articles that had become
very familiar and sweet and dear; the bottles were all sorts of things, the
daily stuff of life. In my lifetime I have seen Protestantism, wearing the
same or but slightly more dandaical vestments, singing the same hymn

tunes and sitting in the same pews, part from hell, fluctuate upon the nature and gravity of Sin, and play the most extravagant intellectual conjuring tricks with the Trinity, now professing to swallow it, now making it vanish, now reproducing it from the head or the elbow, expanding it to fill the stage or rolling it up into a small round pillule. Nothing could better illustrate the dominance of the daily circle of life over its theories and explanations. There is not a heresy in the whole cyclopædia of Christian heresies that has not had the privilege of the Protestant pulpit during my lifetime. The pulpits creaked but remained. Their occupants remained.

From its beginning Protestantism was a departure. It goes on departing. In my young days I was greatly exercised by Matthew Arnold's modernisation of St. Paul, and I am still entertained to find the anxious liberalising clergy trying to find recognition for their guarded misinterpretations of the explicit old creeds in Mr. Shaw's " Blanco Posnet " and " Saint Joan," or extending an uncertain experimental hand towards faith-healers and even towards the spookeries of Sir Conan Doyle. Broad-minded Protestant clergymen are the best of company for a long thoughtful talk in the small hours. All things in earth or heaven become equally credible, and nearly everything is symbolical of something else. In that urbane atmosphere we discover after the flattest opposition that in the end " we all mean the same thing." We never define what that is. We go to bed on that. I find Dean Inge particularly sympathetic. He is a great modern Churchman, entirely honest but extremely devious. He is elaborately uninforming about the Virgin Birth, and courageously outspoken about birth control. His Gifford Lectures on Plotinus betray in every passage his preference for the light Moselle of Neo-Platonism to the emotion-loaded Port of Catholic mysticism. I suppose if he and I were handed over to some tremendous spiritual chemist and each ground to powder and analysed to the last milligramme of his being, the report in each case would tail off with, " Belief in a living personal God—slight vestiges ? " I met him a little while ago at a dinner-party and I found him all that I had hoped to find him—liberal Anglicanism incarnate, lean, erect, and—a little discoloured.

I do not know how Protestantism will end. But I think it will end. I think it will come to perfectly plain speaking, and if it comes to perfectly plain speaking it will cease to be Christianity. There is now little left of the Orthodox church except as a method of partisanship in the Balkans. The League of Nations may some day supersede that, and then the only Christianity remaining upon earth will be the trained and safeguarded Roman Catholic Church. That is less penetrable, a world within a world, it shields scores of millions securely throughout their lives from the least glimpse of our modern vision.

§ 11

PHILIP HENRY GOSSE, the naturalist, made the most ingenious and delightful accommodation between his creed and his scientific beliefs. I read about him ten or twelve years ago in that little masterpiece, *Father and Son*, and my memory went back to a book upon shore life adorned with delicately coloured plates that I discovered in the library at Mowbray. When Sir Edmund Gosse, the venerable critic and poet, was a small boy he used, as he tells us in his memoir, to perch on a high stool and tint those drawings of sea-anemones and sea-mice and sea-slugs for his father. I am no collector, but for a time in my unsystematic way I sought the works of P. H. Gosse; they are rare and expensive now; and I read everything I could find of his. And so I learnt the completest defence of the literal interpretation of the first chapter of the Book of Genesis that has ever been made.

Gosse, the father, lived a simple, austere, and exalted religious life, and was evidently very happy in it—after his fashion. He followed the disciplines of the Plymouth Brethren. It was a life founded upon the English Bible, upon the most complete acceptance of the verbal inspiration of the English Bible. It was necessary, if this life was not to be shattered, that he should believe peacefully and fully in a special creation of the world in the year four thousand and four B.C., in the establishment of the first man and woman in a garden of Eden situated in Mesopotamia, and in their almost immediate disobedience and misbehaviour. But Gosse, the father, was also a naturalist, and as a naturalist fossils and geological stratification forced themselves upon his attention; he was obliged to be aware of the contemporary controversy about evolution and to realise the existence of a mass of evidence that pointed to an enormous past for the world and life. A superficial mind might have considered he was in a hopeless dilemma, a Catholic might have been disposed to flee from natural history as a peculiar invention of the devil and seek refuge in the authority of the Church and Mr. Belloc, but Philip Gosse neither despaired nor retreated. For some time perhaps he prayed and wrestled with the difficulty; in the end he overcame it, lucidly, simply, and completely—in a manner entirely Protestant.

For consider, he argued, what must be the conditions of creating such a universe as ours. It would have to be created as a going concern, for one can imagine it working from the outset in no other way. The honey must be ready for the moth at the moment of creation, the grass for the deer. The tree must be there for the woodpecker with its leaves and fruit abd bark and grubs complete. Consider now the trunk of the tree. It must be a trunk according to the nature that a tree must henceforth possess.

there can be no cheap methods for the Creator ; he gives the best. That tree-trunk therefore cannot be a flat stage-scenery trunk, nor a trunk of featureless pulp-like plaster or marzipan ; it must have the normal structure of a tree-trunk—that is to say, it must have annual rings. What could the grubs of the woodpecker do in a plaster tree ? And yet every annual ring would naturally indicate a year of growth, a year of previous existence. A sceptical fool at the very instant of its and his creation might declare therefore that that tree was as many years old as it had annual rings. He would be wrong.

Similarly every perennial in the garden of Eden, in the dew of the first Sabbath morning must have borne the leaf-scars of leaves that had never budded. At the root of every annual there must have been the decaying scales of a seed that had never been sown. And even Adam himself, at the moment of creation, must have been either an imperfect man—which is contrary to all religion—or he must have had a navel in his belly that had never linked him to a mother, because he had never had a mother. Moreover, since the animals directly they were created were living and modifiable and reproductive, the idea of their procreation and descent was in that instant made unavoidable ; there was instantly projected into the entirely imaginary past their logically necessary ancestry. Fossils had to lie about in the rocks for the same reason that annual rings had to exist in the first created tree. The Neanderthal bones and the Cro-Magnon skulls, therefore, are no more proof of Adam's possession of an ancestry than his navel was of his indebtedness to a mother.

And so it must have been with the whole universe. Mountains of lime-stone arose built up out of the skeletal remains of creatures that had never really lived. The planets and stars spun out of nothingness upon orbits they might have followed for an eternity through phases of expansion and distortion, from nebula to night—if things had been different. Adam opened his eyes and saw the stars, all of them and in their order—though it takes years for the light of many of them to reach the earth. God who made the stars could make the ray. How else could it be done ? The appearance of an immemorial past in the material world, then, no more disproves the simultaneous creation of everything at a specific date than the vistas one sees in two mirrors that are set face to face in a room prove that room to be an endless gallery.

This is logically perfect. One may even carry it a step further. For all that I can demonstrate to the contrary, I may have been created even as I write here, created with the illusion of past memories in my mind. Or the reader may have come into being in the very act of reading this sentence.

By this, to me, quite flawless argument Philip Gosse disposed of all the implications of Darwinism and could go on believing in the special creation of the world and man as the Bible recounts it, and in the doctrines that the Plymouth Brethren teach, and be able to have fresh spiritual difficulties whenever he wished and wrestle with the Lord in prayer in his evenings as he had been accustomed to do, and remain still for all this weight of conviction an honest naturalist collecting fossils and polyps among the rocks upon the beach without concealment or prevarication.

He must, I think, have made his discovery of this wonderful way out while he had been meditating, after the manner of the monks at Mount Athos. At any rate it was Adam's navel and not the annual rings of trees that had first directed him to his line of escape, and so he called his book the navel, *Omphalos*, and wise men still seek the surviving copies of it and read them and treasure them.

But Philip Gosse was a man of exceptional mental power, and few theologians have his clearness of head and his strength of faith. At the London Natural History Museum Sir Rupert told me they seem to show you Piltdown skull and Cro-Magnon remains and suchlike things, but indeed what you are seeing are most carefully and skilfully executed facsimiles. The originals themselves are locked away in safes downstairs, secure not only from fire and lightning, but from a far graver danger— the destructive arguments of the Creator's less intelligent partisans violent in defence of their threatened self-content.

§ 12

I DO not find myself under the same necessity to believe in a special creation of the universe as Philip Gosse, and so my mind takes the easier course of accepting this appearance of an immense antiquity—immense, that is, in relation to my experience—for my world as real. The vast age of the world is as real for my mind as my own individual existence. How far that is to be considered real and what " real " may mean are, as I have explained already, questions I have put outside my contemplation of the spectacle of being altogether.

And as the theological explanations of this spectacle have lost their grip upon me year by year and become unreal and incredible, I find myself passing under the sway of an entirely different set of ideas that seems to be taking hold of the modern imagination more and more firmly. They are called creative ideas nowadays, and they look for thir justification not towards the past but towards the future.

Philosophically I am quite prepared to admit that there is no plot nor scheme nor drama nor pattern in the flow of events as they are apprehended by human minds, but my disposition is diametrically opposed to my philosophy. I have never encountered even a stain on a wall or a glowing cavity in a fire upon which my mind could not impose a design. It is still more natural for me, a moral being inherently, to impose some dramatic conception upon my universe as a whole—if only to get an orientation for my living, a standard of judgment by which to estimate the good or evil of my decisions.

Now the outline that modern science, with an ever-increasing assurance, develops upon this common-sense spectacle of space is the story of progressive life. The black curtain of eternal nothingness rises to reveal the stellar universe, a whirl of matter like a puff of dust particles upon an immense scale, eddying through the endless emptiness of space. On one of its spinning, circling particles comes this life, at first not perceptibly more than a stir of complex chemical reactions amidst a warm wet slime. It is a new process in matter ; presently it begins to display desire and discrimination, to seek nourishment, to seek the light, to move away from things unfavourable. At first it can exist only in warm and shallow waters, but its ability to spread and reproduce itself and to bring recalcitrant substance into the sphere of its desire increases steadily.

I pause and set a note of interrogation against that "steadily." I am not sure how far a case can be made out to show that life has continually grown in range, in knowledge, in continuity of will, in co-operative power. But there is much to support the assertion that life has been uninterruptedly progressive from its first beginning. The thrust towards greater range in space and time and an ever-richer and fuller mental being has been continual. Progression is not the same as proliferation; there have been secular massacres of animal and vegetable life, in comparatively brief geological phases thousands of species and genera have been swept away by rapid geographical change and there have been ages of great hardship for living things. But these severities seem always to have sustained exceptional strides in adaptation and to have prepared the way for a new phase of abundance upon a higher level. The swampy vegetation and floundering, basking reptile life of the Mesozoic Age was extinguished in perhaps a few hundred thousand years of adversity, but it was swept away by the same changes that presently evolved the grassy prairies, the rich forests, and swarming herbivora of the Miocene. Life had won the hills and dry places by the sufferings and disasters of that struggle, and now feathered birds and furry beasts could push their way towards the poles. The geological record, the archives of life's adventures, does certainly seem to so amateurish a reader as I a straightforward story of expansion and progress—and particularly of expanding intelligence. That is the thing these new views press most urgently upon me. Feeling appears, perception, restraint, and judgment, eyes that see ahead, and limbs that pause and hesitate. Mind grows— and grows at an ever-increasing pace.

The first elements of mind were assembled slowly and painfully through enormous ages. Among the invertebrata and among the lower vertebrated animals it is improbable that there are inner worlds beyond the scope of mere incidents ; their most sustained mental operations may have a depth in time of only a few hours, or even of only a few moments, may be no more than a series of little puffs of consciousness connected by no unifying idea. The life of a frog or a fish is probably a life of transient awarenesses dying away at once after flight or feasting or fecundation into forgetting. The probability of a greater continuity than that appears only with the enlarging brains of the birds and mammals of the Tertiary Age. Manifestly these brains brought something quite new into the struggle, and thereafter the drama of life centred upon them. The brains in nearly every order and family of the mammals have enlarged relatively five times, ten times even, since the first appearance of this class in the world.

And it is not only by a mere increase in the size of the brain, we are reminded, that a great mental enlargement is indicated in the mammals. The peculiarity of the mammal, which the bird shows to a certain extent, its continuing contact and fellowship with its young. Wisdom no longer perished with the individual. Quite early in their ascendancy the mammals began to educate. A wolf or a dog is elaborately educated morally and in the tactics of hunting ; a young monkey has a powerful impulse to imitate and learn. With man came an ever-swifter process towards a mental continuum. In a few score thousand years he developed speech, picture-writing, writing, a distribution of documents, printing. In archives and literature he began a racial brain.

Each century, each decade in the last few hundred years, has made enormous additions to the speed and range of interchange between one man's brain and another's, and to the accumulation of more and more available stores of knowledge. Telegraphy was still a wonder in my infancy. Now we can broadcast speech, will presently radiate drawings, and preserve a record of gesture and movement. The trace of the increase in man's powers of communication rises hyperbolically. Our minds are less and less isolated. They mingle and interact in a new common medium of published and recorded and universally accepted ideas and interpretations. A new common medium I write : for imposed upon our minds appears a mind. This is the mind in which exist science, history, and thought. It has the same sort of relation to our individual activities that a regiment or army has to its constituent men. It is a collective human person in whom we all participate and which invades all our personalities. It is no longer mortal as we are mortal. It is life awakening, breaking through the limitations of individuality and growing conscious of itself. We are all presented as contributory units to a Titanic being which becomes conscious and takes hold of this planet.

Is there any reason for supposing that this growing mental being has any limitations yet imaginable, set to the increase of its power, to its expansion, to its invasion of our lives ? I do not find any. It is said that it must be limited in time because it is limited to this planet, and that this planet is doomed to freeze and die with the cooling of the sun. But I do not see how anyone with a knowledge of the implications of modern physics or with any sense of the unknown knowable can believe that life is necessarily limited to this planet for ever. The premises are altogether insufficient. An observer of nature in the Cambrian age might as readily have declared that life was only possible under water, and that in a few hundred million years the last fish would gasp its last gasp as the last puddle on earth dried up. To me it is far easier to suppose that this present unfolding of consciousness and will is only a birth and a beginning, and that I am not merely myself but a participator in a Being that has been born but need not die.

This is the appearance on the face of things that best survives the test of the sceptical acids. It is how I see life. It holds my mind when all the older faiths have lost their last vestige of credibility. It is, I admit, a poet and not a demonstrable idea. To accept it is not to return to religion. Th Being is not to my mind a God, unless we are to invert the idea of Go altogether. It is an objective and not a cause, and since it falls within th frame of time it can only have a proximate and practical reality. But it great enough, I feel, to comprehend the utmost scope and outlook of m life and to rationalise its motives and relationships.

§ 13

I HAVE put this idea of the common mental being of our race, this Racial Man to which all our individual lives consciously or unconsciously are contributory and subordinate, as if it were an outcome of the new biological outlook upon the universe. In what I have just written I have told of it objectively as a history of our world. Seen thus objectively it appears indeed modern. But the same idea comes into human thought from another angle. We find it within us.

In the last million years or so our breed has changed from the most solitary habits to habits more social and co-operative than those of any other animal. The fierce, lonely, egoistic ape-soul has been modified and qualified, and had superimposed upon it an intricate fabric of mitigating and restraining dispositions. The superstitious fear which may not only overshadow childhood but last right into adult life, is only one of the earliest and crudest of these adaptations to social needs. The self-control of the primitive tabus is also among the merely initial amendments of human fierceness. There are not only inhibitions but addenda. The emotions of sexual abandon and maternal and even paternal love as the ape knew them have also been seized upon by nature and broadened and utilised for social ends. There is now in man a desire to serve. There is a pleasure in and a craving for co-operation and associated action. Curiosity has become disinterested, and the constructive impulse has been varied and widened.

The primary form of the human soul is still self-seeking, self-protecting egoism, as the primary scheme of the human body is still that of an ape's. But in contemporary man the gratification of purely egoistic needs is not sufficient for happiness, it does not satisfy completely. In the case of man as in the case of the dog and other social animals, the individual soul has been invaded by the soul of the pack. A man has to be not only gratified but reassured. There is a conscience, there is a moral struggle, a conflict of motives. The cat, which is a solitary beast, is single-minded and goes its way alone, but the dog like his master is confused in his mind. And in our rationalising human minds it seems plain to me there is a continuing conflict between the intense and originally much more intense, crudely and definitely self-seeking factor, and a vaguer, wider, unselfish factor. The two are associated but not unified. They jar, and the rationalising mind struggles to account for the disharmony. I think that this less personal element of the self increases generally as we grow older and our experiences increase and widen, and that it is becoming more evident and important in the world's affairs. On the objective side there appears a race-mind, and this is paralleled on the subjective side by a great extension of individual interest to impersonal things. The race-mind, which is as immortal as the race, continually accumulates interest and attractiveness, and has more to offer the individual and more power over the individual. A large part of the waking hours of many people nowadays is occupied by activities that are of slight or no advantage to them whatever, although they may be of very great advantage to the race. A man may live a quarter or a third of his time in a study or a laboratory keenly engaged upon things that have nothing whatever to do with his intimate personal drama, activities that add only to the common inheritance. He may even neglect his personal drama for these things.

The last time I was in London I met a very stimulating man whom I had long wished to encounter, Dr. Jung, the psycho-analyst. He had come from Zurich to London to give some lectures, and after one of these, the last of them, he had joined a party in a flat looking out upon the Thames at Westminster. I do not remember who my host and hostess were—Dickon had taken me there—but there was a pleasant and interested and not too numerous gathering to meet Jung, and we smoked and drank champagne and whisky and ate sandwiches and talked late. It was very good talk, no fireworks, no posturing in it, but close and clear. Jung's English is excellent, and an hour's lecture at the Queen's Hall had not fatigued him in the least.

I buttonholed the great man because I wanted to know how he regarded this conception of a sort of supermind of the species, and he said that it was entirely sympathetic with his views. He made it clear I had not been following up that track alone ; I had been running beside and responding to contemporary thought. One meets a phrase here and a suggestion there, and subconsciously they incorporate themselves with one's own ideas. I had thought myself original.

I quoted Paul that we were all members of one body, and remarked upon the ease with which one fell into theological phraseology in this matter. Someone mentioned a distant relative of mine, Wells, who had employed many religious expressions in a book called " God, the Invisible King " ; a Manichean book, said somebody, neither Greek nor Hebrew, but Persian. The writer in question had gone very far indeed in his resuscitation of theological terms and in his recommendation of prayer and suchlike exercises. Too far, said someone. I agreed. I had already talked about that with Wells himself, and it was plain to me that this God the Invisible King of his was not so much God, in the sense in which people understand that word, as Prometheus ; it was a titanic and not a divine being. This unseen monarch was much more akin to Nietzsche's Overman than to a normal divinity. Frederic Harrison too, someone remarked, had said that God the Invisible King was merely the Humanity of Comte with a crown on. I had not heard of this before but it struck me as being a justifiable comment.

Yet I would not be too hard on my cousin for his use of the word God. For can it have other than a lax use? If you believe in good as an objective reality, in a sense you believe in God. I doubt if many Protestants nowadays believe in God in any other sense. The human mind has been struggling to apprehend this something behind and above and about individuality for thousands of years and insisting most pitifully upon exactitudes just where exactitude is most misleading. Theology has been experimental, and it has been angry and cruel because it did not realise what an experiment it was. It was worried by immediate practical needs. It has been dogmatic because it felt that its flimsiness could not stand the strains of inquiry. It felt it must take a standpoint if it was not to wander for ever. It has shown all the nervous irritability, rising at times to vicious violence, of a weak, well-intentioned man trying to carry out an important task with a defective equipment. But in all its aberrations it has clung to its essential idea, the denial of individual isolation. The assertion of complete individual isolation is, I suppose, the essential idea of the dogmatic Atheist.

Jung laid great stress on the readiness of people to misconceive these ideas about a greater human being. They did not grasp how that being was supposed to be synthetic and comprehensive. They thought of it as something outside themselves, an individual of the same order as themselves, as someone put over them, and not as a being including and comprehending them as I include and comprehend my own nerve cells and blood corpuscles. Neither Nietzsche's Overman nor Shaw's Superman was really to be thought of as an individual person. Both were plainly the race development, the whole race in progress. But writers with the journalistic instinct to caricature got hold of these ideas and cheapened them irremediably, and the popular interpretation of these phrases, the Overman and the Superman, had come to be not a communion of saints but an entirely ridiculous individual figure, a swagger, a provocative mingling of Napoleon Bonaparte, Antinous, and the Admirable Crichton.

Jung came back to my quotation from St. Paul about our all being members of one body. Evidently he attached much importance to that. He said that not only Christian theology, but nearly all mystical religion in the world, was saturated with the idea of a merger of the narrow self in some variously apprehended greater soul. So soon as religion began to develop theology and pass out of the phase of abject fear of the mythological Old Man, the tribal God, this conception appeared. The believer in the mysteries became more or less the greater being and the greater being became more or less the believer. In the phase of ecstatic communion the believer was lifted altogether out of his sinful and finite self and above all the frustrations of life.

You found this same idea of transcending individuality, in the Mass, in

3*

Mithraism and in many surviving hymns and phrases of ancient Persian and Egyptian cults. It was expressed almost in identical terms by Moslem and Jewish mystics. It was not a clear and cool intellectual realisation with the mystics; it was felt rather than thought, but clearly it was strictly parallel with the inclusion of the individual in a racial being that was so congenial to modern biology. In Christian mysticism it was obscured by the heavier emotional charge of that cult. In the case of women mystics particularly the suggestion of the phrase " the divine spouse " had been excessively powerful, and with such types as St. Hildegarde or St. Gertrude or the Blessed Angela de Foligno, Christian mysticism had sunken a long way towards a mere sublimation of sexual abandon. The Being became very personal and physical and responsive in their imaginings. The egoism was exalted rather than expanded to divinity. That, someone suggested, was what happened when women took to mysticism. A remark which started a detached wrangle in one corner of the room.

Jung listened for a while to that, and then he remarked that by his " Superior Person " Confucius must have intended the same generalised comprehensive man as this we had in mind, the racial and not the individual man. That again was new to me. " Superior Person," Jung remarked, could be translated just as well by Overman; but we Europeans had an unfortunate trick of misunderstanding and making Chinese thought ridiculous and unprofitable by using the least dignified words possible in our literal translations of its phrases. One can do that to European phrases with an equal destructiveness. Caradoc Evans, I remarked, degraded Welsh religiosity simply by translating the shining garments of righteousness as White Shirts. We had still the cloudiest notions of Chinese thought, said Jung, even of contemporary Chinese thought; the Chinese might be getting towards a working philosophy of the modern world, without our aid or sympathy, along a road of their own.

But so it was, whether one turned to the great teachings of China or the sacrificial mysteries of Peru, one found in forms that were sometimes gross and monstrous, and sometimes cold and enigmatic, intimations of an almost universal idea. Every great religion and every philosophy of life throughout the world seemed to have been feeling its way, often in spite of enormous initial difficulties of creed and training, towards this same process, the process of subordinating the egoism to a broader generalised being, the being of communion. Could one doubt that a common psychological necessity determined these agreements, that like parallel streaks on the surface of a great river they show the direction of a current that has been flowing with gathering force for five-and-twenty centuries ?

The realisation of this inner psychological necessity which, under the suggestions of Jung and Freud and their groups of associates, we are now beginning to correlate with a new phase in the circumstances of human life, marks what one may perhaps compare to a coming-of-age. Just as we are disentangling our minds from the last lingering fears and submissiveness that marked the childhood of our race, so also are we growing out of the intense individualism of its romantic adolescence. As our mental range increases we realise that in the end frustration and extinction await everything that is purely individual in us. We are beginning, some of us, or even most of us, to develop a further, a more fully adult, mental stage. This adult mentality of the years ahead will be self-neglectful and scientific and creative in comparison with anything that has gone before. It will be consciously and habitually a contributory and co-operating part in the over-mind.

§ 14

THESE identifications of modern tendencies with old religious impulses are very curious, and I note them here on that account. But I do not find any necessity for religious phraseology to express my own apprehension of the drama of existence. If it is a matter of interest it is still a matter of secondary interest to me that anyone should have thought these thoughts before in other terms or from a different angle. I do not want, I am under no necessity, to be religious and mystical on this point. The science of physics has enough paradox in it for me, and about ordinary life I prefer to be matter-of-fact. I am much more inclined to use such new and unprecedented expressions as "The Adventure of Life," or what for all practical purposes is synonymous, the "Adventure of Mankind," or "of the Greater Man," for my general conceptions of everyday reality than any of the timeworn phrases of the older faiths. Those may be charged with emotion and reverence, yes, but also they are charged with misunderstanding.

"Adventure" is more in the quality of my character than any imperative to live in this or that particular fashion, and it conveys, what the theological terminology fails to convey, the suggestion that after all the limitless will of man for knowledge and power may not prove to be sanctioned by the nature of things. He may fail and freeze after all. He may smash to nothingness in some interstellar collision. Even with the admission of that uncertainty, the adventure is great enough and wonderful enough to hold my imagination completely.

This way of looking at existence differs from any religious interpretation in its entire voluntariness. We are not told dogmatically that we are so-and-so or that we must do so-and-so; but it is put to us, Let us be and do so-and-so. Let us gather knowledge and power, let us communicate and learn to co-operate, let us lay hands on life and fate. Let us at any rate make the attempt.

To give oneself knowingly to the Adventure of Mankind has this much to be said for it, that it is in the trend of current things. Whatever we may think of the universality of progress, there can be little dispute that the current phase of existence is by human standards progressive. We shall be in the movement whether we desire it or not. And since we are thus conscripted in the army of the Titans against the old Jove of chance and matter, since we are obliged willy-nilly to participate in the increase and creative application of knowledge to human ends, we may as well give our lives cheerfully and take a conscious share in the process. We shall be happier so. We shall be happier to extend our motives and desires beyond the tragic uncertainties of the purely egotistic life. We shall be broadened and steadied by that participation, we shall be released, we shall be very largely released from the worst intensities of personal desire and passion and from the bitter fear and still bitterer realisation of futility that haunt self-centred minds.

§ 15

IT may be, the reader thinks that all these sections so far, were written on one wet day at Dickon's desk in his rooms at Bordon Street. The way in which I began this book may have given that impression. What a day's work it would have been! Indeed, I wrote no further there than the eighth section, and then I fell into a profound meditation in the arm-chair before the open-fire—about electrons. And things like that. I had stirred up the long-slumbering curiosities of my adolescence by recalling them. I had a queer little idea, an imp, a paradox, an atom of explanation; I made some notes at last, but nothing to interest the present reader. Those notes will come to nothing; my day for such bright ideas is past. The rest of these pages I have written in my " bureau," as Jeanne will call it, at the Villa Jasmin.

I have revised all that I wrote in London here, and I find myself more and more interested in this enterprise. It is doing more for me than I expected. Autobiography, provided that it is not too severely disciplined, may be, I perceive, an almost inexhaustible occupation. Nothing is altogether irrelevant. Whatever interests one, or has ever interested one, is material. In due course no doubt I shall get to autobiographical particulars.

I have been back here in Provence now for fifteen days and everything is as it used to be last year, the same sunlit peace, the same delicate beauty and kindly freshness in the air, the same lean red-haired Clem, as absurdly insistent that she idolises me and will have no other man but me, invading me whenever she dares and protecting me against a score of imaginary onslaughts upon my peace and comfort : everything is the same indeed, except that my little kitten has grown into a very pretty grey cat with a quite extravagant sense of its own importance. It comes and sits in judgment upon each fresh sheet as I write it so soon as the paper is sufficiently warmed by the sun. At certain passages, upon no consistent principle that I can distinguish, it purrs.

This Villa Jasmin is an old Provençal *mas*, a small farmer's house set upon a hillside among olive terraces not far from Grasse. No automobile can come up to it and it is beautifully difficult to find, but there is a mossy stone track to us beneath the grey contorted trees by which we can supply our timber and coal and suchlike heavy needs. Let me describe it with some particularity. In it I hope to write most of this contemplated book ; it is the foreground to all that follows.

The house is of three stories in front and has a tall bare face ; behind, it nestles its rump, so to speak, into the hill ; its sole decoration is a ripple of plaster beneath its ruddy brown tiles, a great scarlet geranium that sprawls up half its height, and a passion-flower; the narrow windows have wooden fastenings, and old wooden shutters on rusty hinges that a Cornish southwester would wrench off in a minute and scatter like dead leaves. Before the house is a broad terrace where I take my morning coffee and my midday meal. Blue-berried ivy climbs over the parapet; there is a trim close Japanese medlar in one corner, and in the midst, surrounded by a grass-rimmed oval of little respectful rose-trees, there is a very fine and flourishing palm. At the corner is a big olive-tree that now dots the gravel everywhere with its fallen black fruits. Beyond are other olive-trees and some fig-trees; a broad gravel path goes ceremoniously to a large oil-jar in which a genteel, glossy, flowerless plant is growing, and there it comes to a rounded and dignified conclusion. On the other side of the terrace there is a clump of thorny-bladed agaves, green-blue or green with yellow edges, a big stone-rimmed fountain where our washing is done and where Jeanne, in spite of the most passionate remonstrances from Clem, is in the habit of leaving her bowls and brushes and whacking-boards to desecrate our serenity, and there are two delicate grey mimosas, a great old Judas tree, two pretty gracious trees whose names I do not know, and above and behind all a thick, tall hedge of bamboos.

There is always a sound of running water about this house. A stream comes down a little channel from above; close by the wall a mouth of stone, with lips like an angry ape's, spouts water into the big washing fountain; below the terrace a dispersed trickle of water falls from a domed niche adorned with an abundance of dripping hart's-tongue and maiden-hair fern, into yet another basin of stone. There is a third fountain in a corner where irises grow, a little terra-cotta affair put there by my predecessor. It has an inscription in Greek letters, a phrase that Heraclitus made: παντα ρει all things flow. There is no enduring thing.

The hill descends steeply in front of the house, and paths sweep round from the front door on either side of the terrace and are hidden and unite before the fountain of the ferns below, and run straight down the hill in a broad, stony incline beneath now golden chestnut-trees and grey olives, to ruinous yet stately entrance pillars upon the rustic highway.

My study is on the top story and it is as far as possible from the kitchen, for Provençal servants prefer to converse when they are at some distance from each other, and always rattle plates and beat upon pots and pans for a time before they make use of them. It is a calm austere room. Its walls are painted grey and have nothing on them but six engravings, four by Mantegna and two by Dürer; there is a tall fine bureau, a large cupboard in which books are hidden—for the backs of modern books if they are displayed talk overmuch—a table on which papers are scattered, a table at which I write, and some rush-bottomed chairs. The floor is tiled, all the rooms in this house are tiled with time-darkened red tiles ; the carpet is discreetly gay, and in one or two shapely old pots of white earthenware, very delicately crackled and discoloured, Clem puts bright flowers. And there is a stove, a good little hungry warming stove which burns wood and pine-cones.

My window looks almost due south over my palm and Japanese medlar and olives, and my view is wide and gently various upon hills and crests and further hills, a remote ridge from the Estérel and a sharp-edged inlet, a dagger-blade, of water. Beyond the last reluctant distances of the land appears the sea gravely blue and the horizon like the top edge of a blue silk barrier.

The hills are all terraced and planted ; mistily grey olives prevail, but there are many sorts of trees and there are a few vineyards, rusty and yellow now, and other cultivations. The houses are solitary and plain, white or pink or pale yellow with little vertical windows like the toy houses of my childhood. There are many cypresses like black candles, like warning fingers, singly or in groups ; I do not believe the land would be half as beautiful without its accentuation by these cypresses ; and when the day is clear but overcast the trees upon the contours of the hills pattern against the soft grey-blue distances like a border of minute dark lace. Close to me on my extreme right is a single cypress against the butt-end of a lean high grey house ; it is tall and like a plume, and for some reason it pleases me very greatly. A steep edge of precipitous walls above ravines and blank white factory-palaces clustering upon the hillside and partly veiled in haze is Grasse ; it just comes into my view beyond the nearer olive slopes. A slender chimney minaret sticks up here and there, a steadying vertical white line ; its rare, occasional smoke has, I know, the smell of incense. The cathedral tower is single and tall and square and outstanding. Right in the middle of my view behind a ridge and ten miles distant one feels rather than sees Cannes.

The whole of this land is a pleasant and prosperous region very indulgent to mankind. Its agriculture, like its scenery, has a delicate, fastidious quality. I never see a pig here nor any cattle ; there are occasional sheep, genteel-looking sheep, there are disciplined grey geese and immaculate white poultry. Once or twice, in the more open and rocky spaces among the hills, I have met small companies of goats with goatherds. They had a quality so harmonious with the scenery that they seemed rather like elegant quotations from Theocritus than economic facts. The farmer below me is employed in growing jasmin and violets, and a little way along the road there are fields of carefully tended rose-bushes.

In the early morning the stream-beds and valleys between the crests and ridges are filled with very sharp restricted banks of white mist, and then a conical hill some five or six miles away from here becomes an island of romance. All day long there is a quiet soft change in the features of this scene, hillsides hold the sunlight for a time and then fade away, spurs and summits grow from insignificance to prominence as the sun searches them out on its daily round. Towards sundown Mougins upon its ridge six miles away will at times shine out with such a brightness that I think of Bunyan's Celestial City. Everywhere at this time of year there are rubbish fires burning, and their bright down-feathers of white smoke expand and unroll and dissolve away continually and are continually renewed. Ever and again an absurd little single-track railway asserts itself by an acute long nose of white steam that burrows hurriedly across the bluish greens and greys and hangs for a time and fades like an unimportant memory.

Almost always the sky above this land is a pure clear blue or delicately streaked with filmy cloud, and the sunlight is a benediction. Sundown brings a glow of warm contentment. Then presently the nearer houses lose strength, and faint and die and become white ghosts in the twilight. Amidst the darkling scattered lights appear.

I have never known a more intimate sky than this of Provence, by night as well as by day. Even the rain, the infrequent rain, is confidential, with something apologetic and reassuring in its whisper. Last night I saw the morning-star and the old moon close together above the crest of Peyloubet. My bedroom window looks out eastward, and there, in the deep blue of morning, framed in my window-frame like a luminous picture on my wall, was the old moon on her back with the young moon faint but visible in her arms. There is, I suppose, a slight astigmatism in my eyes, for I saw Venus not as the minute disc she is, but as an animated splash of laughing white light that made exhilarating gestures over this grouping. I understood suddenly why Czechs and Danes and Poles and Swedes and Englishmen and suchlike boreal and Baltic men were needed to realise the inhuman remoteness of interplanetary space. The stars and planets of the Mediterranean have no aloofness at all; Diana can still descend upon the hills of Provence, and for all our modern science the heavenly bodies move here as they did in pagan times, harmoniously in crystal spheres.

Possibly I dozed, for when I looked again moon and morning-star were gone altogether and the sky was flushed with the excitement of coming sunrise. I lay for a time and then got up and went to my window to see whether that little hill of mine towards Cannes had got its mists about it yet, and was sitting up and minded to play at islands of enchantment with me.

This is the present foreground of my world. Men have lived among these hills for scores of thousands of years, and one could think that here if anywhere in the world was peace and permanent adaptation. A short automobile journey to the east would take us to the caves of Grimaldi, where some of the earliest of human skulls were found, and Moustiers, which has traces of men even more ancient, is as close to the west. Cro-Magnon, in Dordogne, is five or six hours of motoring beyond. The soil everywhere is rich with human traces, from chipped thin fragments to Phœnician beads, Roman brickwork, and medieval crockery. The newest villas of Grasse stand on old foundations. This, one might say, is man's enduring home. The soil is generous ; there is no persecution in the weather, no implacable animal enemy, and little disease. Here, it would seem, a man can still be born and live a life of immemorial usage, can believe and worship after the fashion of his ancestors, and die under the blessings of his church as a child falls asleep in the arms of a nurse.

But, indeed, this fair and spacious scene is a mere mask of calm beauty upon the face of change. As I sit writing I hear the sounds of chopping and sawing and ever and again a shout and a crash. Under the aged, wrinkled boughs a fire is crackling briskly. A farmer just beyond my cypress plume is busily destroying his olive orchard, and he is doing so in order to plant the ground with jasmin. He will have to stub those tough gnarled roots ; it will be a heavy toil for him. All these peasants seem to be giving up their olives for jasmin, and they are growing that for the perfume factories in Grasse which serve the transitory, unstable world of luxury in Paris and London and New York. A change of fashion in scent, or some ingenuity of the chemist, may abolish the profits of this flower-growing, and then these hillsides will know trouble ; for olive-trees that are gone are gone for ever. No one can wait nowadays for planted olive-trees to reach fruition.

The fate of this countryside, which looks so self-subsisting, is I perceive dependent upon the great consuming centres ; those little hidden railways are like suckers from the urban fungi that have drained away all local autonomy. The rural life here has been insidiously and secretly and completely subjugated by Paris. Ostensibly this land is very like the countryside of a hundred years ago, when its peasants could have gone on living if all the rest of the world had died, but in truth their lives now are hardly more secure upon these hills than they would be if they were dodging the traffic in the midst of the Champs Elysées. They are educated, they are tempted away, they are taken for the army and demoralised, they are pushed out of their homes to make way for artists and winter visitors like myself, they are pushed off their land to make way for villas and gardens and strange new cultivations.

Just out of hearing up the hill behind me is the main road through Grasse from Paris to Nice, along which drives the restless fever of a new breed of rich people, people cut off from the tradition of the past and incapable it would seem of any interest in the future. They have incalculable powers of manipulating the franc on which these peasants rely. Their great fat-tyred cars go throbbing and hooting past, the chauffeur is glassily intent upon the road, the passengers—are passengers. Never were there people so entirely passengers. They are carried along like sacks. The clothes they wear, the very complexions of the women, seem to have been put upon their passive persons by the tradesmen of Paris and London before they were packed off in their cars. One cannot believe that their financial reactions are other than automatic. And yet they control. Or at least they are the instruments of a blind control. It is they who are sweeping away the olive orchards and turning the peasants into gardeners, speculative flower-growers for their perfumeries, and servants for their multiplying villas. Without premeditation, with no definite object, they change the face of the earth. Not merely here.

This window looks south and modern manufactures and mines and forges, the slums and the dismal industrial defacement of the world, are far way behind me and out of the compass of this picture. The plants I have helped to plan and reconstruct, the factories and sidings and warehouses of my group of companies and all our offices are forgotten here. There are hills and mountains gashed and tormented by us for minerals, far away to the right in Spain ; and for all I know, though I should doubt it, there may be labour trouble and bad conditions in the scent factories of Grasse just round the corner of the hill. But such things are the mere fringes of the world of massed toil ; there is no glare of foundry or furnace in this scene ; between here and the equator there are no many-windowed factories lit up to break the visible night. The great masses of industrialism are at the back of this outlook, and as it were below my comfort, away deeply down through my sheltering hills and mountains, through the bulge of the world northward that robs them of our sun. They would be out of mind here altogether were it not that these people, hurrying in their automobiles along the road from Paris and Lyons and Grasse to Nice and Monte Carlo and Italy, and the still greater multitude in the lits-salons and trains-de-luxe that follow each other along the coastal railway, do in some subtle way recall that distant teeming darkness of toil. They come with a haste, with a headlong effect, crowding upon each other, as if they were in flight from things and suggestions and, it may be, apprehensions that they desire to forget.

Well, I at least do not want to forget. But I want for a while to be away from these things to think.

I sit now at my window after the sunset, and my cat is purring before the purring stove, within which the pine-cones have just begun to flame. My little study is bright and clear and secure in the light of my freshly lit lamp, but outside, behind a veil of blue silence that is deepening into darkness, is an incessant hurrying world. The rivulet that prattles beneath my window does not hurry half so fast.

If I could put out an arm of ten miles I could flatten down a little undulation of the land and see the lights of Cannes and Antibes and their hotels and villas-de-luxe, and if I could push away a few unimportant hills with my left elbow I could unmask the lights of Cagnes and Nice and, beyond those, Villefranche and Beaulieu and Monte Carlo and Mentone. From here they would look like patches of burning sand-grains along the dark littoral. In those places the evening is only a beginning. Through the nearer shadows among the hills the peasants are going home from their work, invisible in the twilight ; they will eat and sit and talk for a while and presently blow out their lamps of American paraffin and go to bed. But all along the Riviera the immense ritual of dinner is in preparation, myriads of cooks and waiters are busy upon the endless repetitions of the standard meal, thousands of baths are in progress, hundreds of men are struggling at this moment with their heads in their dress-shirts, and women of every age are enhancing or creating their beauty for the illuminated and significant half of the day. They will eat rather too much of their magnificently commonplace food, they will drink rather too much, most of them, they will dance like automata to imitation negro music, they will flirt without discrimination, they will set out upon timid, dishonest, nocturnal adventures and arrange their poor little adulteries and fornications, they will gamble according to solemnly conceived systems against the facetiousness and disrespect of chance, and so come at last belatedly to inartistic lasciviousness or speechless grossness and sleep.

Nevertheless these people, individually and in masses, seem to make decisions, seem to have the direction of economic change. They have an air of being less mutely the creatures of fate than the peasants. It is hard to believe that it is so.

My mind takes a wider range beyond these Riviera resorts, these patches of luminous eczema upon the broad face of the earth. Out beyond is the Mediterranean, and across it, could my eye see through the smooth curve of the waters to them, go the lit ships from Genoa to the east of me and Marseilles to the west, and trailing my imagination with them go the slender threads of their wakes further and further round the globe, through the straits and through the narrow seas and into the tropics to the harbours and warehouses of India and the far East, and out by Gibraltar to South Africa and to South and North America into distant ports and up great estuaries. My mind hovers for a while over these ships, mere particles upon the homeless wilderness of the waters, and I think of grave engineers watching oiling and pressure, of officers in the chart-room, of stokers, excessively minute because they are so remote, sweating before their furnaces, and passengers—again those passengers !—congratulating themselves upon the calmness of the night and anticipating dinner. What a complex of habits and motives it is that drives those ships, with their ill-assorted cargoes, their vaguely directed passengers and their uncertain profits, about the world !

On my other table lie the English newspapers of three days ago, and the *Quotidien* of yesterday and to-day's *Eclaireur* and *Petit Niçois*. And there are various London weeklies and the weekly *Times* and *Manchester Guardian*. As I recall what I have read in them to-day the view from my window seems to extend further and further, my boundaries sweep forward across the Mediterranean eastward and westward to Oran and Morocco, to the Atlas, to Egypt and the Soudan, to Arabia Petræa and the Yemen and the Hadramaut, to Basra and Ormuz and India and China, and northward across the Pamir uplands, and on and on until at last they enclose the globe and meet themselves again in a shrinking coil and varnish. Over there in Africa, out beyond the hump of the Estérel and across the waters just over the roundness of the world, the Spanish are retreating before the recalcitrant tribesmen of the Riff under Abdel Krim. It is a hustled retreat, and the Spaniards are losing heavily and are likely to lose more. They can be having no rest to-night. Even now as I write some poor peasant lad from Andalusia or Castile may be writhing in agony with a sniper's bullet flattened among his freshly shattered vertebræ. Down he goes, and if there is no ambulance at hand they may have to leave him to the mercy of the pursuers. Or they may not trust that mercy. I can almost see those scattered figures of distress straggling across vast and lonely and rocky places and the crumpled bodies lying still, until the prowling beats discover them. That too, is in my present world as surely as these tranquil hills.

The Spanish retreat is leaving the French garrisons in Morocco very uncomfortably in the air, and all North Africa, I gather, is uneasy and dangerous—more uneasy and dangerous than the papers will admit. This afternoon there has been a great rattling of machine-guns from amidst the hills beyond Grasse. There is a garrison here of neat yellowish men, Malagasy I am told, and they are polishing up their tactics, for who knows what may happen ? The other day as I came here from London I lifted the blind of my sleeping-compartment in the early morning and looked out on that queer contorted country about Toulon, which is so much more Spanish and African than French, and there in the crystalline light of dawn I saw companies of khaki-clad, brown-skinned men with mules and mountain guns engaged among the brown rocks in some manœuvres.

A little further to the east in my outlook to-night there are British warships steaming through the darkness to Alexandria. Egypt also is astir. The Sirdar of the Soudan has been very deliberately murdered in Cairo by a band of students, and the new Tory Government in London is showing the strong hand. Beyond the Red Sea, Mecca is in the hands of the Moslem puritans and the king the British set up has failed to recover the city. All along the festering lines of contact between Islam and the Western world there is crisis now. Out of hearing of me, out of sight of me, and yet wonderfully close to my imagination, there must be scores of thousands of human beings at an extremity of stress and excitement to-night because of reasonless conflicts, disorders of relationship, which are still almost as destructive and fruitless in human affairs as earthquakes and cyclones.

These newspapers just faintly visible in the shadow contain, I reflect, much other disturbing matter. There are particulars of religious riots in India, of the struggles of military leaders for power in China ; considerable armies are in conflict there ; the British Government has refused to ratify its predecessor's treaty with Soviet Russia, and there also trouble gathers. From America there was little to hand to-day except a tale of rising prices and a paragraph about a fight and bloodshed between the Klu-Klux-Klan and a State militia. But all these newspaper headings and items are merely the sudden swirls, the frothings—red frothings they are at times—and rapids upon the surface of the broad incessant rush of human affairs. The rest I apprehend but do not see. Between these various scattered and more or less significant items there are enormous intervals, great distances filled with unrecorded crises and unnoticed change. Everywhere older people have been dying and younger people have been asserting themselves for the first time ; new practices and new ideas have gained a little ground and old ones lost it. The common mind of the world is not what it was last night nor what it will be to-morrow. It might seem that there was no permanent thing whatever in all this onward flow.

The more widely I extend my view from this window the more transitory the spectacle appears. Yet the books and criticisms of life that come to me do still, to a large extent, question change and repudiate progress. Men can still be found to write of the " enduring elements " in human nature and the " undying factors " of human life. Always by life they seem to mean the peasant's life, seed-time and harvest, desire and children, toil and rest. They see it associated with the soil, renewed by the soil, as necessary and inevitable as the succession of day and night. A denial of essential change is, I suppose, almost fundamental to the Catholic faith. And by denying essential change men solace themselves for the shortness

of their self-concentrated careers. To those whose brief historical perspectives have been brought to a focus at the building of Rome and the
Greece of Homer and Hesiod, this peasant life may well seem immemorial.
But in truth there is no underlying permanent stratum to the changes of our
world. It all changes, root as well as flower. Less rapidly, indeed, but
as surely, the peasant changes with the rest of mankind. These terraces,
these olives which now seem part of the scheme of Nature, have not been
here for more than five-and-twenty centuries. And they go.

Before that time this land behind the coast was held by cattle-tending
barbaric tribes. And earlier they were more barbaric. Only a few thousand
years ago this land was an untamed wilderness and its people savages.
The man of the Grimaldi caves was of no European kin, and in his day it
seems there was no sea out there beyond the hills, but a great valley in which
men lived precariously and across which one might walk on foot to what
were then the dense jungles of North Africa. And when one goes back
a few score further centuries, back to the age of the relics that were found
in the caves of Moustiers, then all about here there were bleak and desolate
uplands where the cave-bear prowled, where the mammoth and the woolly
rhinoceros crashed through the frosty thickets, and the only thing to represent a man was a grisly heavy-browed brute beyond our understanding.

Παντα ρει, flux universal. It is only because I may sit at this window
for so brief a time that I do not see this scene dissolve visibly and pass and
give place to other unprecedented and equally transitory appearances.
Of one thing only can I be sure, that all this goes, peasants and pleasure
cities, ships and empires, weapons, armies, races, religions, and all the
present fashions of man's life. Could my moment be enlarged to the
scale of a thousand years, my world would seem less lasting than a sunset
and the entire tragedy of this age the unimportant incident of an afternoon.
I can discover in all my world nothing enduring, neither in the hills nor
in the sea, nor in laws and customs nor in the nature of man, nothing stead-
fast except for this—a certain growth of science, a certain increase of
understanding, a certain accumulation of power.

But there is that growth of science, there is that increase of understanding,
there is that accumulation of power. I do not know why it should be so,
but so it is. It gathered its force slowly before man was. It goes on
now with accumulating speed and widening scope, and on it I build my
working conception of the course of life. Man, unconscious at first, begins
now, in an individual here and an individual there, to realise his possibilities
and dream of the greatness of his destiny. A new phase of history is near
its beginning.

But it has not begun. The world I have surveyed this evening is a world
still unawakened. It flows towards its fate down the chance slopes and

natural gullies of a will-less destiny. It obeys not a purpose but a gravitation. Its wilful contribution is relatively ineffective. Such science as we have brings us suggestions rather than direction. It is not a dawn of power. But it is a small, clear, certain light, a morning star, tacitly hopeful, which it seems to me must surely and certainly prelude such a dawn. Implicit in the knowledge we now possess appears the promise of that comprehensive Greater Being, towards which thinking minds have been reaching for many generations.

I do not so much accept this conception of the coming of a general mind as find myself possessed by it as a natural outcome of all my mental growth. With the readiness of one completely prepared, I fall in with the intimations this new science of psycho-analysis gives us, that a new sector, a more completely adult stage, a stage of fuller self-knowledge and self-direction, is now enlarging the cycle of human life and bringing us into a comprehensive mental community. We become more impersonal, more co-operative, and more disinterestedly creative.

For long ages man has been the rebel child of nature ; it is no new thing that he should attempt to anticipate and divert fate. Already this world is a man-shaped world ; the water that runs beside the stone-flagged paths and the trickle of the soil down these slopes is guided and controlled by terraces and channels. Rain-water and earth go here as they are told. Scarcely a tree about this house but is here because it was planted or tolerated. Every beast that is too big to lurk or burrow is a subdued beast. But so far all this human control has been a control in detail ; there has been no comprehensive control because there has been no comprehensive understanding. Yet can that fail to come ?

Since man in a few hundred centuries has travelled from that lonely savage in the upland caves to the engineer and chemist and psychologist of to-day, since to-day there is a constantly increasing stimulation and enlightenment of men's minds, since there are no real positive obstacles to human progress but only negative ones—ignorance, obstinacy, habit, doubt, and superstitious fear which vanishes before the light—it is not difficult for me to believe that in quite a few generations now, in quite a little time, our race, moving necessarily in the direction of its innate promptings, will enter upon a life that would be altogether wonderful to us could we but anticipate it, that will be broad and gracious and lovely and beautifully eventful beyond anything we can dream of now or desire. That new way of living may be much nearer at hand than many of us dare to suppose, since its coming seems to depend almost entirely upon the conscious co-operation of men. No one has yet been able to gauge what increased power of co-operation a freshly conceived education may yield us. The long centuries that were needed to mould the life-cycle of the early Palæolithic brute-man, darkened and refractory, into our present freedoms, are no measure of the rate of change that is practicable to conscious effort.

As I look out upon this world, upon these hills so tranquil now under the glittering stars, I see as plainly as I see that those stars are rising and setting, our waste and disorder, our petty, distressful, and dispersed life, so intelligent and eager, so hasty and undisciplined and tragically silly, giving place to the advent of a conscious, coherent being of mankind, possessing and ruling the earth.

In the peace of this starlit hour one can see wide and far. I can put in their true proportions the fretting events in those newspapers, invisible now in the shadow beyond the circle of my lamp. That futile excitement about the gambling-tables beyond there is altogether swallowed up in the night, and all the gambling and money manipulation in the world becomes scarcely more significant in this longer view than the rustling passage of a few autumnal leaves down the water-channel beside this house. They may choke a grating for a moment; they may waste a little water.

And the broad vision that I have from here is scarcely more troubled by those poor bodies in the desert twilight. The cracking of rifles and revolvers in the streets of Cairo does not reach up to this serenity. In some manner all men must die, and while their lives remain poor and little it is a small matter whether they die in bed or whether they die in battle. The great guns upon those ships have but a short range in time. That men should finish a trifle more painfully and a trifle less tediously than usual, by shot and bayonet, by gas and great explosions, is little worse than that they should die by fevers and famines and the cruelties of large beasts. Such things are aspects of our phase, and only in degree less transitory than the night-mares that may be troubling a score of pillows among the peasant homes near by.

There is no enduring pain, there is no eternal tragedy. Toil passes like the straining of a rootlet or the opening of a bud. Supreme above wars and disasters, surpassing and at last redeeming all the present torments of man, is the growth of a being of thought. Such circles of light as this beneath my lampshade are more formidable than all the armies and navies in the world, and stronger than the sum of human violence. They have an invincible tendency to run together like drops of oil. They grow brighter. It is because our light is growing that at last we apprehend the shadows. To realise the unacceptable evil in a thing is to begin its cure. Great as are the evils that we can see in life, the power of the will in us grows greater. I see the nearness of an order in the world like the order of a garden, of a workroom, of a laboratory, a clean life and a direct life and a powerful life for men ; the jungle and all its sufferings gone at last for ever.

Nor will the coming to consciousness of this greater life of the race diminish or dwarf or fetter individual lives. They will be different, they will be enlarged. They will be passing beyond egotistical conflict and out of the age of jealousy, as we are passing beyond superstition and out of the age of fear. But they will be just as freely interested. They will be far more various and individualised. Their form of self-assertion will be different, it will have the form of distinctive service and distinctive creation, instead of being a blind insistence upon formal honour, upon possessions, and upon stereotyped advantages. To-day already in a thousand aspects of their lives people about us are anticipating this new phase, this completely adult phase of human life.

This is no act of faith I am making. I am not thinking against my own resistance. I am not declaring my passionate belief in something that the common aspect of things denies. I am writing down as plainly as I can what I believe to be plain matter-of-fact, as I see it directly my nose is sufficiently removed from my own affairs to permit a broad view of my world. This prospect of a saner, greater humanity controlling the world is as real in my sight as that faint light that came a moment since, and now I see has gone again, in a peasant's window there among the hills.

§ 16

I HAVE made a long account of my framework of belief, much longer than I had supposed it would need to be when I began it in Dickon's London room. I turn over the corrected sheets and I still find matter for correction. I did not realise how much of the foundations of my life remained unformulated. At last I seem to have gathered everything together, everything essential, into the view from this window. Here I have got the present moment, the long past, the future, and the deeps of space. Here for a moment I may pause.

It is three o'clock in the morning, starry and immensely still. The moon is not yet visible ; not even the pale stain of its light upon the edge of the sky. It will rise later, a hunted fugitive with the devouring dawn upon its heels. There is no sound in all this dark world but the soliloquy of the water under my open window. But at last I feel I have made my ground clear and disposed of my premises, and to-morrow I will go on writing about the more human things of life, about social organisation and toil and business and possessions, and about the hopes and desires of men and women, their loves and their ambitions, their generosities and disregards, and about the change that is going on in all human relationships. That change in human relationships is to be my expanding and increasing interest throughout. That was what I intended to discuss from the beginning, and it is only as I have set about my task that I have realised how much preliminary explanation had to be made—to myself as well as to the reader.

BOOK THE SECOND

THE STORY OF THE CLISSOLDS—MY FATHER AND THE FLOW OF THINGS

THE STORY OF THE CLISSOLDS—MY FATHER AND THE FLOW OF THINGS

THE SECTIONS

WHEN I was twelve and my brother Dickon nearly fifteen, my father, Richard Clissold, having been found guilty of falsifying the books of London and Imperial Enterprises and sentenced to seven years' penal servitude, committed suicide and died in the passage behind the court just after he had left the dock. He had swallowed a small capsule containing poison which he had concealed in the lining of his waistcoat. While there had been a straw of hope left to him he had fought, but now hope was at an end. A few minutes later he would have been searched and they would have taken everything from him, and his way of escape would have been closed.

Neither Dickon nor I heard of this disaster at the time. Our mother had taken us abroad at the first intimations of the final storm. Probably our father told her to do so. We boys thought at first that we were going for a few days of holiday, but that holiday stretched out perplexingly from days to weeks and from weeks to months, and for all that time things were kept from us or mitigated for us. We went first to Holland and then into Belgium ; we wandered from town to town and from pension to pension. For a time we were at St. Omer, where there were mysterious comings and goings of my mother and various friends between France and England. We settled down at last at Montpellier—by that time we knew of our father's death—and there we began to realise fully that the spacious days of Mowbray were over and that we had entered upon a new life under a new name and more restricted circumstances.

I understood very little about my father's position in the world before our flight from Mowbray, and I doubt if Dickon knew much more than I did. I had known, however, that he was a very great business man. One of our many governesses—I forget her name—told me he was " very, very, *very* rich." Always with three " verys," and the last one stressed. That young woman, I realise now, had an admiration for him beyond her station; she liked to talk about him endlessly, she said he was " wonderful " and ought to have been knighted long ago, and she left abruptly and in tears.

I had still but the vaguest ideas of worldly position in those days. Mowbray effaced Bexhill. There our surroundings had been brightly and prosperously suburban in character ; we had lived in a square-faced red house called " Sunny Beach " not five minutes from the sea-front, with a garden at the back where croquet—tennis had still to become universal— struggled against our infantile occupation of the lawn. There was, I remember, tamarisk about that lawn, ragged and ill-treated, and there was tidy tamarisk in front of the house, and everywhere about us there was tamarisk. Life at Bexhill was being a " kid " in a multitudinous jumble of " kiddies " amidst perambulators and nursemaids and pet dogs and iron seats and sand-heaps and boats and the stray balls of strange children coming out of nowhere into our play, and the legs of grown-up people. But Mowbray was a large and dignified frame for our lives. It conveyed a sense of social perspectives, and there I began to observe something of the relationship of things. I knew there were poor people in the world who had to be pitied but not encouraged, and that there were lower servants who resembled one another closely and upper servants of greater personal distinction like Mrs. Praydo and Jenks the butler, and the current governess between heaven and earth, and mummy's friends who called in the afternoon and were shown the gardens, and daddy's friends, a gay and glittering train who came for week-ends. Some of these were knights and baronets and even lords and ladies, and far away and over them all ruled the old, old Queen, Queen Victoria in Windsor Castle, who lived for ever and was halfway to God. There were a lot of foreigners also in existence ; some of daddy's friends were foreigners, but foreigners did not amount to much unless there was a war. Then the Fleet would protect us.

I had not learnt very much in those days because my education had been so intermittent, but I was curious and fairly quick and I read voraciously. My education was intermittent because my father was imaginative and erratic and my mother fastidious and resistant. Towards the end of our great days he was talking of a public school for me, but he did nothing whatever to get me to one. " Which shall it be, Old Son ? " he would ask. " Harrow and a halo or Eton in a topper and a bum-freezer ? " I had a brief spell at a very select preparatory school near Guildford which I hated, and when I was eleven I began, by a special concession, to be a weekly boarder at Cossington's School. There I learnt to draw and the beginnings of science. I was taken away from that abruptly in mid-term. Dickon was then in the fifth form at Laxton after a good beginning at a preparatory school in Bexhill—his was a much sounder and more normal education than mine—and a few days later he too was jerked home and came back in a state of pleasurable excitement, with no idea of what impended.

" What's up ? " said Dickon. " Is it to be Eton after all ? "

I can still recall something of my mood when I learnt on the Monday morning that I was not to return to school. I went out on the terrace after Jenks had given me my breakfast and contemplated with infinite satisfaction the vast, empty, wonderful day that opened out before me, a surprise gift, a golden globe of sunlit time. It was a bright March day and the clouds were like great ships crowded with canvas that sailed before a strong yet kindly south-west wind. Everything was very quiet, there were no week-end visitors packing off and departing, because my father was away. I had no suspicion that life at Mowbray had come to its last phase of all for me. I decided I would begin by going to see if the primroses had appeared along the bridle-path through the wood.

I must have gone into the park and looked back at the house somewhen then, because it stands out so plainly in relation to this moment of my life. I see again the fair pale frontage under its pseudo-classical pediment, the dignified portico, the dining-room to the right, and to the left five windows of the long room both Jenks and my father always spoke of as the " saloon." East and west were stables and other offices, each with a cupola and a clock. The house was backed by woods, tall brown beeches, red-tipped before the first sharp jets of green athwart their lower branches. I can see it now. I can feel the freshness and release of that spring morning still. After the matter of the primroses had been investigated I proposed to strike back to the dip in the park and see whether the bracken had got its croziers above ground yet or whether I should find them by digging, and what our fallow deer were doing. Our new fallow deer. Only last autumn my father in his splendour had turned the cattle off the park and stocked it with nearly three score fallow deer.

Then probably after that I should cease to be a boy and become a Red Indian or an African explorer.

But the rest of that day and the two days of solitude that followed before Dickon's return have left no clear record in my mind.

Uncontrolled freedom at Mowbray seemed too good to be true to both of us. It was too good to be true, and we received the news that we were to go abroad to Holland " to see the lovely bulbs " with loud protests. " Oh *no*, mummy ! " We had no desire to see the lovely bulbs and our mother's manner did not convey to us any great anticipation of pleasure in the spectacle. We wanted to go on mucking about at home. There was a dismay in our mother's dark eyes and a stress in her manner for which our boyish imaginations had no understanding. We argued that going to Holland was perfectly rotten and we made a stolid passive resistance to packing. One or two incidents before our departure struck Dickon as " rummy " ; Jenks vanished suddenly, and a housemaid found in tears on the staircase said everyone was going to be turned off. She apparently, said Dickon, had been jolly well just turned on. Strange men appeared and moved the furniture about and treated a small boy accustomed to be taken notice of as if he was invisible. Mother appeared to be sniffing furtively that evening. Anyhow, when Dickon asked her if anything was " up " she turned her face away and dabbed her eyes with her handkerchief before she answered in a strangled voice, " *Nothing*. Nothing, dear. I have a little cold."

That first perception of something wrong in the air, something that was being kept from us, was greatly intensified by my mother's behaviour in the brougham on the way to Duxford Station. Dickon had, of course, collared the seat beside the driver but I was inside with mother. The excitement of travel was upon both of us youngsters by that time, we were disposed to forget our recent recalcitrance, but it was painfully evident she intended to continue depressing us. Dickon had made a sort of song about our departure that seemed to me the quintessence of wit, it was so perfectly innocent and justifiable in reality and yet so close to indictable offences. He had made it as we got up and we had been singing it all the morning.

> " We're going to Rotterdam,
> " Rotter Rotter Dam,
> " We've both of us gotter
> " Go to Rotter,
> " Rotter, Rotter (*open out and let yourself go*)
> " *Dam !* "

When I tried to cheer things up inside the brougham with this agreeable refrain my mother quenched me with, " Don't, Billykins, I've got a headache."

We drove down the park road to the town lodge. I sat back subdued but resentful. At the curve where the woods sweep round my mother leant forward and became very still, looking back at the great house she was leaving for ever. It seemed to be smiling in the sunshine with the blandest indifference to her departure. I gave it one glance over her back, noted that her shoulders heaved and stared disgusted out of the other window. What was the *good* of all this depression ? What was the *sense* of it ? It was *my* holiday that was being spoilt by her obstinacy, not hers. I remained stonily averted until we were close to the station.

Then she spoke to me and her voice showed that she had recovered herself. " Come, Billykins," she said. " Take your little bag."

I took my little bag.

Queer how just these scenes of five or ten minutes' duration stand out in one's memory. Queer, too, how broken and intermittent are all my memories of my mother, without prelude and without immediate sequel. It is as if that part of my mental record had been edited by some unknown power with a disposition to suppress her. I suspect a sustained inattention. It is only by an effort even now that I can restore her sufficiently to describe her. She was dark and slender, she was weak and gentle and ineffective ; fear was in her nature and she would not, she could not, stand up to events. I think that both Dickon and I felt that fear in her as a thing excessive, and that it robbed us of much of the natural confidence and love that sons should have for their mother.

Her promotion to Mowbray must have frightened her very much. At Bexhill she had been able to manage fairly well, but Mowbray after Sunny Beach must have seemed like a white elephant after a governess cart. In the course of time she had come to like the place after her fashion and at the end she had become proud of it. Jenks and Mrs. Praydo had made things difficult but not impossible for her during her period of responsibility ; they had never failed to come to her to tell her what orders to give them unless they were very hard pressed. Some of the week-ends must have been terrible—such a crowd of large, bright, brilliant, and various people, yet after all my father was there to manage them and she could wear her dresses very successfully—she had a lovely neck and shoulders—and even get into little sympathetic conversations with anyone who, like herself, seemed to be detached and shy. And in the quiet in between she could almost expand into a great lady and have local callers and see her own friends and take them to see the roses or the orchids or even, if they had suitable dispositions, completely " over the house."

I know very little of my mother's history. My father must have married her when she was very young ; she could have been hardly three-and-thirty at the time of his death. I do not know where he met her nor what her people were ; I may have first cousins quite unknown to me. I have no doubt he came into her world suddenly and splendidly and discovered her quiet, dark loveliness and decided to make her his with the same effective decision with which later he made Mowbray his. And to begin with for a brief year or so I am convinced she must have been a quite happy young woman. He was good looking and charming and confident and kind. I imagine she began by believing him to be just exactly the nice and gallant, high-principled and capable husband that every Victorian young lady expected as her portion in life. Presently she must have come to realise that instead he was a strange and unaccountable animal, that a thousand things in the world could attract and excite him more than she could, that he could be unfaithful to her without a qualm, that without an antagonistic thought for her his proceedings could be utterly regardless of her security and of her standards of right and wrong and of everything she valued in life. I am sure he loved her ardently at first and then began to go away for a little while and then come back more ardent than ever, and so on for longer and longer absences and briefer and briefer spells of compensatory ardour, until it must have become apparent to her that he was developing the habit of forgetting her to very serious proportions. He was never, I am sure, positively unkind to her, he never in any material way neglected her, he showed her the greatest respect, but he forgot her more and more. It was his way to forget things. Negligence was the fault that finally destroyed him. At last it was all forgetfulness and there was no more ardour at all. In his forgetfulness of her he may have inflicted some terrible humiliations. He was a man of manifold activities. He went on with his career as he had been going on with it before he met her, his expansive, enterprising, erratic, dangerous, and occasionally forgotten career.

I think she must have known how dangerous it was, by instinct, by watching his moods, quite early in their life together. I believe she felt the quiver of the coming earthquake through all our comforts and splendours long before it came. In her heart she may have been praying desperately against an inevitable catastrophe.

I wonder how lonely that poor fear-oppressed lady was at Mowbray. She was a helpless nonentity on a ship that she felt might founder. She had no consolation that I can perceive unless it was the sense of temporary possession when my father was away. She did not resort to religion, at least perceptibly; I think she was too shy to take her troubles there. And we two boys must have been very uncongenial offspring indeed, intractable, difficult to pet and in voice and appearance very like our father, Dickon even more than I.

§ 2

IT was at Bruges that Dickon and I were told that there was to be no more daddy and no more Mowbray in our lives.

I have never been to Bruges since those days and I do not know how much that little old city has changed. I remember it as cobbled, with grass and moss between the cobbles, as built of very worn red brick and having a great number of courts in which big trees grew and into which one went through great archways. These I think were called Beguinages and I remember worrying my mother to show me a Beguin. " Mummy, is *that* a Beguin ? " One might lark about among these places—discreetly. There were also numerous green-scummed decaying canals with grassy banks, sustaining a multitude of brightly painted and interesting barges. Also there was a very entertaining Grand' Place, above which rose a tall belfry that continually disseminated tunes like the tunes of a musical-box. It showered chimes and airs at the hours and the half-hours and quarter-hours. All Bruges lived as a vocal exercise to the accompaniment of this almost incessant carillon. One could ascend that belfry, but our mother would not let us do that. High places made her giddy and so they were forbidden us. Always there was a creaking and clatter in the cobbled square below, a coming and going of big two-wheeled waggons with the most interesting loads, a selling of things from booths, a shouting of hawkers and so forth. There was a great traffic of small carts and trucks drawn by dogs ; we had never seen the like before. The dogs would bark at you but they would not go for you because they were fastened to the carts. They were always barking. We lodged in an inn upon the Grand' Place, an inn with some old Flemish name that I have forgotten, and it was in a little bedroom upstairs with an open window giving on the noise, on shouting, barking, chimes and clatter, that our mother told us that our father was dead.

We had known for two days that things were getting worse with mother, but we had said nothing to each other about it. She had kept us away from her as much as possible, sent us out to play, even given us francs to buy anything we wanted in the shops. When we drifted back to the square and the inn she had gone off for a long walk by herself—a strange thing for her to do. At bedtime there had been a storm of affection, more especially for me because I stood it better. " My poor, poor darling little Billykins ! My little Billy ! "

Then she began to talk to herself, a thing she had never done before. " How can I tell them ? " I heard her say as we sat at our lunch.

And also I remember, " I can't even wear black. I can't even do that."

She made us come up to her room after our lunch. We came the more reluctantly because she said she had something to tell us, something very important. We were both now in a state of extreme resentment at her odd and unaccountable behaviour. We knew nothing of her distresses and to her, poor woman, our minds were inaccessible. She had never known how to reach them, how to make herself in any way understood. From our earliest childhood she had never been able to imagine, much less to direct, what went on inside out little skulls.

" Sit down," she said. " No, don't look out of the window, please, *please*, don't. Sit down." Dickon she made take the only chair, and I was perched upon the bed. The room, I remember, struck me as untidy. The poor lady looked at her two difficult, obdurate offspring and stood clasping her hands.

" You poor dear children ! Oh ! dreadful things have happened. Dreadful things. How can I tell you ? "

" You haven't had bad news, mother ? " Dickon hazarded.

" Oom," said my mother, full charged with emotion.

" Boys ! " she recommenced—she had never called us that before " Boys, you are never to *speak* of your father again. Never. You are never to *think* of your father again. You will never see him any more— ever."

Neither of us, I remember, said a word. I glanced at Dickon for a cue and he was sitting stock still, not looking at her but, still hostile, taking in what she had said.

Her lips were compressed. She clenched her handkerchief into a ball and pressed it against her cheek and sat down abruptly upon her big travelling trunk. " Never see him again," she said. " Never go back to Mowbray. Never go back to England not for many years. Live abroad here. And your name isn't to be Clissold any more. None of us are to be Clissold any more. You will be called Walters—Willy Walters. Dickon Walters. Mrs. Walters."

She paused. Then added an injunction : " Whatever questions they ask you, you are not to answer. Not to answer and not to listen. Whatever they ask or whatever they say."

Dickon, it was evident, intended to speak. She stared at him with dark apprehensive tear-stained eyes. Already he was so far his father's heir that she was afraid of him.

" But what's become of daddy ? " he asked. " Why should we be called Walters ? I think it's a *rotten* name."

" It was—it was my name—before I married," sobbed my mother.

" All the same," said Dickon. " And besides—where's he gone ? I don't see it."

I was younger and blunter. I had had what I felt was a really bright idea, and I wanted to get it out before Dickon thought of it. " Is he *dead*, mummy ? "

Dickon glanced at me as though he was minded to strike me. For a long time, as it seemed, my mother said nothing. Her brows were knit and her face was red. There was an immense silence in the room and outside a turmoil, a sudden dog-fight, men shouting, the clatter of cans overturned and trailed over the stones.

" OO !—oom ! " my mother assented at last, nodding her head, her lips pressed tight. She choked, and then spoke very quickly in a sharp squeak : " *He's dead.*"

And then her face flushed transparent red and broke up like an infant's when it gives way to uncontrollable grief. She took refuge from all further inquiries, from all further control of the situation in a stupefying passion of weeping. I had never seen such weeping. I was astounded, I was horrified, I was ashamed. It seemed to me that even the noises in the square outside were stilled in amazement at her grief. " What *shall* I do ? " she cried. " What can I *do ?* "

" Leave me," she said at last. " Leave me. Oh ! my heart's breaking."

How vividly those moments come back to me ! I can see her still, see her thin red clutching hands before her face, and her poor silly little handkerchief so soddened with tears that it oozed and dripped. I can remember such a detail as that, but my own feelings I cannot remember at all. I do not think I had any feelings at all. Was I sorry for her ? Was I sorry for my father ? Was I even sorry for myself ? I do not recall it. I was simply stunned with astonishment at the spectacle of a human being " breaking down." In all my life before I had never seen anyone " break down." And this was mother !

I do not remember the slightest impulse to console or comfort her.

I remember, too, almost as vividly how I walked with Dickon by the side of a canal that afternoon, though how we had got there from my mother's bedroom has quite faded out of my memory. I see Dickon with a white face staring blankly ahead of him, his eyes glassy with unshed tears, and I beside him waiting until it should please him to speak.

He spoke at last in tones of intense bitterness.

" Just as if nobody wanted to blub except her," he said, and wrathfully : " It's *our* father."

I accepted that and remained silently respectful as became a younger brother.

At length after a long interval his voice came again : " What's the sense of our not being called Clissold ? Everybody knows our name's Clissold. Everybody."

4*

That again called for no comment on my part. He brushed his eyes lightly.

Presently he thought aloud once more. " Why aren't we going to his funeral ? It's our Right to go to his funeral. I am the Heir. I am his nearest. I ought to be there. Both of us ought to be there."

Again I had nothing to say. We went on silently side by side, silently comforting one another. We felt a hundred things we could not say. We both understood quite clearly that all we had been told was but an intimation of unspeakable things. The whole world had become dark ; sinister abysses yawned beneath the Belgian cobbles ; our feeble speculations and interrogations were as helpless as a weak wailing in an immensity of night. And we knew that so far as our mother went we should never be told, never be given any shape for his disappearance and death and this enigmatical collapse of our world. Some disaster, some frightful thing ? In that our splendid, meteoric father was lost, dreadfully lost. Our hearts began to ache for him. His voice, things he had said and done were coming back to us. He had gone, gone for ever.

Towards our poor, fragile, incapable mother I can remember only that dreadful hardness of our hearts. It was almost as if we felt that it was she who had taken us away from him. And Mowbray and all we held dear.

§ 3

FROM that time on Dickon and I became the close allies we are to this day. Before then we had not seen very much of each other; we had gone to different schools and lived dissimilarly, but now we were thrown together in an almost constant association; we shared our troubles and antagonisms, we were English brothers in a French school and Clissolds, suppressed but still obstinate Clissolds, crypto-Clissolds for a time, against the world.

We were poor in comparison with the Mowbray days, but not impossibly poor. My mother had property. Years ago my father, in a phase of clear prevision, had settled money upon her, and in particular some parcels of shares and some house property in Belgium and France. She talked freely and frequently during that phase of wandering, about returning this property to his creditors, but no creditors were ever about to take advanatge of her mood. She presently adopted widow's mourning and put crape armlets upon us and established herself definitely in Montpellier as Mrs. Walters, a young English widow, very inconsolable and quite devoted to her two sturdy boys. And we had to be the Walters boys thoroughly and suppress the Clissold in us even in our private thoughts. Imperceptibly we fell into a grouping in which she alone was the mourner amongst us, and we shaped our behaviour more and more easily to her assumption that it behoved us to comfort her and compensate her for all she had been through.

She made no great confidences to either of us. To me she talked rather more than to the silent and often preoccupied Dickon. I was younger and gentler in my manners and more flexible. " Ah, Billykins," she would say. " You're all I've got to live for now. You two dear boys."

And she would pat my shoulder and quite obviously let her thoughts amble away to other things.

A more capable comforter appeared in the late August or early September in the person of her cousin, Mr. Walpole Stent, a tall, shy, thoughtful, knickerbockered man with a very large forehead and an immense appetite for long, deep, confidential talks with her. He used to carry field-glasses in a leather case slung by a leather strap over his shoulders in order to examine distant landscapes with more particularity. Those field-glasses extended our sense of *comme-il-faut*. He put up at a little hotel in the rue Boussairelles not far from our house, and he resumed a severed but never-forgotten friendship with our mother. With him we all went presently for a holiday to St. Raphaël, which was then a comparatively unknown resort. He had persuaded her to this, she explained, and she had yielded

because she thought it would do us good to go to the seaside before w
recommenced school.

He was partner by inheritance in a firm of London solicitors, and
remember that even then I was impressed by the retentive and preservativ
quality of his mind. It was my first encounter with a well-trained lega
intelligence. It was like some great furniture depository, safe from fire
corruption or admixture, nothing seemed to happen in it and nothing eve
got lost in it, and he could, with every appearance of pleasure, reproduc
the most commonplace facts at any time at the fullest length and in th
completest detail. He did all he could to make friends with us in spite c
his preoccupation with our mother. He liked us with the greatest deter
mination. He told me a lot of natural history and scientific wonders tha
for the most part I knew already, and to Dickon he professed a sympatheti
interest in cricket that his performance on the beach did not seem to justify
He was, most worthy man, the completest contrast to our father that on
could imagine, and I perceive that the hostility to his memory that sti
smoulders in my heart is a quite instinctive reaction, unrighteous an
unreasonable.

He reappeared at Christmas and found my mother almost out of mourn
ing altogether, very animated and pretty in a dress of bright grey trimme
with black velvet. She began to make it after his departure but she did n
wear it until he returned. We noted that, but said nothing. A patern
solicitude crept into his manner towards us, and he discussed our futu
careers with us at length. We did not, however, discuss them with him
we were already enormously self-protective towards him. We felt th
coming usurpation. Within a year of my father's death my mother ha
married him.

She told us she did it entirely for our sakes. She said that we two neede
the friendship and guidance of a good man. All boys needed that as the
grew up, but we needed it to an exceptional degree. She was too weak f
us and she knew it. For her it was implicit there could be no surcease fro
tragic memories.

There was a honeymoon in Switzerland while we two remained at Mon
pellier, and then the French phase in our education was broken off abrupt
and we were moved to Chislehurst. At Dulwich College, which was th
a vigorously progressive school just taking up science teaching, we made u
for a great deal of lost ground. We became boarders and went home on
in the vacations. There was never any active dissension between us a
our stepfather, but there was a sort of mutual estrangement. We differe
Even in our holidays it is remarkable how little of our waking time we spe
at home. And in the course of the next three years our mother showed h
further devotion to our needs by securing us first the friendship and guidan

of a small but large-headed baby brother and then of a little sister, and then of a second sister.

Dickon was now nearly nineteen and I was sixteen, and as the Walpole Stent family fulfilled its destiny in this manner we two became more and more aware of our superfluousness therein. We proposed to enter at the Royal College of Science and set up for ourselves in London lodgings, and after a great deal of needless discussion, for our departure was manifestly a relief to everyone, this was conceded. But our stepfather loved weighing pros and cons fully and deliberately, and saw no reason why a foregone conclusion should be treated cavalierly. It was not difficult for our mother to give us an allowance of eighty pounds a year each out of the property my father had set aside for her ; that was a quite possible allowance in those days, and so we two were able to establish ourselves in apartments in Brompton and face the world together.

When everything essential to that removal was settled, Dickon broached a matter of great concern to both of us.

It was late one evening that he found his opportunity. My mother and stepfather had been out to dine with a neighbour, and we had just come in from a music-hall. We found them refreshing themselves with biscuits and some lemonade. The bedroom candles were on the table. We exchanged colourless information about our proceedings. Then our stepfather asked some unnecessary question about the courses at Kensington I proposed to take.

"Oh, by the way," said Dickon with a little catch in his voice and an elaborate casualness in his manner, "now that we are going away from here—and things have blown over a bit—I see no reason why we should keep up this pretence of being Walters. In fact—I'm entering at Kensington for both of us as—Clissold."

"But, my dear boy ! " said our stepfather. "Do you know—do you know anything of the story ? "

"Most of it," said Dickon. "Billy has looked it up in back numbers of *The Times*."

"*Well !* " said our stepfather.

"We don't like sailing under false colours," said Dickon. "We think we ought to stand to it."

"But how can we *tell* people ? " cried my mother.

"You needn't. We can be Walters here. Whenever we come along to see you."

He lit his candle calmly and thoughtfully as though the matter was concluded. His hand was quite steady, but mine trembled a little as I followed him. I was sorry for my mother and I avoided looking in her direction. "There's much to be considered," my stepfather began.

" We've considered most of it," said Dickon and took up his candle
" You coming, Billy ? "

My stepfather made no immediate answer.

Dickon went over to mother and kissed her good-night. " Good-night
father," he said. It was rare he said " father." I, too, saluted my mother
and just for a moment her hand sought mine and failed to press it. Her
furtiveness made me as shy and ineffective as herself. We conveyed nothing
and perhaps there was nothing to convey.

" But——! " said my stepfather as Dickon reached the door.

" If I go out into the world as Clissold," said Dickon, turning to him
" I begin at the bottom—yes. But if I go out under a false name and then
they find out I am Richard Clissold Secundus—where am I then ? "

He did not wait for any further discussion, and my stepfather had no
immediate reply. He had to readjust his point of view. And that he never
did in a hurry.

But presently he began to assemble his considerations. Our bedroom
was directly over that occupied by my mother and my stepfather, and
could hear his quiet, unhurrying voice unfolding the situation to himself
and to her, amply, thoroughly, and needlessly, until I fell asleep.

My mother, I know, loved to have things explained to her. She did not
listen, but she loved to have things explained to her. I am sure that she
was in a muddled way distressed at our going, and that my stepfather's
discourse comforted and consoled her. It was not that it met her fears and
objections so much as that it anointed and soothed her mind. Dickon and
I lay awake in our beds for a long time talking in fragmentary spurts, ex-
changing ideas about our own unforgettable father and about the world and
about that battle with the world that lay before us, or following out our own
thoughts to the accompaniment of that submerged, interminable com-
mentary. I do not remember what we said to each other, but I have a
vividly present in my mind as if I had heard it only a moment ago the
muffled sound of that voice coming up through the floor.

§ 4

I FIND it very difficult to recall what sort of figure our own father made in our minds at that particular phase of our lives.

Necessarily his offence, his disaster, his career, and his punishment completely dominated our early outlook. He bestraddled our start in life like the Colossus of Rhodes ; we sailed out under his shadow into the world. He overwhelmed us, immense and indistinct and enigmatical.

I knew he had died in some " dreadful " way after that scene at Bruges, but it is a curious thing, for which I cannot account, that I did not make any attempt to find out exactly how he had died for several years. I suppose when first I was told I was too young to know how to set about the inquiry, and before I had got the necessary *savoir faire* for such an investigation the habit of not inquiring was established. It was by chance one day at Chisle-hurst that I came upon a succinct notice of his tragedy in a stale Whitaker's Almanack. In those days nothing in print was unreadable to me. There in the Events of the Year my eye caught the name of Clissold, and I read, in small print at the bottom of a column amidst a crowd of other happenings :
" Clissold, Promoter of London and Imperial Enterprises, having been sentenced to seven years' penal servitude by Mr. Justice Ponters for fraud, committed suicide with potassium cyanide as he left the dock."

So that was it ! That was my mother's great secret.

My first impulse was to go and tell Dickon all about it, my next to conceal my discovery from him altogether. For either he knew already and had been keeping this thing from me, or he did not know and we should have only this bare poisoned needle of statement to rankle in our minds and inflame us to painful, futile guessing about the details. Obviously a thing like that, big enough to be an Event of the Year, would be found in the newspapers of the time, and so after a day of consideration I asked one of the Dulwich masters—Graham Wallas it was, who afterwards became a great Fabian Society man and a professor of social science—how one set about looking up old newspapers. He was one of our keenest teachers, extraordinarily kind and sympathetic with anything responsive in his classes, and to him one went as a matter of course in any such difficulty as mine. I recall his little start at my request, his judicious self-control—I suppose he knew who I was really and guessed what I had in mind—and how he hesitated and considered and knitted one brow more than the other, with his kind brown eyes looking away from me over his glasses at infinity and his mouth screwed up in a way he had.

" Perhaps it's the best course," he said.

He could not tell me exactly on the spot how I could consult old news-paper files—I was too young for a British Museum ticket—but he would inquire and let me know the exact particulars. He would inquire.

" It's *The Times* you ought to read—certainly," he said. " You'll get the facts there complete and without—without sensation. Whatever facts it is you want to look up."

And at last at a charge, I remember, of sixpence, in a commodious room at *The Times* office, where a number of blighted, anxious-looking people were pulling big volumes about over the tables, I began to reconstruct item by item my father's dereliction and death.

As I did so a great cloud of long-neglected memories returned to me, memories of a big, kind daddy-giant, who came suddenly out of nowhere into one's childish world with a tremendous " Hello, you kids ! " and banished dulness. He banished boredom ; that was his supreme quality. He is always a large, not very distinctly featured giant to me ; my memory of his face is not clear. Chiefly I remember his red whiskers. My mother destroyed every photograph there was of him, and in those days the portraits of prominent people published in the papers were engravings—photographic reproduction for periodicals did not yet exist—and those I was able to dig up made a lamentable mess of him.

So he remains incurably atmospheric, red whiskers, a flushed complexion, a very reassuring smile, quick movements. A wonderful giver of " pig-a-bags " he had been at Bexhill, and at Mowbray there had been rare, memor-able sprees, a time when a week-end party of grown-ups played rounders with wild enthusiasm on the great lawn, and Dickon, who was only fourteen, ran faster even than men of fifty and got rounder after rounder for his side, and several games of spoof cricket with the end pillars of the terrace balus-trading as a wicket and a walking-stick for a bat and a rubber ball. He dressed up once as Father Christmas for us. He sang the " Two Obadiahs " and " Tommy Make Room for Your Uncle " to us—until my mother implored him not to make us vulgar. He would think of us when he was abroad and in all sorts of places where a daddy might reasonably forget his little boys ; he brought us back delightful flat tin soldiers marching, cooking, camping, in oval wood boxes from Paris, and entertaining earthenware Nativities with kings, shepherds, and irrelevant crowds complete, from Italy. And he sent us coloured picture postcards from the ends of Europe, cos-tumes or animals or railways or ships. He saw to it that we had toy railway trains on rails that really worked, from some special shop he knew of in Holborn. Such deeds fought for him eloquently. It was absolutely impossible for me to think of him as a villain.

I sat in *The Times* search-room with my cheeks flushed and my eyes growing hot and red, reading of growing suspicion and denunciation and insolvency and pursuit and trial, and never had I a doubt that he was an evilly entreated man.

He had almost got away from them. For days he was missing. He had danced off to Paris, taken a ticket and a lit-salon berth for Geneva, and vanished at Culoz. They had found him and arrested him nine days later in a little out-of-the-way inn in Biscay. When the detective broke it to him that he was known and under arrest he had remarked cheerfully : " Good old Scotland Yard ! Have some déjeûner with us ? It's awful stuff."

Us ! He had travelled with a typist-secretary as his daughter. He thought, he said, that was a fresher disguise than wearing a false beard. His levity on this delicate matter told against him at the trial.

And his offence ? That was rather a tangled business for a boy of fifteen. I will not attempt to summarise that complex story here. I could appreciate better the nine days' man-hunt that had preceded his arrest. Even in the decorous Victorian *Times*—a *Times* without headlines—I could detect the sporting zest his disappearance gave the affair, and when later on I looked up the case in other contemporary newspapers, I realised what a bright addition to the British breakfast-table of that spring, the chase of my father must have been. Tall Englishmen of easy manners had been arrested at Marienbad and in Stockholm ; all over Europe his travelling compatriots must have been seeing him, sometimes several times a day.

I saw the chase from the point of view of the hunted. I suppose he knew how hopeless his flight was even from the first. But he was always for giving the thing a trial rather than for giving in. But there he was, dodging about at minor junctions and giving false names at inns and wondering what the devil he should do when his money ran out and, I guess, keeping up the delusion of his pseudo-daughter that she was having a romantic elopement. And treating her as it seems he did—strictly as his daughter. He would not damage her more than he could help. All the while he must have been going over the squalid sequence of rash falsifications and expedients that had ended in his crash. So recently as a year before he had been in no greater danger than that of a rather florid and extravagant bankruptcy. Even then he might have pulled through and recovered his prestige in the City. But he had been unable to face a merely legal failure when just a slight stretching, a further risk, a fraud that good luck would conceal again, might tide things over. He did not want merely to escape ; his hopes grew with his dangers ; even when the game was utterly lost he had still attempted victory. He had been careless in his manipulations, a little contemptuous, I am afraid, of the alertness of his associates, a little too confident of their courage and sympathetic dishonesty.

Towards the end he broke badly. His last exploits were hardly more planned or intelligent than the flurry of a harpooned whale. He plunged from misdemeanour to felony. His last falsifications were puerile, and on those he was convicted.

And so after a futile struggle over the extradition they took my father back to England. I imagine him concealing as much as he could of his chagrin beneath a bearing still hectically debonaire. Back he came to the City of London, where he had been so brilliant, so brilliant and meteoric a figure, and there he stood in the ill-lit stuffy court and was examined and re-examined and wearied and exhibited and disentangled and picked to pieces, picked to discreditable shreds.

I realise now that he had never taken business quite seriously. I perceive from one or two phrases of his under examination that he was immensely astonished that a little more or a little less sharp practice should make all this difference in his treatment by his fellow-men.

Twice the judge, a fellow-member of his club, a successful youngish man who had once looked up to him, had to reprove him for " a certain familiarity " in his manner.

And then it became plain to him that it was really so, that he was in a trap and the springe had closed upon his neck. There was a line drawn between permissible and illegal sharpness, a miserable line, and they could not see how slight a thing, how playful and fresh a thing, it had been to overstep it. That dismally cheerful train journey with the detectives, the restraints of his present imprisonment, this dingy crowded court all eyes for him, were to be only the prelude to a long grey, chill, eventless, under-nourished, unstimulated living burial. They meant it. They had got him and they meant it. Well, he, at least, had had one saving moment of fore-sight. Here the stuff was, close at hand. Here under his finger. Good !

So he held his chin up and answered firmly to the end. Was even humorous once or twice. There was laughter in court.

The Times search-room seemed to contract upon me until it became the waiting-room of a court and the helpful attendant might have been a warder. It was as if I stood in my father's place. I could understand it all.

Death is a very dreadful and tremendous thing to the adolescent mind, but I felt that I could understand. I wished that somehow when he stood up to hear the foregone verdict, alone without an overt friend in a court crowded to overflowing with his enemies and with merciless, curious spectators, he could have known that some day his son would be there beside him in imagination and feeling—not condoning but understanding. He would not have wanted his offence condoned. I am sure there was no nonsense of that sort about him. At last, almost as a relief, after his tedious drawn-out defence, the verdict and the sentence must have come ; the old club acquaintance exalted and aloof, in his antic great wig and scarlet gown, a successful windbag, giving the reporters in particular his carefully prepared phrases, blaming, condemning, pronouncing a sentence heavy and exemplary. Well, some of us have to muddle and lose our game, but why add insult to defeat ? Seven years' penal ! And the rest of life, a few years of discredited, pauperised age. Thank you for nothing, my lord.

And then ?

Did the stuff hurt ? Did it seem as swift a poison as we suppose it to be or did time drag ? Were there some moments, some minutes even, while the capsule dissolved, minutes charged with fear whether it would act at all, and then perhaps a frightful pang, some numb horror or rending agony that none have ever lived to tell about ?

Then the blow of the wall as he fell against it, if ever he knew he fell against the wall, and darkness.

§ 5

IF I had had any faltering of sympathy for my father in his destruction, Dickon's sturdier simpler faith would have sustained me. When I came to tell Dickon about it, he showed, so far as I can remember now, that he knew most of the story. Perhaps he had been put through it by schoolfellows ; at any rate, all his judgments were prepared. " They made him a scapegoat," said Dickon. " They let him down." And, phrase reminiscent of rafts and pirates and all the fierce imaginations of a boy : " He got the long straw."

" They never touched his co-directors," said Dickon. " They were too high up and too near royalty. Lord Duncomby was in it. Two others. What were their names ? . . .

" But they took the stuff all right while it lasted. . . . Trust *them*," said Dickon.

That was what I, too, wanted to believe. Our father had been careless, indifferent, and they had caught him. But he had only done what everybody did. " They don't catch *me*," said Dickon, gauging the realities of life.

Neither of us believed that he was essentially worse than the run of business men. We contemplated a brigand world.

In which after all he had made things that remained. All over London were great buildings he had promoted. He had altered the face of London —criminal though he was. He had been lavish with his architects, and his ideas about service flats and suchlike new methods of housing were far in advance of his times. Many of his failures have since become richly paying properties. And though he flourished in the worst period of English architecture he never put up anything absolutely detestable. I remember Dickon stopping me one day against the heavy but by no means ungainly masses of Cornwall Court.

" That's one of the Clissold offences, Billykins. They called him a scoundrel, but he gave them that. That's just one of his things. Catch a muff like Lord Duncomby doing anything as fresh as that ! "

From the outset, because of our father's fate, we two saw the world lawless and adventurous. We were precocious in that. Children believe that in heaven and on earth alike there is order ; they do so naturally and of necessity, and most young people and many people through life retain this early assumption that there is justice and benevolence behind and sustaining the law, that laws and customs are really wise and good. This is an illusion, or at least an exaggeration ; of great provisional value no doubt in restraining youthful excesses ; but it was one that our peculiar circumstances forbade us to entertain. For if we agreed that the system in which we lived was a righteous one, what could our father be but a rogue ? But if it was un-righteous and casual then he was merely ill-starred.

There was a strong suggestion of the predatory animal about both of us in those days after we had left Chislehurst and set up for ourselves in Brompton. We had a mean furnished bedroom with two narrow beds, a frayed carpet, a small wardrobe, and one washhand-stand, and a sitting-room lit by a central gas-light ; the accommodation was greatly restricted by the mute corpse of a black piano the landlady refused to take away ; and there was insufficient table-room and shelf-room for our books and work. Our elbows were therefore a good deal in each other's ribs. We neither of us betrayed by any word we spoke how sick with longing we were at times for the space, the freedom, and self-confidence we had had at Mowbray, but we both knew what was in the other's mind and our expressed intentions towards the future compensated for our silence about the past. We would talk long and intimately at times, late at night perhaps when there was a noise outside to keep us awake, or on the way to the College, or of a Sunday when we walked in Kensington Gardens or explored the endlessness of London to the north and west, and then through intervals of days or even weeks we would have no rational conversation at all. We would fend each other off with silly nicknames and playful and nonsensical insults and go our own mental ways alone. For days together we would elaborate some fanciful joke—our standing dish about Mr. G. for example—or invent and embroider upon a saga about some odd imaginary personality.

We had an underworld, ten times more foolish than this world of appear-ance, which underworld we called the Boops. The Boops followed the events of the day and the fashions of the time after their manner. The Boops had a Royal Jubilee ; they had an Inventions Exhibition in which Mr. Heath Robinson would have felt at home ; they held reviews of army and fleet ; they worshipped curiously a god after their own image, a Mr. B. In the Boops we guyed much of our astonished chagrin at life and laughed it off. For we both had a cheated feeling about life as if something had been promised and snatched away from us.

Occasionally our excessive proximity got on our nerves. There were forces storming in us that made us want to be alone with ourselves for a time, made solitude an urgent need. Dickon would warn me of a brooding violence. " Billykins," he would say, " your little face fatigues me. Take it right away before I buzz books at it. Lose it somewhere. Pawn it for a day or so where it will be safe from damage. See ? "

" Why the hell don't you go out yourself ? " I would retort, savage but preparing to depart. " Look at the rain ! "

" You're insoluble—worse luck," said Dickon. " The door, my lad, is there."

As he was nearly two stone heavier than I in those days I could not banish him when the corresponding mood came upon me. I would then go with my work into the Education Library in the South Kensington Museum and there until the place closed at ten I would read and write by the glare of great spitting violet-flushing arc-lights of a type that have long since vanished from the earth. Then home to a malignant silence and bed. Or it might be, with the clouds lifting, to a tacit amnesty and talk into the small hours.

It added to the natural restlessness in Dickon's blood that he had still to find his calling in the world. In the meantime he was working, but working neither so hard nor so well as I, first at mineralogy and then at mining. " There's always something doing with mines," he said, but he never seemed convinced that that was his proper line of attack. He would have moments of pure rage against the social system that environed us, that seemed so lax and yet was so difficult and dangerous to assail. I remember him once in Holland Park. " How the devil are we to *get* at them ? " he cried suddenly as though he had been stung. " How the devil ? "

" Get at who ? " said I, in the London idiom.

" In these houses. *Look* at them ! Every one stands for thousands a year. And I can't think of a dodge against them, not a dodge. Idiot and fool I am !—unfit to survive. Like silly fat sheep inside a wire fence they are, and I'm like some brainless wolf. Look at this outfit coming along ! Perambulator, two nurses, and a Newfoundland dog. Large expensive toy elephant and a ball. Fine fleecy blanket. All for one ratty, beady-eyed kid ! . . . You ugly little mite ! Where does daddy get it ? Where does daddy *get* it ? "

I was shocked. In those days I had not a tithe of Dickon's voracity. I did not want money then. I did not want money seriously until after I was married. I was under the spell of pure science then, submerged in it, and while Dickon's work was almost perfunctory I studied with all my strength. I was working in the Physical Research Laboratory under C. V. Boys, then a very young man, pink-skinned and flaxen-haired to the eyelashes, clever-handed, and delicate-minded, inspiringly ingenious, rapidly understanding. How many brilliant and delightful minds have gone and go to the making of science ! Boys in those days was the worst lecturer I have ever heard, so bored, so devastatingly bored, so appalled by the hour of talk before him, but in the research laboratory he had amazing flashes, he threw out sparks that set one alight. I had been taken out of the ordinary class and allowed to do some special work under him upon mineral threads and particularly fibres of quartz, and it is difficult for me to exaggerate how much I owe to him. He developed and encouraged my innate enthusiasm for physical research. I began to dream of papers read before the Physical Society; of the Philosophical Transactions, of broadening explorations below the surface of matter. And my taste for such work reinforced my distaste for money-making.

After all what use had I for money? Given a laboratory and a lodging and a few pounds for a summer holiday, what else was there to desire? Nothing that I permitted to rise to the surface of open and confessed thought.

I tried to put my point of view to Dickon.

"You're dreaming, Billy," said Dickon. "You don't know what you're in for. You think you'll give your life to science. They won't let you. You've found your little corner at the college for a bit—but nobody wants research, pure research, and so there's nobody to pay for it. Try it if you want to, for a bit. Until you need money or the college turns you out to make room for some one else. The world's a scramble and you'll have to come into it. Seeing what you are. Trust me."

§ 6

THOUGHTS are parricides. Each phase abolishes and devours its parent phase. Thought is always trial and selection and discarding and forgetting. I can recall some of the things Dickon said in those old days, and some that I said, and they stand out like fragmentary ruins and seem to illuminate a little the past state of the areas immediately about them, but as for the detailed mass of that development it is gone, it is gone now as completely as the lie of the houses and frontages and ownership round about the Cathedral of St. Paul in London before the Great Fire.

We argued tremendously about Socialism and Individualism, but what I meant by Socialism and what he meant by Individualism are now, I perceive, things almost beyond recovery. I think my Socialism and my passion for scientific work were all mixed up together and that it was my sense of the scientific process that dominated the mixture. I doubt if my views have changed fundamentally in the intervening years, but I perceive that what I called Socialism then is no longer to be called Socialism. Socialism for me was certainly something quite different from those vague aspirations towards a land of Cockayne professed by Mr. Ramsay MacDonald and his party when they are out of office, and still less had it anything to do with the doctrines of Communism that have since swamped it. It was, indeed, little more than the application of the distinctively scientific spirit to human affairs in general. I wanted to be part, an honourable part, of this clean and orderly development of knowledge, strong, unhurrying, wonderful, that I found going on in the research laboratory, and from that point of departure it was easy to envisage the social struggle as an indecent and preposterous inconvenience and to want to extend the honourable openness, co-operation, and collectiveness of the world of science to human affairs in general. The social struggle impressed me even in those days as if I were required to fight for my chemical balance in the laboratory and knock out my competitor before I could use whatever was left of the weights and instruments. It was an intolerable distraction of attention, a destruction of possibilities. I did not stop to consider how it had arisen and whether, perhaps, it was not in some way necessary. Possibly even more necessary than the scientific process. I simply denounced it and demanded that it should be discontinued, that the private ownership of the means of research and economic exploitation should follow the private and secretive methods of the Alchemists to oblivion.

While I clung to the opportunities for pure research that, thanks very largely to Boys' good opinion of my work, I had had the luck to find, I was saying therefore, but only, so to speak, with the sides and back of my attention, " Get on to the Socialist State, the International Socialist State, social peace and world peace, and stop this tumultuous waste. Do in the search for food and comfort and security what we are doing in the search for knowledge." And as I was very much preoccupied then with the crucibles and cross-bows that were our chief weapons against the innate disposition of quartz to settle down into a compact geometrical form, and with the problem of how to fuse that refractory material to as fluid a state as possible and shoot it forth, as swiftly as possible, so as to draw it out into the finest possible threads before it cooled and set, I did not perhaps sufficiently consider the very much less congenial and very much more massive and refractory task I was proposing that other people, conceivably beside me and behind me, should undertake. I just wore a red tie once or twice, called myself a Socialist—chiefly to my private self— and argued at nights with Dickon.

Now Dickon's more resentful turn of mind made him direct his attention to just those things, the blunderings, the casualness, the inconsecutiveness and injustice of the world at large, that I was most disposed to ignore. He was then much more irritated by life, much more *in* life, more combative than I was. At that period of adolescence every year of age means a great difference of temper and will. He had penetrated further into the jungle. And, moreover, he was naturally more energetic and realist than I, more aware of foreground things and less concerned about distant ones.

" You're trying to live in Utopia," he would say. " You're living in a dream and you'll awake with a bump."

Our difference exercised him ; he felt the implicit criticism of himself. He would suddenly break into discourse—at the most unexpected times. His words are all forgotten now, but I will try to give the sort of things he would say ; he would be sitting on his bed, perhaps half undressed, marking his points with minatory waggings of the collar and tie he held in his hand.

" You can't live in a world that isn't here, Billykins ; that's what you don't grasp. That's what's the matter with you. This show is a scramble and it's going to be a scramble yet for centuries. You've got to look after yourself ; you've got to look after the things that you care for, yourself. You may want to do the most disinterested things but you have to do them yourself—as your fad. Poor people aren't permitted to have fads. I'd be a Socialist just as you are if there *was* any Socialism. But it's only just been thought of ; it hasn't begun to come. They call all this about

municipal gas and water the coming tide of Socialism. Coming tide !
It's just a few Fabians piddling under a locked door. The world's a world
of private adventure yet for—far beyond our lives, Billykins. Take it
or leave it, that's what it is. And as I want to live in this world and not
in a world that isn't here, I'm Individualist. It isn't a matter of chance
as you seem to think. It's a matter of necessity. I'm an Individualist
and out for private enterprise—which means in plain English going
through the pockets of some crowd one has coralled by dangling some
commodity before them, or making some other looter disgorge. And then
for freedom—and, if you like it, disinterested service—scientific research—
or anything else—as the mood may take you."

No, that is too clear and quintessential, too hard and definite and contemporary, but it has something very close to his spirit, and it is as near
as I can get now to the discussions of those days. The reality of our talks
was much more loose and inconsistent. We were trying things over ;
we were feeling our way. We used claptrap phrases because there was
nothing else to use, we came home with remarkable discoveries that
evaporated, we went back upon ourselves, we jammed in flat contradictions
and lost our tempers. But what I have written has the clarified essence
of it all.

And here something strikes me. Until I began to write this account
of the ideas of my student time I had always assumed that I was still a
Socialist and Dickon still an Individualist. But now I begin to think it
over and try to write it down I find my Socialism is very little more than an
old railway label on a valise ; it records an important journey, indeed, but
hardly a scrap of present significance attaches to it. What I am writing
here is, I realise, no longer Socialism.

Where is that liberal Socialism of the eighties and nineties now ; that
wide project to turn the expansive forces of the modern world towards
organisation and construction ? It has expanded to simple recognition
and become incorporated in current thought, and it has evaporated
altogether as a movement and a cult. It is not only that Socialism has
become no more than a memory, a used label, in my own life ; it has become
no more than a memory in the world. That journey has been made. It
has gone—gone like Chartism, like Puritanism, like the naturalism of
Rousseau or the civic virtue of Robespierre. And as I consider these
things I wake up for the first time to the quality of the Socialism
that remains. The movement did not realise the wider recognition of
its broad ideas. It became sectarian with organisation, it gave way to
impatient passion, it bore a narrow-souled, defective, and malignant child
Communism, and that child has made away with it.

I am no more a Communist than I am a Catholic or a Conservative.

It is not that I have left Socialism, but that Socialism has passed away from my world.

Socialist, Individualist; it is time we washed these old labels off our intellectual baggage. They are no longer of use to us, and they may easily send our wills and intentions astray.

§ 7

THE Socialism I knew and professed in my scientific days was a project for a more spacious and generous ordering of the world. But gradually that propaganda for a larger, less competitive, scrambling and wasteful way of satisfying the staple needs of mankind gave place to a vehement campaign against existing institutions and usages, lumped together for convenience of invective as the Capitalist System. I seemed to hear more and more of the evils of the Capitalist System at every Socialist gathering I attended, and less and less of anything desirable that could be imposed upon its disorders. Gradually there loomed upon my consciousness the legend of a tremendous book, which was to set all other Socialist writings, teachings, and preachments aside, a mighty book always, spoken of in those days by its earnest young propagandists as " Das Kapital," in which this Capitalist system was discovered and demonstrated upon as the source, the engine, the form of all the oppression and robbery and parasitism of man by man. A new sort of Socialist appeared, energetic, opinionated and intolerably abusive, and the moral and intellectual decline of Socialism began. It ceased to be a creative movement, and it became an outlet of passionate expression for the inferiority complex of the disinherited. So it remains to this day.

It is so much easier to vilify than plan; it is so much easier to fix attention upon an injustice than a hope. All planning these new Socialist derided, and they succeeded not only in feeling themselves but in suggesting the feeling to others that " Utopian " was the word for something contemptible and unphilosophical. What need for planning? Had not the profound and stupendous Hegel, that master intellect, that supreme if slightly incoherent God of Human Thought, made it densely clear that the overthrow of the Thing-that-is was in itself the creative establishment of the Thing-that-it-is-not? And so all our young Socialists went about being tremendously scornful and heroic, no longer working for a world wide organisation of peace and staple supplies, but simply for the Thing that-the-Capitalist-System-was-not, whatever that might turn out to be.

These things came to me intermittently. I had little time for socialist discussion after I began to work with Boys, and I found these new views bored and repelled me rather than irritated me to the pitch of discussion. Now it is hard to recall even the substance, much less the method of various disputes. I remember making a bad impromptu speech at some meeting in Chelsea in which I defended Utopian Socialism and was derisively handled. But I do not think I was quick enough to realise in those days that the Proletariat and Bourgeoisie about which these new Socialists gabbled endlessly were absolutely indefinable classes, and still less to apprehend that this Capitalist System of theirs was a phantasmagorical delusion, a sort of Pepper's Ghost, thrown upon the face of reality.

Nowadays I do not succumb so easily to our human disposition to believe that where there is a name there is a thing, and I have learnt to look behind the logical surface of every argument and conviction. I find now in this retrospect that I can see round quite a number of corners that defeated me in those days. Mere everyday living is in itself a training against false classifications and the habit of accepting unanalysed terms. Which is one reason, I think, why we older people are more penetrating and less logical than our younger selves.

A recent chance encounter, when I was last in London, comes back into my mind, an illustration of all the qualities that make Communism a travesty of intelligent revolutionary theory. It was with a young man with a System to expound. If I had to argue a case against Communism now I should take all the possibilities of delusion that inhere in the one word " System " and rest my case on that.

This word " system " has done extraordinary mischiefs not merely with Socialism but in the whole field of political and social discussion. Its peculiar treachery is the insidiousness with which it imputes deliberate order to entirely unorganised things. A system is properly an organised relationship such as one finds in a system of pulleys or the metric system. But when the learned, confronted with some quite possibly planless, discreet assembly of facts, have sought to classify and arrange these in order to discuss them the more conveniently, these arrangements have also been called systems, whether the facts really responded or not, as in the case of the Linnæan system or the Copernican system. It was easy in the past, when men were entirely possessed by the idea of a supreme designer, to pass from these systems of description to the idea that the things classified were themselves systematically arranged. Men, for example, spoke of the miraculous order of the solar system as though it was something as definitely arranged as a clock, and so hid from themselves the extreme casualness of the relation of the sun to the more or less persistent satellites, the planets, planetoids, comets, meteorites, and so forth that go with it, like midges round a wandering beast, as it drifts through the scintillating disorder of space. And with matters of social arrangement this imputation of purpose and order where there is naturally no order at all, is still extraordinarily mischievous.

I remember how in my schooldays the endlessly complex social muddling of medieval Europe, the swaying smash-up of the Roman Imperium, was dressed up for us as the Feudal System. We were taught to believe that there had existed a neat, universally respected pyramidal arrangement of Society, in which everyone knew to the prettiest pitch of precision his level and his place and his dues and duties. The natural disposition of little scraps of floating wreckage to cluster about and adhere to larger lumps, the obvious phrases, flatteries and conventions of such vassalage, the customary humiliations of the abject and the ingenious devices of the medieval lawyers, were seized upon by the romantic imaginations of later historians and elaborated into a nicely balanced scheme. Hundreds of millions of perplexed, instinctive people lived and died while Feudalism floundered and changed through the centuries of its prevalence, and never had the remotest suspicion that some day earnest scholars would reveal how beautifully systematic were there lives. And to-day millions live and toil, suffer or prosper, and only by reading a very bad-tempered and unattractive special literature or by falling into some propagandist meeting do they get any explanation of what is meant by this Capitalist System under which they are supposed to be living.

Capitalism there is, no doubt ; it is a complex of financial and economic events arising out of purblind attempts to organise the large-scale production rendered possible by modern knowledge and by the enlargement of the modern imagination. But it changes in its general facies yearly, monthly, hourly ; it is never quite the same thing twice nor here and there, and people who scold and blame the Capitalist System and organise a revolution to overthrow it and behave as though the millennium will necessarily ensue when it is exorcised are wasting their strength upon a Protean shadow. They are " seeing things " and fighting phantoms. There is no more a Capitalist System now than there was a Feudal System in the eleventh century. These are systems of description, far remoter from reality than the systems of Linnæus or Ptolemy. There has never been any essential system in the general social and economic life of mankind. Some day men may make these things systematic, but the time is not yet. At present all these things are an immense driftage, with an endless multitude of counter-currents and minor eddies and a limitless variety of interactions. The most immediate task before Man in his great adventure, as I see it, is to make the system that is not yet here, to thrust and weld it upon this chaos of his economic methods and ideas, and subjugate it to his security and creative happiness.

I met a young man the other night at the studio of my nephew and godson, William Clissold, who helped me greatly to understand the working of this system obsession. " A regular intellectual stinker, he was," said William, who affects a remoteness from things of the mind. This young man, at once nervous, convulsive, and arrogant, fell in very illuminatingly with my present line of speculation. He was apparently incapable of thinking of human affairs except in systems. I could not make it plain to him that I believed there was no system at all in economic affairs ; the idea was beyond his intelligence. His main obsession was what he called the Manorial System, a dressed-up revival on the economic side of the exploded Feudal System, and he seemed to regard it as the clue to all existing social and economic relationships, and was honestly shocked when I professed never to have heard of it.

He was a discordant person even to the eye ; he was rubricated at the tips of all his features, he wore rimless spectacles, and his hair was black, wiry, and discursive. His manner had a kind of fierceness, his voice, which seemed to have corncrake blood, was permanently raised, and his occasional laugh was like the wheels of a heavily laden cart. How he generalised ! There is nothing so invigorating as a good generalisation, but it ought to go through its facts and marshal them ; it ought not to fly over their heads and expect them to follow. He floated over the confused procession of occurrences as irresponsibly confident as the spirit of creation once floated over chaos. He did it with such assurance that he did not even know he was floating.

"Oh, you *ought* to know about the Manorial System," he said. "It explains so much."

He expounded it a little. He opened a picture of the Middle Ages as bright and clear as an illuminated missal. There was this Manorial System of his all over the country, with wonderful bailiffs and reeves and the court leet, particularly the court leet. The land in his clear, gay vision of those vanished times was cut up into nice little manors and rather larger little baronies, all dovetailed together, all, it seemed, with vivid, quaint coats-of-arms upon them, and to balance and complete them a Guild System in the towns, sweet and subtle and humane. And happinness and homely justice and art—remarkable art. And the Church kind and grave in an attitude of benediction. And in the sky the stars and all the Sons of God purring together.

I hardly liked to press him to tell me how it was this dear Fairyland of his had collapsed into the evils of our own times. No doubt the Reformation was much to blame for it, but the discovery of America upset things ; the Turks and Mongols were stupidly rough with the warriors of Christendom, and the Black Death took the meanest advantage of the merrie sanitation of the Manorial System.

Fairyland it was, a Scholar's Fairyland, secure and aloof from that dark wilderness which is history. For think of what those days were in reality, the life in fortresses and castles, the towns like criminal slums, the houses crowded together and locked and barred and fortified against each other, bodies unwashed and clad in coarse and dirty woollens as the finest wear, brutish communes here and reigns of terror there, gangs in possession, monasteries and nunneries illiterate and remote, sheer naked savagery in many districts, and mud-tracks through the unkempt roads between the towns, not a road except for some Roman highway in decay, not a bridge except by way of atonement from some powerful dying sinner, fierce dogs upon the countryside, hogs and stench in the streets of the cities, pestilence endemic. And endless breeding of children there was, to fester and die for the most part before ever they grew to youth's estate. Here and there would be a region where some accident of natural kindliness gave life a little space of April sunshine ; here and there perhaps one might find a tolerant equilibrium of lazy lassitude, some lord or abbot in tidy or genial mood. A little space at most and a transitory phase it was in the ugly succession of cramped, distressful lives. And this fellow, blind as a bat to facts that scream aloud at us from every thick-walled, windowless, medieval ruin, from every museum with its instruments of torture and its girdles of chastity, from the stunted suits of armour in the old armouries, and from the flaws and indecisions in the fabric of the patched, unfinished cathedrals that were the chief achievement of that age, talked of his Manors and Guilds and seemed to think a kind of Paradise might be restored by setting back the clocks of history.

I questioned him, but I argued very little with him. I went away to think him over in a mood of wonder.

Wonder ! Yet perhaps not altogether wonderful. A student of physics or biology turns his back on the world at large and goes towards a more concentrated reality—in the chemical balance, the laboratory, the marine station. He must travel and explore. He must serve facts sublimated and released, facts that will blow him to pieces or corrode him to death at the least levity on his part. But a student of history or economics turns his back on his reality when he turns his back on the world at large ; he goes into a cave of the winds in which documents whirl about before imaginative gales. In that cave confident statements are stronger than facts. He may lie, misjudge, and blunder ; nothing will hoist him sky-high or eat his flesh out or stain him purple for evermore. All the circumstances of a scholar's life conspire to turn the mind inward away from the dusty bickering of the common life. For him history is not, as it should be, an extension of reality ; it is a refuge.

Perhaps there is something innate that in the first place disposes a man to become a University teacher or specialist. He is, I suspect, more often than not by nature and instinctively afraid of the insecure uproar of things. Visit him in college and you will see that he does not so much live there as lurk. He must find infinite assurance, infinite compensation for the threatening indignities of life, in the development of his lucid counter-world, so much simpler, so much clearer, so entirely logical. Once he has secured his cell he encounters little opposition; he may bid good-bye to his worst timidities, and set to work secreting his soul's protection. To deny a fact in that withdrawn and protected atmosphere becomes more and more like defeating it, and to impose a system on the confusion almost as good as conquering it. In his classrooms, his lectures, his written controversies, the theorising recluse can soon grow fierce and contemptuous enough; he can at last down and out with his facts that are so intractable in practice, to his own complete satisfaction.

And to live in agreement with a theory for any length of time is like what the Americans call a common-law marriage; you and it are wedded by habit and repute. A man wedded to a system is less and less able to apprehend contradictory realities. He becomes like the dogs and pigs people here in the South of France specialise to hunt truffles; he can at last discover his system at the merest hint of evidence, and all that does not countenance it ceases to interest him, ceases to exist for him; he thrusts past it heedlessly, scornfully.

§ 8

AND now I can come to the maggot, so to speak, at the core of my decayed Socialism—Karl Marx.

To him we can trace, as much as we can trace it to any single person, this almost universal persuasion, which now Socialist and non-Socialist share, that economically we are living in a definable Capitalist System, which had a specific beginning and may have a definite end, and that the current disorder of human affairs is not a phase but an organised disease that may be exorcised and driven off. Then after a phase of convalescence the millennium. For me he presents the source and beginning of one of the vastest and most dangerous misconceptions, one of the most shallow and disastrous simplifications, that the world has ever suffered from. His teaching was saturated with a peculiarly infectious class animosity. He it was who poisoned and embittered Socialism, so that to-day it is dispersed and lost and must be reassembled and rephrased and reconstructed again slowly and laboriously while the years and the world run by. He it was who was most responsible for the ugly ungraciousness of all current Socialist discussion.

I have always been curious about Marx, the Marx of the prophetic London days, and always a little baffled by the details that have been presented to me. He seems to have led a blameless, irritated, theorising life, very much as Lenin did before he returned to Russia in 1917, remote from mines, factories, railway-yards, and industrialism generally. It was not a very active nor a very laborious life he led ; a certain coming and going from organisations and movements abroad in France and Germany must have been its most exciting element. He went to read and work with some regularity in the British Museum Reading-Room, a place that always suggests the interior of a gasometer to me, and he held Sunday gatherings in his Hampstead home and belonged to a club in Soho. He had little earning power, a thing not unusual with economic and financial experts, and he seems to have kept going partly by ill-paid journalism but mainly through the subsidies of his disciple Engels, a Manchester calico merchant. There was a devoted wife and some daughters, but I know very little about them ; one married unhappily, a tragedy that might happen to any daughter ; of her one hears disproportionately. He suffered from his liver, and I suspect him of being generally under-exercised and perhaps rather excessively a smoker. That was the way with many of these heavily bearded Victorians from abroad. He grew an immense rabbinical beard in an age of magnificent beard-growing. It must have precluded exercise as much as a goitre. Over it his eyes look out of his portraits with a sort of uneasy pretension. Under it, I suppose, there appeared the skirts of a frock-coat and trousers and elastic-sided boots. He was touchy, they say, on questions of personal loyalty and priority, often more a symptom of the sedentary life than a defect of character, and the " finished " part of his big work on Capital is overlaboured and rewritten and made difficult by excessive rehandling and sitting over. Examined closely, many of his generalisations are found to be undercut, but these afterthoughts do not extend to Marxism generally.

He tended rather to follow the dialectic of Hegel than to think freely. There had been much mental struggle about Hegelianism in his student days, much emotional correspondence about it, a resistance, and a conversion. He competed with Proudhon in applying the new intellectual tricks to the new ideas of Socialism. He belonged in his schoolboy days to that insubordinate type which prefers revolution to promotion. He was, I believe, sincerely distressed by the injustices of human life, and also he was bitten in his later years by an ambition to parallel the immense effect of Charles Darwin. One or two of his disciples compare him with Darwin ; Engels did so at his graveside ; the association seems to have been familiar with his coterie before his death. And after three decades of comparative obscurity his name and his leading ideas do seem to have struggled at last—for a time—to an even greater prominence than the work of the modest and patient revolutionary of Down. But though his work professed to be a research, it was much more of an invention. He had not Darwin's gift for contact with reality.

He was already committed to Communism before he began the labours that were to establish it, and from the first questions of policy obscured the flow of his science. What did his work amount to ? He imposed this delusion of a System with a beginning, a middle, and an end upon our perplexing economic tumult ; he classified society into classes that leave nearly everybody unclassified ; he proclaimed his social jehad, the class war, to a small but growing audience, and he passed with dignity into Highgate Cemetery, his death making but a momentary truce in the uncivil disputations of his disciples. His doctrines have been enormously discussed, but, so far as I know, the methods of psycho-analysis have not yet been applied to them. Very interesting results might be obtained if this were properly done.

He detected in the economic affairs of his time a prevalent change of scale in businesses and production which I shall have to discuss later. He extended this change of scale to all economic affairs, an extension which is by no means justifiable. He taught that there was a sort of gravitation of what he called Capital, so that it would concentrate into fewer and fewer hands and that the bulk of humanity would be progressively expropriated. He did not distinguish clearly between concrete possessions in use and money and the claim of the creditor, nor did he allow for the influence of inventions and new methods in straining economic combinations, in altering their range and breaking them up, nor realise the possibility of a limit being set to expropriation by the conditions of efficiency. That a change of scale may have definite limits and that the concentration of ownership may reach a phase of adjustment he never took into consideration. He perceived that big business methods extended very readily to the Press and Parliamentary activities. He simplified the psychology of the immense variety of people, from master-engineers to stock-jobbers and company-promoters whom he lumped together as Capitalists, by supposing it to be purely acquisitive. He made his " Capitalists " all of one sort and his " Workers " all of one sort. Throughout he imposed a bilateral arrangement on a multifarious variety. He simplified the whole spectacle into a process of suction and concentration by the " Capitalist." This process would go on until competition gave place to a " Capitalist-Monopolist " state, with the rest of humanity either the tools, parasites, and infatuated victims of the Capitalists, or else intermittently employed " Workers " in a mood of growing realisation, resentment, and solidarity. He seems to have assumed that the rule of these ever more perilously concentrated Capitalists would necessarily be bad, and that the souls of the Workers would necessarily be chastened and purified by economic depletion. And so onward to the social revolution.

This forced assumption of the necessary wrongness and badness of masters, organisers, and owners, and its concurrent disposition to idealise the workers, was, I am disposed to think, a natural outcome of his limited, too sedentary, bookish life. It was almost as much a consequence of that life as his trouble with his liver. His work is pervaded by the instinctive resentment of the shy type against the large, free, influential individual life. One finds, too, in him that scholar's hate of irreducible complexity to which I have already called attention. In addition there was a driving impatience to conceive of the whole as a process leading to a crisis, to a dénouement satisfying to the half-conscious and subconscious cravings of the thinker. It was under the pressure of these resentments and impatiences—and with the assistance of the Hegelian doctrine which tells us that the Thing-that-is is always shattered at last to make way for a higher synthesis by the Thing-that-it-isn't—that Marxism evolved its prophecy of the ultimate and not very remote victory of the idealised worker. The Proletarian would solidaritate (my word), and arrive *en masse*, he would crystallise out as Master, and all things would be changed at his coming. He would put down the mighty from their seats and exalt the humble and meek.   He would fill the hungry with good things and the rich he would send empty away.   The petty bourgeoisie he would smack hard and good. And everyone who mattered to the resentful gentleman who was making the story would be happy for ever afterwards.

It was a wish solidifying into a conviction that gave the world this wonderful and dramatic forecast of the dispossessed Proletarian becoming class-conscious, merging the residue of his dwarfed and starved individuality in solidarity with his kind, seizing arms, revolting massively, setting up that mystery, the Dictatorship of the Proletariat, "taking over" the "Capitalist-Monopolist state " and, after a phase of accommodation, dissolving it away into a confused democratic Communism, the Millennium.   It is a dream story of things that are not happening and that are not likely to happen, but it is a very satisfying story for the soul of an intelligent and sensitive man indignant at the distresses of life and living unappreciated in a byway.

It is for the pyscho-analyst to lay bare the subtler processes in the evolution of this dream of a Proletarian saviour.   Everybody nowadays knows that giant, in May-day cartoons and Communist pamphlets and wherever romantic Communism expresses itself by pictures, presenting indeed no known sort of worker, but betraying very clearly in its vast biceps, its colossal proportions, its small head and the hammer of Thor in its mighty grip, the suppressed cravings of the restricted Intellectual for an immense virility.   This Proletarian is to arise and his enemies—and particularly an educated world very negligent of its prophet—are to be scattered. There will then be a rough unpleasant time for the petty bourgeoisie. Things of the severest sort will happen to them.   After the upper, they will get the nether millstone grinding into them. . . .

The respectable leaders of British Victorian Trade Unionism upon whom Marx sought to foist this monster as their very spit and likeness, seem to have been considerably dismayed by it.   They felt so much more like the petty bourgeoisie.

One need only run over the outstanding names of the movement to realise how little the working man has had to do with the invention of this fantastic Titan or, indeed, with the development of Socialistic ideas at all.   Trade Union and Labour leaders by the dozen and the score have called themselves Socialists and Communists in recent years, just as they have called themselves Rationalists or Eugenists or Single-Taxers, but none of them have laid hands of power upon the central edifice of theory. That, on both its constructive and destructive side, has been the work either of prosperous men bored by social disorder and waste, or of irritated University students and scholars.   Saint Simon was a benevolent aristocrat,

Robert Owen a capable employer, William Thompson an Irish landowner, William Morris and Ruskin belonged to the wealthy middle-class, Engels sold Manchester goods in Germany with reasonable success, and Marx, our Marx of the relentless class-war, Marx, in the ecstatic language of his biographer Loria, " arose in a refined and aristocratic entourage," came from " an extremely ancient stock devoted to the accumulation of wealth " and was " united by marriage to the race of German feudatories, fierce paladins of the throne and the altar." Beer, in his history of British Socialism, says Frau Marx was " related to the Argyles "—related to the Argyles ! it is near divinity !—and speaks of Marx as a " proud mental aristocrat." The intense hatred and contempt expressed in Communist literature for the *petite bourgeoisie* is a further symptom of the element of down-at-heel aristocracy in a state of bruised self-conceit inspiring the movement. The stock Communist insult is to imply that an adversary isn't a born gentleman. I doubt if the theory of democratic Socialism owes nearly as much to real working men as the sciences do, as geology, archæology, and physics, for example, do. It is a product not of the worker under oppression but of unprosperous expectant types irritated by exclusion and disregard.

In a tract by Lenin, *The State and Revolution*, written upon the eve of the Bolshevik seizure of power in 1917, I find the same smouldering resentment against all prosperous or educated people reflecting the economic argument, I find the same resort to the Armed Worker as the humiliator of negligent authority. Lenin discusses with evident distaste the probability that the Dictatorship of the Proletariat may need the services of educated people other than its own prophets. He writes of them with a sneer of the pen, so to speak, as " these intellectual gentry," and dwells with satisfaction upon the fact that they will be at any rate " controlled by armed workers."

Consider the values of that phrase.

A little while after this tract was written Lenin was dictator in the Kremlin and the " intellectual gentry " of Russia, the men of science and art and literature, were at his mercy. They might have starved altogether in these troublous times if Maxim Gorky, the novelist, who had a certain personal prestige with Lenin and a strong sense of the value of things intellectual, had not intervened. There was an attempt to organise their protection and maintenance, and when I was in Petersburg in 1920 I visited an old palace—the " House of Science " they had rechristened it—looking out upon the grey-flowing Neva, to which a number of " these intellectual gentry " had been shepherded. Control of the world of the mind by armed workers did not seem to be a very successful experiment. These men—and some of them had been very important figures in Russia's intellectual and creative life—were manifestly living in great misery and most of them were doing little or nothing. They were ill-fed, scantily and shabbily clothed, detestably watched, and with neither the books, papers, nor apparatus needed for their work. Poor Glazounov the composer was there, very wretched, the shadow of his former self, cold and ill ; he could do nothing with his time because the Armed Workers would not hunt him out any music paper. He played some of his music to me on an old piano and talked of the days that had passed, and he wept. The chief Armed Worker directing the House of Science was a Mr. Rodé, who before the revolution had kept an ultra-smart restaurant on one of the islands, a resort of gay parties during the white nights of the Northern summer. He had adapted himself to a Communist régime and he had a considerable control of the dietary and general comfort of the interned " intellectual gentry." Distinguished archæologists, physiologists, chemists and historians, great mathematicians and brilliant teachers were in his power and fed from his hand. Maxim Gorky also was looking after the place with the breadth of intention and the practical incapacity of a genius and a Slav.

The social breakdown that has occurred in Russia is claimed by the Marxists as their prophet's social revolution. This they do in spite of the fact that he had pointed to England and the highly industrialised countries of the West as the lands of revolutionary promise. In truth the Russian collapse was like nothing Marx had ever dreamt of. The Russian peasant soldiers, having been robbed, starved, massacred, and misled by the Czar and his ministers—six or seven of these poor devils had to be killed in battle for every one Austrian or German—reached the limit of their endurance when they found that the Kerensky revolution gave them no respite from the torture of the war. Two millions of them had been killed and mutilated. They had had enough and they would stand no more. They turned homeward to their villages. Once they had started nothing could hold them. The Russian armies melted away from before the Germans and Austrians and streamed home across the land. For a time Russia was in a state of social dissolution such as this Western world has not seen since the Thirty Years' War ; straggling bands of armed men did what they liked with the country through which they passed ; robbery, rape, and murder went free and unavenged. In many provinces there was a Jacquerie, a château-burning. At times in bad places that Jacquerie rose to an extremity of horror. Yet there was a kind of crazy justice in it.

That was the true Russian Revolution, a social debâcle, a destruction of Czarism by its own weapon, the deliquescence of the army.

Amidst the tumult of the disorganised towns there emerged the Russian Communist Party, the only association of men with any solidarity left in that frightful confusion. They were not workers, they were not proletarians—

5

in Russia there was practically no Proletariat—they were a small body of Intellectuals with a following of youthful workers and students, greatly helped by sailors from the fleet. They grasped at power, they secured machine-guns, they organised forces of their own, including a band of Chinese, they shot, disarmed and restored a kind of order in the towns and as far as the railways reached in the country. " They had to shoot," President Masaryk told me on one occasion. " But they went on shooting."

They went on shooting. They were men of no experience ; many were mere boys ; they had fallen into irresponsible power and they had tasted blood. They had an orgy of blood-lust sharpened by fear. Then they set about the reorganisation of Russia upon Communist lines, declaring that the word of the prophet was fulfilled and the Capitalist System at an end.

They have held Russia ever since. They have held it because the Whites are worse than they are and because they fend off foreign interference and the return of the detested landlordism from the peasants. But there seems to be some uncertainty even in the party about the depth and quality of the resultant higher synthesis. There is a hitch in the Hegelian sequence, no system has appeared. There is no Communist system ; it is a negation, a project-shaped vacuum.

Since I do not believe there is or ever has been a Capitalist System, I cannot get very excited about its alleged overthrow in Russia or anywhere. But I do find myself very deeply stirred when I think of the enormous wastage of good human hope and effort that has resulted from this falsely simple statement of our economic perplexities, this caricature of contemporary human life, as a simple antagonism of two systems that never have existed and never could exist.

I have been twice to Russia since the Revolution, and I was there several times before it. I should find it difficult to give a short general judgment upon the new ensemble there. With all the judgments I have encountered, from the violently adverse to the enthusiastically favourable, I find myself in disagreement. The peasant has got rid of his landlord, and if he is shot more frequently he is whipped much less ; the hysterics of the Czar and his wife have given place to hysterical experiments ; instead of Rasputin's practical interpretations of Christianity one finds Zinovieff's practical interpretations of Marx ; education is more general, but, if possible, less efficient ; the railways are more awful than ever, and if there is more cruelty, filth, and disorder in the prisons there is less misery on the road to Siberia. If, as is highly probable, the Bolsheviki have killed more people than there are members of the Communist Party, we must set against that the far more monstrous war waste of the Czardom. If Zinovieff gets his way, the shadow of a giant war of the steppes against Western Europe may materialise, but many things may happen before Zinovieff gets his way.

I will not attempt to weigh the outcome of the Russian Revolution in the scales of my partial knowledge and possible prejudice—I had some irritating times in Moscow with the younger Bolsheviks and I dislike the type actively. The present " system " there, as I have been able to judge it, is just the same old Russian " system," with many of the parts missing, many of the wheels failing to cog, and many of its former patched-up compromises dislocated. In the old days my businesses could get along in a fashion at the price of a considerable amount of bribery ; now they cannot get along at all ; that is the most evident difference to me. Old traditions still make Russian officials hold one up, but the uncertainties of the new régime make them afraid to do a fair and reasonable blackmailing deal. One is just held up to no purpose. This is naturally irritating to a man who, like myself, has kept a certain pride in his work, and has always been a very temperate taker of profits.

The Communist formulæ obstruct everything and have released nothing. I have been to Russia twice to get some little of the metallurgical wealth of the country out of the mess into which the Bolsheviks have dropped it ; our aluminium works are still in a salvageable state at Dornoff, the only region of the world where there are deposits suitable for the new Manson process—and if only they would do the work properly I would gladly put the Bolsheviks in complete possession rather than have all these carefully adjusted arrangements going to waste. But each time I have been treated with a stupid suspicion, kept waiting about for weeks, watched and followed, my rooms searched in my absence, and in the end I have been thwarted—for the mere sake of thwarting me. I was quite willing to tell them all I knew about the particular matters that concerned me, put all my cards upon the table ; for I want cheap aluminium and light alloys in the world as badly as they want Communism. Why should they assume they are more disinterested than I ? The impudence of it !

But their theory required me to be a subtle and treacherous representative of the Capitalist System, a thievish moneylender and entangler of simple, brave, good workers, and themselves, raw, young, and self-ignorant, the guardian angels of mankind. They had no shadow of doubt about these moral values. Their ambition was to lay me by the heels on a charge of " economic espionage." They had their dirty prison and they had me, and they felt an opportunity was being lost. The career of a good Communist depends upon conspicuous displays of zeal. Were they showing *zeal* ? They would not listen to what I tried to tell them ; that was obviously only a blind. One fool said my science was " capitalist science " as opposed to " proletarian science "—in metallurgical chemistry ! I battered myself against that sort of thing in vain.

5*

What can one do with men who are inexorably convinced, in spite of every material fact about them, that they have, germinating under their hands, a new and perfect social system, the Communist system, which they are defending from the subtle treacheries of a wicked Capitalist System ; and whose entire intellectual outfit is unsleeping suspicion and a stock of ready-made nicknames by which they can misconceive everybody ?

There is no way round these fixed ideas. You are put on this or that side of an opposition between entirely imaginary systems ; and in whatever direction you thrust the end is futility. So there is our stuff in Russia untouched and badly wanted, and our works are going to decay—beautifully planned works they are, though I say it who shouldn't—doing no good to Russia or any human being.

And this is mainly if not entirely an intellectual trouble, a trouble of wrong statement, just as most of the great religious wars of the past were mainly wars of wrong statement. The world splits between Europe and the East and the limitation and misery of hundreds of millions of lives is the by-product of an incoherent argument about the interpretation of social interactions. An imperfectly aerated old gentleman sits in the British Museum, suffering from a surfeit of notes, becomes impatient to set a generalisation in control of his facts, and presently we have this harvest of tares. It is Arius and Athanasius and the camel driver of Mecca I think of in his case, rather than Darwin.

§ 9

SOCIALISM which was creative is stunned, and Communism, which is the sabotage of civilisation by the disappointed, has usurped its name and inheritance. I have accused Marx as the prime mover in the destruction of Socialism. But the teaching of Marx would not have found impassioned and fanatical followers, if there had not been something deep and widespread in the human make-up to answer its appeal. This response came, I believe, from the natural hate of men deeply conscious of their own merits and conscious also of social disadvantages for those whom Fate seems to have treated better. It is a response easy to evoke in all too many people in a world so chancy as ours. Malice is a necessary quality in an animal which has changed so swiftly from solitude to an exasperated gregariousness as man has done. The new Marxist Socialism, therefore, with its confident dogmas, its finality and hardness, its vindictive will, developed an intensity and energy that drowned and almost silenced the broader, more tentative, and scientific initiatives of the older, the legitimate Socialism. Communism, with its class-war obsession, ate up Socialism as Catholicism, with its facile consolations and definitive creeds, the Church militant here on earth, ate up Christianity. Communism may live as long as Islam ; which is most like it of all other human things, as rigid and as intense. It may endure long after the Moscow caliphs have passed away, establishing a second system of fanatical resistances to the comprehensive organisation of the world upon modern lines.

But the constructive conceptions that inspired the earlier Socialism will not disappear with the fading-out of Socialism from general discussion. They arise too easily in the natural development of economic and social life. They may change their phraseology ; they may cease to be expressed in the old terms and under the old name, but they will live. It may have been necessary that Socialism should die in some such fashion in order to be born again, revised, refreshed. There were extraordinary gaps and imperfections, I realise, in the liberal Socialism of my student days. The broad ideas of it, the ideas of a collective organisation of the basal needs of mankind, of a systematic economy of the energy that goes now to waste in competition for mere existence, the idea of a complete abolition of forestalling, of obstruction for gain and indeed of every sort of profiteering, these primary Socialist ideas are more living now than ever they were. They have infected the whole body of modern thought.

But among other obvious deficiences, that nineteenth-century Socialism was almost wilfully blind to the necessity for a scientific monetary method, a proper reckoning of obligations and claims proof against manipulation, if any just and efficient system of production was to work. Owen, indeed, thought of that essential—Dickon has shown me recently a collection of Owen's experimental " labour notes "—but his smaller followers in their little wisdom dropped the question. If anyone mentioned money in a Fabian Society meeting in my Socialist time there would be a kind of general hoot : " Oh, Lord ! Here's a Currency Crank ! " Saying " Currency Crank " in a Fabian Society meeting was almost as deadly as saying " Boor-jaw ! " in a modern Communist gathering. I have seen Sidney Webb, our London Lenin, flushed, flustered, and irritated, waving all that sort of thing aside. Bitter scorn, an earnest scorn. Let us get on to sensible things. Morris to judge by his *News from Nowhere* would have done without money ; his other contemporaries, it seems, thought that any old money would do. But science is measurement, and money as we have it at present is about as good for the measurement of social obligation as an earthworm for the measurement of length.

Equally vague, evasive, and useless was the political attitude of that old Socialism. The Socialists were proposing to " nationalise " the means of production and distribution, but when one asked who or what was to be the operating " nation " they had nothing to suggest. Again came flushed impatience and a hasty waving of the disturbing question away. Socialism, they recited, was an economic not a political reform, which of course explained everything. It seems incredible, but they seem to have believed that economic justice and administrative efficiency were compatible with any sort of political rottenness, division, and absurdity. Never mind about that ; the wise little officials would see anything through. You see while Marxian Socialism was invented by discontented professors, Fabian Socialism was largely the product of hopeful Civil Servants. The psycho-analysis of Fabianism is as destructive to its scientific pretension as the psycho-analysis of Marxism. The only difference is that it reveals a brighter type of soul.

These Socialists of my student days were entirely vague about international relationships. It was uncomfortable for those Civil Servants who did its thinking to imagine a world with quite a different sort of Civil Service altogether. So they did not imagine it. And though they could contemplate the expropriation of most people they had an habitual respect for the possible resentment of rulers and politicians and the governing class generally. None of these nineteenth-century Socialists I heard

and read were clear whether they were nationalists or imperialist or international, or what they were. They shivered at the word Cosmopolitan
and sneered at the phrase World-State. They did not even know whether
they were Protectionists or Free-Traders ; and to this day they do not
know. You will find a Labour paper like the *Daily Herald* scolding
vigorously at the private ownership of land and minerals in one column
and insisting in the next upon the " right " of some little barbaric nationality
to hold its territories and its natural resources, however vast they may
happen to be, against the needs of all mankind. It would wrench the
northern coalfield from the Duke of Northumberland and leave all the
minerals of the Riff to Abd-el-Krim.

The petty industry in research of these Fabians affected to be prodigious,
but in general inquiry their inertias were astounding. They were all
for municipalising and nationalising, and yet they would never consider
with any patience or care the constitution, the methods of election, the areas
of control of the municipalities and parliamentary governments to which
with the utmost recklessness they proposed to entrust the land, the natural
resources, the public services of the community. So long as it was an
elected body and not an assembly of private persons they did not seem to
care. The community was just to elect somebody, somehow, anyhow,
and the clever little official would tell that somebody what to do. Gross
energetic men, it seems, were to wait and plan and spend and fight
vehemently for power—and then, whichever of them won it, would hand
it over meekly and trustfully to the wise, good, quiet " experts " waiting
in their bureaus.

Socialism took over a prevailing belief of the time when it took over
the belief in the necessity for elected bodies. There was no need to take
over that belief, and had the movement been a really full thinking movement it would not have done so. But in the nineteenth century A.D. it
was believed that it was necessary to have some sort of election, any sort
of election, however preposterously conducted, before the affairs of the
community could be administered, as it was believed to be necessary to
have some sort of blood sacrifice before seed-time in the nineteenth century
B.C. It was the current superstition. It fades. When creative ideas
emerge again into a definite system of proposals, I believe we shall find
them completely detached from this delusion that they can be realised
only by, through, or with the consent of elected persons. There will
be no further research for majorities. Realisation of a new stage of civilised
society will be the work of an intelligent minority ; it will be effected
without the support of the crowd and possibly in spite of its dissent.

I am now, more than ever I was, a revolutionary. Every year of my
life makes me more certainly revolutionary. I believe that before the

muddled and very insecure process of the world's affairs now current can be changed into a stronger, broader, happier, progressive organisation, many habitual resistances will have to be overcome and many legally established institutions which will refuse to undergo the modifications and subordinations necessary to adapt them to a scientifically conceived world civilisation will have to be cleared away. The legal standing of such old, obstructive, entrenched rights will have to be changed by imposing—in a manner essentially illegal—a different legal standing upon them. No human legal system has ever voluntarily abolished itself in favour of another. Fundamental changes of political and social method must be effected by pressures exercised by the sort of people who have a will for the better order. There is no way round such a necessity that I can see. This may not mean actual violence, but there will be at least the intimation of superior strength. If that sort of thing is not revolution, then I do not know what revolution is.

I believe that ultimately man, collective man, has to suppress the sovereign independence of any part of the world as against the whole. He cannot get on very much beyond our present sort of civilisation until he has contrived a world currency, a world control of staple production, a world peace—and, in fact, a world state. He has to regard prescription and proprietary claims as entirely secondary and provisional arrangements in dealing with the land, with the natural resources and the material organisation of the earth. No quibbling can make dispossessions and redistributions of ownership and sovereignty, in the face of protest, legal acts ; and no evolutionary process that does not involve death and birth, putting an end to old things and beginning again with new things, can ever bring about the new world implicit in science and in manifested human possibilities.

But when I think of revolution I have in mind something quite different from the idea of a Revolutionary that has dominated the human imagination since those violent days in Paris a hundred and thirty odd years ago. I have no use for that Revolutionary of the Communist placard type, that pithecoid Proletarian, dishevelled, semi-nude, making heroic motions with improvised weapons behind a casually assembled barricade of beams, paving-stones, overturned carts, pots, pans, railings. I look, indeed, for something antagonistic to that. I look to the growth of a minority of intelligent men and women for the real revolution before mankind. I look for a ripening élite of mature and educated minds, and I do not believe progress can be anything more than casual and insecure until that élite has become self-conscious and effective. I do not look to the mass of people for any help at all. I am thinking of an aristocratic and not a democratic revolution.

Except as scavenging or fertilising floods, I do not believe in democratic revolutions. I believe the multitude, when it is suitably roused, can upset anything, but I do not believe that it can create anything whatever.

I quite understand the dismay that comes upon every impatient world-mender when he seeks creative forces among the prosperous people of to-day. Most of them are prosperous by reason of some flaw or direct iniquity of the economic muddle, and they are vaguely aware of that; they do not want any examination of the complex of disarrangements that gives them the advantages of their property; as a class they are prepared to defend the stacked-up instabilities they call the "existing system" very stoutly. But there are exceptions to the conservatism of the prosperous. Many of these exceptions are personally or vicariously curious and spend their resources upon research; many, like myself, are bored to death by the poor mean pleasures, displays, and gratifications our prosperity can buy, and many have a really disinterested creative impulse. It is to the increase in number of these exceptional types and to the spread of an inquiring and adventurous spirit in this class that I look for the continuation, acceleration, and extension of social and economic progress towards a new and finer world order. If the class-war idea is sound and liberated people are necessarily less socially disposed than frustrated and limited people, then manifestly there is no hope for mankind.

No doubt our present social complex is still heavily loaded down by an accumulation of dull and heavy creditors, parasitic, greedy speculators, and unproductive spenders generally, but social life has always had to carry such a burden of selfish and obstructive prosperity since social life began. Relatively I do not think there is more of that burden now than there was two hundred years ago. I think there is less of it. And it has less pride and assurance. Read any eighteenth-century novel and mark the amelioration of social attitudes. There is no reason why we should go running off in a passion to fields, slums, workshops, mines, railway-yards, docks, the forecastles of ships, gaols, and institutions for the reorganisers of society, because the imaginations of the fortunate classes are still largely unstimulated by creative ideas that are hardly a century old. It is true that the lives of the majority of mankind to-day are insecure, anxious, limited, laborious, stunted, unfruitful, and generally unhappy, and that they will remain so until economic order is attained. But because masses of toilers and needy people are thoroughly uncomfortable it does not follow that they are capable of the subtle and intricate adjustments needed to make themselves and mankind free and happy. It does not follow even that they are capable of recognising those who are attempting to make them free. They are very properly disposed to discontent, and many of their livelier minds find the idea of a class-war attractive, but I doubt if their conception of that class-war is anything but vindictive. It is not a better order they want but—witness the Communist hatred of the petty bourgeoisie—malicious reprisals against the slightly more prosperous class immediately and therefore most irritatingly in contact with them. The most dreadful thing about their situation is their evident inability to imagine any better order. They do not want a change ; they want an inversion without a change. They have grown up in a coarse and ugly way of living, and their first impulse, so soon as they realise the coarseness and disagreeableness that has been put upon them, is to extend it to everybody. " See how *you* like it ! " They want that far more than they want a new way of living. They know instinctively that a new way of living would be unpleasantly discordant with their established habits.

One may sympathise with that vindictive impulse, but I do not see that one is called upon to assist it. The sense of frustration in a hopeless toiler may be keen enough to make even sabotage a pleasure, but I have other tastes. For three-quarters of a century Socialism under the spell of Marxism has cherished the delusion that in the masses there is a huge reservoir of creative power. There is nothing in the masses as masses but an unreliable explosive force.

The greater revolution must be a deliberate and not a convulsive process. It has to fight against the egoist and fool in man, the ancestral, instinctive brute, as much in the suspicious and angry mob below as in the timid, mean, and violent propertied classes above. It has a far greater percentage of possible adherents among the educated and able than in the crowd. Just as we depend for the gigantic services of scientific progress upon at most a few score thousand rather unpopular individuals mostly of the middle and independent classes, so the task of bracing, ordering, and clearing this very cruel and wasteful jungle of human affairs may remain for some generations still in the hands of quite a few obstinately clear-headed men and women. They have to work hard and be patient ; there is nothing else for them to do ; they cannot indulge in the emotional gratification of premature organisation and simplified propaganda. They will be men and women of experience, who have learnt about human affairs by handling them ; they will be prepared for formulæ that will not simplify, and for incurable intricate problems. Ultimately this sort of people will acquire the necessary force and knowledge to change things systematically, and then they will set about doing so. Their convictions will radiate into the general mass. They will reshape the general conceptions of economic political and social life.

Their revolution will involve much greater and much more sustained operations than barricades in the streets and little squitterings of machine-gun fire.   They will have a different sort of strategy than the disorganisation of political parties and subtler methods than sabotage schemed in cellars and the misdirection of honest discontent.   I do not see why thwarted pedants and unlicked youngsters should be allowed to monopolise the excellent name of Revolutionary for ever, nor why restless shop-stewards and the sort of defectives who set fire to things should imagine themselves sole lords of human hope.

§ 10

THIS morning my work has been interrupted.

I have been raided and assaulted by Clementina. She has come into the room with an armful of mimosa, iris, and white and purple stock, and stuck this pretty stuff all over the place. She has made a great disturbance because I was not going to have my lunch out of doors in the sun—they are laying it out there now all over again—and her beastly little animated muff of a dog has chased my grey cat up the Japanese medlar. It is the fifteenth of January, and she declares the Provençal spring arrived. But that is no reason why she should constitute herself Primavera and cumber my study with an excess of flowers.

" It's no good," she said. " I can't keep away from you to-day." And she hasn't. She has ruffled my hair. She has also ruffled my mind.

She seized upon some pages of this manuscript. " Oh ! Marx ! " she cried with a note of disgust. " Capitalism ! Revolution ! " She put the sheets down. " I thought you were writing your life. I thought I was going to read something about you. I thought it was going to be about yourself ! "

" This book," I said, " is not for you."

" You told me about it one day."

" In a moment of weakness. It is hard not to talk at times to a woman who besets one as you do me. But what I said was—inexact."

" Obviously. If you are writing about -isms, I'm not sorry I interrupted you. I thought it was to be about yourself and what you had made of the world. I thought I should get an idea of what you were like when you were a young man."

" I have a section to finish. And the door is just behind you."

" I'm not going. I'm not disposed to go. It's spring. And near lunch-time."

" You are going," I said.

I do not know why I scuffle and romp so easily with Clementina. Certainly there is spring in the air to-day. But now she has a better idea of what I was like when I was a young man. She has been at last more or less thrown out of this room in a properly pacified, subdued, and crumpled condition, and I find myself turning over my writing and reassembling the ideas she dissipated by her wanton invasion.

It is true that the last three or four sections have been mainly devoted to Marx and Socialism, but that is no more than a digression from the account of my world than the theology of the First Book. Why should one entertain the idea that a man is no more than his face, his mannerisms, and his love affairs ? A man, if he is to be rendered completely, must begin with the creation of the world so far as it specially concerns him and end with his expectations of eternity. If a man is to be given completely, there must first be the man and his universe, then the man and history, and only after that man and other men and womankind. My struggle to apprehend the social conflict about me in terms of Socialism was at least as much a part of me as the poor little marriage and the poor little half-divorce I shall presently have to reveal—and my subsequent proceedings. It played as large a part in shaping my life—a larger part.

It is plain to me that, having swept aside the Communist idea of a revolution and thrown some passing doubts upon the economic interpretation of history, I am bound to give a version of the human story that seems to me to be truer. I am bound to indicate and in a measure explain my conception of the world of toil and business in which I have struggled and won freedom and security for myself. Every autobiography that is written for more than a special circle of readers must be thus encyclopædic. My eyes are astigmatic ; my mind is no doubt ill-informed and incompetent ; that is all the more reason why I should tell of things as I see them and of all the things I see, and not assume that I see them in some correct and standard fashion.

A writer may affect modesty and deal with these broad issues by reference. But is that modesty ? He may defer to recognised authority. He may declare that so far as recognised authority goes he has no world of his own. He may say, " In matters of religion I follow the teaching of the Holy Catholic Church," or " Upon questions of economics I submit to the superior knowledge of the economists." But is not the good man assuming that he has so complete a knowledge of the teachings of his church or of the orthodox economists as to be sure to think upon all issues exactly as they do ? He commits his church or his science to all his implications. Though he disavows authority, yet he presumes excessively to knowledge.

To achieve the perfect robe of perfect modesty should he not rather say, " I follow the teachings of my church so far as I know and understand them ; I am conscious of limitation and even of error on my part, but I do my best," and then he should go on to set forth his own defective interpretation. " That as I see it," he should say, " is the teaching of the Church. That is my humble reading. By this I have guided myself. I may be in grievous error, but this is what my authority has meant to me." It is his interpretation that matters to us, and claims our interest in him. Or else, why autobiography at all ? The existence of perfect solutions that he may or may not understand does not excuse him. These we can study without his help, but his reaction to them is another matter. We do not want him to give us these things in perfection; we do want to see them in fallible operation. And so we bring his modest gentility back, blushing prettily no doubt, to the full encyclopædic range again.

In the next two or three sections I propose to write a short history of human society as a labour-money complex evolved out of the primitive patriarchal family. They will have to be highly concentrated sections. This book, at any rate, is not going to be a home of rest for tired readers. If presently Clementina repeats her aggressions, she will find sheets of discussion about how toil came into the world and what money did for the Roman Empire. " Old economics ! " she will cry. For the life of me I cannot get either my father's disaster or the business achievements of Dickon or myself into any sort of focus without that background. And as for Clementina——!

Clementina has a mind like one of those water insects that never get below the surface of anything. Water-boatmen they are called, and they flicker about sustained by surface tension. She just flickers about. She professes an affection for me that is altogether monstrous, and she knows no more about my substantial self than the water-boatman knows of the deeps of the pond. She knows as little about the world.

Why is a person with so quick an intelligence and such wise instincts as Clementina mentally so superficial ? Why does she habitually dismiss three-quarters of human concerns as uninteresting ? Is it some sort of mental economy ? For gossip, excursions, household matters, and making love, Clementina has an abundant, swift, penetrating, and indefatigable intelligence. She has subtlety ; she has invention. The poetry she writes shows at least a keen appreciation for poetry in general and also for a certain prettiness in things at large that she has not learnt from pre-existing poetry. But she will not even look at the framework in which such things are set and which is continually affecting and determining such things !

I am reminded of something I was told the other day by a man who is by way of being a prominent historical writer. He was " approached," as they say, by one of these big American film producers. People, the film man apologised, were displaying a certain curiosity about the general history of mankind. It was an unaccountable lapse, and no doubt a temporary one, but it could not be ignored. Would it be possible for my friend to prepare the scenario for a series of films of such a history ? A glimpse was given, carelessly but attractively, of dollars falling in showers.

My friend considered various difficulties, but decided that something of the sort could be done. " The public wants to know about things," he agreed. The film man expressed great optimism about the scheme—but in rather doubtful tones. His reason was in conflict with his instincts and mental habits. The latter were the better exercised and the more powerful. There was a pause in the discussion. It was evident that a difficulty had to be considered.

" I wonder now," said the film man, " if it wouldn't be possible to run some little *story* through this series, something about a boy and his girl and a bit of trouble between them or a revenge or something of that sort. *So as to have a thread of human interest in it.*"

A thread of human interest—in the history of mankind ! The conversation ended in discord.

For Clementina there is apparently no thread of human interest in economics—that is to say in the toil, payment, enslavement, or liberation of scores of millions of human beings. Of history she has much the same opinion as the film man. Geology, of course, means nothing to her but " old rocks," palæontology nothing but " old bones." It is inconceivable to her that anyone should be interested in theology. Sociology makes her impatient and politics rude. Yet though she has renounced all the vanities of the world in order to come and live near me in the less accessible lanes of Provence, she can still muse pleasantly, during one of our rare trips to Cannes or Nice, before a hat-shop window. That, she feels, is " life." As surely as biology isn't. And with her flitting glance she is just a sample of general readers everywhere. They do not care whence they came nor whither they go nor what they are doing. They just flicker about. They will be water-boatmen till the stream dries up. . . .

But it occurs to me that Clementina has had to wait an unconscionable time for lunch. What patience she has shown ! She is almost directly under this window and she has not called up once. Probably with a pensive calm that sometimes descends upon her after misbehaviour she has been eating up the beetroot and olives.

§ 11

FIVE thousand years ago our ancestors can have had no more economics than the animals ; they lived from hand to mouth where the food was. If the food diminished they wandered away. If they could not find more food they weakened and perished like any other beasts. Their gear was just a skin and a stick and a stone or so, not more than could be trailed or carried. A stranger was an intruder and better killed. The old man killed or drove off his sons, and was the lord of all his womankind, lord indeed of his visible universe, until a younger and a stronger adversary came to dispossess and end him. If his equipment was simple his ownership at least was immense ; he recognised no other rights in the world but his own, and he died fighting for them.

The first step towards human accumulation on a broader scale was taken when the Old Man came to recognise the right of another adult male to live within sight or smell of him. This first mitigation of the possessive instinct was the foundation of human society. The women trained their boys in the fear and avoidance of the Old Man, to regard all his belongings and particularly their mothers and stepmothers and sisters as tabu, and in return they persuaded the Old Man to tolerate the existence of his sons, and at last, in the course of ages, even to allow them the right to possess the strange girls they caught and dragged home with them to the family fireside. That is the only credible story of the beginnings of human society I have ever found in anthropology. It explains the primordial incest tabu, and the worldwide traces of marriage by capture, and a score of worldwide primitive customs that are otherwise fantastic. And it marches with most of the complex suppressions that lie at the roots of our modern mentality. It follows that the first private property to infringe the universal dominion of the Old Man was property in a woman.

One can still hardly speak of economics even after the ape family had passed into the primitive human tribe. The tribe personified in the Old Man still owned so far as it ranged ; it hunted in a pack and feasted from one carcass ; most of the implements it used were made by those who were going to use them ; there may have been a little bartering of ornaments and curious oddities between individuals and mutual present-giving, but there was still nothing in the nature of work, of employment, as we understand these terms. Mothers worked for their children and got them food and watched over them, as animal mothers do. Probably children and inferior women were the first human beings made to work beyond this instinctive devotion ; they were sent out to find and bring home sticks for the fire or berries or small edible creatures. The first reluctant worker may have been a fire mender. The first workers were in much the position of the modern labouring man's wife ; they did all that had to be done, and they got no pay beyond their keep and their owner's attentions. Maternity had given woman a greater submissiveness to routine drudgery than man, and probably the greater part of the simple duties of the cave and the squatting place fell to her.

The early Palæolithic human tribe could have been only a stage more advanced economically than a pack of wild dog. They had their fire and implements to the good. They had become more carnivorous and had perhaps grown bigger and stronger than their more solitary ancestors. The expansion of toil as the tribe grew and possessions and elaborations increased, fell no doubt upon the shoulders least able to evade it. There is no natural instinct for toil in man. He likes to make things but with as little trouble as possible. Already in Palæolithic times a considerable and increasing amount of human intelligence and energy was being devoted to shifting toil upon the shoulders of somebody else. As human societies grew larger and better equipped and the necessary labour increased, oppression became more intelligent and systematic. The Old Man in the ape-man stage just killed and maltreated ; the chief of the primitive human tribe directed and employed his folk, the women almost naturally and the men as much as he dared, and punished the idle among them. Sometimes perhaps there was not one single chief but three or four big fellows who had learnt to respect each other.

That was the quality of the " primitive communism " so many worthy anthropologists have seen fit to idealise.

As hunting tribes and herd-following tribes developed into cattle-herding and cattle-driving, and as agriculture, first of snatch crops and then of settled regions, appeared, an ever rising tide of labour poured into human experience. The hungry picnicking freedom of primordial man gave place, age by age, to the more and more regular work and regular meals of the agricultural man, under the guiding compulsion of the chiefs and elders of the community. The children as they grew up found they had to work ; the young men had to work. That it had once been unnatural to have to work was an idea beyond the brief range of human thought in those days. As soon could a draught-horse think of freedom. An anxious industriousness was gradually imposed upon the men of the agricultural regions, a moral impulse towards activity. To be an idler became a new shame almost as great as the older one of being a coward ; one pretended not to be lazy just as one pretended not to be afraid ; and man began to store like the squirrel and worry about the future.

It was only with the development of agriculture that man became a truly economic animal ; the first of the vertebrata, I suppose, to be truly economic. Hitherto the chief economic creatures had been the ants and termites and bees. To become economic is first to become the watchful servitor of vegetable growth ; that is the essence of it. Nomadic predatory peoples never succumbed to the delusion that industry is in itself a virtue. It seems to me fairly certain that there was a barbaric stage in human development when most of the tribe worked on such occasions as demanded work, under the direction of the chiefs and medicine men, and that they did it as a matter of course, without wages or personal reward. The labour was communal—that is to say, only the very strongest could shirk it ; the product was communal—that is to say, the weaker got what they were permitted to get out of it. Probably there was little private personal property beyond wives, ornaments, weapons, huts and suchlike things. The cattle and lands belonged to the head men. Or some cattle on the common land were perhaps ear-marked for individual owners and the rest belonged to the tribal heads.

I think it is a fairly obvious and very important thing that, to begin with, trading had little or nothing to do with the economic life of the tribe. In our present life, trading, with its later instrument, money, is so intimately mixed up with staple production that people are apt to forget the two were once separate processes and dealt with different orders of necessity and desire. A barbaric agricultural people could, if necessary, live a fairly full and complex economic life without any trade or any pay whatever, and with scarcely any private property. Trading was an extra thing, a function, and not the most important one, of such seasonal gatherings as may have occurred.

An early enrichment of the primitive economic scheme must have been the slave, either the stolen child or the spared captive. Just as the stolen woman came into the early Palæolithic human group as the first private wife, so as the Neolithic order developed, the slave came in as a more amenable worker than the tribesman. Before the Neolithic stage there was little use for slaves. A stranger child could be taken along with the tribe like a captured wolf-cub, and petted or ill-treated, outraged or adopted as luck would have it. It was agreeable to have a human being to do exactly what you liked with, a motive which, as the Society for the Prevention of Cruelty to Children knows only too well, still leads queer people to take over the care of orphan children. And all sorts of small irksome services could be put upon a youngster too timid to run away into the wilderness.

That was probably the limit of slavery while man was still a wanderer. An adult male slave was of little use to nomads ; his escape was comparatively easy. If he proved to be a helpful person it was better to make him a member of the tribe. But as agricultural work increased, men and women captives, used hitherto chiefly for sacrifice and torture and suchlike amusing but transitory ends, began to have an economic value. The heads of the tribes got a more tractable service from them. Their spirits could be broken entirely because they were not wanted for fighting purposes like the young men of the tribe. They could be used up more completely. The Egyptian turquoise mines in Sinai, as early as the days of the First Dynasty, were worked by slave labour.

There must always have been great local variations of the early barbaric state. We make a great mistake, we fall into the System myth, when we suppose the early barbaric community to have had a stereotyped pattern. It had certain common tendencies ; it developed under certain common necessities ; all the world over, men's minds are much alike. And though communications were difficult, men were as imitative and perhaps more imitative than they are now. The tradition of the Old Man of the primitive days gave here a God and there a God-King and there a King-Priest. Where-ever agriculture went there went with it the traditions of a blood sacrifice, a human sacrifice. I have never been able to imagine satisfactorily why this should have been so ; but very plainly it was so. In the old world that blood sacrifice became very generally mitigated ; in America, under a mysterious tendency towards harshness manifested by that continent, it developed to tremendous proportions until it obsessed a civilisation. The Maya, the Aztec religions were insanely bloody. With agriculture, too, came an enormously clumsy primitive astronomy to determine the coming of inundations and the propitious phases of the year for sowing. Pyramids and obelisks acted as gnomons, temples were oriented to stars. It is wonder-ful to think how widely and vividly those opening phases of civilisation have been studied and made plain, within my lifetime.

Side by side with the largely agricultural hard-working communities of the warm alluvial countries there developed endless less agricultural and mainly nomadic groups, grazing sheep, driving cattle, and in Central and Eastern Asia keeping herds of horses. They traded, they conquered or were driven out again from the agricultural lands after a phase of conquest ; they developed institutions after their needs, and these came in to modify and confuse and complicate the customs, institutions, habits of mind and points of view that grew up from the ploughed lands. Among the cattle-tending nomads and in mountain glens one may even imagine a sort of justification for that " ancient gentilic (tribal or clan) organisation " which Engels, the fellow-prophet of Marx, declared by some inner light to be the primitive stage of human society. Only instead of his amiable Elders, enjoying " the spontaneous informal regard of Society," there must have been a reality much more after the vivid pattern of a Highland chief. All these things, we must remember, were worked out by thousands of communities through hundreds of generations, over plains, uplands, gorges, valleys, forests, steppes, and deserts, and the more simple and exact we make our classifications and explanations the easier they will be to carry in our minds, and the farther they are likely to be from the truth. Human society did not develop through an orderly progression of stages, but by an infinite diversity of temporary equilibriums and blundering innovations.

All the anthropology I have read seems to me almost without exception to assume that the man of six or seven thousand years ago was more lucid and systematic than the man of to-day. But plainly he must have been very much less so. It is not that he was intellectually inferior—there has probably been little if any growth of the human brain since Palæolithic times—but that he had nothing made ready for him. His language was still a relatively poor instrument, there were no accumulations of recorded and established general ideas. Logical reasoning and systematic thought did not begin until about twenty-five centuries ago ; Plato struggled mystically with the species and the individual, the One and the Many ; and the syllogism is no older than Aristotle. Our classical scholars never seem to be quite sure whether in the dialogues of Plato they are dealing with a Cyclopean clumsiness of argument or philosophical profundities. Before that time men thought, as children and under-educated people still think, by imagination. They tried to express things beyond the immediate daily life by symbols and mythical stories which were promptly misapprehended and retold in a different sense. And there was infantile wonder and emotion still flowing undisciplined through their minds. They could find some numbers beautiful and others flat or obnoxious. They were as childish as that. They were capable of immense inconsistencies. Habit and imitation held people's lives together throughout wide districts and regions in a general likeness. They attempted, they got, they prevailed, or they submitted, they toiled or robbed the toil of others, they feared and hated, killed and triumphed. This was life, they said, for what else could there be ? They bred and passed on the mysterious appeal of life, they loved their children violently and their grown-up offspring less, and they died and forgot and were forgotten.

Seven thousand years ago you had, at a generally more simple level, all the elements of the social problems of to-day ; oppressors and oppressed, luckless wights born to toil and suffering, lucky ones to veneration and delight, genial, kindly recipients of good-fortune, patient drudges, people cruelly misunderstood, souls in wild protest, cunning, wary winners in the game, perplexed losers, and it was all unsystematic, no one had planned it. It had grown unawares as a jungle grows, it had drifted along the stream of time, expanding, multiplying, complicating into an ever broader and vaster spectacle, out of man's solitary past.

It seems to me to be enormously important to stress this casual, complicated, and incoherent quality of man's past. I reiterate it deliberately. I return to it again. It is a conviction fundamental to the edifice of my ideas ; it is as much a part of me as my eyes. I do not believe we can deal properly with our current problems until we are saturated with this realisation. I have watched political thought with a very close interest all my life, and I perceive the urgent need to purge from our minds the disposition to think that at certain phases of human affairs something wicked was done, that a few men, priests or kings or rich men, plotted against the rest to deceive and enslave them. Or that at a definite time something wise was done and a new direction given to affairs. I can find nothing of that sort in my vision of history. What are called turning-points in history are significant and not directive. Life is more muddled and more innocent than we are inclined to think it. Men accept their lives as they find them, and all human beings are greedy, something disingenuous, and inapt to sympathise with the unlike. Some are pressed into the position of devourers and some find themselves stifled and preyed upon. But change priest and victim and with scarcely a hitch the sacrifice would go on.

Man's soul and mind in those days were already a palimpsest. It is only nowadays that psycho-analysis is beginning to work down through the superimposed layers and to reveal the restrained and baffled solitary-minded Old Man of the pre-Palæolithic days, peeping up through all the obliterations of training, custom, law, and religion that have been imposed upon him. But there he is at the bottom of things, the reason why men will combine far more readily for warfare than peace and for persecution than worship, why they are so easily " anti " and only by repercussion " pro," why they must grab beyond their utmost needs, why restraining laws are necessary, and why we all seek instinctively to ensure our own private security against the promiscuous motives of the general herd, that uncertain currish mob-soul of our kind.

§ 12

No other part of history so interests me as the opening chapter before the documents begin. There is no excessive presentation of persons and personal names ; egoism has left nothing but defaced monuments and disconnected boasts, and we seem to come nearer to the realities of human life than we do in many a later age when kings and princes and their policies monopolise the foreground.

Certain great enlargements of human life came about in the period between ten thousand and two thousand years two. They came about very gradually and it is only nowadays that we begin to reconstruct the story of their appearance. One of these enlargements was writing and another was money. Even in the Palæolithic age, thirty thousand years ago, men were very near to writing. They not only made beautiful pictures like those in the Altamira caves, but they simplified drawings down to conventional signs and wrote them rapidly and kept tallies. I remember being shown some tracings of Palæolithic rock paintings in the Madrid Museum five years ago. There was a hunting scene, a dance, some men gathering honey, and what were perhaps hunting tallies done in red paint. I do not know if these latter have ever been published. They might be primitive Chinese ; the sign for man, for example, a swipe of the brush and two legs, is very similar. Matters remained at that stage for a long period. Hunting and herding people need tallies and route pictures but have little other use for writing. As trading developed the need for record increased. The evolution of trust and commercial patience must have been a slow affair. Such things crept into life and became domesticated and familiar by degrees, age by age. As picture writing passed into syllabic writing and became more and more capable of rendering the subtleties of speech, much more extensive possibilities of communication and of the extension of power opened out. Laws and claims and pledges could go farther and endure longer. Men could be documented and " fixed."

With this enlargement our universal disposition to shift toil to other people and get them working for us discovered a rich mine of new possibilities. The man with the upper hand was no longer obliged to beat his slave or peasant to his task and stand over him. He could check his output. Much fine intelligence went to the elaboration and enforcement of " bits of writing " by which men were entangled.

Money, too, came creeping into the elaborating scheme of human economy. It was not so much invented as discovered to be present. We are told, or at least we used to be told, that the first money was cattle. That seems quite plausible. Cattle must have been exchanged for women in marriage and for other desirable possessions very early in the human story. The herdsmen, one can understand, were among the first traders ; the nomads no doubt began merchandising. I suspect that nomads were among the first metal and mineral miners, but I do not know how far archæologists would countenance me in that. In many parts of the world tinker and blacksmith and " cheap-jack " are still gipsies. They brought metals and precious stones along from the mountains and passes and gorges to the alluvial plains where minerals were rare. Possibly the first approach to a coin was a metal tally with a cow stamped on it. But metals were rare in themselves and highly desirable. I have read somewhere that the Hittites and Spartans had money of iron. It is only twenty-five or twenty-six centuries ago, it seems, that coined money came into use in human affairs, and for some centuries it belonged only to the superficial world of trading operations ; it had little to do with the broader, more fundamental economics of the community. Most of the food was grown, most of the houses and temples were made, even possibly most of the ships were launched, without a resort to money.

It has struck me, as a man coming late to such studies, that our histories of mankind do not attach sufficient importance to the gradual but profound alteration of phase, the reorientation that occurred in human affairs as documentation and money, from their first sporadic superficiality, crept into and changed the massive substance of economic life. These two things must have varied and elaborated the fundamental game of shifting the toil enormously. They cast the cloak of personal invisibility about owners. And they fixed obligations with a new relentlessness. As the broad lines of the money convention were more and more widely understood and recognised, as its purchasing power extended from a few to more and more commodities, the novelty of abstract wealth arose. Men found themselves possessed, not merely of cattle, olive orchards, ships, slaves, and so forth, but of an amulet which would call all or any of these things into their service. They could be mortgagers instead of worried owners, and they need keep no slaves, because now every penniless man was at their bidding if they so desired it. Money had generalised slavery. They had no need to insist upon the status of a slave. They found very soon that it was superfluous even to have the coined money in a strong-box ; they need only have the documented promise to pay money or an acknowledgment of receipt from a sufficiently solvent creditor. Parchment money was already in use among the Carthaginians.

Money has always had about it something indefinite.   It varies and has varied widely in its nature. It was not invented by any particular person. There never was, to-day there is not, a complete system of money. That has still to come. Money crept into human concerns insidiously, century by century. It is a variable, many-faced thing. It is a token here, and there a piece of metal of intrinsic value. It will breed like a rabbit where Usury is permitted. The Catholic Church once sought to sterilise it, but now she holds her peace and makes no trouble over a pious legacy of debentures. It breeds, but it is subject to degeneration. It can be debased and manipulated in all sorts of obscure and furtive ways. Men can operate upon its moods and fluctuations and snatch profits, but even the most cunning operators must sometimes guess. In modern life it has become so intimate and so fundamental that most people have a kind of horror of thinking too closely about its uncertainties. We will not even ask ourselves why it should be sterile in our pockets and prolific when we hand it to state or bank. We feel that to speak to a man about his dividends is an immodest act. With most of us money is protected from ruthless investigation by an emotional fear analogous to that which veils sex in the minds of the young. We realise a helplessness.

In the period when Dickon and I faced the world money was fairly stable. We accepted it as a trustworthy measure of values. Most of the world was on the gold standard, fluctuations in exchange were fractional, and there was a slow general fall in prices going on, a fall that scarcely anyone discussed. But the world-wide stability of money throughout most of that half-century before the war was an exceptional phase in its history.

Almost the whole story of mankind from the days of the Roman Empire onward could be told as a history of the fluctuations and variations in the behaviour of money and of its sublimated form—credit. The older civilisations of the Orient did, no doubt, use the precious metals abundantly; all Asia Minor and Greece coined money before Cyrus; the latter days of the Jews were dark with debts and usuries; there was lending and banking in Babylon and Carthage; but the cash nexus first sent its ramifications deeply into the general life of the community in the triumphant years of the Roman Republic. Did men, common men, pay taxes normally in money, anywhere at any time before the Roman days? I doubt it. And with the rephrasing of transactions in terms of money in that age ownership attained a novel fluidity, interest could expand to gigantic proportions, men could borrow with an unprecedented, dangerous readiness, and be ruined and sold up with amazing rapidity. The punishment of the bankrupt was merciless. The history of Rome seems to me to be full of the entanglement and dispossession of small men, of great inflations and explosions of debt, of popular attempts to repudiate debts and of aristocrat suppressions of repudiation, of moneyed men becoming for the first time more powerful than lords and rulers. It is the history of a series of events of a different type or order from those of any previous history.

There are historians—it does not dispose of them to say they are mostly Germans and so, by nature and necessity, wrong—who declare that the Roman collapse before the barbarians was essentially an economic collapse due to crude finance. The slave estates which had succeeded the debt-consumed free cultivator had given way to the serf cultivator, who was born and lived and died the debtor of his lord. And the serf had no spirit to resist the invader. For him a barbarian lord was little different from a Roman lord— himself perhaps only a very imperfectly assimilated barbarian in the imperial service. The outer barbarian had indeed the merit of cutting off the visitations of the imperial tax collector. Disorder and political disintegration were welcome then for the common man, since they meant a disappearance of the taxes and debts and deeds that crushed and held him down. Illegal exactions and outrages might be substituted, but these were, by their nature, transitory things.

This interpretation of the fall of the imperial system seems very plausible to me. It is fairly plain that the money and credit nexus which first pervaded the Roman Empire, and which was ruptured and left in tattered fragments by its fall, was mended very slowly and crept back throughout our Western community again in the later Middle Ages. To-day it is the method of nearly all our economic intercourse. Except the toil of mothers for their children and the toil of the wives of poor men, I can think of no large class of services that are not appraised and paid for in money. Hardly any were so appraised and paid for in the early civilisations three thousand years ago. In the old civilisations one was paid for one's toil by a specific easement or reward; nowadays one is paid by this abstract token, this coin or note, which is understood to carry with it a power of command over a certain quantum of whatever pleasures or possessions we desire. So long as that understanding holds it will work. In the ancient world services were simply and personally reciprocal. They are no longer so. Even the traditions of that reciprocity are lost and I do not believe they can ever be restored. And this has come about not by any revolutionary substitution of one organised system for another, but by an extraordinary growth of contrivances, conventions, tacit, unreasoned acceptances, establishments of usage. Money is not an institution that has replaced simpler and less convenient institutions, it is a tradition that has grown and exfoliated and crowded older usages out of existence.

It is not a safe device. It can fail to keep faith. It has failed and recovered in Russia and Germany. Nowhere is it proof against fresh failures. If men lose confidence in it sufficiently, our civilisation, which is now entirely based upon it and which has no reserved alternative to it to fall back upon, will clog and cease to work.   It is at least as indispensable now as housing and clothing.   Modern cilivisation is like an aeroplane in mid-air, an aeroplane with one sole, imperfect engine which is popping and showing many signs of distress.   It may win to an aerodrome and repairs and replacements.   Or it may make a very unpleasant forced landing presently with little hope of immediate recovery.

§ 13

In the last three centuries there has been a great expansion of the scale of economic processes. This change of scale is one of the outstanding facts in the general scheme of history. It has inaugurated a new phase in human experience. It has an effect as though upon the customary succession of day and night there were to dawn an unfamiliar illumination from some strange new star, a light altering all visible values, dispelling accepted shadows, revealing things hitherto unknown. There seems to be no simple cause of this change. There may have been an almost entirely accidental confluence of favourable conditions.

Through stimulations that I will not attempt to clasify or estimate, European business in the sixteenth and seventeenth centuries was in a state of vigorous renascence. Shipping was pushing with an unwonted boldness round the continents and into unknown seas, there was a great influx of silver from America, towns were growing rapidly. There were also great intellectual liberations, the rediscovered Greek literature was releasing the long-restrained imaginations of men, printing was making reading easier and cheaper ; but how far this mental enlivenment really affected economic developments it is impossible to calculate. The eighteenth century carried on the expanding stir ; there was much experimenting and innovating in financial method ; there was a rush of inventions ; coal was utilised for metallurgy, and that led to a bigger scale use of iron and steel ; the machinery made possible by this opened up new possibilities of organised manufacture, and the facilities of intercourse began an astounding increase in scope and pace that still goes on.

Most of these things seem to me to have arisen detachedly. The more one looks into their history, the less connected they appear to be, and the less ready one is to accept simple explanations. One is apt to think of the steam-engine, for instance, with its intricate, tremendous influence upon transport and upon the development of mass production, as arising out of the scientific thrust. But did it ? Were the inventors and exploiters of steam—Watt watching the dancing kettle lid, for example—really scientific men ? Were they influenced very much by the science of their time ? Did they owe very much to Bacon or the Royal Society ? And for the matter of that, to take a later case, was the aeroplane a scientific invention ? Was it not rather the creation of odd experimenting out-of-the-way people, a little distrustful of the mathematicians' assumptions about the air ?

The proper triumphs of science no one can deny. Indisputably the whole development of electrical appliances arises out of systematic scientific research, and so do most medical progress and most metallurgical and chemical improvements. But it is worth noting that the experimenting, innovating spirit of the last three centuries was also active outside the strictly scientific movement, and that historically the scientific man has rather pursued and overtaken and studied and organised, first in this and then in that province of creative knowledge, than directed the opening inquiries. In the last three hundred years inventions and new ideas have come faster and thicker like flowers in springtime; the scientific man has gathered rather than sown. In the world of psychology he is only now really getting a grip upon the stuff, and in the world of social and economic relationship and in relation to law I am doubtful whether, even at the present time, science has fairly begun. Yet there have been tremendous changes and enlargements in these latter fields, changes and enlargements almost as considerable as those in natural science.

But though I see the expansive forces which distinguish the life of man in the last two or three centuries as multiple in their origins and defiant of any comprehensive explanation, it does seem to me, nevertheless, that one can throw at least two generalisations over the whole. The first of these is the sustained widespread appearance of this change of scale in human possibilities.   Suddenly the world has grown relatively much smaller. Man has acquired new power over matter. He can handle masses and produce commodities by wholesale methods absolutely undreamt of before the present time.   And, secondly, he has now so mastered the utilisation of fuel, wind, and water for the production of power that a large part of the burthen of sheer toil imposed hitherto since civilisation began upon the unwilling shoulders of our kind may now be lifted. Human intercourse need no longer be mainly a toil-shifting tangle.   I take it the main features of the present phase of this property-money give-and-take which is human society are due to the confused and mainly selfish efforts of people to adapt themselves to the releases of these new conditions without any clear understanding of their nature.

This change of scale and all the disturbance and opportunity it brought with it was going on even in the eighteenth century, but it was only becoming the completely dominant fact in the world's economics when my father was growing up.   He was already alive in the early days of railway speculation. I remember he told me when I was a small boy that he was married in the year the *Great Eastern* was launched, which was, I find, 1859. He was showing me a picture of the monster hung up in a bedroom at Mowbray. She was a prematurely big ship of eighteen thousand tons.   I doubt if her engines were up to their task, and I believe she was a financial failure.   She was beyond the limit set by circumstances at that time to the change of scale in shipping.

My grandfather was a not very leading partner of a not very prominent firm of stockbrokers. So my father grew up, indigenous to that dark hive, the City, in the days when London was really the head and centre of the business enterprise of the world. The new phase of civilisation had first become manifest in England; she was leading with iron and steel, cotton, wool, railways, steamships, finance. In those days the English were regarded, not only by themselves, as a people beyond all other peoples, more energetic, more practical, cold and high and wise. And Providence had favoured His new Chosen by putting their coal and iron very close together and planting them in an island at the geographical centre of the trading world. It was their mission to develop the rest of this planet, patronisingly, profitably. France, their most serious rival, was, they declared, " fickle," Spain sunken in Catholic decay, Italy a protegée, Russia barbaric, Germany poverty-struck and impracticable, lost in dreams of music and philosophy; America from north to south a continent of unstable republics, fields for enterprise, of no financial importance at all. The chief manufacture of the United States in those days was supposed to be wooden nutmegs. English schoolmasters teaching transatlantic geography never failed to mention them with a kindly you-may-laugh-now-smile.

In those days all the nations of the world were resorting to the dark and narrow ways of the City for credit to make railways and harbours and to reorganise their industries along the new lines. If any refrained, energetic young Englishmen went to inquire into the matter and if necessary compel them to come in. The solicitation of China and Japan was forcible. French enterprise had a narrower range in the Mediterranean and the Orient, and was always rather too closely entangled with its Foreign Office. In the Far East the Englishman sometimes met a stray American, for a mysterious instinct drove the Americans very early across the Pacific, but in those days they did not seem to amount to very much there, and presently their Civil War engaged them. That was supposed to be the end of all their democratic hopes. North America would " split up " as South America had done, lacking the golden bond of a crown. Amusing it is to recall that in the political cartoons of those days John Bull figured as a wise old giant and Jonathan as his untidy, ill-behaved nephew. Neither American nor German enterprise had ruffled the hustling, muddling self-confidence of London in the days of my father's youth.

The industrial and mining developments of the later eighteenth and early nineteenth centuries were largely proprietary. Landowners prospected for minerals under their own lands; cotton-spinners bought machinery and reduced their cousins and neighbours to economic servitude, and presently resorted to the foundling hospitals and workhouses to increase their supply of tractable cheap workers. There were companies, but they were mainly just multiple proprietors. With the coming of railways and steamships and power machinery, however, the change of scale passed further and further beyond the dimensions of ordinary individual fortunes. Before a man could set about trying to handle this or that still incompletely developed economic activity in the big way he found he had to associate himself with someone who would bring in the large amount of credit needed for the attempt. He had to go to the City.

By the middle of the nineteenth century two contrasted types of exploiter were trying to draw wealth, ease, and power out of the new forces of enlargement; one the reorganiser of employment upon new lines, and the other the operator with credit. The method of the latter was to saddle the new production or the new service with as heavy payments as it could stand—or at any rate to operate and get away with a profit before the limits of payment were apparent. The former was a cheap producer and seller who sought new customers ; the latter was a collector of savings which he led towards investment in the new enterprises, and deflected more or less on the way thither. The organiser encroached upon and destroyed the freedom of the small man ; the financier enmeshed the organiser. That stately process continues. To nowhere in particular. The smaller people, superseded by the new machine and power-using enterprise, had to take care of themselves as well as they could. Most of them the new developments took by surprise and they were impoverished or pauperised before they realised clearly what was happening. After the immemorial practice of mankind, the new labour needed was obtained as cheaply as possible and left to get as much above a bare subsistence from the social economics effected as it could.

Among the early victims of the new drives towards larger scale business were the small cultivators whose way of living was knocked to pieces by the Enclosures Acts, and the weavers and spinners and other workers who were crushed or devoured by the factories. The railways put an intricate and picturesque high-road life out of action, ruined coach-owners, horse-owners and horse-breeders, wayside inns. On the whole the new methods were increasing production very greatly, but they were requiring a smaller proportion of skilled and capable workers among the people they employed. and so the larger share of the increased output went to support a great expansion of population, a proliferation of low-grade human beings. Everywhere arose great new towns, vast sprawls of mean streets and slums, in which the bulk of this additional unspecialised and unselected population sheltered.

It is one of the dearest assumptions of the Marxist theorists that there has been a concentration of wealth in the hands of a vigorously acquisitive and teadily concentrating minority throughout the last two centuries. It is amazing how many of us, with eyes in our heads, with museums, ancestral mansions, and collections of old furniture to refer to, with pictures and books at hand, novels, plays, collections of letters, poems with dedications, have come to accept that concentration as a fact. But relatively to the common lot the life of the rich and noble in the seventeenth century was manifestly finer and ampler than it is to-day. They had far more space and beauty, more respect, more servile human service. Music of the finest quality, delightful art, every sort of decoration—such printing and book-binding, for example, as we cannot rival to-day—mental freedom, existed for them alone. It is preposterous to say that the rich have become richer and the poor poorer in this last phase of history. The increase in produc-tion has gone along quite another channel. It has neither been monopolised by the property-owner nor distributed throughout the general mass. It has merely expanded the general mass. It has been absorbed by blind breed-ing. Since my father was born, in that little space of time, the population of England has doubled. So has the population of Germany. By internal increase and in spite of considerable emigration. Since 1850 the popu-lation of the world must have increased by many hundreds of millions. No one is much better off nor worse off as yet for the change of scale ; there are only more people.

§ 14

SHORT-SIGHTED rearrangements of production under a conspiracy of helpful circumstances, and then blind borrowing and purblind lending, reckless breeding ; evasion of toil and responsibilities above ; congested, reluctant protesting labour below ; and nowhere any clear vision of the whole—that was the substance of the nineteenth-century spectacle, and it followed logically and necessarily in the vein of all preceding social life. Knowledge had so grown by the middle of the nineteenth century that there might have been enough for all and unprecedented freedom for all. But this possibility concerned nobody in particular. The practical fact which concerned everyone was that there was not nearly enough for most people because of the primitiveness and incoherence of proprietary and monetary methods.

Quite the strongest and most remarkable of the impressions of financial men my own dealings with finance have left me is the superficiality and inattention. Men follow science and art, pursue agriculture, organise manufactures, or go upon the seas to trade, *closely*, because these things are profoundly and sustainingly interesting. But no one is in business in the City for the sake of business in the City. Men go there to come out of it again, successful. There is no instinct for arithmetic, no lust for computation, in the make-up of a normal human being ; I doubt even if those abnormalities they call calculating boys get any pleasure from their gift until it is applied ; the only living interests in the City are acquisition and the excitements of risk and conflict that might be pursued as easily at Monte Carlo. The activities of the City and its younger, perhaps stronger, offspring in Wall Street—for who knows now which is leading which ?—affect the intimate lives of all mankind, but this is not present in the consciousness of the City. It is the peculiar quality of money and credit to abstract reality from transactions and remove it to an immense distance. Finance is forgetful of the world in its processes, and the world thinks as little as possible about the finance that thrusts it along and pushes it about. Hardly anyone in the City is going an inch further than he is obliged to do beneath the surfaces on which he moves his pieces. The City has grown up from forgotten beginnings ; City men accept it as it is and follow its rules and traditions. They no more want an inquiry into what lies beneath it than cricketers want people to geologise beneath the pitch.

In the course of my life I have met a certain sprinkling of bankers, and I do not think there is any sort of human being more marvellous and incredible. They take money for granted as a terrier takes rats ; when they see it they go for it ; but they are absolutely immune to any philosophical curiosity about it. From no other profession do men fly so rapidly to the distraction of other occupations ; bankers become collectors, naturalists, historians, critical writers ; the profession is a hotbed of amateurs. The world of banking and finance draws princely incomes from processes it does not understand clearly and that, with a strong self-protective instinct, it will, if it can, prevent anyone from understanding clearly. I can imagine no more preposterous caricature of reality than the representation of the City and Wall Street and the bourses and exchanges of the planet generally as a sort of synthetic, wicked, watchful, many-headed spider, scientifically sucking the life-blood from the world. The spider sucks blood because it wants to do it, but banking does it merely because it does it.

No doubt the activities of the City tangle the whole world, but they do so aimlessly. The men who rush about its narrow ways do not know what they are up to. They would be very angry to be told as much, but so it is. They impress themselves and each other and their clerks and their typists and the anxious, greedy, investing public as strong men and bold men and decisive men and little Napoleons ; some of them are controlling altogether colossal sums ; but in their heads are brains that still remain—it is offensive, but it must be said—inadequately developed. They are youngsters who have never taken time to grow up, youngsters overblown. They have never struggled on to the fully adult stage. They are ignorant of fundamentals, they do not see themselves plainly, they are individualistic in their aims, the sense of being a possible part in one complete social organisation has not come to them, and all these characteristics are the characteristics of immaturity. Their great enterprises, their debts, their loans, their technicalities and methods are solemn vast puerilities ; it does not make them any the less puerilities that all mankind suffers because of them.

The congested City is still the chief credit whirlpool of the world confusion, and thither the money goes and there it must be sought again. About its ways went our father in his time, in a becoming black top-hat and an impressive frock-coat after the fashion of the period, red-whiskered and comely and engaging in his manners, bold and enterprising to his own undoing. And thither came Dickon and I later on, sniffing after the credit and the money which are the keys of personal liberty and without which there is neither food nor freedom nor power in the world.

I will not disinter my father's story here. Indeed, many essential phases of it are now so covered up and hidden and untraceable that I do not think I could, even if I wanted to do so. He seems to have worked with his

father's firm for a time and to have been at first an alert but quite wary specu-
lator.   There were many people in the City who liked him and who kept
their faith in his ability and recuperative power right up to the wild pre-
liminaries of the final disaster.   He did very little with railways ; railways
had been built, had been over-capitalised, had failed to pay, and had been
made to pay—by excursion trains and an educational campaign—before
his time.   The railways were settling down after a wild youth.   But the
new possibilities of large-scale retail trade the railways had created were
still in process of active exploitation.   It was an open question then whether
the greater changes would follow the lines indicated by the increased ease
with which customers could be brought to centres, or those defined by the
increased facilities of distribution.   Bright, pushful men were looking
for presentable aspects of both these possibilities with which to woo the
City and, in co-operation with the City, the investor at large.   My father
was early in this field, and he seems to have done very well along both
lines.

He looked for easily transported goods and hit upon tea ; he brought
together some tea wholesalers, some lead-packet people, and a small retailer
in Clapham named Partington, whose shop it was possible to claim was
" Established in 1810," and out of these ingredients he created " Partington's Pure Packet Teas ; Partington's Own Delicious Blend."   At first
there was to have been a postal order business, but, instead, the packets
were found to be particularly marketable on the counters of small retailers.
People with sweetstuff shops and confectioners and so on, who had never
weighed out tea, could sell packet tea.   Simultaneously he revealed to
Nickleby's, the drapers of Camden Town, that they were the North London
Central Bazaar, " the shopping and social centre of North London Life,"
and got them into a phase of hectic enlargement.   He worked with sustained
energy and very closely in those early years : there was reality and substance
in both these concerns, and it was rather through the pressure of natural
business development than any nefarious intention that by the time he had
altogether disposed of these organisations he had sold them for about ten
times their actual value as going concerns.   Partington's, with a group
of other firms of very unequal value, presently became the London United
Tea Company, and then launched boldly into World Tea Plantations ;
Nickleby's also expanded into London and Empire Stores, with shops at
Brighton and Manchester and a place in Durban, and another, a shocking
failure, in Bombay.   The belief of the investing public, and particularly
of the small investor in associated shop constellations, was growing steadily
all these years, and my father took his own where he found it.

In those days my father was by the best City standards a sound man.
He was watching what he was doing quite carefully.   His reputation for

soundness was greatly enhanced by the Red Gulch and Throttle Load affair. Either he got a tip in some way, or he made a happy fluke with a large parcel of copper-mine shares and was out and away with his profits before anyone had noticed what had happened. It seemed a desperate fling to many City sages. But after that raid he never went near that market again; they never had a chance to get back on him. This resolution as it became more evident turned people's momentary doubts into an accession of confidence.

Nevertheless, it was the beginning of his undoing; his natural belief in his instinct and his luck was stimulated; he became greedy and hasty, he spread himself out over ground he had never explored with any care, he took liberties with his associates and lied where before he had simply exaggerated. He went out for the promotion of seaside resorts, for big housing schemes and especially for service flats in hugh architectural piles, for gas-lighting—more particularly in South European countries—and, arising out of that, for soft coal. I do not even know the succession in time, much less the inter-relations, of Cornwall Court Limited, the London Buildings Company, Seabreeze Estates, the Gas and Metallurgical Coal Group and Mediterranean Gas and South Coast Development; I know only that the mounting pile culminated in London and Imperial Enterprises and crashed. But I know enough of my father through my own nature to know that what was the matter with him was boredom, the frightful boredom of City life, the boredom of enterprises getting more and more remote from any living and breathing reality, the boredom of arithmetic in little offices, of bluffs and misleading statements in board rooms, of deposit-books and cheque-books that one had to remember didn't mean what they appeared to mean, and of remembering what So-and-So didn't know and what Such-and-Such did. Stuff like that in the brain must be like dry chaff in the mouth on a hot day. The City is a trap for human energy; it promises life more abundantly and wastes it ruthlessly. It is like the bottle of nuts with the monkey; he can get his hand in and he can get his hand full, but to get his hand out is another matter. And until he can get his hand out the nuts are uncracked nuts.

My father must have felt that beneath the florid appearance of success his life was passing away. I realise only too vividly his desperate determination to clutch some concrete happiness, some vivid splendour, high place or power, out of that mocking hurry of dingy and doubtful transactions, before age or death overtook him. Our removal to Mowbray was the first early symptom of his possible impatience for realisations and expenditure. Afterwards, nearer the end, there was some gaudy pleasuring; I have heard since of brilliant but costly ladies assisting him to taste " life," and there was a great time in a hired villa at Monte Carlo, of which except for a few postcards no intimations ever reached Mowbray; and a theatrical venture with a now forgotten actress, Lillie Morton, whose private may have been greater than her public charm. I hope it was, for my father's sake. Before he had reached my present age the whole feverish story was over.

And so he passed, and so, with less acutely tragic incident, a great multitude of brave and eager lads have passed through the City, growing old as they passed but not really growing up, a swirl and a superficial consequence upon a deep flood of changes beyond their understanding.

BOOK THE THIRD

THE STORY OF THE CLISSOLDS—
ESSENCE OF DICKON

THE STORY OF THE CLISSOLDS—
ESSENCE OF DICKON

THE SECTIONS

My brother Dickon was physically very like my father, but he had a sturdier quality of mind. His imagination was as bold, but his self-restraint was steadier. Both of us indeed were honest to a greater degree ; our consciences were livelier and more watchful, the sense of an obligation incurred gripped us more firmly and did not so readily slip its hold. Some ancestor of marked integrity must have been latent in my father. We were both mainly Clissold, but physically Dickon was nearer to my father than I. He was a better-looking youngster. He had my father's reddish hair and something of his physical swagger, while I mingled threads of my mother's darkness with streaks of paternal gold.

Dickon, I have told, professed individualism, but he has always been a very sociable individualist ; I was an unsocial Socialist from the outset, with a greater disposition to go alone or with one companion. Clara once said that Dickon was canine and I was feline, and I think that expresses something very elemental between us. Dickon's pink skin freckles at a mere glimpse of the sun, and he has carried my father's sanguine amplitude of limb and body to a considerable massiveness. He is now, in fact, a very fine figure of a man indeed, a stout tweed-wearing man, " Nordic," they would say in America.

In the preceding Book I brought the account of Dickon and myself up to the later " eighties," when we were studying science very unevenly at the Kensington schools, and considering our attack upon the world. Then I went off on the trail of Marx and the economic history of the world. I left Dickon at loose ends.

He did not long remain at loose ends. It was at night in a show called the Inventions Exhibition, while we were sitting watching a crowd of promenaders and listening to a band, beneath festoons of fairy-lights— little oil lamps they were—and in front of a grass plot on which yet other fairy-lights, blue, red, and orange, made a flickering guttering enchantment, that Dickon's ends ceased to be loose and he unfolded to me his plan of campaign. It was to be his life's plan of campaign, but I believe that it had crystallised out in his mind only that afternoon.

That Inventions Exhibition was one of a series of annual shows ; there was one called the Healtheries and another the Fisheries, and others, in what was then a great area of waste land in South Kensington. Now most of that land is filled up by the Imperial Institute and by Museum galleries and buildings belonging to London University, but in those days these exhibitions were able to spread from the Exhibition Road to the Albert Hall, the upper galleries of which building were somehow included in the spectacle. These grounds were put in order and laid out with beds of geraniums and calceolarias ; they were illuminated in the evenings, and the Exhibition was favoured by a succession of fine summer nights.

It would be interesting now to disinter the plans and guide-books, if any copies survive, to that Inventions Exhibition. It was before the coming of the safety bicycle or the automobile ; the gas-lamp still held its own quite hopefully against the dangerous uncertainties of the electric light, and gramophones, cinemas, wireless had hardly germinated in the womb of time. The germs existed, but nothing had come to exhibition pitch. I remember some very attractive omnibuses, driven by compressed air, wallowing to and fro in a confined space. They were the only anticipation of automobiles in the show, and I remember, too, how Dickon that after-noon doubted whether electric traction could ever be anything more than a scientific toy. It might be done, he said, but it could never be done to pay.

Yet what we had seen had stimulated our imaginations considerably, and while we listened to the band in the evening after a frugal supper, we were both much more prepared to expect great changes during our lifetimes than we had been when we pushed through the turnstiles in the early afternoon. Our talk had ebbed for a time and we were smoking unaccustomed cigarettes which Dickon had made with a machine for the occasion.

" It is no good inventing things if you do not get people to make use of them," said Dickon, coming up to the surface, so to speak, after a pro-found meditation.

" No," said I, not in the least aware of his drift.

" There's no money in anything until people have been told of it."

" The money ? "

" No," contemptuously, " the anything."

I perceived that he was taking up his standing problem of " how to get it " again. " I suppose new things have to be sold," I said.

" Exactly. And you have to make people *want* them."

A pause.

" Advertisement," said Dickon. " Advertisement is only beginning. Billy !—I see it. That's where my money is. Advertising."

The distant band was playing a waltz tune just then, for I remember the rhythm of it. (Tra-la-la la pum pum, pum pum. Tra-la-la la pum

pum, pum pum. Tra-la-la pum, pum, pum pum. Tra-la-la-LA pum pum, pum pum, it went. Am I filling in details from my imagination or was it the Blue Danube waltz ?) And the promenaders passed, keeping step to it; mysterious, romantic promenaders, for the fairy-lights were not enough to show their faces plainly.

With something of the manner of an explorer, the voice at my side began to talk of the dark and dismal advertisement of that time and to point out its defects and its possibilities. I understood now why he had been so silent and preoccupied throughout the afternoon. He had been reading all the advertisements in sight and thinking about them. He had been struck by their limitation of range ; their crudity and formality ; their inapplicability to the sale of new devices. A realisation of unworked opportunities close at hand had struck him dumb at first, and was now moving him to speech. He began to talk of advertisement, and to the best of my recollection he talked of advertisement for the next year or so.

That evening I had a lecture on the things advertisers did and the things they failed to do. It was delivered with the dogmatism proper to an elder brother, and with a note of reprehension as though I had in some way participated in the negligencies of the commercial world. I said little, and what I said was brushed aside or crushed. I did what I could to find excuses for backward and unskilful advertisers and was soundly scolded for their sins.

I recall the feeling rather than the substance of his outpourings. I remember that after a time we got up from our seats and walked about the grounds, and Dickon was still weighing pros and cons ; we went into the more or less deserted exhibition galleries, and he held me remorselessly before silent exhibits and denounced the futility of their appeals. He was still at it as we made our way at the close of the exhibition, with other *jusqu'au-bout*-ists, along a tiled subway that echoed to our feet and led to the Metropolitan station.

" Look at that thing ! " he would cry. " Look at that *silly* thing ! What's the good of sticking that here ? "

I recall distinctly my agonised protest. " Damn it ! *I* didn't put it there ! "

It restrained him not at all.

In the small hours he was sitting up in bed. " Advertisement, Billy," he said. " Advertisement ! And the School of Mines may go and blast and burn and fuse and run itself to Jericho. The Voice has reached me, Billy ! Come over and help us ! The Hoardings call to me, the Magazines are moaning, ʌnd I come. I come."

" Oh, *shut* up, Dickon ! Good-night ! " I said, pulling the bed-clothes over my ears.

He dropped his work at the School of Mines almost immediately ; he made no pretence of finishing off his term, and for some weeks he divided his waking time almost equally between an intensive study of advertising methods and brooding in Kensington Gardens upon his course of action. His first definite step was to go, after a very careful and elaborate preliminary exploration of the special field in question, to an advertising watchmaker in Cornhill, to get an interview with him, and tell him why his watches were not selling nearly so well as they might do in the West-end, in various suburbs, among the City clerks, in the East-end, and what he thought might be done to stimulate their sale. He had brought notes and sketches of almost all the advertisements the firm was using, and very politely and clearly he pointed out how stereotyped was their appeal and how mechanical their distribution. He convinced his hearer of advertisements going to waste and reaching nobody here, and of areas neglected there, and in the end he was allowed to make a scheme for a more scientific campaign. Hitherto the work had been done in an almost routine fashion from the office. His scheme was accepted. It succeeded, and his path in life was open before him.

§ 2

I DO not know whether it was luck or some mysterious flair that made Dickon pitch upon Milton for his first attempt, but I doubt if he could possibly have chosen better. Milton liked him from the outset ; and with Milton, Dickon at the ripe age of one-and-twenty fixed up his first contract and began pushing Milton's Silver Guinea by the score, by the hundred, by the thousand, into the waistcoat pockets of the middle-class. Faster than Milton could assemble his watches Dickon assembled his customers. That was only a little while before the mass production of watches was fully under way. Milton's watches, I fancy, came in whole or in part from Switzerland. And when presently the Waltham watches came ticking very loudly from across the Atlantic, Dickon made a brave and successful fight for Milton for some years, with "Milton's Silent Silver Guinea ; each personally tested, numbered, and individually guaranteed."

In the end Milton left the field of popular sales and became a professor of quality. Milton's Limited now sell "watches that are beautiful and intimate," but Dickon still steers the bulk of the output along the path of assertive veracity to the grateful customer. Only last summer I discovered him in his smoking-room at Dorking meditating profoundly over Milton's current advertisement in *Punch*, a most gentlemanly affair.

"Do you remember Milton's in the old days, Billy ? " he said, handing it to me.

"Rather."

"Changed since then. The money I've brought these people ! Used to be cheap stuff."

I considered the page of *Punch*. I know of no other periodical whose advertisements so exactly catch the tone of the morning-room of a good West-end club.

"There are times," he reflected, "when I almost think of buying a Milton. . . . Beautiful and intimate. . . . They seem to be first-rate watches."

§ 3

MILTON'S was only Dickon's point of departure. A great light had come to him, and for a time he saw life wholly as a field of action in which he was to create appetites in people for commodities they had never in the least desired hitherto, or to direct their attention to the great superiority of common necessities when they are labelled distinctly with a proprietor's name.

Immense wealth lay in convincing people that an article could hardly be considered to exist unless it was vouched for by a respectable firm. In the days of our youth an enormous number of things were sold anonymously that are now sold under the brands of makers and packers. Our father had been one of the pioneers in this christening of goods with his Partington's Packet Teas. When I was a child every grocer had his own sorts of tea, his tea-chests with different qualities, and he weighed the tea out and packed it up for each customer. I can remember seeing that done. Almost everything he sold them—bacon, butter, lard, pickles, jams, biscuits—he sold from stocks of his own buying on his own individual reputation. He had pickled onions and cabbage in a great tub, as they still have them here in France. He used to display sugar-loaves in his window and chop them up in his shop ; I would gaze fascinated at the sugar chopping in the Duxford grocer's. And the oilman sold his own lamp oil, and no one asked where he got it. Mustard used to be bought for Mowbray at the chemist's.

But even in our childhood there was already a number of vigorous firms reaching their hands over the retail tradesman's shoulder, so to speak, and offering their goods in their own name to the customer. As an infant I used to love a particularly fascinating Oriental who infested the back pages of magazines, pouring stuff into the mouth of a forked fish in the interests of Nabob Pickles. He seems to have vanished utterly. Colman's Mustard insisted already upon being the only English Mustard. It just stuck up its name in bright letters—everywhere. I do not know if it ever became the only mustard, or if there are other mustards now. There was also a " Keen's Mustard." Is " Keen's " still with us ? " English " mustard that is—there are all sorts of other mixings here in France. But I saw yesterday in the window of an *épicier* in Grasse neat little tins of Colman's, with the same vivid yellow ground and the lettering I remember spelling out from a train window in my childhood. If it is not the only English mustard everywhere, it is certainly that here.

Then there was soap. The great firm of Pears in those days had already thrust an individuality upon soap. *Pears' Soap* marks an epoch; I hope history will not neglect it. It was advertised with an unprecedented swagger; there were magazine and newspaper articles about how the firm did it; Pears bought Academy pictures by R.A.'s to reproduce in a sort of facsimile, gilt frame and all, and were among the first of all advertisers to be funny and laugh at themselves. Harry Furniss did a picture in *Punch* of a dirty tramp writing a soap testimonial: " Two years ago I tried Pears' Soap; since when I have used no other." They secured it and made a great thing of it.

These and a hundred other siren voices had called to me from wall and hoarding and printed page from my childhood up, but it was only now that Dickon was talking about them that I gave them more than a casual attention. I had never yet stirred up a restaurant by demanding Nabob Pickles and rejecting all inferior imitations, nor refused mustard until I was reassured by a sight of the Colman tin; but now I began, if not to clamour, at least to watch and discriminate under Dickon's critical guidance. He was grappling with a multitude of curious problems, and he insisted upon discussing them with me to the exclusion of every other subject.

" You see, Billy, you help me. The things you say—not much in themselves, but they give me ideas."

Queer amusing problems some of them were. Cocoa had come into English life, and a number of firms were struggling to monopolise the market, among them Van Houten, probably a Dutch firm, and Epps and Cadbury. I do not know if Rowntree's came then or later; I fancy they were never very deeply in the cocoa fight, but only came in later with chocolate, but I may be wrong about that. Dickon was making a careful comparison of their different methods. " *Epps' Cocoa, Grateful and Comforting*," Dickon would repeat. " Wonderful words. Wonderful! Genius in them. . . . Billy, do you think *any* of these cocoas are the least bit different from the others ? "

So earnest were our researches that we tried them to see. We sipped our cocoa and regarded each other with grave, inquiring faces.

These were purely English firms, I suspect. The battle of the cocoas, if it was fought in America at all, was probably fought under other names. I doubt if any commodity straddled the Atlantic in those days.

Another of our investigations was an attempt to discover why there was no advertising campaign for a salt or a pepper to put beside the omnipresent clamour about mustard. We never got to the bottom of the pepper problem. We decided that an opportunity was being lost there. " Harvester's Black Pepper Stimulates and Enlivens without Harmful Mechanical Irritation " we believed would have driven nameless pepper from the cruet. White pepper could have been denounced as an effeminate powder. There could have been bright attractive pictures of a stomach curly and vigorous rejoicing in its strength under the cheering influence of "Harvester," and of another, lax as a dead slug, debased by common white. Salt, common salt, we guessed, was deliquescent stuff to pack and handle; that was why no one touched it—except for Tidman's— was it Tidman's ?—bath salt. Salt, for a proprietary sale, would have to be salt with a difference, we concluded, and we came very near to fore-stalling the dry table salts warranted not to cake into lumps, that presently appeared. "Cerebos," I think, was the leader.

I remember him sitting on the hard, wooden seat of a compartment in the dingy, dirty, sulphurous Underground Railway of those primitive times, with three or four magazines on the seat beside him, discoursing of the advertisements of a medicine called, if I remember rightly, "Owbridge's Lung Tonic." Always those advertisements were encircled by a monstrous O. "Now, why that O ?" he demanded. "It individualises. It is also probably on the bottle. If there is any other lung tonic going, it serves to make the other fellow seem an undistinguished nobody. But does it make people want to take the stuff much ? Does it do anything to catch the eye of consumptive people ? Think of anyone with lung trouble and a cough. Suppose he had this advertisement on one side, and on the other side one that said quite quietly, ' Clissold's Lung Tonic soothes and gives peace. And in that peace you heal,' which would you want to try ? Think of those words, Billy, not too big and noisy but put where they seem to catch the eye almost by accident ! Just whisper it. ' *And in that peace you heal.*' "

In that period there was a great clamour of pills and proprietary medicines generally ; I think they were far more vigorously pushed then than they are now. Hardly anything in domestic medicine that was not being dragged out of its anonymous phase in the prevalent research for big business in small things. It is natural that many people should experience a certain internal dullness on occasion, and require artificial animation. In the pre-Victorian days this was almost always supplied by homely remedies ; castor oil which chastened and sweetened the soul, rhubarb pills and antibilious pills, Epsom salts, and, for the defenceless young, flowers of sulphur. One took these things and corrected oneself as a cat eats grass. But no philanthropist ever filled columns with the praises of these more immediate gifts from God. So they were thrust aside by Beecham's Pills, Worth a Guinea a Box (marvellous words, oh ! marvellous words !), Eno's Fruit Salt, and a crowd of other highly named and vividly packed proprietary mixtures.

The age of the secret remedy, says Dickon, is drawing to an end.

Advertisements of medicine decline. Not that people are giving up their resort to a tabloid or a cupful of something out of a bottle directly they feel out of condition, but they are more and more disposed to take known and specified drugs and preparations. This does not mean a return to the little chemist's scales and measures—in Britain the little chemist has been almost syndicated out of existence—but a development of the great-scale marketing of tabloids and capsules, made up to this or that prescription, by firms of manufacturing druggists. Dickon has been pressing manufacturing chemists to bolder and bolder advertisements for some time. He wants them to market attractive little medicine cases for dressing-bags. The ordinary citizen will then have his physic at hand, like a case of golf-clubs, to meet all occasions. He will play upon himself as a conductor plays upon his orchestra, summoning the drums, soothing the brass. Far more entertaining this will be than the tin-whistle solo of the old panacea. There will certainly be great changes of fashion in the contents of these cases, and the objective of the advertiser of the old-fashioned proprietary medicine will be more and more to get and keep a footing in the case; to ensure his position as a contributory instrumentalist, so to speak, in the internal symphony of the citizen. He will become like the advertiser of automobile accessories instead of a principal dealer.

But this is by the way. I was telling of the advertisements of London and the London press of forty years ago as I remember them. Even when they were not concerned with medicines they dealt largely with the comforts of the human interior. In addition to those things I have named, there was in my adolescence much propaganda of Cod Liver Oil; Elliman's Embrocation, always well advertised, flourished then as now; and the abolition of home-made beef-tea and mutton broth was beginning. Liebig's Extract of Meat was widely pushed, but I cannot now remember whether Bovril was already afloat; Oxo I am almost certain came later. We were to watch some pretty fighting presently over those meat extracts. The small tobacconist was still a single-shop adventurer, unaware of his approaching doom; he sold loose tobacco and cigars and matches and walking sticks; the propaganda of cigarettes had scarcely dawned in those days. Cigarette smoking was a picturesque exotic habit that middle-aged people associated with Italy and Spain and the laxer morals of the south; one rolled a cigarette with a luxurious nonchalance and felt oneself a villain; the American machine-made cigarette was just creeping up by way of the shop-boy and art student. No one had heard yet of Russian cigarettes.

Besides these things I have named, and a few others at the same level which I have no doubt overlooked, there was really no very big and sustained advertisement going on at all. Big central drapery and provision stores had not yet learnt to advertise continually in the daily papers; many of them were still developing from moderate sized local shops in the footsteps of Nickleby's. Bicycles had not yet arrived, nor margarine, cereal foods, fountain pens, typewriters, kodaks, automobiles and all their accessories, and scores of other such things.

To compare one of the great American magazines, or even a modernised London weekly, with its equivalent of forty years ago, is an amazing revelation not only of the increased equipment of life nowadays, but of the continuous extension of strongly organised big businesses into what were then the trades and occupations of a great multitude of independent individuals. When I was young, England was far in front of America in the process, but American advertising has long since overtaken and outstripped anything we do on this side. France still follows us—now rather rapidly. Many of these big organisations seemed and still seem to be aiming at monopoly, but their sustained advertisement is the proof of their sustained sense of insecurity. Some have failed to achieve their object. Nobody has yet succeeded, for example, in replacing the small baker, though there have been various well-supported attempts; and cheese remains, like art, above all standardisations.

I suppose that, as far as provisions go, it helped greatly in the concentration of the distribution trade into big stores in England that so much of the food of the country was imported. The shipping of it necessarily accumulated it into bulk, and made bulky handling easy. And the fact that America and other new countries were exporting so much of their food production developed a collection at centres there, and so made concentration easy for them also.

It was after some rather unfruitful work for an advertising shoemaker that Dickon began to interest himself in the bicycle. Big-scale selling of boots and shoes, he said, would come a little later, when machine manufacturing was better developed, but the bicycle would not wait. The bicycle was here and now. So he jumped on to the bicycle and travelled some way on it. The more he inquired into this then fashionable toy, the more convinced he became of its future as a normal means of transport. First it would develop as a holiday amusement, and then it would cheapen down to the daily worker's needs. He attended early shows and races and himself rode with some fury. He was an early believer in the diamond frame which has long since ousted all others. He was in bicycle advertising from the first, and he started one of the earliest bicycling weeklies, the *Flying Wheel*, which he afterwards sold and which still survives in an incorporated state. He made great efforts to organise the advertisement of wayside inns in cyclists' magazines. For a time he was very keen indeed upon what he called consumers' magazines. The ordinary citizen, however, refuses to accept the specialisation implied in a specialised magazine. In the case of bicycles, motor-bicycles, and automobiles, in the world of pet-fanciers and photography, such publications have worked fairly well, but they have never yet superseded advertising to the general consumer.

Quite early in his novitiate as an advertiser, I remember Dickon pointing out to me the interesting conflict between the advertisements in what he called Trade Papers and advertising to consumers. By Trade Papers he did not mean the Trade Papers of such great industries as iron and steel, but the Trade Papers of the smaller distributor. These latter appeal to the retailer, shop-keeper or hotel-keeper or whatever he may be, and the goods advertised are often just those plausible imitations against which the big advertiser is warning his public. Often these less well-known goods are the output of minor packers and manufacturers selling on too small a scale for a public advertisement campaign, but supplying a quite sound and honest article. These typical Trade Paper advertisers want to sell their stuff to the man behind the counter and not to the public; they are on his side against his big enemies, and they expect him to pit his personal recommendation against the pervading public advertisement. The retailers' Trade Paper was in fact, according to Dickon, not advertisement, properly speaking, at all, but anti-advertisement.

But for Dickon, I suppose, I should never have seen an inch below the superficial appearances of countryside commerce. But because of the education he has given me, I recognise still in every wayside advertisement, in every article in every shop, in the steep streets of Grasse here, and upon the highway through Magagnosc to Nice, in the patches of cultivation about me, and the inscriptions upon my wine bottle and mustard jar, the flying fragments, the living details of the great battle between small and big, between the standardising organisation and the huckstering individual, which is still a dominating aspect of human life to-day.

§ 4

ONE of Dickon's main discussions in those early days concerned what he called "media." A medium for him was anything you stuck your advertisement upon—a wall, a hoarding, a railway station, a landscape, a public conveyance, a book, a newspaper or other periodical. Or it might be an Exhibition or a Market Show. And then there was the house display, the shop-window, the imposing premises, the van. He invented for these primitive explorations of what has since become, in America at least, the great science of advertising, two beautiful terms, the *advertisand*, which was what you wanted to sell, and the *advertisee*, who was the person you wanted to sell it to. A good advertisement had to reach as many advertisees as possible as inexpensively as possible; it had not only to reach them but it had to create a buying desire for the advertisand; it had not simply to do that, but it had to make the route to the purchase clear and plain. These were his criteria in his judgments on the advertisements we saw about us, and by this standard he judged his "media."

He would weigh them against each other with extreme gravity. Walls or hoardings lasted longer than any daily or weekly periodical, and he went to great pains to estimate the life of a poster; he would even waylay and talk to bill-stickers. Enamelled metal was already in use; sheets of that, he reflected, talked for years. But they were difficult to place, and if there was any need for a change of appeal they were hard to recall. Also, they tired people by repetition.

" Imagine passing the same plaque every week-day for a year! There's season-ticket holders have to. Horrible, Billy ! "

He was far in advance of the times in perceiving that an advertisement should not bore; the advertisers of those days sought strenuously to bore. He held also that landscape should be respected; he believed that it was very easy to arouse an antagonism to a commodity by rude and blatant methods. He considered the advertisements he saw in stations and vehicles abominably ill-done. They shouted where there was no need to shout. In those days railway advertisements were almost conscientiously ugly, and they vied with each other in the size of their letters. " No need for such an uproar, Billy—no need for it. You've got your people there— they're standing about and their minds are unoccupied. They're quiet and at your disposal. Ready to take an interest. Why bawl at them ? "

He was the first to offer the public anything of length and interest to read upon a railway platform.

Yet he could be compact with the best of them when the medium required it. It was he who thought of advertisements on the risers of the stair-cases going up and down to railway stations, spaces hitherto neglected and mute. How well I remember the excitement of that novel idea, the weighing of considerations, the problem of who to take it to, the feverish hope of great developments. " It must be witty," said Dickon. " Short and witty. I won't have them just yapped at." To whom should he take it ? For a time he hovered between a flea powder and a chewing gum.

It was in periodical publications that the greater future of advertising lay, he believed, and particularly in monthlies and weeklies. They were left about in the house and were turned over again and again by different people. " But advertisement must be fresh and different each time. This sort of thing—— "

Yes, it was. I remember, that same conversation in the Underground Railway I am recalling, and he pointed to a standard announcement in the back pages of some monthly magazine.

" This sort of thing is as exasperating as hiccoughs. It comes up again and again and you can't control it."

He doubted whether the daily newspapers were very much good for proprietary articles. They were good for theatres and amusements of all sorts, but not for an advertisand that had to go on selling. He watched people reading papers in trams and buses. They showed a vulture's eye for the news they wanted and a wonderful capacity for sweeping disregard-fully across the most tremendous displays of advertisements. He declared it was possible to print a newspaper advertisement so big that it was totally invisible. People would not read type that was visible three yards away, Their eyes went through the gaps.

" But any sort of stuff that has a quality of news—' Salmon is exceptionally cheap to-day,' for example, with a reason for it, or ' Mackerel in the Channel and Oranges in the Bay,' would get them. *What* Bay ? There you are ! People would read that sort of thing like any other news."

He weighed that idea carefully. Fishmongering and fruit selling were still far from any syndication or he would have started a scheme for a " Fishmongers' Chalk Board " and a " Fruit Shop Bulletin " in some of the old dailies, a sort of eleventh hour announcement of goods to hand.

And as the grouping of shops into big centralised stores, which my father had done so much to promote, went on, Dickon became more and more keen on what he called bringing the shop window into the morning paper. In those days it was beneath the dignity of the London *Times*, for example, to admit what are called displayed advertisements or break its grave gray expanses with pictures. The other papers in those con-servative days did not care to be very different from *The Times*, and for a

long time, indeed until the great Americanisation of the press by Harmsworth and Pearson, Dickon's idea remained an aspiration. Long before
it was done in England, the stores' advertisements flared all over the
American papers ; there was an interval of a quarter of a century or more
before the big London stores were brought into a similar intimate relationship to the popular press.

How recent all this seems to a man of my age ! I remember when shop
windows were made of little oblong panes, and lit in the evenings by a
few jets of unassisted gas or an oil-lamp or so, and when the aim of the
window-dresser seemed to be rather to impress the amount and nature
of his stock upon the observer than to interest and attract him. Then
came plate-glass and a depth and vastness of window-front hitherto
undreamt of, and gas-mantles and electric light. People found a new
interest in looking at the long array of shop windows, and the enterprising
heads behind them realised by degrees—and there again my father with
his " Shopping and Social Centre of North London Life," was a pioneer—
that it might be wise to allow people to make a resort of the interior of their
establishments without being compelled, as they used to be compelled,
to make purchases forthwith or get out. But for a long time the big stores
were content with the local crowds they assembled, and I believe it was
Mr. Gordon Selfridge, coming from America with the brightest and newest
ideas, who at last realised my brother's anticipation and carried his shop
window into the London daily paper.

My brother has a great admiration for Mr. Selfridge, and I have been
privileged to meet him, an unobtrusive man with something of the shy
quiet of a poet. My brother compares him to Mozart on account of his
interest and variety. " He makes some of the older advertisers sound
like the village idiot at a fair beating on a pan," said Dickon. " A great
artist ! Oh ! a very great and subtle artist ! Some day people will make
collections of those Selfridge advertisements."

So it was Dickon developed. The lax and incidental student of pure
science became the enthusiastic specialist in marketing, an active force in
that change of scale in distributing methods which is one of the most striking
aspects of my immediate world. He began as I have told, with watches
and boots and the early bicycle. He extended his interests into the special
journalism of the bicycle, and then into a great variety of magazine enterprises. He found helpers and confederates, associates with capital and
partners. He has always had the gift of being liked, and, oddly enough,
his name helped him. It gave people a shock to begin with, so that they
always remembered it distinctly, and then as they got to know him they
went about remarking upon the paradox of his sterling honesty. He
always kept faith not only with what he said but with what he thought

the other fellow understood by it.   In a little time he was the essential
partner of Clissold and Breakspear, and he had his active fingers in several
of the most promising of the new popular magazine firms that were then
appearing.

In six or seven years he was already very well off, able to marry
and establish himself in a fine house in the Cromwell Road.   Quite early
he relinquished in my favour his share in the hundred and sixty pounds
a year my mother allowed us, so that I could go and live in more comfortable
apartments near to the Royal College and carry on as a research student
there.   He went eastward to a flat in Bloomsbury until his marriage brought
him west again.

But of that marriage and of mine I must tell later.

§ 5

THERE drifts into my mind the substance of a silly little conversation that must have occurred somewhen in those old days before our divergent marriages had diminished our mutual familiarity. It was before my marriage anyhow, because I see Dickon in my only armchair as he talks, and there is a litter of notebooks and drawing material on the table.

He had been asking questions about the drift of my stuff and confessing himself baffled by it. "You're the brains of the family, Billy," he said a little ruefully. "Undoubtedly you are the brains of the family."

"Different brains," I said. "There is one glory of the sun and another of the moon and another of the stars."

"And another of the hoardings and magazine-covers," said Dickon—still a dozen years from sky-signs and twenty years from smoke-writing on the blue.

He fingered the pages of my first paper in the Philosophical Transactions, a tetter of formulæ, and then ran his eye over the rest of the contents.

"Blastopore of the snail," he objected. "Fancy poking about at the blastopore of the snail! It's—indelicate. And cryo-hydrates! This chap Oliver Lodge seems to be all over them. Wonder what they are! Well, this is your affair, Billy. It's up to you to display the name of Clissold properly in these Philosophical Transactions. If that is the end of life. Not my pitch. Not in the least my pitch. I wouldn't try to sell even a stethoscope through these Philosophical Transactions. No."

He ran his hand over the edges of the pages with a shuddering sound and reflected profoundly. A liveliness became apparent presently beneath his depression.

"But all the same, Billy, one of these days, mark my words, I'm going to cheer up this respectable and awe-inspiring periodical. Just to please myself. I know exactly what I'm going to do. I'm going round to the Secretary of the Royal Society, and I'm going to put such an innocent-looking contrast past him that he won't see for a moment what I'm up to, and then I'm going to give these dull old Philosophical Transactions of yours a real, spirited Christmas number, a genuine advertisement display. I'm going to have everything—coloured inset leaflets, extra sheets in the cover, cosmetics, lip-salves, hair-dyes, wigs, corsets—*men's* corsets!—scents, sensational pictures of lingerie, toilet fittings in ivory and silver and gold, the Parisian note loud and clear, soaps recommended by Lillie

Langtry and Sarah Bernhardt, and complexion stuff by Mary Anderson, ravishing portraits of these ladies in colour, super-colour, bath scenes by Alma Tadema, Lucullus bathrooms, smart restaurants, hotels, plages, Monte Carlo, Ascot week, Cowes, grey toppers, hatters to the Prince of Wales, manicure establishments, turf commission agents, dealers in real diamonds."

I said his advertisers wouldn't like that.

" The poor old dears ! Temptation of St. Anthony wouldn't be in the same field with it ! " said Dickon with the confidence of a man who knows what advertisers will stand. He did not worry about them. He was thinking of grave, earnest men in spectacles, aghast.

" Tonics," he said, as an afterthought. " Cures for debility. Ginger. Do you sing in your bath ? "

Dickon never had a proper respect for the Royal Society. " They lead devoted lives," I said.

" Bah ! " said Dickon. " I know 'em. I know their secret cravings. They'll eat those advertisements. Doctor Faustus asks for his youth again ! Mephistopheles restores it—small bottles, one guinea. You bet."

" Counfound it ! " I remonstrated. " Dignified work ! Vital work ! Why *will* you always insult men of science ? "

And then at the sight of my artless indignation he threw a great fit of chuckles. " Oh, Billy ! " he cried. " Oh, Billy ! I got you," and kicked his legs about. . . .

Always a great lout, my brother Dickon.

§ 6

WATCHING Dickon and watching the world through Dickon's eyes has been at times almost more instructive than watching it through my own. He embarked upon advertising at first, as I suppose most of the early advertisers did, in a cheerfully piratical spirit.   It was to be his way of " getting it "— and that was all that mattered.

But as time went on and his interests spread and his wealth and power increased, he was obliged almost in spite of himself to recognise the part that he and his like were playing in the rephrasing of human life.   They were assisting at a synthesis that was replacing the scattered autonomous various individualism of the past by a more and more intricate interdepend- ent life.   He began to think of advertising less and less as an adventure, and more and more as an integral social function, with obligations and standards of its own.

Temperamentally he had never liked falsehood ; he had disliked even reserve if it misled ; he always kept as clear as he could from the pill and patent medicine field, in which lying and bluff figure so largely, but he had never felt quite happy in his assertion that in the long run it was better to understate than overstate in an advertisement.   It is largely true, but it has never been wholly true, that for the individual in business honesty is the best policy.   For a trade as a whole it is certainly true, but not for the incidental adventurer.   He can achieve his " get away," as the American criminals phrase it, leaving his trade discredited.

Dickon has been a prime mover in the organisation of advertisers into a professional organisation since the war.   He has helped to found lecture- ships and establish examinations in advertisement.   I believe he would like to see a special university degree, Bachelors and Doctors of Advertisement. Some day we may come to that.   Even before the war he was thinking of schemes for making deliberate falsehood, either in an advertisement or in the news columns of a newspaper, a felony.   " If it was felony for our father to issue a false balance-sheet which only caused people monetary loss, it is far more felony to tell some poor old woman in a cottage that the filth you want to sell cures the pain in her back, and so waste her last chance of proper treatment for kidney or cancer."

" Proper treatment ! " said I.   " Where ? "

Dickon stuck to his own line of thought.   " Here we have people making fortunes by keeping people ill, misinforming them about their symptoms, inducing them to trust in misdescribed goods.   Billy, it's a crime against the Empire. It fills the streets with uncomfortable people. Poor mothers, induced to give the children they cared for innutritious muck, so that they grow up disappointing weeds. All these weedy people in the streets, in the buses, everywhere—just because you let advertisers say their muck is flesh-forming and frame-building and bone-making when every competent authority knows that it isn't. The poor mother isn't a competent authority. How can she be ? She finds it out too late. Can't help herself. And in the long run it's bad for advertising. *It's bad for advertising.* The advertising world has to sacrifice its black sheep. *Has* to ! Advertisement, Billy, is too big a thing for lying—too big a thing. Much too big a thing. It's the web of modern life ; it's the call of the flock. For most people, flat statements in advertisements is warranty, absolute warranty. And it ought to be. They take it as they take the news in the adjacent columns. The voice of print, Billy, is the voice of God. To them it is. And it's up to us to see that they get it divine and true."

I raised my eyebrows.

" Divine and true," said Dickon, raising his voice above me massively.

I said I supposed our legal theory was that if there was misdescription there could be an action for damages.

" But how can the poor mutts bring actions against a firm with scores of thousands to play with ? How can they do it ? No, I want the fellows handled by the Public Prosecutor at the instance of a properly constituted Advertisement Society, and sent to jail."

I was amused. It was down at Dorking, and in 1912 or 1913, that he discoursed in this fashion. We had been playing tennis and we were on the terrace above the court. Dickon was sitting in a deck-chair looking flushed and freckled and over-healthy and very, very earnest, drinking an inadvisable whisky and soda.

I raised the old issue between his individualism and my Socialism. What was all this talk about ? Where were his lifelong principles ? He was preaching rank Socialism. Wasn't *caveat emptor* the sound principle for an individualist world ?

" Individualist be blowed ! " said Dickon. " *Caveat emptor* was all very well between two Latin peasants at a bargain in that little old parochial Roman world—as it *was*, Billy, as it was—but the odds have altered now. I'm thinking of those weedy children and the old woman with a pain in her side."

§ 7

THE Great War did much to develop Dickon's conception of his rôle in the world. He expanded mightily upon a diet of propaganda. There was a phase in the Reconstruction Period when it seemed to him that only an adequate advertisement campaign was needed to achieve the Millennium. I have given these vignettes of him in the eighties, in the later nineties, and in the pre-war days as he grew in strength and confidence. Let me anticipate for a section and complete his apotheosis of advertisement. I must recall what I can of a discourse of his towards the end of 1918. Then you will see how the imagination of Dickon the advertiser grew from that of the watch peddler he was forty years ago to its present dimensions.

If the Great War made nothing, it did at least appear for a time to have disorganised everything. The idea that society had been shattered and would need rebuilding was very prevalent in 1915. Everything was going to be rebuilt, fairer, sounder, juster, happier; that went without saying. That was the justification for a war that was otherwise inexplicable; it was a Phœnix flare. By 1916 this had become a standard promise for all the optimists who were engaged in whipping up the flagging enthusiasm of the nation. It crystallised into the word Reconstruction. All our English world talked Reconstruction, from the pro-war intellectuals, who dropped off from the war propaganda into silence or opposition after the collapse of the Stockholm Conference, to the deep *John Bull* bellowings of Horatio Bottomley, most popular of patriots and stimulators. " A world fit for heroes," said Lloyd George—phrase unforgettable. How tremendously that word Reconstruction was bandied about ! It waved as gallantly, it vanished at last as abruptly, as a contested banner in a riot. Many of us can still feel uncomfortable if some thoughtless person chances to revive it.

There was much pitiful moral tragedy in that fiasco, but to begin with Reconstruction embodied some bold and righteous hopes. And it completed the evolution of Dickon. Under its spell he became temporarily a Utopian, more Utopian even than I in my Brompton days, and planned a world which never had been, but which, it seemed to him then, might very easily be. He had realised the tremendous possibilities of handling people in great masses revealed by this war advertising, in which he had played a conspicuous part ; possibilities of teaching hygienic practices for example, suggesting new habits or routines, restating and changing general ideas, altering outlooks altogether. For a time these realisations possessed him completely.

His Utopianism was amateurish ; he had all the crudity of a sudden convert. He wanted to see the energy that had been gathered into the great Ministry of Munitions turned directly to the material rearrangement of the country, the railways re-made, the countryside re-planned, slums swept away, old beauties restored, and much of our present towns and cities rebuilt. Then manifestly the war would not have been in vain. He saw himself directing the demobilising millions back to abundant work, and homes renewed and happy, through a vast advertisement organisation. " A land fit for heroes," he quoted continually—in his profession they call that sort of thing a " slogan "—and it seemed plain to him after the vision of large-scale human co-operation the war had given him, that the whole food supply of the world was capable of control, that population could be poured from district to district like water, instructed in the requirements of its new surroundings and held to its effort. He had some magnificent moments in that Utopian phase of his.

" The war's been a bloody mess, Billy, but at least it's taught us to handle things in the big way," he said : " the advertising way. We learnt it by selling mustard and motor-cars, but these were only the things we learnt upon."

And again : " Advertising ; what is it ? Education. Modern education, nothing more or less. The airs schoolmasters and college dons give themselves are extraordinary. They think they're the only people who teach. *We* teach ten times as much. Why ! even the little chaps who write the attractions in the big weeklies and monthlies, Kipling, Jack London, Bennett, Galsworthy, Wodehouse, all that lot—teach more than the schoolmasters do.

" Schoolmasters ! What do you mean by education ? When you get down to hard tacks. *Just old-fashioned, primitive advertisement done by word of mouth in a room !* Why ! a class-room schoolmaster teaching by shouts ought to be as out-of-date nowadays as a town-crier !

" The only use I've got for schools now is to fit people to read advertisements. After that *we* take on. Yes, we—the advertisers. You may laugh, Billy ; it's true. All new ideas come as a shock at first. Don't just laugh at it like that. Don't sit like an oaf and grin. Tell me what's wrong with it.

" And even *in* the schools we could put ten times better lessons over the heads of the masters now—with a properly organised cinema. Ten times better. But we leave the cinema to a lot of music-hall muckers and close-up chorus girls, as though it wasn't worth using."

He laid great stress upon the cinema, but I do not recall him saying anything about broadcasting in those Reconstruction days. But, of course ! One forgets how fast the world moves. In 1919 there was no broadcasting. With broadcasting I can see Dickon reducing his poor schoolmasters to the last extremity of usherdom—mere conductors on his omnibus to knowledge. Before broadcasting he had at least to leave them an occasional use of their voices. Now they would just hum on the loud-speaker and stand about and mark registers. Gagged, perhaps, to prevent any personal intervention.

His denunciation of schoolmasters increased and intensified, of schoolmasters and the clergy, as his imagination of what might be done with the crowd developed. He would talk to me in his hectoring, elder-brother way, but always with a twinkle in his eye and a touch of burlesque in his tone and an evident readiness to jump overboard from his argument at any time with a sudden splash of laughter if it became too difficult to maintain ; and his argument was always exaltation of the modern advertising method and always contempt for the refinements of the intellectual world.

" These fellows in caps and gowns think you can make things decent by being genteel in a corner and shuddering and sneering whenever you hear a noise. I ask you ! You've got to *explain* your Millennium to people, Billy ; you've got to make 'em want it, and you've got to tell 'em how to get it. Then they'll get it. Just as they get Lucas lamps and safety-razor blades or any other old thing. The advertisand is different, but the method is the same. Why, Billy ! Look at things plainly. With all reverence—— "

He adapted his ruddy face roughly and quickly to express all reverence. It was just an habitual concession unnecessary in my case.

" What were the twelve Apostles ? Drummers, just drummers. Travelling in salvation. Introducing a new line. Why did Paul raise his voice at Athens ? Because he hadn't a Megaphone. And the miracles they did ? Sample bottles. To this day it's advertisement. What is a wayside crucifix ?—an advertisement of the faith. What is Christianity ?—an advertisement campaign. Tell 'em. Tell 'em. Tell 'em all you can. It's the method of social existence."

He turned to biology, to the poetry of life.

" The very flowers by the wayside, Billy, are advertisements for bees ! "

My grin armed the fighting spirit in him.

" Vulgar you think it is ? "

" Frightfully."

" If there's anything vulgar about modern advertisement, Billy, it's because it's been so concerned about pills and soap and pickles. Just a passing phase. A man or a class or a religion or—anything that will not advertise isn't fit to exist in the world. It means it doesn't really believe in itself. To want to exist and not to dare to exist is something beneath vulgarity. . . . That's why I have such a contempt for your rotten, shy sit-in-the-corner-and-ask-the-dear-Prince-of-Wales-to-dinner-once-a-year Royal Society.

" If the soap-boilers did no more for soap than your old Royal Society does for science," said Dickon, " nobody would wash."

§ 8

But this post-war talk is, as I intimated, out of place. I will return to the Period of Reconstruction later. If nothing else was reconstructed then, we were, and our post-war interchanges form a distinct and separate chapter in our history. Before I go on to tell how the war shook up and released and stimulated our ideas about things in general, I must tell of his marriage and of a considerable divergence of our ways of living. When I was three-and-twenty things happened to make me break away from the life of pure research I had seemed destined to follow. I became an employee and later a director of Romer, Steinhart, Crest and Co., I left London to live at Downs-Peabody, and I became more and more involved in the huge industrial developments that have occupied the greater half of my life. The had little or no advertising side. They brought me into a world of associates quite apart from Dickon's ; they carried me abroad for long spells and made me by comparison cosmopolitan.

He remained extremely English. He lived for some years after his marriage in the Cromwell Road, and then he bought Lambs Court near Dorking and became a substantial figure in the substantial suburbanism of Surrey. I, too, married a little while after he did, but marriage, which stabilised him, disorganised all my intentions about life. My marriage was a failure. I will tell of it in due coarse, but for some years a certain chagrin may have helped to make my visits to Dickon's home less frequent than they might otherwise have been. His marriage was heartily successful, ostentatiously successful ; and for a while I suspected him, I think now unjustly, of feeling that I was to blame for the muddle I was in.

Ostentatiously successful I write, but whether it is to be regarded as a perfect marriage I do not know. I doubt if there is any such thing as a perfect marriage. It may happen—as an accident. To this day I find a certain lurking perplexity about my sister-in-law in my mind ; I have never been able to exercise it. There was something extraordinarily fine about her—and something cold and aloof. Nor do I yet see as a clear and consistent thing Dickon's relations to her. He was so incapable of aloofness. He was floridly and magnificently loyal to her and she was profoundly loyal to him, but I do not know, I cannot imagine what there was down there at the very bottom of things between them. Was it love, the tenderness and infinite consideration she had for him ? It was love at first, no doubt. And mixed with his infinite respect for her, his pride and his rare overwhelming tenderness, there was something resentful. Did he always suppress that resentment in her presence ? I do not know.

I will tell as much as I know, what I saw, what I inferred, and leave it to the reader. Plainly there are things here outside the range of my feelings and experiences.

She was a very small person; she had fine exquisite features; she was not a short woman, not dwarfish in any way, but simply made upon a delicate scale; she looked much more fragile than she was, and when I first encountered her she was a little strained and artificial in her manner because she was so valiantly resolved not to be shy. I met her only a month or so before the marriage, and when the marriage was already fixed. Dickon had discovered her in Bloomsbury, and I had a sense that she had been sprung upon me after a period of uneasiness and concealment on Dickon's part. There was a sort of tea-party in Dickon's sitting-room, and she was there under the protection of a cousin, whom I forget altogether, and I had the spectacle of Dickon, my stern, dogmatic brother, almost dishevelled with nervousness, proffering tea, handing cakes, asking me—*me!*—if I took sugar, and watching my face for the faintest intimations of a judgment.

She was little, not very well dressed, guarded. That much I saw at the time. We talked about pictures, about which none of us knew very much, and about music. At Lambs Court there is still a photograph of her in those early days. One had to sit quite still for some seconds in those days in order to be photographed, and so if one did not get blurred one looked like wax-works. She had contrived to sit quite still. How unaccustomed now are our eyes to those later Victorian costumes! She had a collar to her dress that reached to her little ears and great puffed sleeves and a whale-bone figure.

I forget most of the incidents of that meeting now, but I remember Dickon afterwards parting from me at Hyde Park Corner. "You don't see what there is in her at first, old man," he said, for the third or fourth time. Though I had never said a word to betray that I did not think her the most obviously and instantly desirable of all possible sisters-in-law. I had hardly said anything. I did not know what to say.

On our way to Hyde Park Corner he had told me things about her. She was the daughter of a doctor in Bloomsbury, a very competent general practitioner. She was a connection of his early partner, Brakespear. She had passed some examinations—I forget what they were but they were difficult ones. She drew beautifully. She was clever at music and spoke French and German wonderfully well. She was an only child, which, I think, accounts for a sort of reserved inwardness in her manner; she was untrained in the exposures, criticisms, recriminations, and habitual intimacies of family life.

She read, I was to discover later, and she studied, but she was not accustomed to talk. There were moments when I was to watch her listening to Dickon's discourse and compare her in my mind with a passenger waiting for a ferry with the river in flood. Waiting as one waits on a fine agreeable day when waiting is no hardship. Waiting, moreover, with no intention of travelling on the stream. And—to begin with, she was, in a peculiar still way, in love with Dickon and devoted to him. He, too, was in love with her, but just the least bit disappointed, I felt, that she did not make a better show in front of me. Once or twice during those early encounters he tried to draw her out and exhibit her paces, but she had little, scarcely perceptible, ways of stopping that. It was amusing to see Dickon interested in an article that declined to be pushed. He would have been a terrible impresario for a showy woman.

I began to think her a little less undistinguished after a fourth or fifth meeting, and at the wedding I had a feeling that for some obscure reason she had hitherto been concealing from me and the world in general an ability to be, if she chose, conspicuously pretty.

But I still didn't see why it had been necessary for my bright and exuberant Dickon to marry her. I did not see why he of all people should be mated to incarnate restraint.

It was a thoroughly respectable wedding, and the household they set up in the Cromwell Road was in the highest degree respectable. A time was to come when I was to think a lot of Minnie's taste, but in the furnishing of that first house nothing of her sensitive fastidiousness appeared. Perhaps it was not yet fully awake. I suppose Dickon must have just carried her through the furniture shop with him and given her no time to meditate. The house was, my brief disturbing wife declared, when she paid her introductory visit, " utterly and hopelessly *banal*."

I was married, as I will tell later, about a year and a half after Dickon, and my marriage took him by surprise as much as his had taken me. I kept Clara an even closer secret from Dickon than he had kept Minnie from me. Perhaps I felt what his opinion would be of the Allbut ménage. I sprang her upon Dickon and Minnie within a few weeks of our marriage. I took her to call upon Minnie. I went in a faintly irritated mood because Clara had seen fit to supplement her wardrobe from an aunt's supplies, and had suddenly become much more a woman of the world and much less of a hard-up art girl than was seemly in the future wife of a struggling research student.

A natural antagonism flared up at the first encounter of Minnie and Clara. Clara was an effusive human being, and particularly so with strangers. She fell upon Minnie with cries and embraces. " What an exquisite *little* dear you are ! " she said.

I was beginning to forget that Minnie was so very small ; I saw her disentangling herself with an unobtrusive distaste from those swift familiarities.

Clara praised her clothes loudly—they were in the current fashion of the time—insisted upon regarding them as the triumph of a special effort, and then, with an obscure perception of rebuff, turned her enthusiasm to the house and the furniture. " Jolly *good* things you have ! " she exclaimed. " Where did you get them all ? "

" Dickon and I went to Maple's," said Minnie, regarding her strictly later Victorian surroundings for a moment as though she had just seen them for the first time.

Clara looked round for some piece that might be exceptional. There was nothing exceptional. So she pounced on a book.

" *You* read George Meredith too ! " she said.

" Here's Dickon ! " said Minnie, relieved as the door opened. . . .

I became more acutely aware of the sketchy quality in Clara's smartness as Dickon came in. It was my turn now to watch for unspoken verdicts. Clara's way with men was sometimes a little over-confident. . . .

It was not a good call. Dickon, I could see, did not warm to Clara. Minnie seemed deliberately to be refrigerating the conversation, and we left with Clara in a splendid rage.

" So *that's* my prospective sister-in-law ! " I remember her saying on the doorstep.

She paused. " *Watchful !* " she whispered. " She watches."

And then she embarked upon an exhaustive summary of Minnie's deficiencies. The burthen was that there was nothing in Minnie, but for all that it was clear that there was much to be said about her. Firstly, she was personally insignificant. Secondly, she was cold-blooded. Next, her style of dressing was provincial, timid, genteel. She was under-dressed. On such an occasion as this it was rude and offhand to under-dress. One was expected to dress a little. To meet a chosen sister-in-law was an important occasion and ought to be treated as such. One ought to make an effort.

The ashes of our controversy over the borrowed finery glowed again for a moment.

Minnie's furniture and her household management, insisted Clara, had the same limitations as her costume and the same uncivil negligence. The tea, for some reason, had greatly offended Clara. There had been a lack of variety in the tea ; for the first visit of an imminent sister-in-law there ought to have been display ; everybody nowadays gave little sandwiches, cucumber sandwiches, paste sandwiches. Amusing things. Light things one just took in one's hand. It looked skimpy not to do so. And dull. Buttered buns were ridiculous ; hefty things like that ought to be relegated to the nursery. (At tea Clara had " adored " buttered buns, had received them with acclamation.)

And that furniture ! That *heavy* furniture ! Maple's ! Carte blanche to them to furnish, no doubt. No individuality. No character. Where *could* my brother have met her ? No doubt we should have to go to dinner there so soon as we were married. It would be our first dinner party together. Could we last two hours ? What should we talk about ? Even in that forty minutes' call the talk had caught and hung time after time.

" Well, anyhow," reflected Clara " I shan't want much of a frock for *that !* "

I said very little to Clara's tirade, because it shocked and irritated me to hear my own secret judgments on Dickon's wife caricatured, made monstrous and preposterous, and expressed in terms of intense personal hostility. " She isn't so bad," I said. " And she makes Dickon happy."

" *Does* she make him happy ?

" Your brother," said Clara, following up her own question, " would never own to a failure if he felt he could pull it through to look like a success. He's—stiff stuff. As stiff as you are. Obviously she's as flat as ditch-water. Uninteresting. Prosaic. She paralyses him. If she hadn't been there—he would have been different. . . . Sooner or later he'll be going round the corner. You mark my words, Billy. But he'll never own up."

I detested her for saying it, but there was something of a likeness to Dickon in that.

" And she won't either," jerked Clara, suddenly completing her impression.

" Won't what ?

" Own up."

§ 9

THERE with the help of Clara's vivid expressiveness, which sometimes succeeded in being on the whole unaccountably right with every detail wrong, you have a sketch of Minnie. She was neither flat nor prosaic ; she was never uninteresting ; but it is true that she never seemed to take hold of Dickon, and that she did not seem to take hold of life. He had taken hold of her, and she liked that ; it warmed her as much as anything could warm her, but there was nothing about her holding on to him if presently he let go. She was, I had long realised, a creature of fine secondary shades and complicated shynesses and reserves, and I have never known anyone with a less voracious will to live.

I doubted from the first whether he appreciated her fine shades. His natural disposition was towards poster colourings more suitable for display. But gradually I came to see that it was not the delicacy nor the fine shades that he cared about. He had a profound unshakable belief in her honesty, loyalty and common sense, and she justified his belief. Whatever else she may or may not have been to him, she was, so to speak, his treasury, his brake, his wary councillor. And though she was never a brilliant talker in society, I noted that when he quoted her sayings and cited her opinions, there came out a shrewd individuality quite different from his own.

They did not have children for a while. Then in the course of four or five years came a couple of sons and a daughter, and they went to the space and dignity of Lambs Court and took a great flat in Queen Anne's Mansions as their *pied-à-terre* in London. It was only after her death and the marriage of young Richard that Dickon left Queen Anne's Mansions for the chambers in Bordon Street in which this book begins. There were gaps sometimes of two or three years when I would be abroad, or in the north, or in the Midlands, and when I saw little of Dickon and Minnie, and so my memories pass almost abruptly from that rather commonplace, rather nervously self-conscious and apologetic home in the Cromwell Road to a very prettily furnished and well-ordered country house, with a small but very well-dressed and maternal Minnie, keeping a competent eye on her nursemaids and instructing an entirely respectful gardener in the development of the very beautiful terrace gardens she created. The two figures do not merge so completely as they would have done if our acquaintance had been continuous. In that case I have no doubt the earlier, immature, more fragile and shyer Minnie would have been replaced day by day and bit by bit and effaced altogether from my memory.

In that second phase Minnie had far more confidence, far more grip upon the world, than in the first. There was a subtle difference in her relations with Dickon, but it would be hard to define what that difference was. Perhaps she had passed through phases of dismay and reassurance. I thought his attitude towards her was a little more effusive and formal than it had been, and more habitual. I thought that she seemed no longer to be observing him with the happy interest of their earlier time. It was as though she had got used to him and had accepted something that had not been present in the beginning, or resigned herself to the absence of something she had once thought there.

She had become a great gardener, which was rather wonderful after a girlhood in Bloomsbury, and she was also beginning to know quite a lot about furniture and pictures. Later on she was to become something of a buyer of pictures and etchings. She would help struggling artists, until she felt the touch of proprietorship to which the helped are prone. The children were happy and delightful then, in a perfect nursery and with an excellent, kindly nurse ; but I do not remember ever seeing Minnie romp with them, and I doubt if in all her life she ever lost her temper with them. Yet she loved them. Flowers and furnishing, I think, she cared for more than living things ; she could do so much more for them without provoking them to come back upon her clamorously. They did not climb upon her, they did not shout or hammer at her, as human beings might at any time do.

After a time I went no more to Lambs Court. I stayed away for nearly seven years. While Dickon's marriage had turned out successfully, mine had ended in the uncomfortable tangle I will describe later. I was tied to Clara legally for the rest of my life, and unable to marry again. I was welcome at Lambs Court as a sort of bachelor brother, very welcome, even after I had been cited as a co-respondent in the Evans divorce case, but I felt a certain exemplariness in Dickon's attitude towards me and an implicit criticism in the immense discreet silences of Minnie. There were times when Dickon's gestures, pauses, acts seemed to say almost as plainly as though he spoke the words : " My dear fellow, why are you in this uneasy mess ? It is so perfectly simple. All you have to do is to marry Minnie, make much of her, stick to her, stand up for her, stick to business—and keep strange women in their proper place. Out of the picture. And there you are, you know ! "

Quite possibly my suspicions were unjust. At any rate he was habitually proud of her and as good and faithful a husband as most of the rich and rising business men of Surrey.

Then came my attempt to live with Mrs. Evans. That was in the turn of the century and people in England were still unprepared to tolerate a ménage, however stable, of two unmarried people. So long as I was a man of the world, carrying on a series of incidental intrigues almost openly, I was socially acceptable anywhere ; but an attempt at illicit domesticity, with a still undivorced Clara, however disreputable, in existence, was too much for the standards of the time. If I could have divorced Clara and married Sirrie Evans, all would have been well. I wouldn't accept that verdict. I fought. I betrayed excessive resentment. I would not ask Minnie for any help in the matter, I made no attempt to bring her and Sirrie together, I said nothing to Dickon, but I felt acutely their failure to apprehend our situation. Minnie ignored it. She did not know this Mrs. Evans, and apparently she would not know this Mrs. Evans. She asked me to come to Lambs Court alone, and I never answered her invitation. I did not see her again or communicate directly with her until a year or more after Sirrie's death.

To this day that lack of initiative perplexes me. By the time of the Evans affair she and I had become very friendly. She did not know Sirrie, she may not have been prepared to take any very serious risks about her, but still she might have assumed that I should not have become attached to a woman without good qualities, and it would have been quite possible for her to have found out and met Sirrie in some roundabout way before committing herself. But she just did nothing. She was one of a number of people who just did nothing to help us. Something cold and distant there was in that. Or something profoundly timid ? Or some aversion from relationships into which there entered a possible thread of passion ?

Dickon knew Sirrie slightly. One might have imagined that he could have broken down that icy barrier by a word or so. But he did not, and perhaps he could not. The barrier may not have been solely for the benefit of Sirrie ; I do not know. Sirrie may have symbolised many things for Minnie and Dickon that had little to do with me. I continued to meet Dickon in London. We had both become members of the Ermine Club, and we would lunch or dine and gossip together without any allusion to the complete separation of our households. Nothing was ever explained. We belonged to the same group of after-lunch talkers. We gibed at each other's opinions and went to one or two theatres together. But about the rest of his life during that estrangement I made no enquiry beyond such information as he volunteered. I continued to be aware of Minnie only in relation to him.

He varied towards her no doubt. Sometimes when I met him in London Minnie was as remote from him but as necessary to the world and as much taken for granted as the Atlantic or the Equator. At other times he was full of quotations from her and references to her. Then, oddly enough, I was not so sure of his serene and complete assurance about her. It has been the common habit of our two lives never to pry into the intimate proceedings of the other, but I have had a feeling that in these phases of allusion, these passages peppered with " My wife says this " and " Minnie does that," he perceived himself under a necessity to maintain her. Yet it would be difficult to define what it was he maintained her against.

Whatever imperfections and difficulties there were in his married life, whatever hidden relaxations there were of its outward integrity, none of them ever came to the surface as a visible infringement of Minnie's dignities. There were, I happen to know, what the French call *passades*, but the heroines were obscure young ladies, amply compensated and silenced. He was, I repeat, as good and faithful a husband as most honourable, prosperous men.

One spring day in 1910 I found myself put down at a Romer lunch party next to Minnie. I was sure they would put me next to her as soon as I saw her in the drawing-room. She had altered very little ; she was, perhaps, stronger and firmer and better dressed. She looked like very good porcelain amidst the metallic splendours of Lady Romer's assembly.

I put as good a face as I could upon the encounter. I asked after Lambs Court and the children.

" William the Second," she said, " is absurdly like you. He has a gift. He is going to draw—wonderfully. The two brothers together are like Dickon and you—even to the way they insult each other."

She said something about my coming down to see them.

Then in a pause she made a great effort. " Billy," she said very softly, " I was so sorry to hear of your loss."

I was too astonished to say anything.

" I wanted to write. I was stupid. . . . I often don't do—things I want to do."

She was feeling her way towards an apology, and she was flushed and sincere. It was a sort of confession—for one who could not confess. She became more incomprehensible to me than ever. I was quite unable to get her into relationship with that old and now healing sore. I dismissed the attempt.

" I would like to see something of William the Second," I said, after a clumsy interval. " I've neglected my godson."

" Next week-end ? " she said as awkwardly. . . .

It was the most intimate moment we ever had together.

Thereafter our outward friendship—and I can imagine no friendship of Minnie's that except for the rarest moments was other than external—was resumed.

§ 10

BETWEEN that meeting and my later memories of Minnie, streams all the storm, tragedy, and illumination of the war. The war that has changed so much and yet at times seems to have changed nothing.

I never expected the war to happen until it was actually happening. Romer, Steinhart, Crest and Co. were naturally in touch with much pre-war armament business, and armament seemed to us—to me, at any rate, it seemed—a foolish way of using up good metal that fools had got to pay for as highly as possible. I still think the war need not have happened, and that the amount of good that has come out of it is incomparably smaller than the waste and evil. It is easy to be wise after the event and say how inevitable the catastrophe was, but I do not think it was inevitable even so late as July, 1914. More intelligent men in the Foreign Offices could, I think, have averted it even then. But few of us were intelligent and imaginative enough to realise the enormity of the disaster until it was upon us. We expected a quick war, possible humiliations, great changes of the map and far less strain, destruction, and uprooting. Most of our Governments and rulers were as little able to foresee and fear as so many mentally defective children with a box of matches in a powder magazine. At last a match was dropped. Then for a time the skies were darkened, the world was full of thunder, the torrents of disaster poured. There was a clatter of falling things, a flare of burning. Millions of young men suffered detestable things and died and passed. And at last when it had come to seem that no end would ever be possible, the storm was over and the skies cleared magically.

The tornado struck Lambs Court, seemed likely to extinguish the life of Lambs Court altogether, and left it at last—with scarcely a flower-bed ruffled. Dick and William, my nephews, both went into the war and survived it, Dick with a bullet wound and a six months' spell of prison in Germany after Gough's disaster in 1918. Indeed, Lambs Court came through it amazingly. Week-end parties were already resumed in 1919. And Dickon was made a baronet! Dickon was made a baronet and Minnie became Lady Clissold—to my infinite amazement and perplexity.

The war, I say, took me by surprise, but so soon as it was under way my rôle was marked out for me. I was too old for the earlier enlistments, and I doubt if in any case I should have volunteered. I gravitated naturally to technical work, and was presently involved in the new-formed Ministry of Munitions. I did four years of bitter contentious work, and I should suppose that Roderick and I between us saved the British taxpayer many, probably negligible, millions of pounds. My estimates of current honesty and current intelligence were considerably lowered by those experiences; I conceived a passionate contempt and distaste for the higher ranks of the British Army that I still have trouble in controlling, and I came to consider and treat the military, naval, and aerial expert, salaried adviser of the War Office to-day and highly salaried official of an armament group to-morrow, as the moral inferior of a Constantinople tourists' dragoman.

At the end I dodged the shower of honours with considerable difficulty. There were a number of people who were deeply concerned that I should get something and be generally soothed, pacified, implicated, and shut up. I transferred a particularly persistent suggestion of a K.B.E. to a useful subordinate who might have been passed over, the sort of man to appreciate it, and I tried to use whatever claim to attention I might have in hunting down one or two exceptionally scandalous cases. In that I failed completely. The Press would not touch my entirely convincing facts. Nobody would touch them. One of my worst offenders married his loot to American money and became a bright ornament for any London dinner party; another took the fancy of Royalty; another embarrassed me by appearing on the board of an allied steel firm with which we had the friendliest relations. After a while I realised that I was being unreasonable and self-righteous. I began to laugh at my own virtue. If there was to be a real inquisition into stolen goods, where should we end?

Dickon was more surprised by the war even than I was. He had never believed that these European armies were really in earnest, and he had been inclined to approve of German imperialism as of something pleasantly flamboyant and picturesque in an age inclined to be prosaic. It advertised amazingly. When the guns began to go off he was outraged beyond measure at the breach of faith. It was as though a large bill-stickers' hoarding had begun to kill and eat people. There seemed nothing for it at first but violence with an axe.

He was furiously indignant against the Germans. So indeed was I in the early months. So was all England. At this resurrection of war. The awakening of England in the autumn of 1914 may have been uncritical and foolish, but it was thoroughly honest, and so far at any rate as the million odd volunteers were concerned, heroic. By the end of the year Dickon had somehow contrived to get into khaki. He was fully fifty, and I do not know how he managed it, but he did. He had once in the early bicycle days spent some months in that now forgotten supplement to the military might of Britain, the Volunteers. He was keen then on cyclist riflemen. He may have exaggerated his former standing in that force. At any rate, he was taken on. I cherish a snapshot of his substantial figure with a lieutenant's star upon his collar, looking very earnest and unsuitable. Afterwards, for some reason of etiquette in connection with supplies, they jumped him up to be a temporary colonel, and at that he could stand beside the stoutest of them, stouter than any and taller than most. He was trained at Checkershill and then on Cumberbatch Moor, but that was as near as he travelled on the road to the trenches. He went to France, indeed, but by a different route. They found they wanted him on the commissariat.

A man who could advertise things for retail sale was naturally supposed by the military authorities to know how to buy and distribute anything. He did some thoroughly sound work for them, and afterwards he became a great factor in civil food-control organisation. He worked hard under Rhondda, an able, ailing, concentrated man who might be alive to-day, perhaps, if it had not been for the strain of that work, and after Rhondda died Dickon went on with Clynes, a Labour leader, who had joined the Government. Through Dickon I met Clynes on two or three occasions. He was a little intelligent-looking cockatoo of a man, who, like Brer Rabbit, kept on saying nuffing all the time, in the face of every conversational allurement. Perhaps, like one or two others of his colleagues, he needs a platform, a large hall and adequate interruption, before he can really express what is in him.

" Does he know anything ? " I asked Dickon afterwards.

" He knows what he doesn't know," said Dickon.   " He's perfectly satisfactory to work with."

A foretaste of the Labour Government of 1924.

Dick, my elder nephew, volunteered before his father at the beginning ; William was taken later, protesting, but without bitterness, that it wasn't his fight ; Lambs Court was presently filled with convalescents and a trained staff, and my niece Winnie was sent up to London, out of sentimental range, to work with great energy at the manufacture of bandages, a little resentful because her mother would not allow her to drive a car for the Ministry of Munitions. Minnie presided capably at Lambs Court, and presently, after strains and endless petty hardships, scanty food, darkened homes, tiresome air-raids, gleams of leave for the boys, almost overwhelming anxiety over Dick's disappearance—he was " missing " for three weeks— and a sort of universal neurasthenia, the war came abruptly to its hysterical end. Down either side of Pall Mall hundreds of captured guns were displayed, the streets of London were alight again and swarming with a vast, wearily enthusiastic multitude which laughed and shouted because it did not want to howl and cry, and the war was over. And Dickon was talking with passionate conviction of a Britain born again out of these troubles and of a " reconstructed " world.

That was the background so to speak to the affair of his baronetcy.

I realised that he did not intend to refuse it, with an indignation that now strikes me as excessive. At the time it seemed extravagantly important to me that my brother should not accept this thing. I suppose I was over-worked and worried, in a state of inflamed honesty, more indignant and less cynically patient than I have ever been before or since. I was in conflict with my business associates. Perhaps I should have been better employed in watching them. Brampsheet particularly—he had just got his peerage—was against all post-war scandals and enquiries, and my anger extended to the social world which was sheltering the men I wanted to expose. This had been the war that was to end all that sort of thing. These exasperations made me see Dickon's title as a sort of treason to the insurgent radicalism that had always been implicit between us.

" Dickon ! " I protested.   " That old livery !   In an age of Reconstruction ! "

" Historical, time-honoured."

" Everything we want to say good-bye to."

" All the same—— "

" You mean to take it, Dickon ? "

" Yes. Yes, I think I may take it."

" You'll have to kiss the king's hand ? " I invented.

Dickon pretended not to hear.

" You'll have to kiss his hand," I jeered.

" No more than kissing a book."

He went off at a tangent to answer unspoken objections of mine. " You live in a sort of dreamland, Billy," he said. " Science and the future and all that. Even now. In spite of your business and money. But I live in the present time. I'm here and now. I'm contemporary. A child of the age. This sort of thing is the fashion of our time. It's just a symbol of success and service. Very well. It may not be the best of media, but it's one way of saying ' I'm here ! ' That's how I look at it."

It was as if we were back in our Brompton diggings. That, I remembered suddenly, had been his standing argument against my Socialism.

" It's bolstering up the old order. You take the honour, yes—but you give your adhesion."

He said I lacked *savoir-faire*. That if one went on those lines one would become a " lone wolf." One didn't bolster up the old order. On the contrary, it acknowledged itself subdued. It stood on one side to make way for one. Saluted. And besides—with a quick change of line—he wanted Minnie to be Lady Clissold.

" Have you asked her ? "

" And the old man's name," said Dickon, with a second flash of deafness. " I've always had a feeling about the honour of the old man. Here it is at last—his name rather than mine. Sir Richard Clissold, Bart. After the way they let him down. After that last scene at the Old Bailey."

" Sir Richard Clissold Boop," said I.

" Eh ? "

" Boop. The Boops and their Jubilee. Good God, man, you haven't forgotten the Boops, have you ? All this, Dickon, strikes me as the most infernal Boopery. You'll have to wear a little Boopy sword. And silk legs ! And the Boops will stand round in their little Boopy robes, dressing-gowns and tea-cosies and table-cloths and curtains and antimacassar wigs and newspaper hats, all very solemn and solemn, to welcome you. Don't you remember ? "

He did. But he didn't want to do so. He embarked upon an insincere defence of royalty. "They" were so hard-working, so devoted. " Hardest-working couple in the Empire."

" To no purpose," said I, " except to stick on."

" So much to do," said Dickon. " Reconstruction everywhere. Why divide people by quarrelling with that ? "

I told him that people of his sort defended the crown because they were too lazy to set about getting it out of their way. They only pretended to like it. It obstructed the traffic. It falsified realities.

" Bit too many royal visits and processions just now, I admit," said Dickon. " Still—they *are* the decentest ! "

He shrugged his shoulders, and tried to look indulgent and reasonable and as much like *The Times* and *Punch* and a white top-hat in Ascot week as possible.

It was not only the traffic in the streets, I said. It was the traffic in men's minds. It put the common people wrong about the purposes of the State.

" They love it," said Dickon.

" That's just it," said I. " It's a lumbering perversion of human respect. A modern community can't afford to waste its respect like that ! "

That consideration has been my unwavering objection to monarchy and has made me that rare being, an English republican. I am puzzled by the readiness of liberal-minded English people to acquiesce in and con-form to the monarchy. The king is necessarily the head and centre of the old army system, of the diplomatic tradition, of hieratic privileges, of a sort of false England that veils the realities of English life. While he remains, the old army system remains, Society remains, the militant tradition remains. They are all bound up together, inseparably. The people cannot apprehend themselves in relation to the world while, at every turn and crisis of the collective life, the national king, the national uniforms, the national flags and bands, thrust blare and bunting across the realities. For millions these shows are naturally accepted as the realities. They personify and intensify and ensure the national distinction, the separation of the marching, fighting, grabbing Empire from the general business of mankind. How else can a monarchy work considering how monarchs are made and trained and flattered ?

For a time Dickon and I wrangled over the issue between monarchy and republicanism. The United States, said Dickon, could be republican and intensely nationalist ; France—this was in 1919—was republican and militarist. Americans, I said, were not nationalist, but were obsessed by an unavoidable sense of difference. As for France——

" King ! " said Dickon, with a nimble change of front, " but after all what's the king got to do with my baronetcy ? I shall scarcely see him long enough to make a face at him. He'll ask, ' Who's that fine man ? ' And forget when they tell him. It's L.G.'s affair. You're taking the whole of this business too seriously, Billy. You are indeed. You're putting it on too broad a basis. You're so fierce a republican I doubt if you'd read a book if you found it was printed on crown octavo."

He followed that up. " It isn't as though L.G.'s titles were so damned serious as all that. There's something like derision in most of his creations. They're just a flare up at the end. The last dance of the old costume ball. Before it is all swept away."

" In that case Lady Clissold becomes a comic title."

" If it was only for the pleasure it would give the servants at Lambs Court I'd take the title," said Dickon.

" You won't take it," I said.

" I'll do it—if only to annoy you."

I laughed.

" It's just like buying a fur coat for Minnie. It's a decoration. It's a way of putting her over the heads of a lot of showy, chattering bitches that aren't worth a tenth of her."

" There's no need to make Minnie a Lady by the King's grace," I said. " And as for putting her over those other—ladies, you're just putting her among them. And that reminds me : have you asked her about it ? "

He had not. And I realised in a flash he was not quite sure what she would say about it. That was why he was trying over the proposal on me first of all, to get a review of the possible objections.

" She won't let you," I said. " She won't let you."

But she did let him. Dickon took his baronetcy.

§ 11

MINNIE died very suddenly in the early part of 1920. She died under an operation that no one had thought very dangerous. But though she told it to no one, she had a feeling of danger, and she did a thing that was to reveal to me as nothing else could have done, the real quality of her relations to Dickon and the world, their aloofness and their filmy tenderness.

Her presentiment of death was very strong. But I do not think she was very deeply troubled at the thought of dying. I suppose that people who live with delicacy rather than intensity can die without any great mental agony. She was troubled about Dickon much more than on her own account; she thought her possible death might be a shock for him, and she feared that shock. So she wrote him a letter—a letter that was only to reach his hands if she died. Otherwise it would just have vanished like many another thing she must have thought of and done in that reserved life of hers. I saw that letter. He was impelled to show it to someone, and he showed it to me.

I was at Dorking with him after the funeral, and he suddenly came into the library with it in his hand. It was already a little worn with much re-reading. He looked at me with eyes that were distressed and perplexed.

" Billy," he said, " I want you to read this. I want you very much to read this. From her. After she died."

I was inclined to demur.

He pushed it into my hand. " Read it," he said, and again impatiently as he went out of the room, " *Read it.*"

A pencilled note, it was, but in a firm, clear hand. Written without haste. Punctuated, so that one seemed to hear Minnie's characteristic little pauses for deliberation. No outpourings. No abandonment to her impulses, no confidence in her impulses. A skilful letter written carefully for a definite purpose.

It was Minnie come back to life. It was Minnie quintessentially. Except for one or two phrases at the end that stuck in my memory, I cannot remember much of its exact wording. I read it only once. But it was, I think, the tenderest of all imaginable caresses that she reached across the grave to give him. Like Minnie, like all of Minnie, it was faintly aloof from complete participation in life. Because it was faintly aloof it was also faintly insincere. Insincere, I mean, in the sense that she did not seem to believe completely even in her own life and death. But not in any egoistic sense insincere. She was not posing. She did not seem to be thinking about herself at all. She said not a word of any unwillingness to be torn untimely from life. So far as she was concerned, I feel she was capable of saying : " Have I to go, then ? Very well, I am ready," even with the faint shadow of a smile upon her lips.

But Dickon in distress, Dickon left alone, big Dickon with his capacity for vivid remorse hiding a heartache, and with no possibility of a word to cure it, was another matter. That had got through to her as a real and dreadful possibility, and she had done her best with it.

" If I have to leave this queer, wonderful existence," she said, " I want you to know how happy you have made me in it."

That was the text of it, that was all she wrote about, the value he had given life for her. Nothing else.

I thought of many things between them. I saw for the first time as I read her letter with what comprehension she had understood his quality. I saw how well she knew him, and how she feared his easy and abundant remorse. She said nothing of any contentious things, harped upon no forgiving for the derelictions she must have known he had committed, but she said how happy and full she had found every hour with him, she reminded him of many kindnesses and generosities he had shown her, and of the great joint adventure of their worldly success. She recalled a score of little intimate delightful things, mostly from their early years, that she had treasured in her memory.

" The fun we have had, Dickon ! The dear boys and Winnie ! They were such fine and happy things to have launched into the world. And they get their brightness and courage, my dear, from you."

All things must end, she said, and if this was the end of this strange, lovely, difficult world for her—well, she was sorry to leave him, sorry indeed, but thankful for all she had had, and thankful to him.

" Dear Dickon, my own, be sorry—I known you will be sorry for the parting ; but do not grieve, dear Dickon. Do not mind too much about things that never really mattered, do not mind about them. Think of the life that has been so good with you and not of the death at the end. Think of the work that lies before you and the big tasks you have to do. You are only beginning. I know there is endless work before you yet. I wish I could have watched you and stood beside you a little longer. Dickon, my *dear*, thank you and thank you and thank you. . . . And again, dear Dickon, thank you and God bless you, and, if it must be, good-bye."

In that manner, in such words, it ended.

Dickon stood before me again and I gave him back the letter.

" You've read it ? "

I nodded.

" Well. . . . Tell me something. . . . Was she really happy, Billy ?

Did I really make her happy ? As she says I did ? "

" Certain, Dickon."

" Then why should she doubt ? "

" Doubt what ? "

" About what I should feel. If she didn't think that perhaps I had seen that she—she wasn't quite as hard and happy as she braved it out she was. There were times—— "

" You're tormenting yourself."

" But isn't she just saying those things—— She may be just saying those things—— Thinking of me. . . . She did things like that. She couldn't bear—hurting. Anybody being hurt. She'd a kind of terror of anybody being hurt—or remorseful. . . .

" You don't know, Billy, at times when I've been a bit disposed perhaps to be heavy-handed with the boys—how she's stood in. . . .

" And the thought she had—for old servants. For people in trouble. . . . I could tell you things. . . . Noticing when an old housemaid wanted glasses. Feeling when people were overworked or burthened. Things like that. Always for going gently. . . ."

He stared at me. " A man lives with a woman all his life, Billy. Eats with her, sleeps beside her. Happiness. Tears. Endless. . . . And he doesn't know much about her. At the end, he doesn't know much about her."

" She loved you all right, Dickon. More than you deserved, old man. And you made her happy. I've watched her. She was a happy woman, proud of you, proud of the opportunities you gave her, proud of this house and life here—and content."

" But you know, Billy, and I know—— I've been like most men. . . ."

" So far above such things, Dickon," I said ; " they never touched her."

" But many a time I must have been—a bit of a lump to her. . . . A man's so much rougher and clumsier."

" She didn't feel it like that."

" Eh ! " he said, and then for the first and last time in my life I saw my brother weep.

Never in our childhood and boyhood had I seen his tears, not even when our father died. But now he did not conceal his distress. " Tears won't bring her back," he said. " Not tears. Not wishing. Not repenting. . . . Nothing will bring her back to me. . . . Not for a word. Not for a moment —to tell her . . . *What could I tell her ?* "

He went to the window and stood there with his back to me to hide his face.

" If I could be sure," he said. " If I could believe it ! That I made her happy ? "

He became quite still, an immense broad back against the park and the sky.

"Kindness," he whispered to the unresponsive heavens. "Kindness, tenderness, the years of it, from the beginning to the end. . . . That quiet kindness."

He turned and addressed me—how can I put it?—as though I wasn't there.

"Nobody knew her but me," said Dickon. "Nobody knew anything about her really but me. Nothing at all. Nobody thought enough of her. Nobody had any idea. I've been her husband for thirty-one years, Billy— I've never found her lying to me or herself. And courage—I've never known her flinch. A little thing she was and she could look pain in the face. Take it as something one had to take. And when Dick was missing— that April! Three weeks we had of it and never a flicker because she had to stand by me. I just saw one day how white her face was. Or else I might have thought she didn't feel. . . . But she felt. . . .

"What a time that was! . . . Loyal! Strong! And I've let her be in the background. I've let it seem as though she wasn't anything so very much . . . didn't matter. . . .

"Billy, I was silly to take that old title, but don't you see how desperately a man may feel that his wife ought to be honoured? Somehow. When she won't take any honour! So that he sticks tinsel on her—in desperation. She let me do it. She understood. . . . My lady! Princess she was! Princess—with something cool and sweet. Like moonlight. . . . Silver. . . . All my days ought to have been gratitude. . . .

"Oh, what *good* is it talking?"

He looked out of the window again and I could have imagined he was expecting a reply from the twilight.

"Silence," he said, at last.

§ 12

WAS she a cynic ? I think the answer is Yes. On that basis I can explain her but on no other. Hers was a cynicism fine as carved ivory, but it was cynicism. It had neither aggression nor insult in it, but for her I do really think that Virtue, as the Ancient Cynics meant it, and Freedom, were the only good things. She was as completely disillusioned about the pomps and vanities, the received values and accepted gratifications of the life we live as I, but in addition she was disillusioned, as I have never been, about the power of the life within us. She was weak in effort and she knew it. So she would not thrust out to blunder. She accepted. She accepted good and avoided evil. She thought fighting evil was itself an evil. It made one hot and angry. So one went by on the other side. She could not understand the sort of drive that achieves, even if it achieves blunderingly. She could not understand the " dust and heat " of endeavour.

Because of that way of thinking she came a little to underrate Dickon, I suspect, after his first glamour had faded. His infidelities, his urgencies, his sudden changes of direction, his excessive admirations of questionable leaders—of Lloyd George, of Milner, of Northcliffe, for example—his storms of combative energy that had to find an outlet and so often found a wrong one, were incomprehensible to her. Yet as that last letter showed, she kept an infinite kindliness for him to the end.

Dickon, as people say, "adored" her, and yet he never seemed to me perfectly self-forgetful and at his ease with her. Even if she did not under-rate him, his tender conscience made him feel she ought to do so. He was capable of a good deal of expressive coarseness in his conversation, but in her presence he was always rather carefully decent. He never talked before her of his sincere enthusiasm for his calling. The rising tides of Advertisement broke and recoiled from the gates of Lambs Court. The best conversations I had with him during her life were away from her, and it is since her death that he seems to me to have developed most interestingly and boldly. Dickon was incapable of amateurism, and not only his life, but his whole view of life, had to centre upon his occupation. Even more than in my own case, his activities had to be related to the beginnings of things and the utmost star. But he felt her gentle irony at the gravity of his prolusions, her scepticism of the values in his drama, her recognition of his egoism. She was terribly, because so unconsciously and inevitably, a delicate lady, and not an actress upon the stage of life.

This contrast between them intensified as the years went on. At first he carried her with him much more than he did in their later years. He talked most of his thoughts to her. When he talked to her he could per-suade her. Then, I think, he became shy of something passive in her assents. She approved, but she never came to meet him. He felt that in her presence his ideas became huge and clumsy, sweaty and crude—as new things must be crude, and that he forced them on her. So he ceased to force them on her. There is a vein of self-distrust deep in Dickon's nature.

His ascendency over me was established so early and so firmly in our student days that it only dawns upon me now that at times Dickon must have been sensitive to my opinions. Innovation, experimenting, " giving the thing a try," were the quality of his life. He felt the risk in some of his views and acts. And she so manifestly favoured ripened and finished things, fine old furniture, works of art rather than works of science, polished conduct and acts as perfectly adjusted from their very inception as the muscles of a Persian kitten.

Dickon was greatly stirred by the war and by his own experiences of the war. As I have told, he was attaching very broad ideas to advertisement even before the war. Propaganda was an immensely stimulating discovery for him. And the idea of Reconstruction after the war seized upon him, interwove with those expanding ideas about advertising, and for a time possessed him altogether.

The Period of Reconstruction is still only five or six years behind us, and already it is difficult to revive its emotions and expectations. Even more difficult is it to recall the mental states of the war.

We began with heroism and sacrifice. I shall insist to the end of my days that the last months of 1914 were a tragically splendid phase in European experience, months of high, heroic, terrified living for a great multitude of people. I do not think that so far as we English were concerned the war degenerated greatly until the latter part of 1916. Then with conscription the mirage of greatness vanished. Like a mirage its disappearance was imperceptible. One became aware that it had gone. The war was discovered to be a daily tale of stupid and beastly destruction, moral even more than physical.

And then it was that the clamour for Reconstruction became strong. All this bloodshed and waste was the agony in which a new and fairer world was to be born ; the war was to end war and social injustice. This slaughter was the seed-time sacrifice from which we should reap the brotherhood of man.

In the years immediately after the war, with the frightful squalor and sufferings, the fear, pain and stress, the atrocious wastage and tragic heroisms of the struggle fresh in our minds, it was a moral impossibility not to think that there must have been something more than mere destruction, mere warning, in this immense disaster ; that somehow a price had been paid and a gain achieved. I suppose I am an exceptionally sceptical man, but I confess that was my conviction for some time. Only very slowly did I begin to accept the possibility that the abyss had swallowed up that enormous wealth of life, effort, and material accumulation, that it was gone for good, gone never to return, without recompense or consolation.

Now we can begin to face that monstrous verity. The war did no more for mankind than the Black Death or a forest fire. It solved nothing, inaugurated nothing. At best it swept away illusions. The Period of Reconstruction was the hectic death of one of the greatest of these ; that good arises automatically out of suffering.

But while my resort to the consolation of the Reconstruction Period was at least temperate, Dickon's acquiescence in that idea of a comprehensive and forward movement in human conditions was passionate and complete. " A world fit for heroes," he reiterated. " Magnificent phrase, Billy ! And it's alive. It will do things."

He did think it would do things. But what he thought it would do I still do not find very clear.

Across the seas came Woodrow Wilson, with that large, gaunt face of his, solemnly inscrutable, bringing his schoolboy essay in politics, his Fourteen Points. We knew nothing then of his vanity and narrowness nor of his limited authority. Nor did he. He seemed to promise the organisation of a world peace. Within the framework of security this ensured, there was to be a sort of voluntary collectivism. It was not to be Socialism we were assured—because a great number of influential people had declared they were not Socialists, and it would be embarrassing for them to contradict themselves—but it was to have the effect of Socialism. There were to be world-wide labour laws, health laws, protection of women and children, protection of races at a disadvantage, throughout all the planet. Just how it was to be done Dickon seemed to regard as an unimportant detail. He was too full of the spirit for any such particularisation. He would do his job of propaganda and preparation and the other fellows would do their jobs. In that magic word Reconstruction there was no really definite constructive idea at all, no taking apart and putting together again, but instead there was undeniably an enormous amount of what Americans call " uplift." Something was to be done, very large, very generous, very beneficial and splendid ; and that was all it amounted to.

I write something was to be done, but now I come to consider it, I believe that what we really thought was that something was going to do itself. And we were to be its ministers and henchmen.

The Lytton Stracheys of 1990 or so may find in this Period of Reconstruction material for much amusing writing. My own failure to be thoroughly amused by it is due, I admit, to a want of humour. I am still too close to it and its immense, if irrational, disappointments. It was a movement of the extremest incoherence and inconsistency. Men full of undisciplined individualism were rushing about talking about collective effort and the subordination of every enterprise to social ends. Men of the rankest patriotism were rushing about talking of the League of Nations. Schemes for re-housing the people of London in great and admirable buildings in London jostled amicably with schemes for scattering the population of London over the countryside. Everywhere beautiful houses were promised for the populace, and nowhere did they appear. Also there was to be a great exportation of the unemployed to the Colonies. On scientific lines. And a colonisation of England that would render emigration unnecessary. There were to be wonderful new high-roads. London was to have a railway clearing-house and save incalculable acres of wasted building land. Civil air transport, moreover, was to make both roads and railways superfluous. Productivity at the touch of the new spirit of collective organisation was to leap up like a man who has sat on a wasp. Everything was to fetch a good stimulating price, but then wages would be enormous. Charing Cross bridge was to be rebuilt very gloriously as a war monument, and everybody was to go to school up to the age of sixteen. The output of blue prints must have been enormous in those wonderful days. The projects were upon every scale and with every amplitude of scope.

Entangled with a number of self-mobilised business men and jarring upon them every moment was a miscellany of young University "authorities," economists, sociologists, professors of political science, very convinced and guiding and empty ; and there were temporary and permanent Civil Servants in the movement, all mysteriously devious with the devious discretion of men who have to think of their chiefs and their departments ; and journalists and novelists turned statesmen, making generous vacant phrases for us in the utmost abundance ; and inventors of this, that, and the other implement for altering human life completely ; and so down to pure faddists and founts of richly printed matter with which one's letter-box was choked, beings who filled the souls of men of affairs with terror and contempt, and drove them back in panic from their new viewpoints to their old business ways.

And the moral hotch-potch was just the same as the intellectual. Mixed up with the entirely honest types like Dickon were the complicated and half-honest ; and about these again a considerable crowd of adventurers who were not honest at all, who canted reconstruction and presently canted de-control, and whose one clearly apprehended reality in the pother was an opportunity to snatch. Some of them snatched amazing handfuls. Though perhaps it is not for me to complain of that, seeing the derelict Government undertakings that have fallen back into the hands of Romer, Steinhart, Crest and Co. and their associated enterprises.

§ 13

THEN there came a chill. There is a book of Tarde's called *Fragment d'histoire future*, which Mr. Brereton has translated into English as *Underground Man*. It describes the unexpected extinction of the sun. A sudden extinction, like a gaslight being turned off. It is springtime in France, the almond blossom has come, the birds are nesting, people are going afield, when the catastrophe occurs. The sun rises already shorn of its radiance, cools to a red orb at midday, is dulled to a sullen coppery glow, and a snowstorm that grows thicker and thicker fills the air, driven before a cold and devastating wind. The young elder leaves, the almond petals whirl past and are forgotten. Everyone is presently in flight for shelter and searching frantically under cover for fuel. The icicles gather along the eaves and fall clattering like broken glass before the freezing gale. The plants bud no more, the birds sing no more, a great darkness comes upon the world. Naturally those who have fuel cling to the fuel. The quicker-witted start for the coal-mines and begin to burrow down towards the central heat.

In much the same fashion did the hope of Reconstruction vanish from the sky. Peace conditions had returned and the phase of ready borrowing was at an end. The golden sun of credit veiled its countenance. A heavy ground swell in the European currencies gave place to a storm. The States had over-borrowed and mankind was collectively in debt.

Even during the war the belligerent States had rarely dared to take men's possessions outright. Lives and bodies they had taken freely and recklessly, handing over millions of men like cattle to their poor bluffing and blundering military chiefs to waste and torture as their fear and folly determined, but the property of men these Governments would not conscript. Because, you see, *human society is a labour-imposing, labour-shifting, property-money complex, and life, the more or less of it, only an unpremeditated by-product*. It ought not to be so, perhaps, but it is so. The human complex has grown in that fashion according to its nature, and it is not to be hastily and easily changed into some different play of relationships.

When they might have taken the warring Governments had bought, often at exorbitant prices, and they had borrowed to pay. The bills of these usuries were now being presented. Dickon and I and a number of others of us, business men first and money men afterwards, went to and fro in the year of the Versailles Conference, making a great noise about

Reconstruction, putting heart, temporary heart, into a multitude of depressed people ; and we no more realised what our real circumstances were than so many bumble bees in a roomful of spiders' webs. But as the grey filaments wrapped round us and wrapped round us, the note of our buzzing and booming changed. Only those who have hard and vivid memories know how much it changed. But it would be interesting to take a newspaper of the year 1918, let us say, and another of 1924, and count how often the words " Reconstruction " and " Debts " are to be found in each.

The era of Reconstruction faded out, with practically nothing to show for its enthusiasms ; it gave place to the era of Debt-collecting and what is apparently a strained and painful attempt to restore the comparatively stable state of affairs that had prevailed in the three or four decades before 1914. Finance and the manipulation of money became the burden of life. The voice of the " constructive " business man died away ; nobody wanted to hear it any more ; he himself did not wish to hear it any more ; and all the world watched the quiet whispering goings to and fro of the bankers and finance ministers.

But though debt and debt-collecting now dominated our thoughts, I do not think that the rapid evaporation of human hope was entirely due to the entanglements of finance. It was certainly not due to any plotting and scheming and foresight on the part of the financiers. No little, diabolically intelligent knot of men had waited at the centre of the threads and said, " Patience ! Presently all these poor fools will be in our nets. Then we'll stop this nonsense of hope."

Finance is not a malignant conspiracy ; it is only a malignant stupidity, a studpidity we all share actively or passively. It is a persistent, timid adherence to conventions and methods that cannot possibly work out beneficially for the mass of mankind. I have lived near and in business and finance for a large part of my life, and I here declare with the fullest deliberation that I do not believe there are any men of supreme intellectual quality, good men or bad men, now active in the world of finance. There are no doubt many very energetic and quick-witted men, but their acquisitive process is essentially automatic, arising out of the current methods of monetary issue and credit. Every human being alive is something of a toil-shifter, and happier in getting than in yielding ; most human beings have, in addition, a sneaking craving for power and precedence over their fellows, and the weaknesses of the system are found out by the pressure of these common tendencies, quite mechanically, just as the weaknesses of an embankment are found out by the weight of every particle of water it restrains.

Dickon, as he saw his dream of heroic Reconstruction stained and crumpled and spoilt and defeated, was disposed to be very fierce about the Money Power. He would talk of the Money Power throttling the Productive Power, and assert that at last all great combinations of industrial plant fell into the uncreative grip of the banks. He deplored his share in popularising loans when he ought, he now declared, to have been explaining and steadying the country under the " conscription of wealth." But I was never with him in that direct antagonism between money and productive organisation. Finance, I agreed, had sewn up the world in a shroud of debts, but it did that almost as innocently as a blow-fly lays eggs in a carcass. Without a carcass a blow-fly is a merely secondary nuisance easily driven away. When you end litter you abolish flies. Had there been sufficient constructive will and knowledge in the world it would have made short work of that web of debts, that enslavement of the world to the counting-house.

It became very plain to me as things went on that Dickon and I were impractically vague in our intentions. Yet we two were among the more clear-headed and capable of the active hopes of the Reconstruction movement. He had considerable prestige as a propagandist. I was a successful industrial organiser. Until we came to this test we had neither of us realised that in practical affairs we were mere fortunate amateurs following the inertias of our early successes, and no longer in the habit of solving novel problems. We were two samples of a body of perhaps a few hundred, or at most a few thousand, would-be Reconstructors. All of us, individually and collectively, were entirely inadequate to the task we imagined we were attempting. Opportunity gleamed upon us suddenly and found us unprepared—and passed.

How shallow was our conception of Reconstruction !—was every conception of Reconstruction I ever encountered ! To most of the hopeful people of that time Reconstruction meant simply—all they wanted—at once. Labour, for example, demanded an immediate shortening of hours and a rise in wages, and was blind to any necessity for intermediate phases or auxiliary constructive effort. In England, trade after trade struck vigorously, and got its advances, its eight hours' day, and crowded off at once to see the cinemas and football matches, leaving the working-out of the Millennium to anyone else who chose to bother. Nobody chose to bother.

I do not blame labour ; it acted according to its nature, just as the creditors and investors acted according to their nature ; but the Reconstruction collapse was, I think, brought to a crisis quite as much by the failure of labour to understand as by any exactions and obstructions of finance. Neither the unhelpfulness of labour nor of finance was the primary factor. The primary factor was that the organising and administrative people like Dickon and myself, men of concrete affairs as we professed to be, men who ought to have known if anyone did, how to set about reconstructing things, were caught without a scheme of action—without the ghost of a scheme of action. We had no sense nor measure of what was happening to us and the world. We ought to have known that labour would be obdurate, and finance insist upon its pound of flesh at any cost to the body politic. Labour always has been and always will be unwilling, and creditors will cling to their claims, and have to be dispossessed as firmly if as gently as possible, to the very end of human existence.

We learnt our measure in those days. We were as planless as the Bolsheviks in Russia. We were planless for exactly the same reason—because there never had been any plan. There is no plan. There is no Capitalist plan ; there is no Communist plan. There is no plan at all. We have traditions and usages on which we innovate timidly, and they have the claptrap of Marx and Lenin. Both capitalists in the West and the Bolsheviks in Russia extemporise and experiment—with an air of knowing all about what they are doing. We big business men had seemed to be running the economic system in Britain, but, put to the trial, we showed we had no power over it at all. Things had happened and we had happened in consequence.

I do not see that we Western Reconstructors have much excuse for looking down upon the Bolsheviks on the score of failure. They failed to reconstruct from the ground upward amidst the ruins of Russia, and they had a very bad famine and a series of foreign raids to complicate the job for them. We in a shattered and impoverished England failed just as much as they did. But since everything was smashed in Russia before they took on the attempt at reconstruction, their failure showed starkly. In the West nothing was smashed, although everything was strained, and the social and economic inertias carried us through. Our gestures and essays in reconstruction were swept aside by the virtual resumption of the old order, and there was no open revelation of futility. In March, 1925, under Mr. Baldwin—we seem almost back in March, 1914. The difference between the failure of the constructive spirit in Russia and in the West was the difference between a man on a desert island where there is nothing to eat and a man on a walking tour in France who finds he has forgotten to put food in his knapsack. Both may have intended to be self-sufficient, but the former starves, the latter takes refuge in an inn and says no more about it. He eats his dinner and reads of the other fellow's death with a feeling of superiority. But the money with which he pays may be borrowed money, and financially his balance-sheet may be even worse than that of the dead man. Debt is not so bad a thing as death, but it lies in the same direction. It is a parallel road to frustration.

There was no plan and there is no plan.   When the restless, enquiring minds among us have worked out the broad lines of a plan—and that is being done now, and in a generation or so it will be sufficiently worked out—when we have painted and established upon the screen of the future the realities of human possibility in terms that will convince and compel, then the real Age of Reconstruction will have begun, and this queer phase of hope and insufficiency that came to mankind in the beginning of the age of confusion that followed the great war, will be recognised as the first uneasy stirrings of the sleeping world-state before its conclusive awakening.

§ 14

LOOKING back at it now, as it settles itself into the general perspective view of our lives, I see that this effort, this disappointment of the Reconstruction Period and the reaction that followed, was a cardinal phase both for Dickon and myself ; a being born again or—a better image perhaps—a coming-of-age. It is easier for me to see the change that happened to Dickon than to trace it in my own case. So far as one's own self is concerned, when one gains new perspectives and get one's conception of things expanded and cleared, the new vision is apt to swallow up the old, and so one forgets one's earlier limitations. But I remember Dickon before the war as fragmentary and dogmatic and instinctive, in comparison with his more recent self. He took the world for granted then, he took it as established and in all its broader aspects beyond his control. The stress, excitement, hope, and frustrations of the last ten years have pulled him together.

Before the war I was a revolutionary, a theoretical revolutionary, decidedly unreal and amateurish in my views, and he was not. My insistence upon change and the need to change, such as it was before the war, he was always putting aside until to-morrow. It was interesting but impracticable ; it was Utopian ; he lived for the world as it was. But after the reconstruction effort, and particularly after the death of Minnie, he changed—almost fundamentally. The world had hitherto been open to criticism indeed, but good enough for him. He could still take a baronetcy in 1919. He is no longer like that.

The war was the beginning of this new birth, but like so many violent accidents, its real quality and consequences were masked by the immediate shock. Even now they are only beginning to come through.

It is curious how irrelevant the actual details of the war seem to be now, and how enormous the effects we begin to realise. I could tell a hundred stories of the war, of our special productions, of hunts for raw material, of ingenious substitutions, of our tragic explosion at Lembury, of our replacement of men by women workers, and how good the first lot were and how bad all the others, of the spies we suspected and the spies we had, of our poison-gas work, and of how we sank a hundred tons of that filth in the North Sea after the war was all over, because there was nothing else to do with it—stories interesting enough in themselves but of no wide significance in my world now, even to me.

Nor do the accounts of the air-raids we stood, the persistent attempts of the German raiders to localise our works and particularly the plant at Downs-Peabody, seem to matter very much now. One moonlit night of crashes and vast silences, in a wide empty street near Victoria, I came upon a man clinging to a railing and mooing like a cow, and his intestines protruded from his waistcoat; he had just been torn open by anti-aircraft shrapnel; I made up a bed for him with some cushions I borrowed and went off into the wilderness of Pimlico to find an ambulance, and when I got back he had disappeared and nobody knew what had become of him— or the cushions; I had to pay for the cushions; and I was dining not a hundred yards from Buckingham Palace with Stetson during an air-raid when a naval shell, which happily proved a dud, I suppose from some boat in the Thames, danced in from somewhere at the back, made a vast smash of falling brickwork and broken window-frames, and came to rest among the hats and umbrellas in the hall without injuring a soul; but these things are now like something seen in a show or dreamt or read about. They join on to nothing. They are like travel snap-shots or like the promiscuous collections of picture post-cards my nephew Dick used to make when he was a very little boy. They call for no more than a passing allusion here. What is of infinitely more moment is the revelation that they brought home to us of the undirected instability of the world's affairs, the realisation that we were not mere passengers but as much responsible navigators upon the ship of human destiny as anyone.

In the winter of 1920 Dickon and I had a long discussion. We had indeed several, we were much together at that time, but it will suit my purpose best to concentrate the substance of it all into one conversation. It crystallised out a number of ideas that I had had in solution for some time. That week or so of discussion marks the establishment of the new phase, the definitive phase, of our attitude to life. I find as I recall it, already well in evidence, the embryonic but recognisable form of that revolutionary project which it is the main object of this book to state, and to which I shall come after our own story has been sufficiently told.

It was influenza that had thrown us so much together, and fever maybe quickened our ideas. It was in the early days of the Bordon Street Chambers. Deland, to whom we were a great find, could not do enough for us. The influenza of that year was rather more feverish and bronchial than the current one and a little more prone to unfavourable developments. Deland would permit us to take no risks. We sat indoors of an evening, and before us was a big copper kettle steaming on a bright coal fire. We had screens about us, screens that Deland had insisted upon, and we drank hot whisky and Dickon opened his thoughts to me abundantly and frankly.

He certainly said or implied most of the things I am now going to make him say.

I remember him sitting in the low armchair, in a blue dressing-gown under a shaded light, that made his head by contrast look like a great orange, ruffled by eyebrows and split by a smiling mouth below, and with the unusual trick of producing two level blue eyes from below the eyebrows at salient points of the conversation, and I remember, too, that he grunted more than usually when he moved. At his elbow Deland had put a low table and the tray and all our convivial material. And his discourse, which arose out of his complete admission of the failure of the Reconstruction Movement, went in this fashion :

" Addison "—Dr. Addison was the Minister of Health then—" won't get his half-million new houses ; he won't get sixty thousand, and Fisher " —the Right Honourable H. A. L. Fisher was to have been the great light of a better education—" won't get the school-leaving age raised to sixteen. That's all as dead as mutton now, Billy. Addison may make some sort of fight for it, but it won't be any good, and Fisher will let it go because he's that sort of a chap. Then it's ages since we heard a word about that State-controlled milk-trade which was going to save ten thousand babies a year, and your people and people like you are going to take over those national factories that Chiozza Money said inaugurated a new economic system, take them over at scrapping prices, and run them on strictly profiteering lines. O ! I've been watching you, Billy. Well, perhaps not strictly profiteering. Business lines. I've been watching you and I've been watching Brampsheet follow his nose. What a nose he has ! And it's true there's no one else to run them. No one. But the mines are different. That's not true about the mines. Nothing is going to be done about the mines either. That's a clear miss. The mine-owners are mucking along in the dear old fashion in spite of the Sankey Report—and elementary common sense. Public health is as you were, or a bit worse, and nobody will get anything much done except the money-bugs. And so we go on. Reconstruction was quack medicine, and Lloyd George is a liar, and here we are bilked and done."

" And men of our age," I probably remarked, " ought never to have believed that anything else was possible."

Dickon reflected over his tray.

" And yet, for all that, there is a lot in this idea of Reconstruction," he said. " I've acquired that idea of Reconstruction for good. It's like being vaccinated."

Some sound of guarded assent from me.

" Bigger job than we thought it was," said Dickon, shaving delicately at the lemon peel with the razor Deland had brought for the purpose.

" We aren't going to make over this old muddle of a world yet for a bit," he said, and cut a translucent slice and rejected a pip fastidiously. " I shall leave you to put the sugar, Billy. . . . No. . . . But it's been a lesson."

He completed his duties as host.

He made a compelling gesture towards me with the open razor to hold my attention until he began. Then he composed himself to talk.

" I perceive, Billy, that this little old world of ours has been ready and asking for a revolution, a complete and thorough revolution, for three years. Three years. Since about the middle of 1918. The market was ready, the demand there—and no supply. What has been missing has been somebody to know what was wanted and able to produce it. The world had its mouth open. It was scared tame. Lord ! Billy, how funny all this is really. The expectation ! The result ! That solemn goose of a Wilson laying his addled egg in Paris. Day by day, each day a little more of it out. Mankind awe-striken. Go on, Great President ! Go on ! And the Bolsheviks—— Not even an egg—— "

He sought for an image.

" Making a mess," I suggested hastily.

" Making a mess—a little weak mess—in the middle of the remains of Russia."

He shook his head at the fire. " Tremendous pause. Mankind puzzled. ' That is all, gentlemen. No, there is nothing more ; nothing more at all ! ' And then, presently the old things, the dreary things, the slow and pompous things, the shams, the vested interests and the ancient rights, the kings that mean nothing and the uniforms that mean nothing, come crawling out of their shelters and hiding-places, scarcely able to believe they are still alive. As they are, Billy. As they are ! "

" Yet there *was* that pause," said Dickon. " There was a time when the door stood open."

He surveyed history at large. " I suppose there never has been much imaginative greatness in the handling of human affairs. The greatest of men is still an ape—what was it ?—' imperfectly depiled.' Good phrase that ! All damned nonsense about the dignity of history. Dignity hasn't begun yet. We've had great figures stuck up for us. Cæsar and Marcus Aurelius. Really no better than Winston or Wilson. It's always been this sort of thing really—or worse ? "

Dickon returned to his main discovery. " These have been extraordinary years. If there had been a clear project ready and men to put it over, it could have been put over. It was the psychological moment for a great change. . . . I for one thought there was going to be a really great change. A new age. Here and now, Billy. . . . We seemed to see the promised land. And now where is it ? "

" But isn't there something still to be done ? "

" I don't know," said Dickon, and added—as though he poised the name in his hand—" there's Northcliffe."

" Northcliffe ! " said I, and sat amazed.

Then I reflected that Dickon saw all the universe through a haze of publicity. Hadn't he called the temples of the world God's advertisements ?

He began to talk about that great newspaper adventurer in tones of affectionate perplexity. In some obscure extensive way outside my sympathies, Northcliffe had taken a very steady grip upon Dickon's imagination. He had become more than himself for Dickon ; he had become a symbol for forces Dickon partly apprehended and partly hoped for in the world about us. He spoke of the " New Men," the " New Adventurers," and at a scrutiny of these phrases he always fell back on Northcliffe. Northcliffe was still the master of *The Times* then and of a powerful group of newspapers, but for a year or so he had been making a poor figure in the world's eyes on account of his concentration upon a bitter personal feud between himself and Lloyd George. This after clambering courageously through a phase of great unpopularity to a commanding influence in national affairs. His war services had been enormous and on the whole sound. There was a story that Lloyd George had led him to hope he might go to the Versailles Conference and had then disappointed him. At any rate, Northcliffe had behaved like one who had been stung by an intolerable treachery. For a time his conspicuous vindictive resentment had robbed him of any largeness of effect. It had disappointed and estranged many who like Dickon had hoped for great things from him. But Dickon stuck to him. " He is a big man," said Dickon stoutly, " he is a big man."

Northcliffe, said Dickon, had never known what a big man he was going to be until his greatness was upon him. Opportunity had taken him by surprise. As it takes most successes nowadays by surprise. He had found himself powerful before he had had time to turn round and realise what he wanted to do.

"That's more or less the history of all our sort," said Dickon. " We strive with all our little mights—just to get freedom, just to get out of the ruck—and what we thought was a wall of stone and iron turns out to be cardboard and *phut* it goes, and we find ourselves right through, with power in our hands and nothing in the whole universe between us and the ironical eye of God."

" Mr. G.," I said.

" God I mean in this case," said Dickon.

He sketched out the adventure of the Harmsworths. The father was an Irish barrister who had come to London and been called to the English Bar, and who had died before success could be won there. He seems to have been an able man who died too soon, with a restless, ambitious, stimulating home and a wise, strong, patient wife. His chief delight, I have been told, was to speechify in a mock Parliament in some Camden Town tavern.

From that he hoped perhaps to clamber to the other mockery at West-minster.   Alfred, the son, went to a little private school in St. John's Wood, and began a journalistic career with a jelly-graphed school magazine. The schoolmaster knew how to seize an aptitude and develop it, and he pro-moted Harmsworth's purple smudgings to the dignity of print and periodicity.

" I've seen some numbers," said Dickon.   " It was pretty common stuff ; cricket scores and school news and so forth.   Northcliffe never wrote a dis-tinguished line in his life. . . .   Well—writing distinguished lines isn't —everything.   Though, of course, it helps."

While still in his teens, young Harmsworth launched out with a weekly paper called *Answers*.   Then came some awful things for errand boys, and the cheapest public, *Comic Cuts*, that crying outrage.   " Great money makers, I'm told," said Dickon.

The *Daily Mail* followed and was a brilliant success.   The world became aware of a personality different from the ordinary newspaper personality, an influence and an energy.   Then came opportunity, and this Harmsworth of *Comic Cuts* secured a controlling interest in *The Times* and became a power, presently a very considerable power.   The peerages of himself and his brother were formal recognitions of his substantial success.   North-cliffe and Rothermere became the golden flowers on the stem of Harmsworth Brothers.   He pushed forward to something like a commanding position in the country among the uncertainties, hesitations, and novel occasions of the war.

" It makes our little rush up look quite a gentle ascent," said Dickon.

Dickon had become associated with Northcliffe during his propaganda activities.   There was a real liking between them.   He's got imagination, real imagination, the quality that makes a great man, Billy ; almost the only man he is with a touch of greatness in our public affairs.   The only one."

" You don't think there's something great about such a type as Arthur Balfour ? " said I.

" That damned Madonna lily ! " said Dickon.   " He grows where he's planted," and came back without further comment to Northcliffe.

" He knows that we are a new sort of men, and that this is an age of new things.   He knows there is the possibility of great reconstructions in the air. He's not clear about it, but he feels it.   He's alive to it.   He's not afraid to change the world.   That's what makes him signify, Billy."

Dickon gave me a little vignette of Northcliffe and himself sitting in a room in Crewe House, a fine townhouse of the old régime that had been requisitioned for propaganda headquarters against the Austrians and Germans, an easy spacious town-house with a garden of its own up behind Shepherd's Market in the heart of the West-end, full of eighteenth-century dignity and eighteenth-century furniture. "They talk of revolutions," Northcliffe had remarked in that soft whispering voice of his. "Our being here *is* a revolution."

"That," said Dickon, "is Northcliffe near his top note. A bit exalted. None the worse for that. But seeing things. Seeing changes. Seeing forces."

He leant forward, poked the fire, and spread his amplitudes before the blaze. "In a sense," said Dickon, "it was true. In a sense—it was nonsense."

"Potential revolution," said Dickon. "There I agree."

He frowned; he shook his elder-brother finger at me and frowned. "There is something wrong about Northcliffe, Billy. Something grotesque and tragic. Like a string that jerks him back."

The man, he said, had moods, alternations of moods that went beyond the limits of sanity. At times he had to go away and hide from everything. He would fly off to his wonderful old mother at Totteridge. His brothers, his secretaries and subordinates took charge. Dickon knew of these dark interludes already three years before Northcliffe died insane. But all through Northcliffe's life was a succession of moods and phases—vast inequalities. His boldness, his vision, seemed to come in phases and vanish again. Sometimes he had the assurance of immense power—"and it's there for his using," said Dickon—and at others he was just vain and empty, in the air, "posturing or frightened, fat and frightened, and no sort of good at all."

Dickon shrugged his shoulders. "And there you have—in his hands —with no one really able to control him, a gigantic Publicity, the supreme power still in modern life. Yes, Billy, there is no power now, none in all the world, like the power to speak plainly and uninterruptedly to the crowd. My God! the power he and the other big newspaper people could exercise even now, if they chose to take it up and use it. Even now—still—to-day— the empire and the world are absolutely in the hands of the big press owners and the new men they ought to work with. This is their time of opportunity. The situation stiffens; it stiffens every day, but it hasn't congealed yet. There may be years yet before it has completely congealed."

A note of lamentation crept into his voice. "Not twenty men," he said. "And nine-tenths of the British newspaper sales in their hands. And all concentrated in London, not scattered like the American papers in a score of places. They might march this country wherever they chose and the rest of the world would follow. If they had the dignity of their power. Who could stop them? How could you stop them?"

But they drifted. They achieved nothing except great, clumsy, over-whelming fortunes. Opportunity was a touchy visitor if you didn't go down at once to receive her. Northcliffe felt that, but the others didn't. That was where he was different.

I suggested that Dickon over-estimated the strength of these newspaper proprietors. They would lose circulation at once if they tried to put big things over. Dickon was convinced they would not. " The public likes initiative," he dogmatised. " Wants it. And besides, altogether, they control the paper supply and distribution. And there's still no one yet with the courage and decision to stand up against them if they chose to begin ! "

And even if the public didn't like them it would have to stand them, now. Who would they lose circulation *to* ? The public must have some sort of paper. No other sort of paper was possible at the present time. These press barons had the power surely enough. But they had no common idea. They had no idea of themselves. And the power slipped away from them. It was like that moment when Wat Tyler, the Kentish rebel, was killed. The crowd stood irresolute. There was the Press, as the prince had been, mounted and in full view, capable of saying what it chose to say and take control. And there it was with nothing to say—exposed in that expectant silence.

" These men," he remarked, " came up by being new. If they stop being new, they fall back into a position of subordination to the old gang, and cease to matter. They amalgamate with the old crowd and are lost. . . . They don't know their opportunities. They are afraid of their opportunities. Too big for them. . . . Except possibly Northcliffe. I'm not so sure of Northcliffe."

Dickon made a gesture of despair and dismissal, with a glass that was fortunately nearly empty.

" They could say what they like," he said, " even now. The whole world still listens for an idea."

He went on to a general review, an irritated, exaggerated, influenza-touched review, of what he called the new forces in English affairs : " The men like us." Those new forces had never realised their quality and their outlook. That was our trouble. No mental synthesis, no clear understanding, was there.

I give Dickon's views as well as I can. They are not precisely my views, but they are the brothers of my views. He saw things from the angle of a great advertiser, he overvalued the conspicuous, and his choice of new men was very different from mine. But I do not remember that I argued with him that night. I let him cite his own cases.

Lloyd George, Dickon insisted, was one of the " new forces." In 1920, certainly, he was still a very big figure. " In politics he's just what I am in advertisement, and Northcliffe is in journalism, and you in metallurgy—a new sort of man with new scale methods." None of us could have existed in 1880, neither Lloyd George nor Northcliffe, nor ourselves, nor any of the prominent men of the day under sixty. Asquith and Balfour and Grey were by comparison just dignified statesmen in the Victorian tradition. They had learnt to be British statesmen at the Universities under the best tutors. They were incapable of freshness or adaptation. "Locums," said Dickon. They had been pushed aside for a time, and all their type and tradition could still be thrust aside. Thrust aside for good. An active figure like Lloyd George made them look like historical monuments.

But in Lloyd George also there was something that made for futility. "He's just a magnificent weed. In flower. Where one might have a great tree. He lives from hand to mouth. He's as clever as six foxes. Sane— too sane. Meanly sane. What's the matter with him? Just the opposite of Northcliffe. No end of cool, clear brains, but they don't seem to be in the right place or the right way up, or something. No length of vision. No imaginative warmth. There Northcliffe has the pull of him. And Lloyd George can't wait. You must have long views before you can wait. Temperamentally he can't wait. And he's broken with Northcliffe. He ought to have let Northcliffe take a hand in the Government and sent him to Paris. It might have changed the course of history if Northcliffe had gone to Paris.

"But, of course, the Paris show was too big a temptation for George, just as it was too big a temptation for Wilson.

"And here we are!" said Dickon.

He passed the other great powers of the British newspaper world in review and dismissed them all. Imaginative insufficiency. They could do so much if they chose. And they did not choose.

"Riddell—a clever man. A cynic. Laughs at his peerage. What is he after in life? Beaverbrook? He has as much brains and imagination as anyone. But—he's impish." Where Northcliffe was disposed to be grandiose. "Northcliffe," said Dickon again, "that's the *big* man." Beaverbrook was devoted to Bonar Law—they came from the same Canadian village, Dickon believed—and he meant to make his friend Prime Minister. "Possibly he will. And beyond that, so far as I can see, he regards the world as a playground, and isn't quite sure of his fun. Eager, feverishly eager, to be all alive, and no idea what life is. Will he ever grow up? If he grew up. . . . He's young still."

Dickon turned away from that.

Lord Burnham of the *Daily Telegraph* was a good sort, with a greater sense of public obligation than the others. But no inner light, no drive, and no desire. His idea of a newspaper, a pillar instead of a power.

"Lords of Journalism," said Dickon. "Newspaper nobles."

8*

Scott of the Manchester Guardian was a star apart. "But you can't do very much as a star apart," said Dickon. "Twinkling is good enough for him. He doesn't *want* to do." The *Manchester Guardian* and the *Corriere della Sera* of Milan were after their fashion the two finest newspapers in the world, but anything might happen to them at any time because of their isolation. So Dickon prophesied in 1920. For the *Corriere* now it is prophecy no longer.

Dickon sees as drama what I see as process. He sees it as a drama of publicity. What is not seen and known by the public is not reality for him. That night he reviewed our political world entirely as a display of these newspaper adventurers and "new men" of his—Lord Birkenhead, with his careless freedom of word and act, and Lord Reading, who was Rufus Isaacs, almost as "new" in type, he held, as Lloyd George or Northcliffe—and he declared that only a realisation of their common interest in a boldly reconstructed political and social order could prolong and stabilise their adventure. The old things were biding their time, reaction impended, and these new men were attacking and undermining each other, doing nothing revolutionary, and letting the weeks and months slip by. They did not seem to think they had anything to fear from the old conservatives. "Wait," said Dickon. "I've seen and heard a thing or two."

He made me realise the latent power of what he called the "old gang" in things British and American, less audible, less brilliant, slow and tenacious, the old gang of long-established property, of banking and rent, the implacable gold standard and the unwearying creditor, the old gang who want nothing more to happen for ever. He made an acute guess that found its confirmation in the General Election of 1924, when almost all the residue of his "new men," battling one against the other, were swept away or driven into secondary positions. The chill of the coming day when Mr. Asquith would become an earl and a Knight of the Garter, Lord Birkenhead a minister-journalist, and Lloyd George a comparative nobody was upon him. Though he foresaw the coming phase of reaction, he was not yet reconciled to its inevitability. He still clung doubtfully to his hero, Northcliffe, a loyalty that was so soon to be shattered by a pitiful death.

THE fever and the whisky and the quinine that were working together in Dickon's blood that night seemed only to give his mind a wider sweep. He generalised with unusual freedom. He expanded his discourse upon British affairs, until it became an exposition of a world-wide struggle to remake. He saw that struggle everywhere as a triangular conflict. First there were these "new men" of his, the Sons of Light, still uncertain in their quality ; and next there were the "haves," the holders, the creditors, the financiers, the antagonists weaving the nets about these extraordinary Sons of Light he had chosen ; and thirdly there were the "have-nots," labour that would not labour, that did not want anything that anybody else wanted, but did not know what it wanted, the retrogressive obstruction, the massive veto, the eating, breeding crowd.

We two had grown up in an age of rapid progress, and we were too much disposed to take progressive change as the natural order of the world. We were only beginning to realise that the rush of progress had brought also a stimulation of the defensive, a strengthening of the resistances that protected established things. The forces that had been disturbing and enlarging the scale of human affairs for four or five generations might have exhausted themselves in the catastrophe of the Great War. "Crashed," said Dickon. It was an unpalatable line of thought for him, but he followed it manfully for some time. The owner was resuming his loosened grip everywhere ; the creditor was recovering from his earlier dismay and confusion, and there was no residue of creative force to resist his return.

Perhaps we were in for a phase first of stagnation and then of retrogression. It was, yes, it was possible. It might last as long as the forward rush and undo much of its achievement. The conservative forces wanted, indeed, only to fix and retain ; they were as unwilling to go back as to go forward, but you cannot fix and retain without stagnation, you cannot have stagnation without decay, and you cannot have decay without disorder. For a while Dickon was morbid. Life asserts itself in the unused organ as putrefaction or cancer. Decay meant conflict even more certainly than did such an excess of energy as had led to the Great War. But the conflicts of a phase of decay had not even breadth of motive. The creditor, the property-owner, might avert the confiscations of a creative revolution, but at the price of reviving the brigand. "That begins already in Italy," said Dickon. China, India, had passed through "ages of confusion." Why should not our Western world do the like ? Why should there be any recovery at all in human affairs ?

But this was too depressing for Dickon's temperament. I have never known him keep a purely pessimistic poise for long, and presently he was saying that the real age of Reconstruction—which he had tacitly restored to the scheme of things—might still be centuries away. To talk of the world not really going forward was for him just talking ; it signified nothing at all—a polite gesture to the insanities of possibility. Wasn't he himself going forward ? . . .

He sat staring into the glowing coals.

The influenza germ reasserted itself.

" Unless you have men to tell people how things stand and what they have to do——" he said, and broke off.

" Where are the other men to be looked for ? " he said. " Where shall we find the new forces ? Perhaps this is naturally a conservative and creditor country. But—for example—America ? "

He returned to his main hope. " Northcliffe is talking of going round the world," he said. " I wonder if he will. He seems to have this same feeling we have that a big reconstruction is due. Somewhere that isn't perhaps London or England. He wants to look for it. He talks of greater Britain, of the Empire. I wonder if that's it. I wonder what he will find if he does go round the world. I wonder what he expects to find. Banquets he will get everywhere. Flattery. An immense publicity. No rest. No thought. But his instinct is sound. That man, Billy, is like a big lonely wasp at a grocer's window-pane. He knows there is something important to him behind it, but he doesn't seem able to get through. He tries to find a way. Perhaps he will never get through."

He never did get through. Two years later that poor giant with the feet of clay, that great vulgar man of energy whom Dickon had idealised to the level of genius, went round the world even as he had proposed. His progress is to be found recorded with a straining amplitude in the files of his *Times*, and as he journeyed his exorbitant brain glowed and became more and more confused. The problem was too vast for him, he was too utterly uneducated, he staggered with a fundamental instability. His desire to do great things in the world gave place to alternations of childish grandeur and frantic suspicion. The little folks about him whispered and soothed him and tried to put as seemly a face as possible upon the dismal business, and then presently, close home again in Germany, suddenly he became hopelessly mad and violent and was overcome and restrained and passed altogether out of the comity of men.

I doubt the reach and power of imagination that Dickon ascribed to him. But I agree that there was greatness in him and that his story is a tragic one and his destruction a loss to the world. And I agree, too, that he did embody forces that are still operating largely about us.

From his exposition of Northcliffe, Dickon began in a large febrile way to seek through all our world for what he called " creative far-reaching men." The world needed them ; the world was ripe for them ; these " new men " of to-day were only the precursors of the men who had to come. To him it seemed essential that they should appeal to a great multitude of hearers, be audible to the ends of the earth. Until a thing had been put through to the multitude and had taken hold of the multitude, it had not, from his point of view, been done. From the very nature of the case it was manifest that the primary thing in the career of these redeeming advertisers would be that we should know about them. And we did not know about them.

For a time he discussed the American publicity people and such great newspaper men as Hearst and the Pulitzers. From that he spread out upon a general comparison of English and American. " I've met Hearst," he said, " as often as I've met Rothermere ; I've spent days with both the Pulitzers, and do I begin to know anything about them ? No. I've not the faintest idea of what they are up to, or what they *think* they are up to. Billy, why are Americans, all Americans, Americans without exception, such mysteries to us ? European race. More often than not *our* race. Our language. Conditions after all very like ours. A bigger country, of course. A different pace. Difference of phase. But while you seem to get Englishmen and Frenchmen all round and through and through, half an American is in a loud glare and the other half is darkness. It's like seeing things by the beam of a searchlight after you have been seeing them in a light that is soft and grey and generally diffused.

" That's it, perhaps, Billy. A profound difference in their publicity, using publicity in its widest sense. From the way that a child gets looked at and talked about, onward. They're lit up differently, inside and out. And what is life but a consequence of illumination ? When you go to America and see headlines and interviews with a girl about her engagement, or with a professor about his resignation, you at first say, ' Good God. There's no privacy here at all ! ' And then you discover that outside that crude, cheap, hasty, flat, misleading lighting-up of salient objects and events, there's abysses of darkness, immense pits where much goes on and nothing is exposed—and people, rich people especially, unobserved in them and doing the most extraordinary things.

" In Europe a man may have a private life, yes, but in America he has a secret life, lit by sudden shouting judgments and flashes of journalistic lightning. In which you get an impression—vivid enough but wrong. Things about him that would be plain here are invisible there, even to himself. And other things come out with a kind of scream, all out of proportion by our standards. It's because of that, Billy, that to our European senses Americans never seem quite real. The quality of the exposure, the method of illumination to which they have had to adapt themselves, account for nearly everything between us. That sort of watchful reserve they have, mixed up with a desire to make general, over-simplified explanations of themselves. The queerness of these greyish-faced, slow-speaking Americans in grey, who watch your face as they talk to you ! If the searchlight jumps round upon them they are ready all the time. They talk about themselves as we never do. They try and hide their nakedness behind autobiographical statements. They instance themselves as types. They snatch suddenly at your verdict upon them. They have none of our sense of sustained scrutinies and slowly maturing judgments ; none at all."

Was there any such gathering and influential body of men and women in America set upon Reconstruction as we two were set upon Reconstruction ?

" Allowing for all the differences in pace and phase," he said, " the fact remains that we and they are going along the same road in the same direction." The need for a great reconstruction was common now to all the world ; there were only these differences in phase. Business had grown there faster and bigger than it had grown here, and their banking was rapidly overshadowing ours. They were bound to lead the world's affairs for a time. But how far were they able to keep the lead or do anything with it ?

He sized up the prospects of a world under American leadership. Were the Americans producing an American mind that would be large-thinking and powerful enough for the whole world ? In certain things they were broader-minded than Europeans. The United States had always been more curious and intelligent about China and Eastern Asia, for example, and more restrained in its imperialism. It had been far ahead of the European intelligence in its grasp of the importance of a properly regulated currency and credit system to economic life. It had got currency into politics long before Europe suspected there was such a thing as a currency riddle. But, nevertheless, it was—shallow. All its energy—and its energy was tremendous—seemed to be on the surface. Woodrow Wilson was typical of the American quality that perplexed us. The idea of some great settlement of world affairs, some world peace organisation, was magnificent. Quite beyond the scope of the European outlook or the compass of European statesmanship. One saw the United States leading the world into a new age. Then for the realisation of that vision, the Fourteen Points, as trite and superficial as a magazine article.

And after that—America the Creditor.

" And while we sit here asking, ' Can the Americans develop a world mind and lead the world ? ' there may be just such another pair of brothers as we are, Billy, in Indianapolis or Chicago saying, 'Why don't the Europeans show a sign of a world mind?' I believe our sort of ideas are fermenting in the world everywhere. We're not such original chaps as to be very far from the general trail. What brings us here will bring others here. And Americans most of all. . . .

" It's just that we don't know about them. They aren't talking yet. . . .

" This new reconstructed world, Billy, is like a big dragon-fly jerking itself bit by bit out of its larval skin. Jerking and then resting. It's wet and quiet just now, a little disposed to quiver, making no noise, but it's nearly here ; it's almost out ; it's coming on."

" And presently, all at once, it will spread out its wings and buzz," I said.

" And then we shall know about it."

He looked at me with that queer experimental expression of his, like a small boy who has given his little brother a dose and does not quite know how it will agree with him or he with it. I looked back at him and laughed. " You'd like to be sure."

" There is a lot in what your friends the Communists call the economic interpretation of history," said Dickon. " If material needs make political and social forms, then big business and international finance will presently develop a soul of its own, become really conscious of itself and make itself known to the world. The same experiences will beget the same ideas. There must be fellows not only in America but Germany and France who are getting, as we are getting, towards their idea of positively making a new world system—not letting it happen merely, but making it happen."

Dickon reflected. " China ? Japan ? India ? It can't be all aimless mooning. Here two or three are talking, there someone is writing. Convergent thoughts perhaps. Surely convergent. Every day there must be someone pushing the new ideas just a little further, clearing up, rounding off, maturing, making possible and practicable. That is the real Reconstruction. But for the world in general they are still inaudible, smothering, unable to speak out yet within the swelling, uncomfortable old institutions. Then someone says something, definite effort is started, the trouble begins."

He paused, a little troubled by his growing and distending metaphor. He was always begetting these metaphors and finding them too much for him.

" Then is the time for the man-midwife," I suggested, " the propagandist, the advertiser, to set about his task, and bring the new order into the world."

As we talked we replenished our glasses with a reasonable moderation from the decanter and the kettle on the hob, and I think we talked on at last partly because the influenza made us feel as physically lazy as we were mentally flushed, and disinclined us for the little effort needed to get ourselves from the fireside to our waiting hot-water bottles. And it was interesting to have my brother spreading out his general ideas to me again after so many years. It was interesting to see how close he had come to certain speculations of my own.

At last the little clock upon the mantelshelf pinged one o'clock in the morning, and Deland, whom we had supposed asleep, coughed rather markedly in the passage. He would not go to bed before his precious charges were safely tucked away.

Dickon stood up, a great bulk, and stretched out his freckled fists.

" That whisky and the talk has done me good, Billy. Well, the Reconstruction of the world is going to be a long job—but it's going to be done. Even if *we* die—futile. The present muddle isn't going on for ever. . . . Reconstructing the world. It's interesting. And besides, Lord ! *what else is there to do with life ?* "

He drooped and stood with his hands in his pockets staring at the fire.

" Minnie. And the children married and scattered. It's passed like a dream."

§ 16

So, in effect, Dickon talked and thought four years ago—nearly five years now.

I think it was Dickon who first hit upon the image of Vishnu, Siva, and Brahma, the Indian triad of fundamental gods, to express the main forces in the world about us. We found that a very happy symbolism for our ideas. Neither of us can stand a dualism in politics or social life, a mere antagonism of the ins and the outs, the haves and have-nots. Both of us have an instinctive hatred of eternal rhythms. Dickon, even more than I, insisted upon the triangularity of human affairs. The war of Vishnu, the stubborn conservative, against Siva, the democratic destroyer who ploughs up and inundates, would mean only a dreary alternation of dulness and catastrophe, if it were not for Brahma the inventor, the creative spirit, for whom politics has so rarely found expression. He is the innovating thing ; he is always young and being born into the world, always struggling to become effective. That Hindu trinity is far nearer to political and social realities than the Persian dualism of light and darkness, the dualism of the good and the bad, that the party system suggests.

Like modernist theology, like all such applications of ancient and time-worn phrasings to new necessities, it fails a little under scrutiny. Dickon's treatment of Lord Northcliffe and Mr. Lloyd George as Sons of the Morning, lit by the spirit of Brahma, is decidedly unsatisfactory. Something has gone wrong there. I make identifications in quite another direction, but of those I will tell later. My identifications, too, are provisional and for want of any better. But I think they are nearer than Dickon's. Mr. Baldwin is better as Vishnu's Prime Minister, and there is much to be said for the view that the Duke of Northumberland is a modern incarnation of Vishnu. But the genteel Ramsay McDonald and the inexpressive Clynes, man-of-the-world Thomas, and Catholic Communist Wheatley are not very good as—shall I say Sivatheria ? Siva keeps his temple, if he keep a temple anywhere, in Moscow. Does Siva tolerate temples ? One thing I know, that in the heart of every youngster forced at the very dawn of adolescence to accept a destiny of obedience, inferiority, and uncongenial toil there is a potential altar to Siva with the red fire waiting to be lit.

Perhaps it would be better to stress the eternal intermingling of the triad. The spirit of Vishnu—that is to say, the stiff, fierce cowardice of established advantage, the spirit of Siva, the wild resentment of exclusion and imposed inferiority, the spirit of Brahma, the urge of curiosity and creative experiment; all these in varying degrees work everywhere and in all of us. Wherever there is ownership and government Vishnu installs himself; wherever there are dispossessed masses Siva reigns. Brahma, who makes all new things, dominates neither ruler nor crowd, but moves throughout the universe, progress eternal. . . .

If Vishnu rules among the creditors and conservatives and Siva is the god of debtors and the parties of the left, does it follow that Brahma is to be identified with liberalism?

This is a matter for discussion not so much for me as for the bright young gentlemen, often now quite middle-aged, who spend their vacations reviving the Liberal Party in conferences and summer schools. I admit that liberalism has always attracted me, and even in my socialist days as a student I called myself also a liberal, I still call myself a liberal and my views liberalism, but the repulsion of the Liberal Party has been as strong as the attraction of its name. When I dabbled in politics in that rather excited and uncritical reconstruction period after the war, I joined the Labour Party—I do not now recall exactly why. Possibly because of the little bunch of intellectuals who gave it a delusively constructive air. Under democratic conditions all parties are the same stuff and all politicians are alike; the game they play is the same for all of them, and every team must be made up of much the same sort of men. But nevertheless—though Mr. Vivian Phillipps, Chief Whip I understand of the surviving fragments, would not own me—I am a liberal. And so is Brahma the Creator. Though I do not think he would own Mr. Vivian Phillipps.

Of all kinds of men who have ever been active in affairs, I suppose the English Whig of the eighteenth century is most after my heart. Yet I doubt if the real Lord Brahma is very like an eighteenth-century English Whig. . . .

Since Dickon took to monetary reform as his special and comprehensive task, he has, I remark, restricted Vishnu more and more to the creditor spirit and the power of gold. And if he were pressed for some evidence of the existence of Brahma, he would find it in the projects for a regulated currency as they have been sketched by Mr. Maynard Keynes. But where he will find the spirit of Brahma expressed in the public affairs of America I do not know. I hesitate between Mr. Henry Ford and ——. But why should I be thus specific about men so far away from my continual observation? Let me keep my personal allusions for the lands I know. Here in France they are quite sure that the one God of America is Vishnu, the Transatlantic Brahma is as inaudible to them as he is obscure to us, and Siva, they gather, is either detained at Ellis Island or safely in gaol.

A golden incarnation of Vishnu rules America, as they see it from these broken European countries, rules America absolutely, sitting upon a

Treasury full of gold. Indeed, the American Vishnu sits, in this vision, like a golden weight upon all the world, smiling gold stoppings at the figure of Hope. But I am an Anglo-Saxon myself and I know that I do not know America. More may be hidden in a market-place than can be hidden in a desert. America seems to be leading the world now, and seems likely to go on leading the world for some time, in the reconstruction of economic life upon this new scale, the scale of the great modern business combinations. It cannot do this, I hold, without producing, in addition to a vast encumbrance of merely wealthy common persons, a great number of energetic and capable directive men and women of a definable type, people who will ultimately be bored and irritated by existing political institutions and current ways of living, and who will set themselves, more and more intelligently and co-operatively, to the entire reconstruction of human affairs.

At present such types are still ineffective in America, because, among other difficulties, they have to struggle towards understanding through thickets of mind-destroying slang and swamps of verbose cant. You do not hew your way across a great continent in three generations and carry your vocabulary intact. America has partly lost the ancient gift of rational speech. American thought is more hampered than we realise by the necessity of expressing itself in a language that is habitually depraved. It is kept at a low level by the universal resort to the common school, with its badly trained teachers and poor equipment, and by those peculiarities of illumination upon which Dickon expatiated, which sacrifice clearness so ruthlessly to vividness, and precision of dealing to harshly dramatic effect.

§ 17

ONE other aspect I want to give of Dickon before his picture is completed, a glimpse of something very deep in him. What I have to tell may seem extraordinarily nothing to the reader, but to me it is the very heart of Dickon. It was one day, at most two years ago, after my very first discovery of Provence and before he went off to Brussels, that this incident occurred. I was sleeping that night at Bordon Street, and when he came in I was reading by the fire.

It was late. He was a little flushed and crumpled, in dinner dress and with his decorations. I did not know at the time where he had been ; I learned that afterwards.

There had been a great dinner of Advertisers—I rather think it was one of the organisations he had created—and he had spoken and let himself go. A little warmed by champagne and professional fraternity, he had spread out his dream of the Advertiser as prophet and teacher to a pleased but incredulous gathering. Someone had laughed, and he had sounded a prophetic note in reply. " We are the masters of the newspapers and they know it," he had said. " We and we alone have the ear of the world. We can dictate what shall be known and what shall not be known, what shall exist and what shall not. We can educate the people or degrade the people, exalt right things and humble base things. We can be the guide, philosopher, and friend of the common man—working together (renewed laughter). Why should we not rise to the full height of our possibilities ? "

Then he had paused and come to something like an anticlimax.

" Are we never to reach beyond motor-cars and medicines, cigarettes and pickles ? "

He lowered impressively for a second or so and then sat down.

The Organised Advertisers cheered and hammered the tables, but also they looked curiously at one another and glanced at Dickon, flushed and already doubtful of the wisdom of what he had said. They had heard some of this before from him, but not so much nor so plainly.

" There was moderation in all things," commented a subsequent speaker. " Our energetic and masterful friend to whose organising fervour our profession owed so much," was he thought, a little prone to exaggerate. It was not perhaps altogether a fault in an advertiser (laughter) within limits (renewed laughter). But though it might be good business to exaggerate, it was not wise to threaten (hear, hear). We had our share, a great share, he would indeed go so far as to say a vital share, in stimulating and in sustaining the currents of trade, the prosperity of our mighty empire, but it was a share—in subordination. It had its place and its limits. There was such a thing as taking one's bit too seriously. . . .

Possibly through sheer clumsiness he had circled about and repeated this thought three or four times. But he was encouraged by " Hear and hear " and some gentle rapping on the table. What had been intended as a friendly reproof became an attack upon Dickon, and at the end what they call a trouncing.

Dickon was a respected and popular figure in the advertisement world, but his was the reluctant popularity accorded to success. His associates liked him but they felt at times, I think, that he did a little to compel them to like him. This talk of their high responsibilities after dinner had not so much flattered them as made them feel uncomfortable, and the gathering fell back very readily into a sympathetic deprecation of " exaggeration " and " lack of humour." They applauded warmly; they nodded their approval. Later speakers showed an increasing disposition to echo and even exceed the trouncer, and a funny man saw his opportunity, and the applause and laughter grew.

The arrow still chafed in Dickon's hide. He stood before the fire and brooded immensely before his explosion.

" This damned sense of humour ! " he cried suddenly and violently.

" Eh ? " said I, looking up from my book.

" You might do a decent thing that would make you look a bit high-falutin'. And so you do a shabby, lazy, second-rate thing instead, and grin and say, ' Thank God I've got a sense of humour.' That's what it amounts to."

" Is this me, Dickon, you're talking to ? "

" Oh no, Billy ! I never talk to you. I was thinking. Man I heard speak to-night. Took me up—for blowing a bit too strongly about advertisement. . . ."

" Perhaps I said too much. . . . Perhaps I did."

He went on as if he addressed some third person.

" But *Modesty !* Knowing your place in the world ! Rot it all is ! Rot I tell you. Cringing, shamming, shirking muck they bully into boys in public schools. And from an Advertising Man of all people ! An Advertiser ! Think of it ! Modesty ! Not going all out for the things that have to be done ! Let a child drown under your eyes ! Thank God *you* don't profess to be a swimmer. *You* don't take upon yourself to rescue all the drowning kids in Christendom. If some presumptuous silly ass who can hardly swim at all chooses to go into the water and gets himself into a mess, *you* aren't going to do anything but smile. Flick a pebble at his head as he comes up for the third time. You're a quiet smiler, you are ! "

I leant back in my chair to appreciate my brother better. There was nothing else to do. I was still at a loss to know what it was all about. He was just the slightest bit drunk, but mostly this was, I perceived, a rational passion.

" Sense of humour ! " said Dickon. " There isn't much of that poison in Advertisement, anyhow. . . . "

He seemed to recall my presence.

" You may laugh, Billy ! But that blamby-pamby idiot to-night has got my goat. I've been a hot man to-night in a world of quiet smiles. Fuming. He let me up to seeing what all this gentlemanly grinning and smirking and enjoying the fun of it quietly and unassumingly really means. Why should a man be guyed for taking himself seriously ? What else *is* there to take seriously ? Those chaps who won't take themselves seriously ought to have been headed off by birth control and never begun. All this half-doing things ! All this living with the guts out ! . . . A joke's a joke in its place, but most of this not taking yourself too seriously is a dirty sin against heaven."

And suddenly Dickon soared above me. He became a pulpit and my admirable armchair a pew. His voice mingled expostulation and passionate assertion in the most extraordinary way.

" Because one sets out to do big things, Billy, because there are big things to be done, because one works until one gets ragged and sore, it doesn't follow one is presumptuous. We two are successes, Billy ; life has pampered us, petted us, put its best carpets under our feet. Have we a right to be anything but serious men ? *Damned* serious men ! It's no want of modesty to attempt everything one can ; to play as big a game as one can ; it's a sense of obligation. What we *are*. . . . That's another question.

" Don't we know each other through and through, Billy ? Do we pretend ? Do we put on airs ? Don't I know what asses we are, I who can't leave a scrap on my plate and you who brighten at the swish of a girl's skirt ? But you *do*, Billy ! Everyone sees it. Don't we know how we blunder, how we lose our little tempers, the endless *silly* things we do ? Yes, and all the same, with all our weaknesses upon us, we've got to be in deadly earnest and do our biggest job.

" If we don't, who will ? Look here, Billy. . . . Is there a race of Gods among mankind, that you and I can slack ? Which will do things if we don't ? If we stand aside, smirking in our elegant modesty, who is there to take hold of things ? A sense of humour, I tell you, Billy, is no fit possession for a decent man. Let the failures have their damned sense of humour ! Cuddle it and nurse it. They need it. Let them snigger and sneak and steal, and make funny faces behind the backs of the men in earnest. That's *their* road, the low road. But for us—things have been put before us, Billy, and we have to take hold of them. We may not be aristocrats ; our luck may be all chance ; but for good or evil, God has put us among the masters in the affairs of men. And a master I mean to be. Oh, I'd rather—— "

He paused to assemble it.

" I'd rather be a skunk and set myself to outstink this drain into which I have fallen, stink and stink hard, instead of making for fresh air, than be one of these damned sense-of-humour business men."

Queer how Dickon could be stung at times !

He was quiet for a moment. " I know I'm a fat ass," he said in an altered voice. " Oh, I know I'm a fat ass and deserve to be grinned at. Don't I *know* it ! "

He went on talking to himself in broken sentences. " Take the second plateful. . . . Go to the club. How can one help eating too much at the Ermine ? Sleepy afternoon. . . . Half one's efficiency gone. . . . Things like that. Temper over a tight collar. . . . The times I've shocked Minnie ! Such a poor *comic* thing ! . . . "

The muttering died away into an incoherent rumbling that was presently ended in a nod and a " Yes."

Then he stood quite still. And suddenly whispered something that gripped me strangely. He whispered it quite forgetful of me, as one whispers a phrase that one has thought out and chosen long ago and repeated many times. I perceived at once that it had been his ultimate consideration on many such occasions of trouble.

" *Weak as we are,*" said Dickon, " *those others are weaker.*"

I stared at him. I had known Dickon all my life, and suddenly it dawned upon me that in some things I hardly knew him at all.

He woke up again.

" Pity I got in a temper ! " he said. " Oh !—a damned pity !

" I could have murdered that fool. . . .

" I showed it and they grinned at me. . . . I'm glad I had you to blow off to, old man. . . .

" I shouldn't have slept all night. Sometimes cursing him and sometimes cursing myself. No one knows the nights we spend, some of us, Billy. . . .

" You see, Billy, what I said wasn't exactly what I meant to say. I overdid it. What I said was right, but somehow I overdid it. I gave him a loophole. I don't say things exactly. It's too beastly hard to say things exactly.

" But they got what I was after all right. . . . Damned sight too much for them. . . .

" They like being funny little nibbling beasts. They *like* it. . . . "

I forget what else he said. I was not listening any longer. I was turning over his astonishing aphorism in my mind. " *Weak as we are, those others are weaker.*"

That, I think, is the quintessence of Dickon.

§ 18

It is curious how the social uses of Lambs Court have dissolved away since the death of Minnie. Richard Clissold Junior has married now, and Winnie has gone to live with her husband in Italy, and young William, my godson, is something of a rebel and a painter (but, I begin to think after my last visit to his studio, a very good painter), and until my great-nephews and great-nieces repopulate it Lambs Court above stairs is an empty place, left more and more to the routines of old and trusted and conservative servants.

Dickon's life, for all our early divergence, reverts to the pattern of mine —the life of a man who has come through the ordinary drama of the world with the sense of a part played out, who is yet full of vitality and anxious to get things done, who still has strong and deep desires, but who is no longer swayed by that intensity of personal reference that narrowed his life before. In that period of renewed intimacy that followed Minnie's death we discussed almost as if we were students again what we were doing with the years that still remained to us. Both of us were at loose ends. Both of us were becoming acutely aware of our dwindling handful of life, and both of us were asking ourselves, as it soaked away between our fingers : " What am I doing with it ? What is the best that I can do with it ? "

We were pulling ourselves together for the last lap of coherent living. We were entirely vague then about our objectives. I had been so for some years ; but with Dickon the phase was more acute. And more decisive. Since then Dickon, with characteristic concentration, has settled down to a task of his own, a task that will need all that is left of him to accomplish, and I, for more complicated reasons, am no longer under the same cloud of feeling that then made me unhappy. But for a while it was as if something long forgotten—anxiety of youth, anxiety about the purposes of life—had come back to us out of those far-off adolescent days.

I find myself wondering how many of our contemporaries have experienced such a fresh start, such a phase of doubt and resumption in their middle years. I question if many intelligent people escape that sort of trouble in adolescence. It is so universal that I would call it distinctively " anxiety of youth." Then for most of us comes immediate necessity, the pressure of events ; we are caught up and hustled along and excited and distracted and amused, and many of us, perhaps most human beings, never reach those open and interrogative silences again before death ends the storm of experience. Unless there is a space of leisure, a release from the thickets of need, I do not see how that trouble can return. And some happy souls hear no more of these interrogations, because, like Sir Rupert

York, they have answered them once for all. It is well I have already given a picture of him in this book, because there at least you have one man who has said, simply and completely : " This work is good enough for me." He will go on unhurryingly, with his bones and his other specimens and the subtle and satisfying problems that concern him, until at last one morning he will not get up, but lie, peaceful and done.

He is one of a number of men of science whom I know to be men serene in their souls and happy in the essence of their lives. But scientific work is a world apart, a magic island cut off from futility. Music, too, may be another magic island, cut off not only from futility but from reality. There is a protective isolation about most of the arts. But Science has most of this precious detachment. And is yet profoundly real. Scientific workers work to the end, though a last they may go gently like a boat coming home as the wind falls in the evening. I was once upon that island of enduring work. Had I kept upon it I should not have been writing this book now and making these half-envious, half-admiring reflections.

Even when there is a space of leisure I doubt if that phase of middle-aged unrest happens very generally. It is natural for me now to find the quality of middle-aged people's lives particularly interesting I am impressed by the present proliferation of the middle-aged. They form a larger proportion of mankind than was ever the case in the world before. And I am more aware of them.

Quite as important in human affairs as that change of scale upon which I have been dwelling in recent sections is the prolongation of life now in progress. I do not think I am being led away by my own circumstances to exaggerate its importance. The average age of the English, for example, has risen steadily for the last century. For that, at any rate, we have fairly trustworthy figures. In Elizabethan times one was mature at thirty and old at forty ; Shakespeare was already a worn-out, unproductive old man in retirement at fifty. Everything was earlier and younger then ; Romeo had the years of a raw undergraduate, and Juliet was a child. One loved and loved again and married and had children, and by the time they were of age the game was done. The ordinary man of fifty was fat or grey or bald and his teeth had gone beyond repair. There was no repair.

Young people died freely at all ages ; more children died than lived to maturity. There was a fever, therefore, to get to the crises of life before the chance was snatched away.

> " What is love ? 'tis not hereafter;
> Present mirth hath present laughter;
> What's to come is still unsure:
> In delay there lies no plenty:
> Then come kiss me, sweet and twenty,
> Youth's a stuff will not endure."

That was the note of it.   To be old and hale was remarkable.   It was to be distinguished and isolated.   The aged of fifty and upward formed a dwindling chorus to the song of youth.   They sat and looked on at the dance—a little outstaying their welcome.   The literatures of the world still preserve the spirit of that more transitory time, and its tradition dominates us to-day.

In all classes now, but particularly in the prosperous classes, people do not die as once they did.   More and more hold on.   And they are cared for and mended ; it is not merely life that is prolonged, but vigour.   Vigour and the desire for living.   An accession is developing to the human life cycle ; a stage after the family life, which itself grows less and less prolific and uses up the available energy less and less completely.   And this elder stratum has no traditions as yet to shape its activities.   Literature has not prepared us for it, and we come through to it with a sort of surprise.   As soon as they have done with loving and getting, the novels, the plays dismiss us with a phrase.   We are supposed to be enfeebled, sated, and done.   We discover we are not so easily dismissed.   We have not finished.   We are not enfeebled.   We demand a better rôle than to act as chorus to the next generation and offer it out-of-date advice.   Here I declare on the edge of sixty is living still to be done, in a new mood and for a new end.

I believe that as civilisation develops this elder stratum is going to play a determining rôle in human development.   In the first part of this book I told of a talk I had with Dr. Jung of Zurich.   Among other things that I brought away from that evening was the fruitful idea that the prevalent states of mind of quite grown-up people in past ages are preserved as phases in the development of the immature to-day, and that a new, more fully adult phase is spreading from the fifties and forties downward in human experience.   This proportionate increase in the elder stratum will contribute greatly to the intensification and extension of this new adult phase.   It will ultimately make life more disinterested and more deliberate and less romantic.   It will make novels and plays that set out to present life aspects of history instead of stories of mating.   But that will only be when this stratum has developed a consciousness of its distinctive quality and rôle.   Then it will impose its standards upon the younger generation and assist it sooner and sooner to maturity.   At present things are still the other way about, and the elder stratum is dominated by the over-emphasised standards of the younger generation.   At present it has still to realise itself. It is like a new actor thrust upon the scene before a part has been found for him.   For a time it is a conspicuous encumbrance even to itself.

What an extraordinary spectacle of waste do the lives of the great majority of us middle-aged and older prosperous people present to-day !

An immense proportion of the property and spending power of the world is now in the hands of old folks, who would in every previous time have died and left things to their heirs. The heirs remain allowanced and functionless, going about the world in a state of arrested reality. They are amateurs of everything, provisionally active, waiting for a call that lingers.

About here in Provence, and especially along this coast from Saint Raphael to far beyond Genoa, there is gathered an abundant assemblage of this old, prosperous multitude for my astonished observation. Under eighteenth-century conditions not one per cent. of these people would be alive. Now their still peculiar sham youthfulness sets all the fashions of living. The amount of altogether futile vitality upon these hills and coasts is incredible, until one has gone to and fro through it and mixed with it and watched it.

There is, first of all, a very considerable resident population here of oldish wealthy people. They build, they own or lease beautiful villas with great gardens and lovely prospects. There must be hundreds of thousands of such people along these coasts ; from England and America alone they must number scores of thousands ; and they must represent an aggregate income of hundreds of millions of pounds. They employ the lives of hundreds of thousands of servants, they spread their gardens over great areas of land, they send up the cost of living for everyone, and they crowd the pulmonary refugees out of the sunshine. They are often men and women who play a vigorous game of tennis, stand the fatigues of whole days of motoring, they come and go among themselves, lunching, dining, assembling, dispersing, and I cannot find a soul among them that is doing anything of large importance in the world or stretching its energies to the full, in any direction whatever. They declare they have played their parts in the world and finished. There are women who have borne and brought up one or two or even three children, and women who have produced none. I could assemble a score of men within an hour's motoring of this *mas*, younger men than I, who say they have " retired." Under that phrase they contentedly rule themselves dead for all effectual ends. They are just playing about, the little innocents, until Nurse Angel-of-Death comes to put them to bed.

Close to me here is a fairly representative sample of these Riviera residents ; she is the widow of old Sir Ralph Steinhart, and she was a niece of the original Romer ; she inherits an interest in the activities of Romer, Steinhart, Crest and Co. and their subsidiaries from both sides. Every time I have done a hands-turn for any of our concerns I have made her richer. Here she is, within half an hour's drive of me, silver-haired—the natural grey made an even white by skilful bleaching—high-coloured and bright-eyed. She is a little bent and restlessly active. Her gardens are very spacious and fine. We pass them usually when we go to Nice. She has, I observe, obstructed a number of the peasants' paths to make her domain more secluded ;

she threatens them on boards with *pièges à loup*, and they must go round by a longer way outside her fences to do their business.   Inside one rarely sees anything moving among the olive terraces and the frequent stone jars ; it is still and deserted except that sometimes in the cool of the evening a manservant is visible taking a pet dog for its sanitary stroll.   Nearer the house there are great hedges of agave and cactus, groves of palm and glimpses of glorious colour which, save for herself and a few guests, delight, only God and her gardeners.   She has bought and evacuated half a dozen peasant houses, she told me one day, to assure the amenities of her view—which, on the whole, is not so good as mine.

I am obliged almost in spite of myself to know something of her house and her life.   When she is here—for two-thirds of the year she is not here and the house stands empty except for a caretaker or so and a casual priest or so, a luxurious blank on the face of the earth—when she is here, she makes continual efforts to cultivate my acquaintance.   It is not that she likes me or that I even pretend to like her, but because she is inordinately curious about my relations to Clementina, and because generally I perplex her and because, more than anything else, she has nothing better to do.   She persists in raiding me with parties of high-coloured, bright-eyed, observant Romer and Steinhart nieces and in-laws.   Or with a literary party of those beastly little cigarette dealers who write novels for the English county families, and their crumpled and dishevelled womenfolk.   Or with a scratch lot from the dramatic world.   Or even with one of her selected collections from the aristocrat Catholic circles of Paris.   But these last are rarer.   That is the side of her life she turns away from me.   Her car does its best and sticks inside my pillars, and up they all come on foot, either quietly agog and staring about them, or else with an impelled reluctant look, according to their race and breeding.

As soon as the car is observed below, Jeanne flies upstairs to put on what is known with us as a Lady Steinhart apron, and while I entertain the party upon the terrace with a taciturn amiability, tea is served in cups of coarse Provençal ware.   The party is made to spread a peculiarly fluid and difficult cherry jam on toasted crusts with large holes in them, through which the red stuff drips on anything below it, and I converse about the Provençal climate—which has recently developed Anglomania—and intimate my readiness to hear the purport of the visit.   If Clementina is present she is silently polite, and regards the visitors in a way that serves at least to embarrass their scrutiny of the books, newspapers, and other oddments scattered about the terrace.   Her dog goes a little way off and yaps pro-testingly and usefully, in a tone that shows that the whole affair is to be considered unusual.   After a time something seems to break, and her ladyship and party gravitate down the hill again. I never ask her to repeat the visit, and she always does.

She cannot understand why I should live here for so much of my time in a house that I rent for three thousand depreciated francs a year, wearing dirty old flannels and employing a solitary servant. She knows that I pay ten thousand pounds a year or so in super-tax and income-tax, and this way of living seems to her like a wicked waste of God's bounty. She cannot understand why I sit for so many hours in this upper room to which her way is always barred. And, above all, she cannot understand why Clementina sometimes isn't here and sometimes is ; why she has so many meals here, and why she sits dangling her long legs over the wall of my terrace and smoking my cigarettes with an air of complete domestication, while I am upstairs writing. As I never explain Clementina to anyone, as I shall probably not explain her completely even in this book, it is natural that to Lady Steinhart she remains unexplained.

Consequently Lady Steinhart never quite knows whether she really knows Clementina and whether she may, or possibly even ought to, invite Clementina to lunch, and what would happen if she did. And all that is excellent exercise for Lady Steinhart's mind.

Visits like this seem to take up a large part of her time. She and a multitude of other people are always rushing about this country seeing each other ; and I will confess I cannot imagine a less interesting series of sights. Like all Romers and Steinharts, she is addicted to discovering and dropping young musicians, and for these special parties have to be assembled. And also she gets through a considerable amount of time altering her house and garden. She is always digging something up or laying something down, or planting out something or opening out a vista, and if she can manage it she takes you to the spot affected and asks your advice. And while you are giving your advice she is thinking of the next thing she will bother you about. She pursues and buys old furniture, pictures, pottery, and jewellery remorselessly and voraciously. It's a clever little fifteenth-century pot that gets away from her once she is on its trail. And when she has bought a thing she glories in it for a little while, and shows it to her friends and makes them guess what she gave for it, and puts it in her already very congested house, where it presently sinks down out of sight among the other stuff ; and when she has forgotten all about it, as she must do, I hope her tremendous and implacable major-domo steals it and sells it to someone to sell to her all over again. Then there is also much to be done about her clothes and her dresses and her hair. So her days are always emptily busy and the net result of them is exactly nothing at all.

But you must not think that Lady Steinhart's life is wholly consumed by these activities. She is a very moral woman ; there is no talk of a lover for her although she is still short of sixty, and she does not dance more than two or three times a week. But the gap thus left is filled in by a rather distinguished serious side. This serious side she does not let me see as much of as I should like to do. It is the one thing she does not press upon me, and it is the one thing about her that interests me. She is a little bashful with me about it ; I do not know why. It reaches high and far. You might imagine that a born Romer, who is a Steinhart by marriage, would be a Jewess, but this is not the case with her. She is hostile to Jews. She is a Catholic. She is substantially one of the old noblesse. She is a Catholic and a reactionary, and it is alleged that she made even Sir Ralph a Catholic after he became speechless before his death. She is involved in French politics at an angle proper to an aristocratic and pious woman. Priests, bishops, monsignori are to be found at her house, moving about quietly, speaking in undertones, forming little black clumps in the bright flower-gardens, obscurely active, mysteriously wary. She has done much for the Church, and she may do more.

And the Church which has always had a weakness for pious women of property makes her a great concession. She has a private chapel of her own to play with ; it is her dearest interest. She buys it petticoats and lace and ornaments and jewels and metal pots and pans to put on and take off. It is in the house somewhere, and often when one goes in, one is reminded of her serious side by a whiff of incense from some recent function. She can go there alone and meditate, and I suppose she can regale herself with special services, but what she thinks of God when she meditates is as hidden from my imagination as what God can think of her. There is usually a subdued-looking priest or so at her table. Not excessively pampered. The Romer blood is in her veins, and you feel, and you can feel they feel, that they have been paid for.

That private chapel is the crown of her life. It is a great privilege, and she must have sought it for many years. It is the consummation of her bric-à-brac. No doubt the Church weighed the matter and decided that it was worth while to respect her spiritual possibilities to that extent. Perhaps the Church does not know the Romers quite so well as I know them. Anyhow, she has it. The chapel is her distinction. Take that away and substitute a lover, or bridge, or the higher amateurishness in art or criticism, or a specialised collecting mania, or a cherished illness, or just blank interludes, and you have the life of quite a large number of these great ladies of the Riviera. And the men, the " retired " men, the resident sort, cultivate their gardens also, play tennis, make love in a vague, furtive way, indulge in wistful reminiscence of the days when they were alive, and are on the whole much less animated than the women. Some are vicious in an elderly, elaborate, Roman way, and their establishments are barred and secret, and their rather too smart men-servants go about visibly clad in light and becoming blackmail. French journalists are modest upon such questions, and the Riviera has no Suetonius. There are not many married couples in constant association among our residents. The prevalent thing is a single personality engaged, with the widest, most dignified, and expensive of details, in futility.

But the residential side of the Côte d'Azur is not, after all, its most typical aspect. Where the big hotels cluster, the multitude grows dense. Sooner or later everyone in the Western world who has more than three thousand pounds a year must come to the Riviera. An invisible necessity seems to bring us here just as the souls in the Swedenborgian books go undriven to their ultimate destinies. I am here, and, after all, I am rather pretending not to belong to it than honestly detached. For so many of us there is nowhere else to go—quite remarkably there is not. To the north are murderous climates and to the south murderous discomforts. A few come once or twice and then not again, but most who have come continue to come. A middle-aged hunger for the sun is an active, physical cause. The transients come and go tremendously. Many of them still function in some reduced or inattentive way elsewhere ; some of the younger set between forty-five and sixty are frankly recuperating; but most have altogether discontinued any contribution to the world's affairs. In the hotels we sit and watch them, guessing ages. The average is astonishingly high. Golden lads of sixty step it briskly with gay girls of forty-five. The grey heads bob to the black music. The other day we found an incessant couple in a Cannes hotel, who golfed all the forenoon and danced together until one in the morning, and both were over seventy. The only young people here seem to be subsidiaries. I make no objection to all this activity on the part of old people. I would rejoice to see them dancing and generally active at ninety and a hundred, but my perplexity is their universal disregard of anything else in the world but amusement taken in a quasi-juvenile form.

For a large proportion of this multitude the belated juvenility finds more questionable expression than golfing and dancing, Darby and Joan. Since they have yet to discover that there is any graver business in life than getting, they must gamble, though they are rich and easy ; and since they know of no livelier desires they still want most desperately to go on with the adolescent modes of love. With a little care and effort much may still be effected in that matter. One can still be jealous and vindictive, still charm here and break-off there, be cold and cruel and fitful and make the yearning lover realise the wretchedness of an insecure allowance. When one is no longer over-anxious to steal away with one's dear mistress, one can still be seen about with her. Which accounts for the prevalence here of a large number of really very beautiful and brilliant and highly decorated young women between the ages of fifteen and forty, and a large variety of utterly detestable young gentlemen. A mistress must look the part and have a lavish and pampered air. And for some of those who have had a hard struggle to win to this Paradise of ease and power, there seems to be a peculiar charm in gilt edged passions ; Russian exiles, often with quite genuine titles, nobility from almost everywhere, countesses, duchesses, princesses divorcing or divorced, royal bastards (in profusion and with every degree of authenticity), ex-royalties, and even precariously current royalties are here, and only too ready to oblige. The Americans, they say, are particularly generous and abject paymasters to such people. That is probably a libel on the Americans ; there are merely more of them with money.

And, thirdly, there is the sport, the mechanical gratification of shooting pigeons, the assembling to look on at racing, polo, flying, fencing, tennis. The worship of tennis becomes more amazing every year. The papers that come here, even the *Manchester Guardian* and the *Nation* discuss it earnestly, deeply. Photographs of its heroic figures fill the illustrated weeklies. The women have a sort of wadded look about the feet and ankles ; the men's faces, in the absence of a ball to hit, are alertly empty. We study the characters, the mannerisms, of these gifted beings. Minniver, it seems, is amusingly short-tempered ; he insults his partner and swears. You can hear it all over the court ; you can hear about it all over the world. Judkins has a peculiar penetrating sniff. It is, I understand, to be broadcasted.

In relation to all these things cluster the shop-folk and all sorts of dealers, the professionals, the teachers of dancing, the manicurists and complexion specialists, the hoteliers, restaurateurs, and so forth, with their own sympathetically imitative tennis and sport and private vices out of business hours.

It is still full season down there on the beaches, for I got my *lit-salon* reservation for next week from Cannes at only eight days' notice—I have to run to London for some business and leave this writing for a few weeks. But presently this widespread crowd of aimless property will begin to pour home like a sluice along the roads and in the expresses *de luxe*, and so to Paris and more especially to England in May and June, to the Paris dressmakers and body-makers and face-makers and on to the jostling splendours of the London Court, and the culmination of all things at Henley and Ascot—especially Ascot. Grave men will wear grey top-hats with the serious elation befitting such an act, and every sort of dress except the old and shabby will be displayed. The King and Queen, those perfect symbols of the will and purpose of the British Empire, will be gravely presiding over the parade amidst the clicking cameras. Wherever there is a foreground there also will be the Countess of Oxford and Asquith, and no doubt some oaf of a Labour member will be well in evidence in a white bowler hat and a loyal grin—just to make it clear that there is nothing different about Labour. And if you study the photographs and pictures of this immense inane gathering you will see they represent mature and oldish people in an enormous majority, deliberately and gravely assembled, dressed with extraordinary attention, and doing nothing, nothing whatever except being precisely and carefully there.

In the wane of the season here, to replace our first-class assembly, there will come a char-à-banc crowd of the merely prosperous, also middle-aged and getting on with it, filling the Monte Carlo Casino at reduced entrance fees, gambling at five francs a go, and learning how to be rich from the margin. They will envy, they will emulate, they will peep over the villa walls and up the Casino staircases to the private rooms. Some may even go up those staircases. Adventurously. The wives will return to Sheffield or Main Street or Pernambuco marvellously changed about the hair and the skirts and the souls. These are the reserves of the great spending class. They are learning. They spread the stratum wide and deep into the general life. Tons of illustrated papers go out weekly to them to keep them in touch ; books and plays of a special sort are made to satisfy their cravings. They have no God, and Michael Arlen is their prophet.

I have written of the " elder stratum," but when I think over my occasional glimpses of life at Monaco and Monte Carlo and Nice I am doubtful whether " elder fester " would not be the better expression. When one traces it away from here to Paris, London, Vienna, New York, California, to Biskra and Egypt, to High Savoy, to Biarritz, Palm Beach, and endless other places, to race meetings and summer resorts, to Scotland and New England, and so to its town houses and country-houses and its places of origin, one realises something of its scale and significance in our Atlantic world. It is all that pays super-tax ; it is the surplus of the world's resources. Yet extensive and impressive as it is, it is nevertheless, so far as its present characteristics go, almost as new as the great growth of advertisement in Dickon's lifetime. Its precursors in the town and Court life of the eighteenth and seventeenth centuries were relatively younger, more actively self-assertive and more assured, and incomparably less abundant and diffused. They were a little intimate community, and this is an auriferous flood. I do not believe that its present development is anything more than one distinctive feature of a transitory phase in the great unfolding of human society that is now in progress. This way of living is no more permanent than the way of living one finds recorded—in caricature indeed, but in illuminating and convincing caricature—by Petronius in his *Satyricon*. It is an overspill of gathering human energy like the spots on an adolescent face. No state of human affairs that releases so vast a splash of futile expenditure can be anywhere near equilibrium. It must be, it manifestly is, undergoing rapid changes. Intelligent people, even the intelligent people in the rich elder stratum itself, will rebel against this mode of life, as Dickon and I have rebelled. And all those who are outside of it have only to learn of it to desire to end it, because it is so plainly a vast waste of spending power by essentially powerless people.

Circumstances may have made Dickon and me rather tougher and more refractory stuff than most of our class, less afraid to lie awake at night and look what used to be called the Eternities in the face. But none of these people can be of a very different clay from Dickon and myself, and what has happened to us must happen with slight differences in quality and quantity to most of them. There is a great dread of lying awake at night manifest everywhere. The activity to escape mental solitude is remarkable. Most of the rushing about in motor-cars is plainly due to that. The rich, ageing Americans in particular seem constantly in flight across the Atlantic from something that is always, nevertheless, waiting for them on the other side, whichever side it happens to be. There would not be all this vehement going to and fro if they were not afraid of something that sought them in the quiet places. And what else can that something be but just these questions that have confronted us. " There is only a little handful of water left now. What do you mean to do with it ? What under the stars is the meaning of your life ? "

" Oh, hell ! " they say at the first intimation of that whisper, " where are we going to-morrow ? "

Below and behind and all about the petty glittering activities of the elder fester a sane and real next adult phase must surely be preparing even now, the realisation that life can be lived indeed to the very end, and that learning and making need never cease until the last hour has come. Surely there dawns the immense undying interest of social development, of the establishment of a creative order, of the steady growth of human knowledge and power upon the blank outlook of the present. Can these poor, raddled, raffish, self-indulgent, aimless, wealthy types of to-day go on existing as that grows clearer ? There is no need of any great convulsion to chase them from existence ; they will fade out of the spectacle. Some will learn, some will be expropriated ; many types among them will be made impossible by less speculative methods of production. In that direction things must be moving now.

If I could return to this countryside in only a hundred years' time, I am sure I should find the villas, hostels, roads, promenades of all these places, and all the life that fills them, changed profoundly. The buildings will be for the most part rebuilt and less miscellaneous in their quality. Villa Cocotte in its louder variations may have gone ; the gaudy casinos and dancing restaurants will have been cleared away ; the gardens will be more beautiful and less strenuously exclusive. The present fences of wire, the *pièges à loup*, and fierce little intimations against trespassing will have been abolished noiselessly by a general amelioration of manners. The peasants' homes will have got bathrooms, and their cultivations will be less laborious and more skilful.

These bathrooms may be already close at hand. Jeanne tells me that one reason given for the cutting down of olive-trees here is that the olive harvest comes in winter and that picking olives swells and stains and chaps the hands. Enough labour cannot be got for the picking. People will not lend their hands to such work. A new phase of civilisation is near when the human hand has won to this much respect.

Swift, silent cars will run about this fairer land on smoother roads, less numerously perhaps, and with a greater appearance of purpose. The advertisement boards, like a clamour of touts that ruin so much of the roadside scenery, will be banished altogether. This Provence is too kind and lovable not to remain the resort of great multitudes of people, but they will no longer be living days of busy inconsecutiveness and pursuing the shadows of unseasonable pleasures.

Perhaps my hopes run away with me, but it seems to me that even in so short a time as a hundred years there may be a far larger proportion of true adults amidst the retarded adolescents of our elder stratum, and that their tone of thought and their quality of conduct will have soaked far into the whole social body. Youth is eager and passionate, but youth is not naturally frivolous, and at present an artificial and meretricious frivolity is forced upon the young by the greedy urgency of their aimless seniors. Youth also may be something graver and stronger a hundred years from now.

However evident its approach, it is certain that the coming adult phase is not yet in the ascendant. And since it has still to come as a general thing, and since its essential quality is a merger of one's romantic, adventurous, individual life into the deathless life of the being of the species, manifestly it is not to be attained in its fulness by a few isolated pioneers. The men of science of this time are as a class more nearly able to be adult-minded than any of the rest of us—so far, that is, as their science goes. They are more in touch with an enduring reality ; they have their side of the world comparatively organised, and they are joined up into a kind of collectivism. The rest of us are rather people who have heard of this way of living and are seeking it than who are actually living in the new stage.

Meanwhile all the available forms and conveniences necessarily remain those of our stratum. We must wear the clothes the fashions prescribe unless we want to have our lives eaten up by minor troubles and explanations. We must live in the usual way, for how else can we live ? If we want to travel we must travel by trains-de-luxe or go slow and dirty, catch colds, and be crowded, stifled, and disgusted ; we must go to the hotels that quiver to the strains of jazz, for there are no others at present to go to ; and eat either in restaurants amidst processions of mannequins or with dancers jogging our elbows, or perplex our poor stomachs with questionable fare. And if we want air and exercise, is anything so convenient as tennis ? Which demands all sorts of conformities.

So we two Clissolds go about the world looking like any other fairly rich spenders—crypto-adults at the best. If I live upon the hills here, and very simply for a part of the year, it is only because I have hit upon a remarkable young woman who has seen fit to make it possible for me. And Heaven knows how long that will last ! It is only here that I can live like this—it is a little abnormal adventure of my own—and for the rest of my existence there waits a setting of hotel managers and porters and maidservants and valets and all that is *comme-il-faut*.

Yet we appear to be much emptier worldlings than we are. We are both, after our fashion, refusing to accept the fundamental stigma of the elder stratum—which is the cessation of all serious work. We have no blank enjoyments and we work as long hours as ever we did. Longer perhaps. Dickon grapples now day and night with the mysteries of what he calls the Money Power. To release our dear Lady of Business from the paralysing grip of the Creditor is the final quest of his life. He is thrusting in a sullen, persistent way through a dark jungle of finance round about her in search of something vulnerable. He believes there is a concrete dragon somewhere in that darkness to be slain, and if so he will slay it. Wherever there is a promise of light upon these obscurities Dickon goes. Last November he was in Detroit in earnest conference with Henry Ford, who possessed, he thought, a peculiar point of view and special experiences about the evil thing. He crossed the Atlantic in winter for that. And he is developing an angry, industrious patience with currency and credit theorists. When he catches me in England he makes me talk about them. He wrangles with me and will not be denied. He talks now about money just as he used to talk once about advertisement—continually, with his heart as deeply in it.

I am quite unable to estimate what his activities amount to, whether he is just hammering at a door which isn't a door but a rock, or whether he is getting through to some working generalisations. In the past Dickon had a way of getting out results, but this is an immense business.

Apparently he cannot wring anything fundamental out of the bankers. I have heard him in his wrath denouncing them as " beastly little Abacuses ; rotten little roulette wheels, bagging the odd zero chance." He clings to it that they are automata and have not the least idea of their rôle in the general economic life of the world. He compares them with the Freemasons, who

" had some sort of a secret once and have forgotten it." He talks of " going into banking " to find out. A pretty manager he'd make for a local branch ! The district would wake up.

I cannot write down his opinion of various Chancellors of the Exchequer. The Treasury he sometimes reviles and sometimes only bemoans. " Some of these chaps seem to think," he says. " Seem to be able to think. But being officials by nature—they won't let on. They control it. Or they might hit on something important and upset their nice little lives." He wants to have the Treasury " dug up and replanted." It is " pot bound " —which is, I believe, some sort of horticultural metaphor. (I am no party to these criticisms.) Certainly he has hit upon nothing definite yet, or we should have had him at once setting about to " put it over." Just as once he " put over " Milton's Silent Silver Guinea.

May he do so before I die ! I dream at times of my dear old Dickon, so amazingly stout and still so amazingly active, engaged upon his last and greatest campaign, leading a band of big manufacturers and engineers, Titans of industry, mammoth distributors and cosmic shippers, piling Pelion on Ossa, newspapers on hoardings, and cinematographs on wireless, shaking all the markets and shocking all the mints in the world, in a stupendous effort to scale and storm the Olympus of Wall Street and the City and dethrone the golden usurer who reigns there.

As for me, I work along a different line. I doubt if this simple treatment of the Money Power as the One True Devil gets to the bottom of things. We need a true sound money, yes ; but that is only to be got with quite a number of other developments that belong together. I have failed to find any place in politics, which is just as well for me ; I have satisfied myself that I was in a state of dangerous fog about economics and education, and at last I have come to this quiet and seclusion in the sunshine—I said last year, to think things out, and now as I get them thought out, I say, to write my mind clear and try my creed over by making this book.

END OF VOL. I.

Waterlow & Sons Limited, Printers, London, Dunstable & Watford.